THE BOOKSELLER OF KATHMANDU

ANN BENNETT

Andaman Press

BOOKS BY ANN BENNETT

The Runaway Sisters

The Orphan House

THE BOOKSELLER OF KATHMANDU

For Mandy

1

CHLOE

Kathmandu, 2018

PARADISE BOOKS WAS hard to find if you didn't know where to look. Housed in an ancient house with crooked walls, elaborately carved shutters and a casement that jutted out over the pavement, it was tucked away in a tiny alley in the centre of downtown Thamel, a network of narrow, busy streets right in the beating heart of old Kathmandu. The bookstore was sandwiched between a temple and a shop selling handmade jewellery, and silver and ivory models of the Buddha and Hindu gods. Some visitors stumbled across it unwittingly, while others – committed booklovers – would often make a beeline for it. Either way, once they stepped over the threshold, people would quickly be drawn in by the bookshop's charms.

It was easy to be seduced by its unique atmosphere. Some customers would spend hours wandering through its three floors of labyrinthine rooms, poring over obscure, well-leafed volumes; breathing in the unique aroma of the place. The smell of freshly brewed coffee, which was served in a tiny courtyard at the back of the shop, mingled with incense wafting in from the temple, the musty smell of old books and the faint scent of the two resident cats, Rex and Queenie, who had inhabited the place for as long as anyone could remember.

Chloe had first discovered the shop by accident. She'd been looking for books about the Gurkhas and their part in the Burma campaign during the Second World War, when she was researching her grandparents' wartime experiences. She'd scoured every other bookshop in Kathmandu with little success, but serendipity had led her to wander through Thamel late one evening when bats were gathering on the telephone wires for their nightly flit around the district, the light in the sky was fading fast, and the smell of incense and woodsmoke permeated the air. She'd stopped concentrating on her surroundings for a few minutes and, before long, was lost. But she didn't panic. It had happened before and she knew if she just kept walking she would probably stumble upon somewhere familiar before too long.

She'd happened to turn into a narrow alleyway, which looked to be in the vague direction she was headed, when there it was in front of her: *Paradise Books,* its brightly-coloured sign lit up in flickering, white fairy lights.

The owner, a bent old Nepalese man called Rohan Dev, stood in the doorway, and when Chloe wandered towards the shop, intrigued, he'd given her a cheery wave and welcomed her warmly.

'Come in, come in, my dear,' he'd said, his face wreathed in smiles. 'I was just about to close, but as the gods are still sending me customers I've changed my mind. How can I help you?'

She'd stepped over the threshold and looked about her, over-awed. There were shelves lining the walls from floor to ceiling in every direction, containing books of every shape, size and colour, and written in every language under the sun. They stretched from the front of the shop to the back, completely filling three tall rooms.

Chloe had told the old man what she was looking for and he directed her to a room on the second floor. Books were piled up on every step of the carved, wooden staircase, and on the first floor were three identical rooms, groaning with yet more volumes. Above that, at the very top of another winding staircase, were *another* three rooms, just as full, these with sloping ceilings and casement windows glazed with diamond panes.

There, in the very top of the building, Chloe discovered a whole column of shelves labelled: *WWII IN SOUTHEAST ASIA; THE FALL OF SINGAPORE, THE JAPANESE OCCUPATION OF THE REGION, AND THE BURMA CAMPAIGN.*

'This is just what I was looking for! I can't thank you enough!' she'd said, turning to the old man, beaming.

He had been wheezing a little from the climb, but he beamed back. 'I'll leave you to it,' he replied, 'while I feed the cats. Please... take your time.'

That was two years ago. After that first visit, Chloe had returned to the shop every day for several days running. Towards the end of the week, the old man, who asked her to call him 'baje', or grandfather, had casually mentioned that he was looking for an assistant, and Chloe had been only too happy to apply for the job. At that time she'd been working for a charity for the victims of the 2015 earthquake, but almost all had been rehoused by then, and the pay was desperately poor. With her husband, Kiran, an earthquake victim himself, unable to work for several months, she'd needed something that paid a little better, and Paradise Books had suited her down to the ground. She loved meeting people, especially fellow bookworms and travellers; she loved being able to browse the bookshelves when the shop wasn't busy; and she quickly fell in love with Rex and Queenie, who – because it was her job to feed them – would follow her around, rubbing their backs against her legs and purring.

When Rohan had wanted to retire a year later, Chloe used some of the money she'd saved from selling her grandmother's house in England to buy the business from him. He'd been delighted to pass on his beloved bookshop to Chloe and became a regular customer himself. He could often be found relaxing in the corner of one of the rooms in a wing-backed armchair under a potted palm, flicking through a volume in Sanskrit, cradling one of the cats on his lap.

Chloe had made a few changes since she'd taken over. She'd advertised the shop in local newspapers, with the tourist board and in tourist shops, and she'd started selling books online too, which had helped her cash flow considerably. And she'd introduced a small coffee shop in the courtyard, where customers could take books to browse. One of Kiran's many great-aunts, Gita, worked there each day from morning until early evening serving coffee and cakes. It had proved a great success.

Inside, she'd added several houseplants – including potted palms, aspidistras and giant ferns – to the rooms, as well as a few artefacts that enhanced the quirky feel of the place. A stuffed yellow-and-blue parrot in a cage stood at the top of the stairs on the first floor. Chloe had spotted it in a second-hand store and known instantly it would be right for the shop. The cage contained a sensor and a tape machine, which whenever anyone approached, sprung into life with a wolf whistle or a random parrot phrase, such as *Pretty Polly* or *Ahoy there.*

Chloe had also installed an ancient fortune-telling machine. She'd bought it at an auction where she'd gone to purchase shelving, unable to resist bidding for the piece. It now stood in the corner of the main room on the ground floor. Housed in a large wooden box with a window in the front, behind which sat a model of a fortune teller complete with veil, bangles and multiple necklaces. It had reminded Chloe chillingly of the fortune teller she herself had visited near Durbar Square, when she'd been retracing her grandmother's footsteps. As she'd predicted, customers loved the machine, putting a few rupees into the slot to receive a slip of paper on which was written a prediction.

Most evenings she kept the bookshop open until nine or ten at night to catch the foreign visitors taking a stroll round Thamel after their evening meal. Tonight was no exception, but she was tired after a whole day on her feet serving customers. She'd sent her assistant, a young student, Shova, home a couple of hours before, and now she was keen to get home to Kiran. He was working as a tour guide again and that night he was due back from his first long trip since his accident; taking a group of tourists up to Annapurna Base Camp. Chloe couldn't wait to see him and was planning to cook his favourite dish, chatamari, or Nepali pizza.

The jeweller next door began to close up – Chloe could hear him dragging his outdoor tables inside and rolling down the metal shutter over the front of the shop. She took that as a cue to do the same.

It was Friday, and on Friday evenings she usually permitted herself a dabble on the fortune-telling machine. She rarely understood the messages the machine churned out, but it gave her pleasure anyway. She went to the corner of the shop, pushed a coin into the metal slot, listened to the burst of traditional Nepalese pipe music from inside the box, then after some clanking and whirring from the machine, collected her fortune card from the other slot. She looked at it, smiling. *Behind every enigma, an untold story awaits*, she read. What did that mean?

She went outside and began to bring in the crates of books she'd had on display that day – second-hand guide-books on Nepal, and large-scale maps for trekkers. She'd managed to heave two inside when she heard footsteps in the alleyway. Her heart sank, but she held her breath. Perhaps it was a late worshipper bound for the temple next door. They came at all hours of the day and night bearing flowers, incense and offerings of food, and the temple never closed its doors to them.

But the footsteps stopped in front of the shop, and Chloe heard someone walk up the steps. She straightened up and smiled at the new customer.

'Good evening,' she said.

It was a Nepalese man, greying at the temples, probably in his mid fifties. His face looked vaguely familiar, but Chloe couldn't place him immediately. He wore a navy-blue suit that was shiny with wear, scuffed brown shoes and a white shirt that looked creased and grubby. He had a careworn look, his eyes were tired, the skin under them smudged with fatigue, and when he looked at her she saw a great sadness in them.

'Good evening. You are Mrs Rai, aren't you?' he said, holding out his hand.

She took it automatically and they shook hands.

'Yes... but?'

'I am Rajesh. Rajesh Desai. A distant relative of your husband's on his father's side. Second or third cousin I think.'

'Of course,' she said, smiling, 'I remember now. You came to our wedding, didn't you?'

'I did! How kind of you to remember!'

She only had the dimmest memory of him from the wedding. He was just one amongst the maelstrom of new faces she'd been introduced to that day; dozens of Kiran's extended family on both sides, friends, colleagues, members of the local community. But this man had looked so different back then. He'd been dressed very smartly, and now she recalled he'd been there with his wife – a rather beautiful, elegant woman – and his father, who'd been very old and walked with a Zimmer frame.

'Well, good evening and welcome to Paradise Books,' she said.

'Thank you. I've heard a lot about it. Many of my fellow academics at the university sing its praises. I had to come and see for myself!'

'That's good to know,' she said, recalling he was a professor of Nepalese history at the University of Kathmandu. 'Is there anything particular I can help you with?'

'Well, actually, I'm not here to buy a book. I heard on the grapevine that you sometimes take away second-hand books to sell. When... when old houses are cleared, for example.'

'Yes. We do that if the books are suitable for our shop. Do you have some books you want to get rid of?'

'Yes.' He dropped his gaze. 'Sadly, my father died a couple of months ago. I'm clearing his house. He was a great reader and also a great hoarder, I'm afraid. He has many, many books. Some quite valuable, I think. Not that I would want payment,' he added quickly with the trace of an anxious frown.

'I'm so sorry to hear about your father,' Chloe said. 'How very sad. But I could come and have a look at the books, if you like. I store any collections I take in the basement here until I have time to sort and classify them.'

The man's face cleared. 'Oh, excellent. Thank you very much indeed. I've been worrying about them. There are so many, you see... could you come by tomorrow by any chance?'

'Yes, I should think so. If you give me the address. I could have an initial look and then come back and collect them another day, if that's OK. What time would be convenient?' She handed him a notepad and pen.

'Sometime in the morning? Would eleven be alright?' He scribbled an address.

'That would be fine.'

'Perfect,' he said. 'I shall look forward to seeing you then. Goodnight, Mrs Rai.'

'Chloe, please,' she said. 'And goodnight.'

She watched him walk down the front steps and out into the dimly lit alleyway, then make his way back through the passage opposite, between its closed and shuttered shops, towards the main street. He walked with a deliberate stride, his shoulders drooping slightly. The death of his father must have hit him hard, Chloe thought as she watched him.

Suddenly, the pain of losing her grandmother two years ago resurfaced. She took a deep breath. Lena had been like a mother to Chloe after her own mother had died, and the pain of Lena's loss had a habit of popping up randomly, blindsiding her. She supposed it would never really leave her completely, she just had to learn to ride out the painful moments.

Sighing, she went to the tiny kitchen at the back of the shop where Auntie Gita made the coffee during opening hours, took cat food from the fridge and emptied out a tin for each of the cats. They'd been asleep on armchairs upstairs for the past couple of hours, but now they materialised instantly, rubbing themselves against her legs, miaowing and purring in appreciation. They lived in the shop, each had a little basket in the corner of the kitchen, and a cat-flap enabled them to go outside. They were good at discouraging mice and rats from the old building, and they were quite happy to be left at night. They were used to it.

Chloe put the day's takings into the safe, then, before she switched out the lights, she glanced at the address on the notepad that Rajesh Desai had left. *Rani Durbar, Nursery Marg, Lazimpat.* She knew Lazimpat to be a wealthy, tree-lined neighbourhood, home to embassies and government buildings. She hadn't expected such a prestigious address, especially having witnessed Rajesh's down-at-heel appearance.

Tucking the paper with the address on it into her pocket, she locked the front door, pulled down the metal grille over the front of the shop and closed the padlock. Then she walked through the silent passage and out onto the busy street beyond, where lights from shops were still blazing, and motorbikes were honking and nosing their way between the evening crowds of shoppers and diners.

She loved the walk home along the thronging streets, through the busiest part of Thamel. She and Kiran had moved into a flat on the edge of the district to be near the shop, and because they both loved the vibrant energy of the area. She drank in the scene, passing the shops with their colourful wares hanging from their awnings, selling everything from exotic food to bright silks, jewellery and mountaineering equipment. She walked by street vendors doling out food from huge cauldrons, stalls selling multiple varieties of nuts and beans, banks of candles flickering outside shrines and temples, which were nestled amongst the shops, several in every street.

There was almost a carnival atmosphere. The streets were still full of people; tourists rubbed shoulders with shoppers and worshippers; sherpas, bowed under the weight of heavy loads, pushed their way through the crowds. Fairy lights and multi-coloured prayer flags were strung from the roofs of medieval buildings, folk music blared from shops and cafes, clashing with the discordant sound of temple bells. As she walked, Chloe waved to people she knew: shopkeepers, food-stall owners, two women wrapped in shawls who sat on the steps of the temple in front of piles of tomatoes, onions and garlic. They were all there every day.

At last she reached Amrit Marg, where she and Kiran had made their home in an apartment on the top floor of an old building. She stood on the opposite pavement and looked up, and her heart leapt to see lights on in their flat. He was home! She climbed the stairs two at a time and arrived at her front door breathless and bathed in sweat.

She let herself in and looked around her. Kiran was dozing on the settee. She tiptoed across the room and stroked his hair, pushing back his glossy black fringe, looking down fondly at his beautiful face, so soft and relaxed in sleep.

She'd worried about him on this first long trip since his accident. He'd been unconscious for days after the earthquake, and had remained in hospital for several weeks. It had then taken months of rest at home for him to recover. He still complained of headaches and fatigue, but nothing she said would have stopped him doing what he loved – guiding foreign travellers into the mountains and helping them discover the astonishing beauty of the land of his birth.

He opened his eyes, frowned for a second, then smiled when he saw her looking down at him. 'Chloe!' he said, reaching up and pulling her towards him. 'I didn't know you were back. I fell asleep. I was so tired.'

She kissed him on the lips tenderly, feeling a rush of affection. It was so good to have him home. 'You stay there. I'm going to cook this evening,' she said, straightening up. 'Do you want a drink?'

'Beer would be good.'

She fetched two Gurkha beers from the fridge, prised the lids off with a bottle opener, and handed him one. Then she went across to the galley kitchen and started to prepare the food.

Their apartment was roomy and light during the daytime and cool in the evenings. It consisted of one huge open-plan living room and kitchen, a separate bedroom and a bathroom. Because it was on the top floor, it also had a roof terrace above, with fabulous views over the city, which was where they took nearly all their meals.

'How was the trip?' she asked, measuring out flour and water.

'Oh, fabulous as usual. It was great to get out there again,' he said. 'The rhododendrons were out of this world. The group was great too. Aussies and Brits, mostly,' he said. 'No trouble at all.'

'And how are you feeling?' Chloe asked anxiously, mixing the batter in a bowl.

'Wonderful!' he said. 'It's done me the power of good.'

'That's great,' she said, turning her attention to chopping onions and coriander. But she was still concerned. Kiran was always so upbeat about his health, but was he telling her the truth? She knew he hated her worrying and she tried not to ask him too many questions, but she couldn't help being anxious.

She'd almost lost him once and she didn't want to go back there ever again.

Later, when they sat out on the terrace, tucking into the spicy chatamari and sipping beers, she tried to relax.

'It's so beautiful out here,' she said, resting her eyes on the sea of twinkling lights beneath them that was Thamel by night.

'It is,' he said. 'I'm so glad we found this apartment.'

Beyond the city, pinpricks of light winked at them from high up in the mountains surrounding the Kathmandu valley, and above them stars were sprinkled across the velvety night sky.

'A lot better than your old place,' she said, smiling, and they both laughed at the memory of his tiny studio flat near the bus terminal, big enough for a single person who only spent a night or two at a time there, but far too small for a couple. They'd both quickly realised they needed somewhere bigger.

'How's it been going at the shop?' he asked, biting into his chatamari.

'Good. Things are really picking up,' she said. 'The café is a big draw now and the takings have been good this week.'

'It's the start of the high season,' he said. 'Was it mostly tourists?'

'Mostly, but this evening I had a visit from someone you know. A relative, in fact.'

'Really? There are a lot to choose from...'

She smiled. 'It was Rajesh Desai. He came to our wedding. But he looked... well, he looked rather sad and lonely, to tell you the truth. He told me his father died a couple of months ago.'

'Oh, that's too bad. Old Uncle Anil. Quite a character. He was very old – must have been in his nineties. Poor Rajesh though. His wife died suddenly last year. Cancer, I think. Ammah went to the funeral.'

'Oh, how terribly sad. No wonder he looked a bit lost. And rather... well as if he doesn't take care of himself.'

'Poor guy. Did he buy a book?'

'No. He actually came to ask me if I wanted his father's old books. I'm going round to the house tomorrow morning.'

'House?' Kiran said, sipping his beer and smiling broadly. 'It's actually a palace! Uncle Anil married a Rana princess. Even though the Rana dynasty were deposed, some of them managed to hang on to their grand residences.'

Chloe stared at him, open-mouthed. 'I saw the address was in Lazimpat, which I thought was rather upmarket, but I had no idea it was actually a *palace*.'

Kiran leaned back on his chair. 'I remember going to a couple of parties there when I was small. It was a beautiful place then, all lit up for the evening with footmen serving drinks and local musicians playing. Uncle Anil's wife, Aunt Manjula, loved a party.'

'What about her?' Chloe asked. 'Is she still around?'

Kiran shook his head. 'No, she died about twenty years ago now. Then the parties stopped. I think the old man became a bit of a recluse.'

'How sad,' Chloe remarked.

'Come to think of it, Uncle Anil was in the Gurkhas for years. He might have some books about them that would interest you.'

'Oh, how fascinating,' Chloe said, thinking instantly of her grandparents and how they had got to know each other on Gurkha recruiting trips into Nepal for the British Army during the war. 'I can't wait to see the place.'

Later, when they went to bed in their tiny room above the street, they held each other tight and kissed for a long time. Then they made love slowly and gently.

'I've missed you so much,' Chloe said afterwards as they lay together watching the shadows from the streetlamps play on the ceiling.

'I've missed you too,' he told her, kissing her hair, his voice already heavy with sleep.

Soon his breathing told her that he was fast asleep. She was glad he hadn't mentioned the subject that had become a slight bone of contention between them before he'd left, and wondered how long it would be before it raised its ugly head again. Perhaps he'd come round to her way of thinking. She sincerely hoped so. She hated any conflict between them.

Chloe sighed and turned over, listening to the night-time sounds of the city – distant horns honking, motor bikes accelerating and dogs howling. She closed her eyes and imagined a beautiful old palace, once the scene of glamourous parties and celebrations, now uninhabited; its grand rooms that had once echoed with music and laughter, now empty but for pile upon pile of dusty old books.

2

CHLOE MANOEUVRED her little Isuzu van into a small parking space on Nursery Marg, as close to the rusting wrought-iron gates of Rani Durbar as she could get it. She locked the van, then walked back along the pavement beside a high stone wall towards the gates. By the time she'd reached them, Rajesh was there, unlocking an enormous padlock that secured some heavy-duty chains around the bars of the gates.

'Ah, good morning, Chloe,' he said.

'Good morning.'

'We have to be careful about security now the place is empty,' he explained. 'We don't want squatters.'

'Of course,' Chloe said.

He pushed open the tall gates with much squeaking and scraping, and beckoned her inside. The gravel driveway was full of weeds. Evergreen trees, luxuriant flowering bushes, jacaranda and rhododendron encroached on its surface, obscuring the way and forming a tunnel of grey-green light. Chloe followed Rajesh between the bushes. They crunched along the gravel and as they rounded a bend in the drive there it was in front of them in all its splendour. The Rani Durbar.

Chloe took in a sharp breath. The palace soared above them. It had a white pillared portico atop a flight of crumbling steps, and beside that a wide wing on either side, each featuring three floors of tall, shuttered windows. The paint was peeling, the pillars crumbling and moss grew between the cracks. The front of the building was stained with green algae from a leaking gutter. Yet despite that, the place looked majestic, like a grand old lady, still proud and elegant in spite of her advancing years.

'It's beautiful!' Chloe exclaimed. 'What an amazing place. Did you grow up here?'

'Yes,' Rajesh said with a wistful smile. 'It was a charmed childhood in many ways. But the upkeep of this place was always a strain on poor Ma and Pa. And now they're both gone, I'm afraid I'm going to have to sell it.'

'I can see how expensive it must be to maintain,' Chloe mused as they walked up the front steps, stepping over the weeds.

'Yes. Pa rather gave up in his latter years. And it would be far too much for me on an academic's salary I'm afraid.' Rajesh chuckled. 'Some developers are interested in it, though. They want to turn it into a hotel.'

'I'm sure it would be a wonderful place to stay,' she replied.

'I can't sell it to them yet, however. There's a bit of a problem with Pa's will and the lawyers are being slightly sticky about it.'

'Oh no,' Chloe said.

She was about to ask him more, but by that time he had unlocked the double doors at the top of the steps and they swung open, revealing a dark, cavernous entrance hall beyond. They went inside and Chloe stood for a second, her eyes adjusting to the gloom. The place smelled damp and musty, but it wasn't cold. Rather, the thick walls seemed to have trapped the stifling heat of the city inside. Looking around her, she could make out a large, vaulted room with a huge staircase rising up in front of her, the pillars of a minstrels' gallery running around the top.

'Wait, I'll put the lights on. The electricity is still connected,' Rajesh said.

Chloe heard him trying a few switches without success, then suddenly an ornate chandelier lit up above her revealing the huge room. It was carpeted in deep-red pile and the walls panelled in dark oak.

'It's a bit gloomy in here, I'm afraid,' Rajesh said, smiling apologetically. 'Partly because the shutters are closed at the moment. Another security measure. I'll show you where the books are.'

He beckoned her down a high-ceilinged, tiled passageway which led off the entrance hall. Here there were skylights, so it wasn't dark, but they gave it a slightly subterranean feel. They passed several closed doors before Rajesh stopped before one, produced his keys, unlocked it and put on the light.

'Come on in.'

Chloe stepped inside a large, square room, every wall of which was lined with oak bookshelves stretching from floor to ceiling.

'Wow!' she said, running her hand along one of the shelves, feeling the cool of the leather-bound volumes under her fingers.

'The books are mainly in English,' Rajesh said. 'My father spoke and read English very well, whereas I don't read it quite so well, I'm afraid. That's part of the reason I have no need of the books myself. I will keep the ones on Nepalese history, of course.'

'Some of these look very valuable,' Chloe said, examining a leather-bound set of Shakespeare's plays shelved beside a full collection of early Encyclopaedia Britannica.

Rajesh shrugged. 'I don't want anything for them. They're yours to take and to get what you can for them.'

Under one of the windows stood a reclining leather armchair, a reading lamp and coffee table beside it, the surface of the table ringed with stains. The room smelled faintly of smoke.

'My father used to spend hours sitting there reading – and

puffing on his cigar,' Rajesh said fondly. 'When he wasn't in his study upstairs, that is.'

Looking at the scuffed chair, Chloe could just imagine an old, bespectacled Uncle Anil sitting back in it for hours poring over a book, a cigar burning down in an ashtray beside him while the sun moved across the window.

'He must have been an educated man,' she remarked.

Rajesh shook his head. 'Sadly, no. He was self-educated. He missed out on formal schooling almost completely. He was recruited into the Gurkhas as a very young man during the war and spent around thirty years in service. When I was small, he was often stationed abroad. He always loved reading, but it developed into a passion when he left the regiment.'

'That's interesting,' Chloe said. 'My grandfather was a recruiter for the Gurkhas during the war. He used to go up into the hill villages in search of volunteers. I wonder if your father was one of the young men he recruited?'

'Quite possibly. What a fascinating thought,' Rajesh said, crossing the room. 'Look, on this shelf you'll find all his books about the Gurkhas. He was an avid collector of everything about them, fiction and non-fiction alike.'

Chloe followed him to a shelf on the opposite side of the room and stared up at Uncle Anil's Gurkha collection. There were probably twenty books there in all and some of them looked quite old. There were histories, diaries, factual accounts, glossy coffee-table books and adventure novels.

'I can't wait to have a closer look at these,' she said. 'Thank you, Rajesh. I'm honoured that you thought about me and Paradise Books.'

He bowed slightly. 'You have an excellent reputation,' he said. 'And when I discovered you are family... well, that clinched it for me. What do you think? Do any of them interest you?'

'Yes,' she said. 'It looks to be a fascinating collection. I could probably take most of what's in the room. If you have any cardboard boxes we could make a start on packing some of them up today and I'll come back later in the week to collect them. I need to be back at the shop by lunchtime, I'm afraid, so can't do much today.'

'That would be wonderful,' he said with a smile. 'Now, shall we go and have a cup of coffee in the kitchen before we make a start? I have some cardboard boxes in the storeroom I'll dig out. There are more books up in Pa's study, but let's concentrate on these first.'

He took her to a large, old-fashioned kitchen even deeper in the bowels of the great house. She sat at a scrubbed, oak table while Rajesh put a kettle on an ancient gas stove and brewed some coffee.

'Do you know where your father served during the war?' she asked.

'In Burma, I believe. The Battle of Kohima. He would never speak about it, I'm afraid. He must have had some terrible memories. Then after the war he was posted to Malaya during the Malayan Emergency as it was called. He was sent home from there and after that he was in Hong Kong for a time, then Indonesia until he was posted back to Nepal around 1970 to train other Gurkhas.'

'What a fascinating life,' Chloe murmured, sipping her coffee, thinking of her grandmother, Lena, who had volunteered for the Women's Auxiliary Service, Burma (or the Wasbies), handing out tea and cakes to the troops during the Burma campaign. She wondered if they'd ever met.

'Yes, but we didn't see that much of him when I was growing up, sadly. Ma and I missed him terribly. Strangely, I only got to know him properly after his retirement. But even then he was always something of an enigma to me. In recent years he became very reclusive. Only interested in his books and pottering round the house.'

When they'd finished their coffee Rajesh found some flat-pack cardboard boxes, which they took back to the library.

'It's hard to know where to start,' Chloe said.

'How about here by the door and then we can work our way round?'

'Good idea.'

They made up a few boxes with parcel tape and began to fill them with books from the shelves beside the door. They worked in silence and, before long, Chloe's hands were covered in dust. Some of these books couldn't have been taken off the shelf for years.

They carried on, quickly filling several boxes and soon reached the shelves holding the books about the Gurkhas.

'I think I'll box these up separately,' Chloe said, but at that point they realised that they had run out of boxes.

'I'll fetch some more,' Rajesh said, disappearing.

Chloe began to take down the Gurkha books from the shelf. Idly, she flicked through some of the older tomes. One, a leather-bound volume, brown, with elaborate gold lettering, entitled, *Land of the Gurkhas; or, the Himalayan Kingdom of Nepal*, looked as though it pre-dated the Second World War. Fascinated, Chloe opened it and, to her surprise, found a letter tucked inside the front cover. It was yellowing with age, the ink on the envelope fading.

Intrigued, she closed the book and peered at the envelope. It was addressed in flowing writing to: *Major Anil Desai, c/o Gurkha HQ, Kathmandu, Nepal*. The date stamp was hard to make out, but Chloe could just about see that the post mark was *Ipoh, Perak, Federated Malay States* and the letter was dated March 1950. She was itching with curiosity to pull out the letter, but held back. This was private correspondence and it wasn't her place to read it.

Just then, Rajesh came back into the room with another pile of flat-pack cardboard boxes. He put them down on the floor, then looked up at Chloe.

'What's that?' he asked, seeing the letter.

'It was inside one of the books. It's addressed to your father.'

She handed it to him, and he stared down at it.

'As I told you, he was stationed in Malaya during the Emergency. But this looks to have been sent to him when he came back to Kathmandu. I know he used to travel back to Malaya sometimes, to see old comrades out there... perhaps it's from one of them.'

Chloe waited. It would have been rather impertinent to ask him to read the letter, but she couldn't help being curious as to its contents.

Then he smiled and handed it to her. 'Why don't you read it?' he said.

'Wouldn't you prefer to?' she asked, nervous now.

He shook his head. 'Truly, reading English is not my strong point. And the handwriting looks difficult to decipher. Why don't you read it out to me instead?'

'If you're sure...' She pulled the letter out of the envelope and opened it up. It was only one page long. 'My dearest Anil,' she read, then looked up at Rajesh. This seemed very personal, and she wanted to be sure he was happy for her to carry on.

He nodded gently, his eyes on her face.

Chloe cleared her throat and read out the letter.

I hope you arrived home safely after your long journey.

It was such a wrench to say goodbye that last day in Butterworth. I stood on the quayside watching your ship until it had completely disappeared over the horizon, not quite believing that you were gone! And I still can't believe the army sent you home before your posting was finished. It seems so unfair, especially in the light of your outstanding record.

I hope one day you will be able to visit. I live for the day that I can hold you in my arms again.

Please write soon with more of your news.
Your ever loving,
Alice

CHLOE FELT her cheeks colouring as she read out what was obviously a love letter to Rajesh's father. When she looked up, Rajesh was staring at her, colour draining from his face. He sat down heavily in his father's armchair and put his head in his hands.

'What date did you say that was again?' he asked.

'March1950,' she replied. It was written at the top of the letter too.

'That was shortly before my parents were married,' Rajesh said slowly, as if he was trying to make sense of it. 'It sounds as if he and this lady, Alice, who sounds as if she was British, were very close. He never told me about it...'

Choe put the letter on the bookcase. 'There's no reason why he should, is there? It was only after my grandmother died that I discovered that she and my grandfather had both been in love with other people before they got married. Theirs was a sort of marriage of convenience. They kept that a secret for the rest of their lives.'

Rajesh smiled sadly. 'It was no secret that Ma and Pa's marriage was arranged by their parents, but it was successful despite that. They truly loved and respected one another. But it would be good to find out more about Alice. Who she was... how they met... It might be painful, I suppose, but I'd like to know.'

'Do you think there are other letters from her here?' Chloe asked. 'It would be odd if there was only one...'

'You're right,' Rajesh said, rubbing his chin. 'Perhaps we'll come across more as we pack. It's all very mysterious, and a bit hard to take in, to tell you the truth.'

Chloe felt a sudden pang of guilt that she'd been the unwitting cause of Rajesh's confusion. It must be a difficult thing to find out about your father. Once again she thought about her grandmother's diary and the revelation that she'd fallen deeply in love with a British soldier in Darjeeling, a secret she'd kept to the grave.

They carried on packing books into cardboard boxes for a while, but soon it was one o'clock.

'I'd better go, I'm afraid,' Chloe said, reluctantly. 'Much as I'd love to carry on. Could I come back on Wednesday morning? That's usually a quiet day in the shop and Shova will be able to cope for a few hours without me.'

'Of course. I can carve out a bit of free time then. Shall we say ten o'clock?'

'Perfect.'

Rajesh walked her down the drive, unlocked the gates and showed her through. They said goodbye beside the van.

As she drove away, she glanced back at him in the rear-view mirror, a lonely figure, waving goodbye. Behind him stood the crumbling palace. What an extraordinary place, and what an extraordinary man Anil Desai must have been. Chloe thought back to the letter, going over and over the words again in her mind. Who was Alice Lacey? And how had she and Anil Desai come to fall in love? She felt a little sorry for Rajesh, discovering these intimate facts about his father while he was still mourning him, but it was a tantalising puzzle.

She didn't want to push it, for fear of upsetting him, but perhaps they would find more letters tucked inside other books when she went back on Wednesday? She couldn't wait to find out.

3

When Chloe returned to Rani Durbar on Wednesday morning, she was still full of hope. Alice's letter had been on her mind a great deal since she'd left there on Saturday; she couldn't let it go. Why was she was so interested in a love affair between a Gurkha soldier and a British woman in the 1950s? Perhaps it was because she'd been so fascinated to find out about her grandmother's past from her diary and this was tantalisingly similar? Or perhaps there was another reason closer to home. There were echoes of her life there – she too had fallen in love with a Nepalese man – and she was fascinated to find out how Anil and Alice had met and fallen in love, and what had happened to that love in the end.

Once again, Rajesh was waiting for her outside the palace gates and welcoming her warmly as he unlocked them and showed her through. She was careful not to mention the letter at first, in case it would upset Rajesh, but before they'd reached the steps to the palace, he'd introduced the subject himself, and Chloe couldn't help smiling.

'I've been thinking about the letter we found,' he said. 'It was a bit of a shock at first, I don't mind admitting. Probably because I'm still grieving for Pa. But I've thought about it a lot over the past couple of days, and I've decided I'd like to check to see if there are any more letters. I'd like to find out what happened between him and this woman, Alice, if at all possible.'

Chloe nodded. 'We might need to look through the books we've already packed again,' she said, 'just in case we missed something. I thought you might not want to find out more though?'

'I didn't at first, but I've changed my mind. As I told you, my father was a bit of an enigma to me,' Rajesh said. 'He was away from home a lot when I was young, then when he was here, he was always buried in a book. If there are more letters, they might help me to understand him in a strange way. Does that sound odd?'

'Not at all. I only really understood my grandmother after she died and I read her diary from the war. It's a similar situation.'

They were now standing inside the grand hallway, and Rajesh led Chloe down the passage and into his father's library. He put the lights on.

'Shall we make a start then?' he asked. 'We can go through the books we've already put in boxes first, then tackle the ones still on the shelves. Once we've checked each one, we can put them straight back into the boxes.'

'Sounds a good plan,' Chloe said. 'But just a thought; do you know which books were your father's favourites? He'd be more likely to slip a letter into a book he read often, wouldn't he?'

'You're right. Why don't you finish looking through the Gurkha books then, while I take the ones on the history of the British Empire? It was a subject he was endlessly fascinated by.'

They quickly made up some more cardboard boxes then set to work. Chloe checked carefully through each of the books about the Gurkhas, then packed them away in a separate box. Although she searched thoroughly, there was nothing to be found in any of them. Then she started to search back through the many boxes they'd already packed. It was tedious work, checking inside the cover of each book then holding it up by the spine and shaking it in case a letter had been slipped in between the pages. It was only the hope of finding another letter that kept her going.

Rajesh straightened up from packing a shelf of books into another box. 'That's all the books on the British Empire done,' he said. 'Nothing in any of them, I'm afraid. I'll make a start on the shelves over here.'

They worked on for a couple of hours. Chloe's stomach began to rumble; she hadn't thought to bring any food, and she'd told Shova she'd be back at the shop by lunchtime. She stopped work, pulled her phone out of her handbag and sent a quick text to Shova to let her know she would be back later than expected.

'Are you hungry?' Rajesh asked suddenly, as if reading her thoughts. 'It's way past lunchtime. I brought some snacks from home just in case. They're in the fridge.'

They left the boxes in the library and went through to the kitchen.

'Sit down, sit down, please,' Rajesh said.

Chloe took a seat at the big table again. Rajesh put the kettle on, then produced some plates from a cupboard and a large storage box from the fridge. When he opened the lid, a delicious aroma rose from it and Chloe saw that it was full of homemade Tibetan momos. She'd always loved them. They reminded her of small, spicy Cornish pasties.

'I hope you like these?' he asked.

'I love them,' she replied, her mouth watering.

He put two out on her plate, then made two mugs of tea and put them on the table. Chloe bit into one of the momos and chewed for a couple of seconds. It was truly delicious. Succulent and spicy, the meat tender, the pastry soft and fresh.

'Did you make these?' she asked.

Rajesh nodded. 'I got quite good at cooking when my wife became sick,' he said, his voice suddenly sad. 'She died about eighteen months ago now, but she was ill for a number of years before that. She was up and down. We tried every available treatment, but in the end nothing succeeded.'

'I'm so sorry,' Chloe said, her heart going out to Rajesh. He looked so sad, but she wasn't sure of what to say. 'You must miss her terribly.'

'I do,' he said. 'Very much. We were soulmates, and I think about her all the time. But, still, I have to try to remain positive,' he added briskly. 'She wouldn't want me to stop living. Cooking gives me a bit of an interest outside my work.'

Chloe smiled at him. She understood now why he sometimes looked forlorn and a little lost.

When they'd finished eating, they returned to the library and continued with their search. They worked on silently for another hour or two, still finding nothing, and Chloe was beginning to despair of there being any more letters at all. Her back was aching from bending and stretching, and she was beginning to worry about the shop. She'd never left Shova to cope alone for so long before.

'I think I've found something here,' Rajesh exclaimed suddenly.

Chloe turned and saw he was holding up a book about British Malaya in one hand and an envelope in the other.

'This book had been put back in the wrong place,' he said. 'It was amongst the maps and travel books, rather than in the section on the British Empire.'

'Fabulous!' Chloe said. 'Is it the same handwriting as the other one?'

'Yes. Same handwriting, same postmark, but it isn't addressed to Kathmandu. Its addressed to an army base in Malaya and it's postmarked a couple of years before the other one. June 1948 to be precise,' he finished, peering closely at the envelope. He handed it to Chloe. 'Could you read it to me?'

She pulled out the letter. Like the previous one, it was only a page long, though a little shorter. She opened it up and realised her hands were trembling with excitement as she looked down at the text.

THE RESIDENCE, Rimba Valley Tin Mine
  Perak, FMS
  10 June 1948
  Dear Major Desai,
  I wanted to write and thank you for coming to see me at the house today. I am very grateful to you and appreciate your concern for my safety. After what happened, it is especially reassuring to know that your brave platoon of Gurkhas is close by, patrolling the area night and day. Without that, life here would be impossible.
  I know you are a long way from your home and family and have few creature comforts in your army quarters. You are more than welcome to drop in again for tea, whenever you are in the vicinity. I would appreciate some civilised company.
  There is no need to write beforehand, just call in whenever you have time. I look forward to seeing you again sometime soon.
  Yours sincerely,
  Alice Lacey

'SO THIS ONE was written a couple of years before the other letter,' Rajesh said. 'It sounds as though they didn't know each other very well at that stage. In the later one they sound extremely close... more than close, perhaps. I wonder why there is such a time gap?'

Chloe folded the letter and put it back inside the envelope. 'Are you thinking there might be more letters?' she asked.

'Exactly so,' Rajesh said. 'Let's continue to look, shall we... that is, if you have time?'

Chloe glanced at her watch. It was two o'clock and she hadn't heard from Shova since lunchtime, when she'd texted to reassure Chloe that everything at the shop was fine. She guessed that no news was good news.

'Of course,' she said. 'There are only a few shelves left to go through. Let's finish off, shall we?'

It didn't take them long to check and pack the rest of the books. But there were no more letters between the pages of any of them.

Chloe looked down at the boxes anxiously. They almost filled the floor of the library and she wondered how she was going to fit them all into the basement at Paradise Books.

'I'll help you take them out to the van,' Rajesh said. 'But I'll open the front gates so you can bring it up to the house. It will be easier that way.'

'That's a good idea,' she said, still thinking about the letters, not wanting to give up on the search quite yet. 'Is there anywhere else you can think of where your father might have hidden more letters?' she asked Rajesh.

He thought for a moment. 'There are some books in his study upstairs, and an old desk with lots of drawers in it. Shall we have a quick look up there?'

'Let's do that.'

The study was upstairs at the back of the house. They returned to the entrance hall and Chloe followed Rajesh up the grand staircase, onto the galleried upper hallway, then down an oak-panelled passage. He opened the double doors to a small, square room which was filled with sunlight that was filtering through a tall, dusty window that looked out on an overgrown garden. Under the window was a huge, mahogany desk, covered with papers and books, an ashtray filled with cigar butts and numerous empty glasses. More bookshelves lined the walls, and polished floorboards were covered with a thick, burgundy, Nepalese rug. When Chloe breathed in, the air was heavy with the sweet smell of cigars, tinged with the faint odour of alcohol. Was it whisky or brandy? She couldn't tell.

'What a lovely room,' she said, looking around.

The shelves weren't completely filled with books like the ones in the library – there were a few reference books on them, but mostly there were ornaments. It looked like the collection of a well-travelled man. Carved face masks, ebony statuettes of gods, ivory elephants, stone figurines of men with spears. Two brightly coloured Indonesian shadow puppets hung from one shelf.

'This was his favourite place, apart from the library of course,' Rajesh said. 'I haven't had the heart to go through his personal papers. Not yet. Everything's in such a fearful mess, it's hard to know where to start.'

'I can sympathise with that,' Chloe said, remembering with a shudder the daunting task of clearing her grandmother's house and how long it had taken to work her way through Lena's disorderly paperwork.

'I'll need to tackle it soon if I'm going to put the house on the market,' he said with a sigh. 'Although with this problem with Pa's will, I might have longer than I'd originally thought.'

'You mentioned a problem the other day. Do you want to talk about it?' Chloe asked.

Rajesh leaned against the desk and passed his hand over his face. 'My father's will had a strange stipulation in it. One that nobody can understand and has the lawyers running round in circles. He left all his money, goods and property jointly to *his children*. But I'm his only child. It has caused all sorts of problems.'

'Do you have any idea why it was written like that?' Chloe asked, intrigued.

Rajesh sighed again. 'I did have a baby brother a couple of years younger than me, but he died before he was a year old. The will was made around that time and I suppose it was never changed.'

'Have you explained that to the lawyers?' Chloe asked.

'Of course,' Rajesh said. 'I had to produce my brother's birth and death certificates. But they're still insisting on advertising in the press, to see if anyone else comes forward. I have to wait until they complete that process before I can put the place on the market.'

'How frustrating for you,' Chloe said, remembering the hours she'd spent with Lena's lawyers administering her estate. It had been quite straightforward in comparison, although she did remember how resentful her cousin, Daniel, had been to discover that Chloe had been left Lena's house. 'People's last wishes often cause problems.'

'Oh well,' Rajesh said with a resigned smile. 'I'm sure it will all work itself out in the end. Anyway, let's think about finding those letters. Shall I go through these books, quickly...? Although there aren't that many...'

'Why don't I do that?' Chloe said. 'While you look through your father's desk? I wouldn't feel comfortable doing that.'

She'd noticed a couple of family photographs on top of the desk; one of Anil and his wife on their wedding day, he in full Gurkha uniform and she in a richly decorated saree with brocade trimmings. She also wore a gold tiara, which held her veil in place, a sparkling almond-shaped jewel hanging over her fore-head. They stood arm in arm, a little stiffly, and both wore slightly fixed smiles. They looked every inch the traditional Nepalese bride and groom.

'Your mother was very beautiful,' Chloe said.

'Yes, I suppose she was,' Rajesh said. 'She had a big, generous heart too. She was so full of life. When she died, it was as if the light had gone out of the world.'

He started to open the desk drawers one by one while Chloe flicked through the books on the shelves, but there was nothing in any of them.

'Here's something!' Rajesh said, closing one of the middle

drawers. He was holding a slim book with a cardboard cover. 'Although not what we were looking for. This is my father's Gurkha service record.'

He opened it up and scanned the pages quickly. 'It's all here. He signed up in Pokhara in 1940, served in Burma, then back in Kathmandu, then Malaya between 1948 and 1950, followed by Hong Kong, then Indonesia, then Kathmandu again in 1970.'

'Does it say whereabouts in Malaya he was stationed?'

Rajesh peered at the book. 'Yes, it does. Gurkha HQ, Batu Gajah, Ipoh. Just like the address on the letter.' He handed the book to Chloe, then went back to looking through the cluttered drawers of his father's desk.

Chloe scanned the entries in the book outlining Anil's career with the Gurkhas. They were just words on a page, dates and addresses, but she realised they meant so much more. Bravery and hardships, battles fought and won, rebellions suppressed, civilians protected. Anil must have been a good, brave soldier, prepared to risk his life for thirty years in the name of peace and freedom.

'There's nothing else in any of these drawers, unfortunately,' Rajesh said at last, his voice tinged with disappointment. 'I guess we'll never know.' He leaned back against the desk and folded his arms, staring down at the floor.

'Never mind,' Chloe said. 'It was worth a look.'

She noticed Rajesh frowning as he focused on the floor. Then, to her surprise he got down on his knees.

'What's this?' he muttered, lifting the edge of the rug and running his hand over a floorboard. 'This board is scuffed. It looks as though it's been prised up and the nails removed.'

Chloe's heart sped up. She moved closer.

Rajesh got to his feet. 'We need to shift the desk a little to the left so we can lift the board. Could you take the other side? It's rather heavy, I'm afraid.'

Chloe did as he asked and, with much grunting and straining, they managed to slide the heavy desk a few inches to the left. Then Rajesh lifted the rug and they both stared down at the scuffed floorboard.

'I'll need a screwdriver or something to prise it up,' Rajesh said. 'I'll go downstairs to the cellar. There'll be one there.'

'Why don't you use this?' Chloe said, picking up a metal paper knife from the bureau.

'Of course!'

They both got down on the floor again and Rajesh inserted the knife between the boards. From the grooves on the edges of the wood it looked as though it had been used for this very purpose many times before. It didn't take much effort for Rajesh to lift out the board; he laid it down on the rug and they both peered into the void.

'Eureka!' he said.

There, beneath the floorboards, was a stash of yellowing envelopes, covered in flakes of black dust.

There must be more than a dozen there, Chloe thought, looking at the pile. There weren't just letters in there, but small packages too. And all were addressed in the same flowing hand-writing as that on the envelope they'd already seen.

'You were right,' Chloe said. 'There *were* more letters!'

Rajesh reached in and took them out, a few at a time, and piled them up on the rug. At one point a photograph fell out from between two of the letters. It was a black-and-white portrait of a young woman with pale, translucent skin. Her dark hair was swept off her forehead and fell in gentle waves to her shoulders in a fifties' style. She was smiling, showing perfect white teeth behind the lipstick, and looking at the camera at a slight sideways angle.

'This must be Alice,' Rajesh said, turning over the photograph.

There were a few words on the back: *To my dearest Anil. Never forget.*

He slipped it back into the pile of letters and they both stared at them, amazed their quest had actually borne fruit.

'I don't know where to start,' Rajesh said.

Like Chloe, he seemed almost afraid to touch the letters. Perhaps he was worried about what they might reveal?

'Why don't we sort them into date order?' she suggested.

He agreed, and they spent the next ten minutes deciphering the date stamps on each letter and package, and putting them in piles according to the year they were written. They spanned the years 1948 to 1956.

'I wonder what happened after the mid fifties,' Chloe said.

Rajesh shook his head. 'I don't know. My father married my mother in 1950 and I was born in 1952. Perhaps that had something to do with it...'

'I'm sorry, is this painful for you?' Chloe asked.

He gave her a reassuring smile. 'Not at all! It's far too long ago to worry me. I'm intrigued, that's all. I want to read them to understand more about what happened. But, like I said, the writing is tricky to make out.'

'I could read them to you,' Chloe offered instantly. 'Just like the others.'

'Would you?' he asked. 'That would mean so much to me, really it would.'

'Of course, I'd love to. But could we possibly start another day? I need to get some of those books back to the shop and check on how things are going there.'

'I'm sorry. I've kept you far longer than necessary. Please forgive me.'

'No need to apologise. I'm so glad I stayed. I can't wait to read the letters.'

Rajesh got to his feet. 'I'll help you take the books back to the shop. If I come with you, I could help unload them at the other end.'

'Kiran promised to come and help. He's taken some tourists out to Patan today, but he should be back by now.'

'Well, we could both help. I'd love to catch up with Kiran again.'

'I'm sure he'd love to see you too,' Chloe said.

They piled up the letters and left them on the bureau, went downstairs, along the drive and out to the street. Chloe drove the van through the gates and up to the front steps of the house and they carried out around half the boxes and stowed them in the van.

'I'll have to come back tomorrow for the rest,' Chloe said, slamming the back doors.

'Are you sure?'

Chloe shrugged. 'The shop is open every day and, besides, Kiran is taking another tour group out tomorrow. I'd like to get them all back to the shop as quickly as possible.'

'So if you come back tomorrow, would you read some more of the letters?' he asked.

She turned to him smiling. 'I'd love that,' she said. 'In fact, I can't wait. Thank you so much for asking me.'

4

ALICE

Rimba Valley Tin Mine, Perak, Malaya, June 1948

DEAR MAJOR DESAI,

I hope you don't mind my writing again out of the blue. Once again, thank you for coming to let us know about the protection the Gurkhas will provide our property during the current insurgency.

Since we are virtually neighbours, my husband and I would like to invite you to return for a longer visit, for a meal this time, if you are able to spare an evening?

If it suits, how about tomorrow evening? That is, this Saturday? I'm inviting one or two of the planters from nearby estates and it would be wonderful if you could join us.

I look forward to hearing from you.

Yours sincerely,

Alice Lacey

ALICE SIGNED THE LETTER, dabbed off the excess ink with blotting paper, and put it in an envelope. She addressed it to Major A. Desai, The Gurkha Base, Batu Gajah, and sealed it up. There was a little bell on her writing desk, which was meant to enable her to summon the servants without getting up from her seat, but she'd always baulked at using that; it seemed so imperious. She may have grown up on a cantonment in British India, surrounded by servants, but she'd never quite got used to it.

Instead, she crossed the drawing room, went out of the double doors and into the hallway where Suleman, the Laceys' aged bearer was cleaning the ornaments on the armoire with a feather duster. Alice cleared her throat and Suleman looked up from his work.

'Memsahib?' he asked.

'Could you ask one of the houseboys to take this down to the Gurkha base in the village, please?'

Suleman took the letter and regarded it suspiciously for a few seconds. 'It may be dangerous for the houseboy to leave the property, Memsahib,' he said.

'I don't think so, Suleman,' Alice countered, keeping her voice level. 'The insurgents only want us Brits. You and the other servants are perfectly safe. Major Desai told us that specifically.'

'Hmm.' He shuffled off, grumbling under his breath.

'Oh dear,' Alice muttered to herself, feeling exasperated and guilty in equal measure. She could tell Suleman didn't set much store by Major Desai and the Gurkhas who'd visited the house the day before and even now were guarding the gates and patrolling the perimeter of the property. She couldn't be sure, but she had a feeling it was because Major Desai wasn't a white man, and Suleman had never encountered someone like that in a position of authority before. It was the kind of paradox that Alice, a daughter of the British Empire, had encountered many times, and one which she would never understand.

It had been a tense time, these past couple of weeks, since three British plantation managers had been killed by communists in Sungai Siput. Admittedly, that was a long way from the tin mine where Alice lived with her husband, but it was still British

Malaya, and it was clear the communists – who were agitating for a violent uprising – had supporters everywhere. She returned to her writing desk, her heart lifting a little at the thought that the Gurkhas were there to protect them.

MAJOR DESAI HAD ARRIVED in an army jeep, unannounced, with a couple of other soldiers. Alice was in the drawing room doing paperwork when he drew up. Surprised to hear an engine, worried the communists might have broken through the security her husband had hastily put in place on the gates, she'd stood behind a curtain and watched as a slender, athletic figure dressed in khaki got out of the jeep and strode across the drive.

The soldier mounted the wooden steps, crossed the veranda and rapped on the door. Her heart raced. They hardly ever had visitors, and they lived so far from other Europeans that a surprise visit was virtually unheard of. So much so that she was certain the servants would be elsewhere and wouldn't have heard the knock.

She suddenly felt uncomfortable, but she smoothed down her skirt, tucked a stray hair behind her ear and took a deep breath. She crossed the empty hallway and opened the door. The soldier outside had already taken off his cap and stood with it under his arm. When he saw Alice, he gave a little bow.

'Good morning, madam. Are you the lady of the house?'

'I am,' she said. It felt a little awkward admitting to that, even after two years. Alice was only twenty-four and didn't feel worthy of the title 'lady of the house'.

'I'm Major Anil Desai. I'd like to speak with you and your husband, if that's possible.'

She hesitated. Bruce was down at the mine office, and he didn't take kindly to being disturbed. But this looked important.

'Why don't you come inside? I'll ask one of the servants to

fetch my husband. Please, take a seat...' She gestured to one of the polished chairs in the hallway that were rarely used. Whoever sat down in a hallway? But she was reluctant to ask the major into the drawing room. It wasn't the Gurkha she was worried about; it was her husband. She had an inkling he might object to her entertaining a strange man, especially a foreign one, in the drawing room in his absence, even if that man was a soldier who was here on official business.

'Thank you,' the major replied and the chair creaked as he sat.

She went along the passage towards the servants' quarters. She rarely ventured down there, so to give them fair warning she walked heavily and coughed loudly as she went.

She found Suleman in the kitchen, smoking a bidi and chatting away to Cook who was busy preparing the evening meal. When she asked him to fetch the tuan from the mine office, he looked suspicious.

'It is most urgent,' she added. 'Tell him to come quickly.'

With a shake of his head, Suleman shambled off to do her bidding, and Alice was forced to go back and speak to the major until Bruce arrived.

She returned to the hallway and saw that he was flicking through an old copy of *Country Life*, which he put down hastily when Alice appeared. He got to his feet and gave a small nod.

She noticed he was quite young for his rank, probably around thirty. He was well-built and he had pleasing open features, along with deep-brown eyes that had an arresting honesty about them.

'That's a very British magazine,' he said. 'It must be a reminder that you are very far from home.'

She laughed. 'Not me. I was born in India. I went to school in England, but it never felt like home.'

'How fascinating,' he said. 'And which part of India, may I ask?'

'Barrackpur Cantonment. My father is a colonel in the British

Indian Army,' she said with an involuntary shudder. Just mentioning him revived unwelcome memories.

'Barrackpur. Near Calcutta. I know it well,' he replied.

'I used to love going into the city,' she said. 'Now *that* felt like home to me.'

'It's an impressive place,' he said.

She smiled at the memory of the teeming streets of Calcutta – the aromas, the clamour, the gleaming white buildings – and fell silent again, not really knowing what else to say to the stranger. He smiled too, then with horror she realised his gaze was resting on her arm where there was a purple bruise just below the elbow. She felt the heat of shame rushing into her cheeks and hastily pulled down the sleeve of her blouse to cover it. He looked away, but she couldn't help noticing his frown and the slightly bemused expression on his face.

'My husband won't be too long,' she said, now feeling more awkward than ever. Should she invite him into the drawing room anyway and perhaps just leave him there on his own? At least then she'd be able to put some space between them.

She was just about to voice an invitation when she heard Bruce's Land Rover squealing to a halt on the drive outside, the door slamming and his boots thumping up the veranda steps. He burst through the door, his face red from the heat and glistening with sweat. There were damp patches on his shirt, and his khaki trousers were spattered in oil from the machines. What a contrast he was to the dapper major.

'What the devil did you call me back for, Alice? You know not to disturb me!'

Alice glanced at Bruce in trepidation, but when Bruce saw the officer coming forward to meet him, hand outstretched, his face relaxed and he smiled.

'I'm Major Anil Desai from the 6th Gurkha Rifles, Mr Lacey. I wanted to talk to you and your wife about security on the estate.'

Bruce glanced at Alice. 'Well, I don't think we need to trouble my wife with these matters,' he said. 'Why don't you and I go into my study and talk man to man.'

'On the contrary, since your wife is as likely to be a target of the guerillas as you are, I think it would be very useful for her to be present,' Major Desai said.

Alice clenched her fists anxiously. Bruce didn't like being contradicted.

But this time he didn't seem to mind. 'Perhaps you're right,' he said.

They went through to Bruce's study, a small, stuffy room at the back of the house that smelled of alcohol and cigarettes. Bruce threw open the window and turned on the ceiling fan.

Glancing at the shambolic piles of papers on his desk, he said, 'Sorry about the mess. I've been rather busy lately, and these attacks have put quite a strain on us.'

'Of course. I understand,' Major Desai said.

'Do take a seat,' Bruce said, holding out a packet of cigarettes.

Desai shook his head. 'Not for me, thank you.'

Bruce rummaged in his desk drawer and produced a bottle. 'Brandy, then?'

Major Desai smiled and shook his head. 'Not while I'm on duty, I'm afraid, Mr Lacey. But thank you.'

Alice sat down in a chair beside the window. Bruce poured himself a hefty measure of brandy and sat on his leather chair behind the desk. Alice was dismayed to see him lean back and put his booted feet up on the desk amongst the papers. She glanced at Major Desai to see if he was offended, but his expression was inscrutable. He was watching Bruce steadily, a faint smile on his lips.

'So, fire away then, Major,' Bruce said, lighting a cigarette.

'As you are aware,' Desai began, 'there have been several attacks by Chinese communists across Malaya over the past few weeks. As well as three planters having been killed in Sungai

Siput, bungalows have been ransacked on several other plantations.

'The insurgents are now being called the Malayan National Liberation Army. The government has declared a State of Emergency across the Federated Malay States and Straits Settlements, so we are stepping up our activities to protect all the mines and plantations in affected areas.'

'And we're an affected area, are we?' Bruce asked, taking a puff of his cigarette and blowing a smoke ring.

'I believe every British mine, plantation, factory or place of business is at risk of attack,' Major Desai replied. 'Following the very serious incident at the Elphil Estate in Sungai Siput a fortnight ago, we have been asked to provide protection around the clock to British establishments, and that includes yours, Mr Lacey.'

Bruce blew smoke out across the desk, then took a glug of brandy. 'Well, that's a relief, I suppose. I put some of my men on the gates with hunting guns, but God knows what they'd do if there *was* an attack. They'd probably run a mile. And there was no way I could defend the whole perimeter.'

'It was a wise move, but you can ask your men to stand down now. By the way, at the moment we think the British are the main targets. Your servants and workers should be able to come and go as they please. But of course... that may change, and the MNLA might start targeting those who work for the British as well.'

'Good God,' Bruce said, taking another swig.

'We will take over the security of your estate from this evening, Mr Lacey. I will put men on the gate, have sentries patrol your fences.'

'Ha!' Bruce laughed. 'This mine occupies the best part of one hundred acres. It's bordered by jungle on three sides and a rubber plantation on the other. I know you're trained soldiers, but I really don't know how you're going to patrol all of that, frankly, Major.'

'I have studied the map of the local area myself, Mr Lacey,' the major replied. 'It will be a challenge, I agree. We will patrol *inside* the fence, rather than outside it – that way we won't be impeded by the jungle. And there will be no need to patrol the border with the rubber plantation because the external borders of that estate will also be protected. We will put checkpoints and roadblocks on the roads into the mine, to check everyone coming in.'

'You seem to have thought of everything, Major. I'm impressed. Will your men be billeted here?'

'No, Mr Lacey. They will continue to live in the camp we've recently established at Batu Gajah and will come and go by truck every shift.'

'So, that just about wraps it up, doesn't it?' Bruce said, putting his feet back on the floor and draining his glass. 'I need to get back to the office. If that's all?'

'Just one more thing... I presume you both have guns?'

'A couple of hunting guns, yes. Oh, and I have a pistol too.'

'And does your wife know how to use them?'

There was an awkward pause. It was the first time Alice had been mentioned since they'd entered the room, and she felt heat rise to her cheeks as both men turned to her.

'I'm afraid I don't know how to use a gun,' Alice said, shuddering at the memory of her father returning from *shikar* in the jungle in Bengal, the carcases of tigers, stags and leopards strung on wooden poles being carried home by a multitude of servants. She loathed the senseless killing of game and had always refused to handle a gun.

'Well, you'll have to learn how to now, *darling*,' Bruce said, emphasising the last word sarcastically. 'But God knows when I'm going to find time to teach you. The mine is at full tilt at the moment.'

'I could give your wife a lesson... with your permission, of course, Mr Lacey.'

Bruce was just reaching for his cigarette packet, preparing to get up from his chair, and at the major's words his hand stopped in mid air. Alice watched him, her heart pounding with trepidation. He frowned, peered at Major Desai carefully for a second, then burst out laughing.

'Why not? Why not indeed, Major Desai. I'd be grateful. She's a timid little thing, though, and needs careful handling.'

Major Desai didn't reply at once. Alice, her cheeks aflame, could barely look at him.

'I could return on Monday morning to help Mrs Lacey,' the major said. 'I'm afraid at the moment I'm busy setting up all the patrols on local properties.'

Bruce strode round to the other side of the desk. Major Desai got up and the two men shook hands.

'Monday it is then,' Bruce said. 'Thank you, Major.'

'Let me know if you have any problems in the meantime. Here is the address and telephone number of the base.' The major handed Bruce a card, then, bowing to Alice, left the room.

Bruce followed and Alice waited, listening to them saying goodbye at the front door and then the engine of Major Desai's jeep roar into life.

Bruce came back into the study, swiped up his cigarette packet, tapped one out, and lit it before throwing the packet down on the desk. 'Well, that was an interesting little interlude, wasn't it?' he said, his eyes on Alice's face. 'Quite the pukka little gentleman wasn't he, our Major Anil Desai? I saw the way you were looking at him.'

'Whatever do you mean?' Alice said.

'Oh, come on, Alice. You couldn't keep your eyes off the fellow.'

'Don't be silly,' she said. But she knew nothing would stop the jealous rage that was about to erupt. She'd seen it so many times before.

'He jumped at the opportunity to teach you to shoot, didn't he?'

'He was just being polite. For goodness' sake, Bruce, if you think that why on earth did you agree to it?'

Bruce took a deep drag on his cigarette. He was standing only a yard or so away, and she could smell the heat and sweat on his body, the alcohol on his breath. She wondered what he was going to do, why he was studying her face the way he was. She braced herself for a push or a thump, her heart beating fast.

'I wanted to see what happened, that's all. And, besides, you do need to learn to shoot.' Bruce drew on his cigarette again and blew the smoke out in front of him, straight into her face.

She flinched and looked away.

'I think I'd like to get to know this Major Desai a bit better,' Bruce said, taking a step away from her and going to the window. 'If he's going to be around all the time guarding us from the commies, I'd like to know who we are dealing with. I've an idea! Why don't you invite him to supper? We could ask the Blanchards and the Watkins. Their plantations are close by, so I'm sure they'd like to get to know him, too.'

She stared at him and swallowed hard, wondering how she could dissuade him from this bizarre plan. On those rare occasions they'd entertained before, Bruce had got drunker and drunker, and more and more boorish, as the evening progressed, insulting Alice and his guests in equal measure. All the ex-pats they knew from the club in Ipoh were used to him, and didn't usually take offence, bandying insults as if they were harmless banter. But she didn't want to subject the seemingly cultured and impeccably polite Major Desai to such treatment; he was bound to be offended and humiliated. How could she possibly bear a whole evening of it?

But once Bruce had decided on something, she knew it was virtually impossible to dissuade him. However, she decided to at least try.

'Is it a good time to be entertaining, Bruce? I mean, there's a

State of Emergency on, isn't there? Surely people should be staying at home rather than going to dinner parties.'

'Nonsense. We need to carry on as if nothing has happened. Show those blighters we're not going to let them change the way we live our lives. I'm sure all the fellows in the club think the same way.'

He walked towards the door and Alice breathed again. Somehow, the ugly scene had been averted.

'So I'll leave it to you then, shall I?' he said, his hand on the doorknob. 'Saturday evening?'

'Yes, alright,' she said.

He left, slamming the door behind him.

Now, Alice stood at the drawing-room window and watched the houseboy, actually a man of forty-five, pedalling away from the house and down the long drive on his black bicycle to deliver the letter to Major Desai at his camp. The servant wobbled along, one hand steadying his red songkok, or traditional cap, on his head, his white robes flapping about his legs.

The evening before, Alice had telephoned both the Blanchards and the Watkins on the adjoining estates and asked them to dinner on Saturday evening. Eve Watkins had been very polite, if a little reserved in her usual manner, and had accepted straight away, but Diana Blanchard, with whom Alice was a little in awe but closer, had been incredulous.

'You're having a dinner party, my dear? You're joking? When there are armed guerrillas lurking in the jungle just over the fence? That's not like you, Alice. You hardly ever entertain at the best of times!'

'I know,' Alice had said. 'It's Bruce's idea. He wants to get to know our new Gurkha officer, Major Desai.'

'Oh yes. I've met Major Desai. Dreamy looking chap, isn't he?

But what the hell's Bruce up to this time?' Diana mused. 'I mean, knowing your dear husband, there's got to be something.'

'I'm not sure,' Alice said. 'But you're right. He's bound to have an agenda.'

There was a pause at the other end, then Diana lowered her voice and said, 'Don't you worry, Alice. We'll be there on Saturday evening. You and I can have a heart-to-heart after dinner. You can tell me all about it.'

'Thank you, Diana,' Alice said before she put down the receiver.

She thanked God for Diana, her only true friend amongst the ex-pats. A good ten years older than Alice, she seemed impossibly sophisticated and worldly wise. She was as outspoken as Alice was retiring, her bleached-blonde hair always coiffed in the latest style, always dressed in flamboyant clothes with a cigarette in her hand and a witty anecdote on her painted red lips.

Alice spent the rest of Friday morning organising the servants for the following evening; she decided not to ask Cook to prepare anything elaborate, knowing that always ended in disaster. Instead, she asked him to make satay for a starter, his signature Malay chicken curry he did so very well, and tropical-fruit salad for dessert. She spoke to Suleman and asked him to ensure there was enough alcohol in the cabinet, that there was soda and fruit juice for cocktails, and that the icehouse behind the house was fully stocked. Bruce would never forgive her if they ran out of liquor or ice while they were entertaining. She also asked Suleman to ensure the drawing and dining rooms were cleaned on Saturday morning, that the vases were full of flowers, and the table was set with their best silver cutlery, cut glass and china.

Suleman, Cook and the rest of the servants responded to the challenge with gusto; she guessed they were glad to have something to take their minds off the anxiety about the insurgency. The house was soon a hive of activity; cushions and rugs being dragged outside and beaten, floors swept and scrubbed, furniture cleaned and polished.

Alice put on her battered old raffia hat and went outside, deciding to take herself away from the house for a couple of hours until things had calmed down. She let herself into the garden at the side of the house, where the lawn was shaded by bougainvillea, casuarina and lotus trees. She would often while away time here lounging on the wide swinging sofa, but today she wanted to get right away, to be by herself to think for a while.

She also didn't want the servants to see where she was going. Suleman and Bruce were as thick as thieves and the bearer often reported on her whereabouts or what she was doing to his master.

There was a gate out of the garden on the other side, and beyond that was a little path, crossing some rough, scrubby land. It then wound through a patch of jungle and climbed up the hill that sheltered the house. From the top of that hill, you could stand and look out over the great scar in the red earth, the enormous pit that was the tin mine. Alice assumed the path had once served as a back route to the mine before the pit had been excavated so deep it had become redundant.

Alice was glad when she was out of the fierce sunlight and walking through the relative cool of the jungle. The path was narrower here, encroached upon by huge ferns and clumps of bamboo. It started to rise, and she skidded a little on the uneven earth in her flimsy sandals as she climbed, pushing her way through. At last she emerged a few yards from the top of the rise where the trees stopped abruptly, and a wire fence had been erected around the rim of the mine.

Alice had found a gap in the fence long ago, and over the months had widened it until she could slip through without ripping her clothes. She often came here to be alone, to stare down at the activity beneath her, to think or to dream. It was an odd place to come, she knew that. It wasn't peaceful. Beneath her the pit was teeming with workers, and the rumble and roar of the tin-dredging machinery was constant. But what was good about this place, was that nobody else knew about it. Not a soul. And she knew that if she came here, she would never be disturbed.

Today she'd needed to get away. Not just because the house was being turned upside down by the servants, but because the encounter with Major Desai and the subsequent tension with Bruce the day before had unnerved her. And something about the whole episode, probably the conversation with the major about Barrackpur and the mention of guns and shooting, had reminded her of her father. She needed to sit calmly and let the thoughts and memories overwhelm her for a while. Only then would she be able to get a grip on herself again and put them to the back of her mind where they belonged.

5

Barrackpur, India, 1946

THE FIRST TIME Alice set eyes on Bruce Lacey was when her
father brought him back to their house on the Barrackpur
Cantonment after a night of drinking and gambling at the club.

She'd been unable to sleep that night; the weather was so hot
and close. The monsoon was about to break, and the electric fan
that revolved lazily above her bed wasn't strong enough to cool
the stifling air. She got out of bed and went to the window,
leaning out to catch any stray breath of breeze outside. But it was
as hot and still out there as it was inside the house. She could
hear the night-time sounds of the nearby jungle, the buzz of
cicadas and the whoop of monkeys. It was the sound of home.

It must have been after two o'clock in the morning, and she
was surprised to hear the rumble of a rickshaw on the road.
When it rounded the bend, she saw there were two people riding
on the seat behind the rickshaw-puller and her heart sank.

Alice wasn't surprised to see her father stumble down from
the seat and pay the driver, but she was surprised to see another
man get down beside him. This was a far younger man, tall and

well-built, with a mop of blondish hair. He was also unsteady on his feet.

She stared, intrigued. This wasn't Father's usual sort of night-time companion. Normally it was a woman or, more precisely, a girl. He'd been known to bring the wives of his junior officers home with him. They must have been crazy or bored out of their minds, or both, Alice thought, to even consider a dalliance with her father. Perhaps it was because of his rank. Perhaps they thought it might assist their husband's career. Either way, she found it distasteful. But far more often than young British women, it was an Indian girl he would bring home with him. One of the girls from Sonagachi, the red-light district in the north of Calcutta. Father would travel down there in his staff car before dark and return in the middle of the night with one of these girls in tow. Just the thought of it made Alice's flesh crawl. Most of them were far younger than Alice herself. Once, she'd caught sight of one the girls emerging from Father's room in the early hours of the morning; a scrap of a thing, dressed in an elaborate red saree, bedecked with cheap jewellery, her dark eyes ringed with kohl. They'd exchanged a brief, awkward glance before the girl had darted back into the room. Alice had never forgotten the look in her eyes: terror, guilt and shame in equal measure.

But Father had never brought a man home, and Alice had never seen tonight's companion before. She heard them stumble onto the porch and come in through the front door, cross the hallway with heavy footsteps and go straight into her father's study. The door slammed, but she could hear the rise and fall of their voices echoing through the still, quiet house. Were they arguing? She strained to hear what they were saying, but couldn't make out the words.

Overcome with curiosity, she pulled on her silk dressing gown and crept down the stairs, wincing at every creak the boards made under her feet. But judging by how loud the conversation going on in the study was, she needn't have worried; they would never hear her.

She crept over the oak floorboards of the hall, across the blue Kashmir rug that felt cool and silky underfoot, and came to a stop in front of the study door. Still the voices were muffled, so, feeling guilty, but unable to stop herself, she put her ear to the door.

'Look, my good man,' her father was saying in his most authoritative voice, 'I simply cannot pay you that sort of sum. I might look wealthy, but I can assure you I'm just an army officer and hardly have a penny to my name. Here, why don't you have a brandy.'

Alice heard the chink of glass and the glug of liquid being poured.

'So why the devil did you invite me back here,' said the other man, 'if that's all you've got to tell me?'

'I thought we could thrash it out away from prying eyes at the club. I can offer you a bed for the night. Our guest room is very comfortable and it's a bit dreary down at the club, isn't it? And my cook does a damned fine kedgeree for breakfast—'

'You've got to be joking!' the other man burst out.

There seemed to be a brief scuffle, during which Alice heard a chair crashing to the floor. She imagined the newcomer holding her father by his collar, their perspiring faces eyeball to eyeball.

'I don't want your blasted kedgeree and I'm quite happy at the club. I want what you owe me, you old bastard.'

'Calm down, calm down. I'm sure we can work this out.'

There was silence for a few moments and Alice heard the creaking of chairs. They must have both sat down.

'Who's that?' the stranger asked after a pause.

'Who?'

'That girl in the photograph. Here, on your desk. She's beautiful.'

'That's my daughter,' said Father. 'You leave her out of this.'

Alice felt a prickle of self-consciousness rush through her and her cheeks heat up. It felt strange to be spoken about like that.

'I'd like to meet her,' the man said.

'She's too good for the likes of you,' her father said to Alice's surprise.

He'd never said anything like that to Alice herself. In fact, she couldn't remember him ever paying her a single compliment.

'Well, I'd like to meet her. Is she here?'

'You'll meet her at breakfast tomorrow morning,' Father said. 'I think we should get some sleep. We can sort out our little difference of opinion in the morning when we're both sober.'

'No,' the stranger said. 'Let's sort it out now. While it's fresh in our minds.'

'If you insist. But I need to pop to the dining room for more brandy first. This decanter is nearly empty...'

Suddenly, her father's footsteps were coming across the study floor towards the door. He would be furious if he knew she was eavesdropping on him. She darted back across the hall and fled up the stairs, terrified of his temper. She'd just reached the top when the door to the study opened and her father emerged. She could see him from where she stood on the landing upstairs, her back pressed against the wall. He was standing in the middle of the rug, his head on one side, listening intently.

'Hello?' he said. 'Hello? Is anybody there?'

The stranger came to the study door. 'Everything alright, Colonel?' he asked.

'I thought I heard a noise, that's all. Probably one of the servants creeping about. Wait there. I'll fetch the brandy.'

Alice slid silently along the landing and back into her room. She shut and locked the door and threw herself down on her bed, her heart thumping ten to the dozen. Whatever had possessed her to creep downstairs and spy on her father? The fact she'd nearly been caught in the act made her both hot and cold with fear. She wondered what exactly her father owed to the stranger. It would be a gambling debt for sure. Father was known for his hard-drinking, hard-living ways and when he'd had a few drinks at the club, he would often gamble deep into the night.

But then her mind turned to the stranger, and she felt a thrill go through her when she remembered his words. *She's beautiful.*

No one had ever told her that. Father never had. Perhaps Mother might have done if she'd lived, but Alice could barely remember her. She'd died of typhoid fever when Alice was only three and Alice had been raised by a series of Indian amahs. She was often aware that the eyes of the younger officers followed her around the room when she was at the club, and two or three of them had asked her to dance during the drunken Saturday-evening dinner dances. She'd even been outside with one of them, but he'd pressed her against the back wall of the club and kissed her violently, thrusting his tongue into her mouth, before she'd pushed him away and run inside. But none of them had told her she was beautiful.

The stranger's words had surprised and intrigued her, and in spite of the bizarre circumstances of his visit, she couldn't wait to meet him at breakfast. She hadn't managed to get a proper look at him when he'd stumbled out of the rickshaw. True, he was drunk, which wasn't a good sign, but she was impressed at the way he'd stood up to her father. Not many people dared to do that. Especially not the people on the cantonment, most of whom were inferior in rank, or owed their livelihoods to him in some way. This man must be new to Barrackpur and, Alice guessed, probably had nothing at all to do with the army.

Later, she heard her father and the stranger stumble upstairs. The stranger went into the guest room opposite hers and her father to his suite along the passage. The house fell silent, and Alice finally dropped off to sleep.

IN THE MORNING she dressed carefully for breakfast, in one of her pretty summer dresses the Barrackpur tailor had run up for her at the beginning of the season. She brushed her hair until it shone, and even applied some subtle eyeliner and a touch of lipstick. She felt a flutter of nerves as she went downstairs and approached the dining room.

To her surprise both her father and the newcomer were already seated at the long, oak table. Both men stood up when Alice came into the room. Her father looked a little bleary-eyed, but was clean shaven, his moustache freshly trimmed. Every morning the army barber came to the house at seven o'clock to shave him. This morning the man must have nicked Father's skin as there was a trickle of blood running down his cheek.

'Good morning, my dear,' Father said, his eyes on Alice. 'We have a visitor. Mr Bruce Lacey. Mr Lacey is here on leave from Malaya where he manages a tin mine. Bruce, meet my daughter, Alice.'

Alice turned to look at the newcomer, who clearly hadn't suffered as Father had from the night's excesses. He looked as fresh and well-groomed as if he'd drunk nothing but spring water the night before. His dark-blond hair was combed back off his face and he had arresting blue eyes and a square jawline. He held out his hand and Alice shook it.

'Good morning, Mr Lacey,' she said.

'Good morning, Miss Wilkinson. It's very nice to meet you,' he said.

The men sat down, and Alice went to the sideboard under the window to get some food. The cook had laid on a sumptuous spread which was set out on silver platters. Scrambled eggs, bacon, mushrooms, toast, porridge and, of course, kedgeree. Alice helped herself to egg, bacon and mushrooms, and sat down at the table. To her amusement she saw that Bruce Lacey was tucking into a huge plate of kedgeree.

'Mr Lacey will be staying with us for a few days,' Father told her.

She put down her fork and looked at him in surprise. She'd expected the visitor to be leaving straight after breakfast. The two of them had clearly resolved their difference of opinion; both seemed quite relaxed. But she couldn't ask about it because that would risk giving away the fact that she'd been eavesdropping the night before.

Instead, she said innocently, 'And what brings you to Barrackpur, Mr Lacey?'

'I needed a break – some time away from the mine. We've been very busy lately. I didn't want to go back to England – it's far too far – and I served with an officer during the war who is now stationed at Barrackpur. He invited me to come and visit him here.'

'Oh really? Who's that?' she asked, not really interested in the answer but wanting to continue the conversation.

'Jamie Buller. Lieutenant. We were together during the Malaya Campaign, at the fall of Singapore and in a Japanese POW camp for three years in Thailand.'

'Oh, how terrible,' she said. She'd heard the horror stories about those camps; the starvation, the brutality of the Japanese, the men being driven like slaves to build a railway through the jungle, the multiple deaths from tropical illnesses.

'It was,' Bruce said quietly, dropping his gaze. 'The only way you could get through was if you had a mate, and Jamie was the best mate any man could have. I owe him my life.'

Alice now regarded Bruce Lacey in a fresh light. Just looking at him – a well-built, strong, vibrant man – you would never guess he'd been through such an ordeal. He must have only been released a year or so before, and he seemed to have already rebuilt his life. Looking at him closely, though, she could see there was something strange lurking behind his eyes, something almost switched-off, that betrayed he'd seen evils few men would have guessed at. That look tugged at Alice's heartstrings. And in that moment she wondered if she could find a way to make it disappear.

6

AFTER BREAKFAST, Colonel Wilkinson stood up, shook out his napkin and said, 'I must be off to the parade ground now. Alice, I would appreciate it if you could show Mr Lacey around. Perhaps get the syce to take you both into town? I don't think Mr Lacey has seen much of the place so far.'

'I'd really appreciate that,' Bruce Lacey said. 'But only if you have the time, of course.'

Alice looked at him and smiled. If only he knew how bored she was, how the days dragged here. Most mornings she would ride out alone on one of the two horses father kept in the stables behind the house. But apart from that she'd only had books to occupy her since the war ended.

As soon as she'd come home from England in early 1940 she'd busied herself with war work. She'd found a job as a telephonist at Regimental HQ and she'd enjoyed everything about it: the daily routine, chatting with callers, relaying – sometimes vital – information, being part of a team. But all that had ended shortly after the war. With men coming back to base from the front in Burma, they no longer needed women to fill in for them. She'd found herself at a loose end; alone in the house, shunned as a spinster by the young married women her age, and ignored by her father – who would prefer to be at the club gambling and drinking than spending time at home with her. Her only friend was Jamila – the daughter of Sita, her former amah – who was the same age and had been Alice's childhood companion.

'Miss Wilkinson?'

She returned to the present and realised Bruce Lacey was waiting for her answer.

'I have the time,' she said simply. 'Do you ride, by the way? We could go out on the horses, or we could take the car into town. Which would you prefer?'

'Let's go for a ride,' Bruce said. 'I don't have riding clothes with me, though.'

'I'll ask one of the servants to dig out some of Father's. I'm sure he won't mind. You seem to be an honoured guest.'

Bruce Lacey laughed, his eyes brightening, and in that moment the blankness behind them that had confused and frightened her at first went away.

They rode out that morning, side by side, and for Alice it was a real pleasure to have someone to share her time with. Both the horses were old and heavy, easy to handle, so they chatted as they rode. It was such a contrast to Alice's usual mornings that it made her realise how lonely she'd been for years.

'I hope you don't mind my asking,' Alice said, 'but if you're here to see Lieutenant Buller, won't he be expecting you to be spending time with him?'

'Ah. Well, Jamie is married now, and they have a tiny baby who never stops crying. And he was unable to get much leave in the end. So it was a choice between staying in his house with his wife and baby or coming to stay at your father's place. Your father and I hit it off straight away in the club last night.'

Alice had to swallow an incredulous laugh. From the conversation she'd overheard, she would hardly have described it as hitting it off. She was itching to ask him what arrangement they'd come to about her father's debt, but couldn't find a way of broaching the subject. In the end, she decided to leave it. Bruce and her father were obviously getting on well now, so the matter must have been resolved to both parties' satisfaction.

They travelled along Riverside Road between the plane trees that lined it, past the officers' houses that sheltered in shady grounds behind high, white walls. At the end of the road, they turned down a track that led towards the river. Delicious cooking smells wafted towards them and they passed street vendors selling fruit and cooked dahi puri – battered doughnuts stuffed with spices. A few rickshaw wallahs were gathered there, resting on the seats of their rickshaws under the trees, smoking bidis and waiting for customers to alight from boats crossing the great River Hooghly, which was so wide the buildings on the opposite bank looked like toys.

'This way,' Alice said, 'I know a path by the river.'

Beside a jetty, they turned and rode along a narrow trail that wound between the walls of the mansions on one side and the river on the other. It was low tide, revealing muddy water flats beside the path.

'I've always loved this ride,' she said, turning in the saddle to look at Bruce.

'I can see why,' he said, looking out across the water that was dotted with patches of waterweed, where herons skimmed the surface and flocks of egrets rose from the muddy banks. Dhobi wallahs stood knee-deep in the water, beating colourful washing against concrete steps, the droplets from the clothes forming a rainbow in the sunshine.

When the path widened, Bruce drew alongside Alice.

'It's beautiful here. I'd never have guessed,' he said. 'Jamie took me into Calcutta to see the Victoria Memorial and the Maidan and that was about it.'

'Well, I'm a native,' she said, smiling. 'I've lived here all my life, so I know all the secret places. Where do you come from, Mr Lacey?'

'Oh please. Call me Bruce,' he said. 'I come from England. The West Country. I was an engineer in Bristol before the war. I signed up for the army and was posted to Kuala Lumpur.'

'Bad luck, eh?' she said.

'In some ways...' He nodded. 'But despite the horrors of the Malaya Campaign and being a prisoner of war for three years, I got a taste for the place. So at the end of the war I applied to manage a tin mine there. I've been doing it for about a year now.'

They rode on in silence, and Alice feasted her eyes on the beauty of the river. She loved the ever-changing colours of the water; the deep blues and greens, the way the fluffy white clouds were reflected in the surface and the sun shimmered on the silver rapids. It never ceased to fascinate her.

After a while, Bruce asked, 'Have you ever been to Malaya?'

'No. I've travelled in India and been to England, but nowhere else, I'm afraid.'

Then he surprised her by saying, 'I think you'd love it there.'

'Do you think so?' she asked.

'Oh yes. If you love it here... Malaya is vibrant, exotic, full of colour and the Malays are a beautiful, welcoming people.'

'It sounds charming,' she said, trying to picture it in her mind.

Just then a small boy on an oversized bicycle approached along the path from the other direction. They had to pull the horses onto the grass so he could pass without spooking them. When they resumed their ride, the subject of Malaya had been forgotten.

Back at the house, after they'd changed out of their riding clothes, the servant brought them tiffin in the drawing room; pakoras and samosas, followed by teacakes and a large pot of tea.

'This is all so civilised,' Bruce said, looking around him at the elegant room, the chintzy furniture, floral curtains and hunting prints. 'I'm afraid my house on the tin mine is a bit unhomely. It lacks a woman's touch,' he added, his eyes on Alice's face.

For some reason, she couldn't meet his gaze. Instead she took a sip of tea and changed the subject.

'What would you like to do this afternoon? We could get the syce to run us into Calcutta? Or we could play tennis? There's a court at the end of the garden and no one's used it for ages. Father doesn't have time to play, and I don't have anyone to play with.'

'Let's play tennis then,' Bruce said eagerly, but then his face fell. 'Although, of course, I don't have any whites.'

'Father has some,' she answered. 'You can borrow those.'

Bruce played well, but Alice was rusty, and – inexplicably – she was a little nervous. She'd never been particularly good at tennis, but she'd always enjoyed the game. Bruce gallantly let her win several points and she soon relaxed and began to enjoy herself. The sun beat down fiercely, though, and before long her dress was sticking to her and sweat was pouring down her face.

After about an hour, she said, 'Let's call it a day, shall we? It's far too hot to be running about.'

They went back to the house to bathe and change. By that time a servant had arrived from Lieutenant Buller's house with Bruce's suitcase. When they were back downstairs, Alice's father was home and it was time for cocktails on the veranda.

'I must say, you two look as though you've been enjoying yourselves,' Father remarked, sipping his gin fizz.

'We had a wonderful time,' Bruce replied. 'I haven't enjoyed myself so much for ages. Your daughter is the perfect hostess,' he added, his eyes on Alice.

She felt herself blushing and took a sip of her gimlet.

Bruce stayed with them for four days, and in that time they rode out each morning by the river, and in the afternoons Alice showed Bruce the sights of Barrackpur and Calcutta. He was fascinated by everything, the Hindu temples, the native bazaars

and the grand imperial buildings. She found him easy and conge-
nial company, and was glad to see that the desperate look in his
eyes was there less and less as time passed.

On the fifth morning, to Alice's disappointment, he said he
must go back and spend the day with Jamie Buller and his family
before leaving for Malaya the following evening.

'Jamie has taken a day's leave to spend time with me,' he
explained to Alice. 'Otherwise, I'd far prefer to stay here with
you.'

She didn't know how to respond. Wordlessly, she smiled up
into his eyes while delight ran through her in waves. She couldn't
remember when she'd been as happy as she'd been over the past
few days, and she was dreading Bruce leaving. She wondered if
she would ever see him again. The thought she might not put her
into a frenzied panic. Life would be so empty without him.

He left after breakfast with Father, who was going to drop him
off on his way to the base. Before Bruce left, he kissed Alice's
hand, his lips lingering on her fingers for a moment longer than
necessary. He looked up into her eyes and said, 'Thank you for
showing me something of the real India, Alice. I will never forget
these few days and I will miss you.'

'I will miss you too,' she replied. She stood on the front porch
to say goodbye, and as she watched him getting into the back of
the car with Father, and waving to her through the rear window,
she felt tears pricking her eyes. 'Don't be absurd,' she told herself,
turning away. 'Forget about him.'

But she spent the next twenty-four hours in a state of misery.
She lay on her bed in a torpor, staring up at the ceiling fan,
hardly moving, wondering how she would get over him. She had
no appetite for food. She didn't even want to read, or to ride.

In the end, the morning after she'd said farewell to Bruce, she
decided to seek out her friend, Jamila, in the nearby Indian
village. Alice had neglected Jamila since Bruce's arrival, and she
felt a little guilty. So she took her bicycle and cycled through the

shady roads of the cantonment until she came to the turning for the native village. It was where all the Indians who served the army base and the homes of the soldiers lived; barbers, dhobi wallahs, gardeners, shopkeepers and those servants who didn't have quarters with the families they served. Some of the houses were built of brick, but others were wooden, corrugated iron or even made of wattle and daub, insulated with cow dung. Jamila's house was neater than most. Her mother, Sita, was a careful housekeeper. Alice pedalled quickly along the bumpy road between the ramshackle dwellings. She passed children playing in the dust, chickens and dogs rooting about, Brahmin cows wandering in the road, old men lying on charpoy beds on their porches, smoking or sleeping.

When Alice drew up, Jamila was sitting on the porch with her mother, preparing vegetables. Jamila shaded her eyes and looked at Alice when she approached.

'Hello, stranger,' she said, jumping up and embracing Alice.

'I'm sorry I haven't been round for a while. We had a visitor,' Alice explained.

'It doesn't matter. I've been busy anyway,' Jamila said with a mischievous smile.

'Go on, daughter, tell her your good news,' Sita coaxed, getting up from where she was squatting and smoothing down her saree. 'I will go inside and make some tea.'

Sita disappeared into the house and Alice sat down cross-legged beside Jamila. This place was like a second home to her. She'd spent hours here as a child, eating with Jamila's family, playing with her and her brothers, Vikram and Ramesh. She spoke their language, Bengali, fluently, because as a child the servants had been her closest companions.

'Well? What is it?' Alice asked.

'I'm going to be married,' Jamila burst out, her voice full of joy. 'Baba and Ma have found a boy in a village across the river.'

Alice stared at her friend, who was brimming with excitement. She couldn't suppress the twinge of envy and sadness she felt at those words.

'Have you met him?' she asked, through a fixed smile.

'Not yet. But I've seen a photograph,' Jamila said. 'Look. Don't you think he's handsome?'

Alice took the proffered photograph and examined it carefully. The boy was beautiful, with liquid dark eyes and smooth skin, a perfectly shaped face. He looked very young.

'He is,' Alice said and hugged her friend. 'Congratulations, Jamila. What's his name?'

'Viraj,' she said. 'He's the same age as you and me. Baba said we were lucky to find anyone, because I'm so old. Viraj was in the army for the last two years of the war, fighting in Burma.'

'When are you going to meet him?' Alice asked.

'This weekend. We're all going to his home. I can't wait!'

'I'm so happy for you,' Alice said.

Jamila and her happiness meant everything to her, but she couldn't help a selfish, niggling twinge from creeping in and spoiling it. It was traditional for married Indian women to live with their in-laws. Jamila would be moving away. Admittedly only across the river, but there were few bridges and the journey would take several hours. When Jamila left, Alice would be more alone than ever before.

She tried not to let those thoughts spoil her visit. They sat on the porch sipping tea and eating sweetmeats as they'd done countless times before, as if nothing had changed. But every time Alice looked into her friend's eyes, she could see in the new way they shone that Jamila was looking forward to her new life and had already moved on. It brought home to Alice that these precious moments, that until now she'd completely taken for granted, were now finite.

Later, she rode slowly home, her mind full of sorrow. In the space of a few hours she'd lost two people who meant a lot to her.

She hardly knew Bruce Lacey, of course, whereas Jamila was a beloved friend, but Bruce had entirely captivated her. She couldn't forget the way he'd looked at her, the touch of his lips on her hand, or the magical words she'd heard through the study door: *She is beautiful.*

It was late afternoon by the time she rode into the drive and lodged her bicycle in the shelter beside the house. When she let herself in through the front door, Amrit, the bearer, was standing in the hallway.

'There is a gentleman to see you, Alice mem,' he said.

'Gentleman?'

'Yes. Mr Lacey.'

'Mr Lacey?'

Why was he here? His ship was sailing from Calcutta this evening, surely. Perhaps he'd forgotten something. Her heart soared at this unexpected chance to see him again, but she instantly realised her hair was unbrushed and she'd made no effort with her clothes or appearance that day.

'He is waiting for you in the drawing room,' Amrit said. 'He has been here for almost an hour. We didn't know where you were, mem.'

'Thank you, Amrit. I'll go and speak to him,' she said, trying to compose herself and to marshal her scattered thoughts.

When she entered the drawing room, Bruce was sitting in an armchair smoking, but as soon as he saw her he stubbed out his cigarette and stood up.

'I thought you were leaving this evening,' she said. 'Is there something wrong?'

'I am leaving this evening,' he said. 'But I had to see you, Alice.' He walked forward and stood in front of her. 'I don't want to leave you. I want you to come with me.'

'Come with you?' she repeated, frowning. Did he mean to the docks to see him off?

'To Malaya. I want you to come with me. I want to be with you, Alice. I've fallen in love with you.'

She stared up at his earnest eyes, dazed. What she'd not dared to hope for these past two days was actually happening. Was she dreaming?

'What are you saying?' she heard herself asking.

'I'm saying, dear, beautiful Alice... will you marry me?'

Alice was glad he'd took hold of her arms, for she suddenly felt faint.

Bruce smiled and tipped his head, his eyebrows raised. 'Will you?'

Those arresting blue eyes pulled her in. It felt as though she was falling...

'Alice?'

She blinked. 'I... I'm sorry, I...'

'I'm the one that should be sorry,' he said, still holding her by the arms. 'Caught you by surprise.'

He chuckled, and she found herself smiling, her heart pounding like never before.

'Yes,' she said, 'of course I will marry you.' But then she remembered. 'What about Father?'

'I've already asked him,' Bruce replied smoothly. 'And he agreed.'

'Really?' she asked, wondering fleetingly when that conversation had taken place.

He nodded. 'I haven't got a ring yet and we don't have time to get married here, but if you come home with me we can get married in Kuala Lumpur before travelling back to the mine. I've taken the liberty of booking you a single cabin for the crossing.'

He took her in his arms then and gave her a tender, lingering kiss, worlds apart from the only other kiss she'd experienced. She wanted it to go on and on, but she heard the sound of the front door closing and within seconds Father was entering the room. They broke apart.

'Your daughter has accepted my proposal, Colonel Wilkinson,' Bruce said.

Father didn't look at all surprised, rather, what she saw cross his face was a flash of something else. It took her a few moments to realise it was relief.

'Well, congratulations,' Father said, coming forward and shaking Bruce's hand before kissing her on the cheek. 'I expect you'll need to be thinking about getting off, if your ship leaves this evening, won't you?'

'We have a few hours,' Bruce said. 'Time to pack at least.'

Alice suddenly remembered Jamila. How could she leave without saying goodbye?

'I need to tell my friend. I'll be back in twenty minutes,' she said, and left them both standing there.

She pedalled as fast as she could through the busy streets to Jamila's house. Jamila was still sitting on the porch, just as she'd left her. It had been less than an hour since Alice had left but it seemed like a lifetime.

'Jamila!' she said, leaving her bike on the ground and running up the front steps. 'I need to talk to you.'

'What's happened?' Jamila stood up.

'You know I mentioned we had a visitor? Well, he has asked me to marry him and go with him to Malaya.'

Jamila's mouth dropped open. 'And you are going?'

Alice nodded and Jamila threw her arms around her.

'So we will both be married! This is such good fortune. We are both truly blessed.'

Alice hugged her friend back, grateful she didn't give her an incredulous stare or utter words of warning about marrying a stranger, but then she supposed Jamila herself was about to do the same thing.

'But I won't see you for a long time,' Alice said.

'We can write!' Jamila said. 'Write to me here at Ma's house. Tell me all about your life. I will always write back.'

'Of course I will,' Alice said.

Sita came out onto the porch and added her congratulations. 'What does your father say?' she asked.

'He's given his blessing,' Alice replied.

'Then you have mine too,' Sita said, hugging her.

Back at the house, Alice threw as many possessions as she could think of into the trunk she'd brought back from boarding school in England. She added photographs of her mother and father's wedding, a portrait of her mother, a picture of her and Jamila sitting on the porch at Sita's house, and several novels to read on the journey. When she was ready, the servants brought it downstairs, took it out to the drive and strapped it onto the back of Father's car. Then the staff all lined up on the porch to bid her farewell. She found she had tears in her eyes, shaking hands with these loyal men and women who'd cared for her since babyhood, and whom she regarded as family.

Father held both her hands and said, 'I'm no good at goodbyes, Alice. I won't come down to the port. I know I haven't always been the best parent in the world. I hope you'll be happier where you are going.'

'Oh, Father,' she said, biting her lip. He was right; he'd been a negligent, distant parent, he'd always put his needs first, but she was so full of emotion in that moment that she was prepared to forgive him anything. 'Thank you.'

Darkness was falling as the car drew away from the house and she looked back for a last glimpse of her childhood home. Father was standing on the porch with one hand raised in an awkward wave.

Bruce took her hand and said, 'It must be tough, leaving home. I'll take good care of you, though, Alice.'

Later, they stood together on the deck of the P&O Liner, the HMS *Carthage*, as it slipped out of Kidderpore Dock at high tide onto the Hooghly and started its long voyage downriver to the

Bay of Bengal. Alice felt a twinge of sadness at leaving the land she'd grown up in and loved fiercely. But looking up at Bruce's face and feeling his arms around her, she felt as though she'd made the right decision.

7

ANIL

Malaya, June 1948

ANIL DESAI DROVE QUICKLY and expertly along the jungle road towards the Rimba Valley tin mine that Saturday night. It was a hot, still evening and the sky was dark, the only light from the low, pale moon. The headlights of his jeep were dimmed for camouflage purposes, but their weak beams still lit up the jungle plants and cast fantastical shadows on the rough road in front of him. He kept his eyes peeled for any strange movement in the undergrowth, any stirrings amongst the huge ferns or outsized bamboo clumps that encroached on the carriageway. His pistol lay on the passenger seat beside a huge bunch of white lilies he'd bought from the bazaar in the kampong next to the camp.

He wondered what the evening ahead would hold. Bruce Lacey had seemed to him an odd, rather difficult man, and Anil had abhorred the disparaging way he'd spoken about his wife in her presence. But his wife, Alice, was something else. From the moment he'd set eyes on her, Anil had been struck by Alice's innocent and natural beauty. Her perfect skin, clear blue eyes and the delicate shape of her face were extraordinary. The way her cheeks dimpled, and her eyes shone when she smiled. There was something unexpected behind those beautiful eyes; something sad and vulnerable that seemed to speak to his heart. And judging by the way her husband had treated her, and the bruises he'd spotted on her wrists before she'd hastily covered them, he had a shrewd idea what it was all about.

British Malaya was the last place in the world he might have expected to be drawn to a woman. Most of the British memsahibs he'd encountered in Burma and India, and even here in Malaya, had struck him as singularly unattractive, both physically and personally. He far preferred the Nepalese girls he'd met in Kathmandu, whose dark, flashing eyes held untold promise.

But Alice Lacey was different. When he'd left the Lacey residence after his first visit, he'd been intrigued, and had caught himself thinking about her again and again over the subsequent hours. And when he'd received her letter inviting him to dinner that evening, despite any misgivings he had about Bruce Lacey, he simply couldn't refuse. It would give him another chance to feast his eyes on Alice Lacey's perfect features.

As he drove, he thought back over the past couple of weeks, and how it was that he came to be driving down this road in the middle of the jungle, thousands of miles from his native Nepal. When he'd been called into his colonel's office on their base in Dehradun in India, where they'd been stationed since the end of the war, he was surprised to be told he would be leaving a couple of days later for a posting in Perak in Malaya. He'd never heard of Perak and knew precious little about Malaya either.

'You and your company will be responsible for guarding a district against the communist insurgents,' the colonel told him.

'Communist insurgents?' Anil asked, surprised. He had to admit to not being fully abreast of the unfolding situation in

Malaya, although he did know the country had been beset by strikes and civil unrest for over a year.

'Yes. The colonial office in Kuala Lumpur is expecting trouble from them in the very near future,' the colonel explained. 'That's why we've been asked to send troops there without delay. We're sending as many men as we can spare. You will be tasked with guarding and maintaining security on all the local tin mines and rubber plantations, of which there are many.'

'Is it expected to be a short posting?' Anil asked, slightly bemused. A few communist guerillas would surely be dispatched very quickly by a single battalion of well-trained Gurkhas.

'We will assess timings as events develop,' the colonel replied, eyeing him steadily. 'I know you served bravely during the war, and that you are a fearless and experienced soldier under fire, Major Desai. But a word of advice... underestimate this particular enemy at your peril.'

'Yes, sir,' Anil replied, standing up and saluting the colonel before returning to the barracks to prepare for his departure. Despite what the colonel had said, as he walked away from the office, he assumed he and his men were being sent to Malaya to undertake something akin to a peacekeeping role.

By that time, Anil had been a Gurkha for around eight years, during which he'd been on active service in Burma, fighting against the Japanese, for almost three years. He'd seen sights that had shocked him to the core; in Kohima he'd been under siege, almost starved out by the enemy and under constant Japanese fire for months. He'd lost many close comrades in that fight to the death and counted himself lucky to survive. So a few communist guerillas bent on sabotaging civilian properties hardly held any fear for him.

He left Dehradun with his company of fifty Gurkha soldiers two days later on an army transport plane. After a six-hour flight, the plane circled a group of jungle-covered hills and landed at the airbase in Ipoh, which itself was hewn out of the jungle.

Looking out the window as they came in to land, Anil was struck by how much the country reminded him of his first impressions of Burma.

He'd spent the first few days settling his men into life at the hastily erected camp just outside the small town of Batu Gajah, which although makeshift, was well equipped. It even had a Hindu temple in one of the bamboo huts where Anil prayed and made offerings each morning at dawn. He'd also got to know the area, visiting the local planters and mine owners in the jeep that had been allocated to him. It was important they understood what the Gurkhas were there for. Most had greeted him with polite disinterest, and he got the distinct feeling that, for the time being, none of them understood the gravity of their situation. To his mind, the planters and mine managers –and their wives – were completely convinced of their inviolability, and were also more or less interchangeably dull.

But during their very first week on the base, just as Anil's men were getting settled in, news came through of the first guerilla attacks on rubber planters at Elphil Estate. Listening to the news reports, he wondered if he'd misjudged the situation. Perhaps the threat from the communists was more serious than he'd initially imagined.

ANIL SLOWED DOWN for the checkpoint ahead of the gates to the Lacey estate, showed his badge to the men on duty, who saluted and waved him past. His jeep crunched along the gravel drive towards the house, and as he neared it he saw that its balconies and eaves were lit up in tiny white lights. He groaned inwardly. This really was an invitation to the guerillas, and he would have to have a quiet word about it – although not tonight, of course.

He parked in the front drive, pocketed his revolver and picked up the bunch of lilies. Then he mounted the steps to the front porch. As he knocked on the door he could hear the clock in the hall striking the hour. He hesitated for a moment. Was it considered impolite by the British to arrive precisely on time? He'd vaguely heard something like that mentioned once. It must be some bizarre British custom – he knew he would never understand some of them. But before he'd had time to think about it, the door was opened by a portly servant in white uniform wearing a red fez.

'Good evening, I'm here for dinner with Mr and Mrs Lacey,' he began.

He heard footsteps on the stairs, and Alice Lacey appeared behind the servant, who bowed and stepped aside. She looked radiant in a filmy powder-blue silk dress. Her shoulders and arms were firmly covered in embroidered tulle, which looked a little out of place in the heat of the evening. He wondered why she'd taken such pains to cover her skin, but it only took him a few seconds to guess the reason.

'Good evening, Mrs Lacey. I hope I'm not too early,' he said, handing her the bunch of lilies. 'These are for you.'

They smelled beautiful and as Alice Lacey took them and thanked him he realised – as he picked up wafts of some sort of fresh lemon-scented perfume – *she* smelled delicious too.

'Come through to the drawing room,' she said. 'My husband will be with us in a moment. He's just finishing up some paperwork.'

Anil followed her, wondering if Bruce Lacey was actually sitting in his chaotic study, his feet on the desk, smoking and fortifying himself for the forthcoming evening with a stiff brandy or two. As they were crossing the hall to the drawing room, he caught sight of Bruce slipping out of his study and standing at the end of the corridor to the servants' quarters. He was dressed in filthy khaki working clothes.

'Suleman?' he bellowed, clearly wanting help getting changed.

The bearer came running and they both went upstairs.

Mrs Lacey flushed, and led Anil into the room, invited him to sit down and offered him a drink.

'You do drink alcohol, don't you?' she asked tentatively, her eyes both anxious and embarrassed.

'I would very much appreciate a gin and tonic,' he replied, laughing.

She looked around vaguely for one of the servants, but when none appeared, walked over to the drinks cabinet to mix the drinks herself. When she'd done so and handed one to Anil, she said, 'Please make yourself comfortable, Major Desai. If you'll excuse me, I'll just take the flowers to the kitchen so they don't wilt.'

Instead of sitting down, he paced the room, drink in hand. There were some shelves, crammed with books that completely covered one wall. Anil had always loved books. His room in his parents' house in Kathmandu was filled with them. He bent down to look at the spines and recognised some of the titles and authors. Just then he heard Mrs Lacey return. He straightened up.

'Are these books yours or your husband's, Mrs Lacey?' he asked.

'Oh, they're mine. I love reading,' she replied with an earnest smile. 'You know, if you're not careful, time can drag here on the estate. There is no one else nearby and the club is in Ipoh, which is a bit of a drive. But it doesn't bother me. If I have my nose in a book, I find the time just flies by. I was just the same when I lived in India.'

'Me too! Me too!' he said smiling with enthusiasm. 'I have read all the books of William Somerset Maugham,' he said. 'I see you have his short story collections here.'

'Oh yes. I ordered them as soon as I got to Malaya. I'm afraid they don't always paint a flattering picture of British colonial life, do they?'

'Far from it,' Anil replied, smiling. 'I'm surprised they haven't put you off completely.'

They laughed, but then there was a cough from the doorway. They both turned to see Bruce Lacey standing there, brandy glass in hand, dressed in his dinner jacket, his bow tie a little skew-whiff, his face like thunder.

'Bruce!' Mrs Lacey said, instantly stiffening.

Anil walked forward to greet him, his hand outstretched, and by the time he took the mine manager's hand the anger had disappeared and Bruce's face was composed.

'Welcome, Major,' Bruce said. 'I see my wife has been keeping you entertained.'

'Yes, she has,' Anil said pleasantly. 'I must thank you for inviting me this evening, Mr Lacey. I've already met your neighbours, I believe, but it will be good to get to know you all better.'

'My thinking entirely, Major,' Bruce said, going over to the drinks cabinet and topping up his brandy.

'And this might be the last time such an event is possible for a while, I'm afraid,' Anil continued. 'Next week it is likely curfews will be put in place around the district.'

'Really?' Bruce said, taking a hefty swig. 'What a dashed inconvenience. Still, I suppose we don't go out that much anyway, do we, darling?'

'No,' Alice said, dropping her gaze.

'As she was telling you, my wife is happiest of all with her nose in a book. And I like my liquor of an evening.'

Anil smiled politely and there was an awkward pause during which, to Alice's obvious relief, the doorbell rang.

'Oh, that will be more guests,' she said and hurried out to the hall.

Diana and Tony Blanchard followed Alice back into the room. When Anil had visited their estate, he'd thought Tony a solid, dependable type, a typical British planter, and Diana an interesting, if slightly unnerving, woman who seemed to have no hesitation in speaking her mind. Tonight she was elaborately dressed in a scarlet, strapless evening gown that showed off her bare shoulders and ample cleavage.

The Watkins followed close behind and soon everyone was installed in the drawing room, primed with drinks and the conversation flowing. At some point Alice left and when she returned and stood in the doorway she looked pale and a little shaken.

'Dinner is ready, if everyone would like to come through,' she announced.

Dinner got off to a good start. Everyone had had at least two cocktails by that time and seemed happy to talk. Satays were served on silver platters. When Anil bit into his, it tasted delicious; the chicken was cooked to perfection and the peanut sauce just the right level of sweetness. The guests all appeared contented and relaxed. It seemed to Anil that they were glad to have left home and be letting off steam after the tense events of the past few days. Talk was all of the Emergency, what had happened so far, what might happen, how long it might last and what the British government might do about it.

'You know they've called it an Emergency to avoid calling it a civil war?' Tony Blanchard said. 'That way anyone who suffers damage will be able to claim on their insurance. If it was called a civil war, the insurers would refuse to pay out.'

'How clever of the government,' said Diana, raising a glass to her husband.

'That's about all they've been clever about,' Bruce Lacey said. 'They're not doing half enough to defend our property. A few half-hearted roadblocks? Do they really think that's going to deter these bloody commies? No offence, Major...'

Anil looked at Bruce, a fixed smile on his face. The man was insulting him and his regiment. He clenched his fists under the table. If only he wasn't his host...

'We are doing our best, Mr Lacey,' he said.

'Of course you are, Major,' Hugh Watkins said, then he turned to Bruce with a reproving look. 'The major's a good man, Lacey... we're lucky to have him.'

'Things need to be stepped up though,' Bruce said. 'The high commissioner isn't taking this half seriously enough. He needs to call for reinforcements. He needs to really clamp down. It's an outrage that innocent planters were shot dead by these commie blighters in their own homes and offices where they should have been safe. Far more needs to be done.'

Anil watched Bruce Lacey as he talked. He looked flushed and belligerent, his eyes slightly glazed, a vein pulsing in his forehead.

'You know, we fought alongside those Chinese communists during the war,' Hugh Watkins said. 'When Malaya fell to the Japs, some of us in Special Ops went behind enemy lines. We worked alongside those communists, we trained them in jungle warfare and even armed them. But now they've turned the tables on us. Some think they didn't give all their weapons back at the end of the war. Now they're fighting us with them. It's a damned rum do, in my book.'

'My men are trained in jungle warfare too,' Anil said. 'We fought in Burma against the Japanese. We can take on the guerrillas, fight them at their own game, but sadly there are not enough of us here.'

'Like I said,' Bruce chipped in, 'we need reinforcements from Blighty. And fast. We can't rely on a bunch of native Gurkhas to look after us.'

Anil saw Alice turn to look at him anxiously. He sat perfectly still, staring down at his plate, doing his best to remain calm.

'Now come on, Bruce, that's hardly fair,' Tony Blanchard said. 'The major here might take exception to that remark. The Gurkhas are the toughest soldiers on the planet. And the bravest.'

Bruce laughed. 'Well, if they're that tough they're going to be thick-skinned enough to take a bit of light-hearted criticism, surely. Isn't that right, Major?'

'You're quite right, Mr Lacey,' Anil said with another forced smile. Why was his host hell-bent on trying to rile him? What was his game? Whatever it was, Anil wasn't going to give him the satisfaction of rising to the bait. 'And I agree, we do need reinforcements urgently.'

At that point they were interrupted by the servants bringing in the main course, and to Anil's relief the conversation moved on.

Later, during dessert, it was Alice's turn to be the object of Bruce's criticism. The talk had turned back to the Emergency and the need for all planters and mine owners to be armed.

'My father taught me to handle a gun before the war,' Diana Blanchard said. 'Fat lot of good it did me against the Japs, though. Still ended up in Changi Jail for the duration.'

'I know how to handle a gun too,' Eve Watkins said. 'Hugh taught me the first time he had to take a trip away. You can never be too careful in this country. What about you, Alice?'

'I'm afraid I've never learned,' Alice said, blushing.

'But Major Desai has volunteered to teach you hasn't he, my dear?' Bruce said in a pointed tone.

'Yes,' she said, looking down at her fruit salad.

'You need to be careful of my wife, Major,' Bruce said then, slurring his words. 'She eats men for breakfast.'

There was a shocked silence, and the women gasped. At first, Anil had no idea what Bruce Lacey meant by the colloquial phrase, but seeing the faces of the others, the truth began to dawn on him.

'I say, Lacey, that's no way to speak about your other half,' Hugh Watkins said. 'You need to apologise to poor Alice right away.'

'I'll do no such thing,' Bruce said, 'I'm only telling the truth.

I'm not surprised *you're* defending her though, Hugh. I've seen her making eyes at you at the club.'

Hugh Watkins stood up so abruptly his chair crashed on the floor behind him. 'I'm very sorry, Alice, but Eve and I are going to have to leave. I can't listen to any more of this insulting nonsense. You certainly don't deserve such treatment.'

Alice Lacey stood up too. 'Don't go, please. Bruce doesn't mean it,' she stammered.

'Of course I meant it, you little fool,' Bruce said. 'Let them go. Their company is as dull as ditchwater anyway. They're no loss.'

'Really, Bruce old man, steady on,' Tony Blanchard said.

Anil wanted to lunge across the table and punch Bruce Lacey square in the jaw, but he knew such behaviour would be punished by the regiment, whatever the provocation. He might even lose his posting and be sent home. Although it pained him to do so, he continued to sit rigidly on his seat, staring at the tablecloth.

Hugh and Eve Watkins left the room and could be heard talking to the bearer in stifled tones in the hallway before the front door slammed, and a car engine started up outside. Everyone around the table remained silent, listening to the car draw away.

Diana Blanchard broke the awkward silence by picking up her spoon and tucking in to her dessert. 'I must say, your cook has really excelled himself this evening, Alice,' she said. 'Every single dish has been absolutely delicious.'

Everyone picked up their spoons and began eating, and, gradually, the tense atmosphere in the room dissipated. Conversation didn't return to normal, but everyone tried hard to resurrect the evening. Even Bruce Lacey seemed to have calmed down, and started talking about High Commissioner of Malaya, Edward Gent.

'The man just isn't up to the task,' he said. 'He simply hasn't got the mettle. We need someone with a bit more backbone.'

'I couldn't agree more,' Tony Blanchard said.

Anil nodded in agreement. 'This situation certainly needs a strong response,' he said.

Gradually the atmosphere thawed, largely through a shared discontentment with Edward Gent and his leadership, and by the time they'd finished eating it felt as though relations had been restored.

At the end of the meal, the bearer came in to pour brandy for the three men and Alice and Diana got up to leave, as was the custom. Anil had no real desire to sit there drinking and smoking with Bruce Lacey – although Tony Blanchard seemed a decent enough man – but politeness compelled him to stay until the bitter end. Once again, they spoke about the Emergency, about the need for security on the estates and how well armed and prepared the guerrillas were.

'It was only when I arrived here and saw what they were capable of that I began to realise the extent of the threat,' Anil said. 'I know now they're a formidable fighting force, well trained, disciplined and well armed. The pact the British struck with them during the war has backfired rather.'

'You don't say!' said Tony. 'It all seemed too good to be true at the time, and now we're paying the price.'

The party broke up at around eleven. Anil stood up after a second brandy.

'I'm afraid I must be heading back to the base,' he said. 'I'm on duty early in the morning.'

Tony Blanchard said goodbye, and then Bruce stood up.

'Well, goodbye, Major,' he said.

Anil wondered if he would say anything about the unfortunate events of the evening, perhaps even apologise for his behaviour, but he seemed completely unrepentant. Perhaps he thought such behaviour was normal.

They walked out to the hall together and were just shaking hands when Alice appeared from the drawing room.

'Ah, Mrs Lacey,' Anil said, bowing slightly. 'Thank you very much for a wonderful evening.'

'Thank you for coming, Major.'

He would have taken her hand and kissed it, but he could feel her husband's eyes boring into him and he didn't want to spark another jealous outburst. As it was, Alice looked pale and agitated, but she managed a wan smile.

'I'll see you on Monday morning then,' he said. 'Would ten o'clock suit you?'

'That would be fine, thank you,' she said quickly, clearly wanting the encounter to be over.

'Goodbye then. And thank you again,' he said, leaving the house and crunching over the gravel drive to where his jeep was parked.

He got into the vehicle, started the engine and turned to head down the drive. As the lights swung round and lit up the front of the house, they caught the Laceys standing on the veranda. Frozen in that moment, the misery on both their faces was plain to see.

8

ALICE

Dear Major Desai,

Thank you for your very kind note. And thank you also for coming to dinner and the lovely flowers.

I feel I must apologise for my husband's behaviour on Saturday evening. Due to the stress caused by recent events, I'm afraid he had rather too much to drink and said some things that were regrettable. I am sincerely sorry for this. I hope it didn't cause you offence and that we can put it behind us.

I'm looking forward to seeing you on Monday morning at ten o'clock as we discussed. I hope you'll accept my apologies, and I'd be grateful if you wouldn't mention to my husband that I've written in these terms.

Yours sincerely,

Alice Lacey

ALICE LICKED THE ENVELOPE, addressed it and went out onto the veranda where one of the servants was sweeping. She asked him to take the letter to the Gurkha camp.

'Me, madam?' He looked nonplussed.

'Yes you, Abdul. And there is no need to mention this to Suleman,' she added. 'This is between you and me.' Looking around quickly, she slipped him a few ringgit coins from her pocket.

His eyes widened in surprise, but he took them swiftly. She could see from his expression he understood her meaning. He left his broom and went off to find his bicycle.

She sat down in one of the basket chairs with a deep sigh and put her head in her hands. The events of the previous evening came back to her in a jumbled rush.

She thought back to when she'd popped into the dining room to check everything was ready. She'd lit the candles then spotted the lilies Major Desai had brought. A servant had put them in a glass vase on the sideboard as she'd asked. The luxuriant white flowers dwarfed the small vases of roses from the garden the servants had dotted about the room – they were truly beautiful. Alice went over, buried her face in them and breathed in their delicate perfume. When she looked up, to her surprise, Bruce was standing at the end of the table.

'Did *he* bring you those?' he asked.

When she didn't reply he strode forward and grabbed her by the wrist, closing his fist around it. She took in a sharp breath.

'Major Desai? Did he bring them?'

'Yes. But what of it?'

'I'm watching you, Alice,' he said, loosening his grip. 'So be very careful.'

'Please, Bruce,' she said, her heart thumping in her chest, 'don't make a scene. Not tonight.'

He snorted, but let her go, and she walked back into the drawing room, trembling all over. She could feel him walking right behind her, his breath on her neck.

She stood in the doorway and cleared her throat. 'Dinner is ready, if everyone would like to come through,' she announced. Then she stood aside and let the guests walk past her towards the dining room.

When Diana drew close, she whispered in Alice's ear, 'Are you alright, Alice? You look as pale as a ghost.'

Alice swallowed. 'I'll tell you later.'

As she'd feared, the evening went from bad to worse, with Bruce getting increasingly drunk, first insulting Major Desai, then going on to insult her. When he said 'she eats men for breakfast', it was the final straw. Shame and humiliation had washed through Alice in great waves. This was worse than ever before. How could she bear it?

Tentatively, she'd glanced at Major Desai, but she couldn't see his eyes. He was sitting rigidly on his seat, staring at the table-cloth. Diana was giving her sympathetic looks from the other side of the table. When Hugh and Eve Watkins could bear the insults no longer and left, Alice wished the earth would open and swallow her. There went two more kind, decent people she'd called friends, alienated by Bruce's behaviour.

At last it was over. She'd heaved a sigh of relief when the servants had come in to clear the table and to pour brandies for the men.

'We'll take our leave then,' Alice had said, and she and Diana had taken themselves to the drawing room.

When they sat down side by side on the sofa, Diana had put her arms around Alice. Alice had felt a great heaviness descend on her and she let the tears flow freely.

Diana didn't say much for a while, she just rubbed Alice's back and said 'There, there' in a soothing tone. But finally, when Alice's tears had subsided, her friend said, 'He really shot his bolt this evening. He was worse than ever. What was all that about, do you think?'

'I have no idea,' Alice said. 'He seems to feel threatened by Major Desai. Though I've no idea why.'

'As I said on the phone, Major Desai is a very good-looking man. He is a highly respected soldier, clearly well-bred and has impeccable manners. Bruce is the opposite of all those things.'

'But what should it matter? He's so jealous and I've no idea why. I've never so much as looked at another man.'

'Well, no one round here would blame you if you did, my dear. He treats you abominably. And he hits you too, doesn't he?'

Alice closed her eyes, trying to control her tears. She felt Diana's fingers on her sleeve, pulling it up, revealing one purple bruise above her wrist and another just beneath her elbow.

'I worry for you, Alice,' Diana said. 'It can't go on.'

'It wasn't like that at the beginning...' Alice said. 'I don't know what happened.'

Diana got up, went to the drinks cabinet and poured two brandies. She returned to the sofa and handed one to Alice.

'Tell me about it,' Diana said, leaning back and taking a sip.

Alice took a glug of brandy too and the fiery liquid coursed through her veins, instantly relaxing her. She tried to think back to when things had started to go wrong for them.

'When we first arrived in Malaya, things seemed perfect,' she'd said, remembering how she'd fallen in love with the country just as she had with Bruce, how happy she'd been to be mistress of her own house, and how she'd set about making it more of a home, motoring in Bruce's old Austin into Ipoh, the nearest sizeable town, to buy paintings, artefacts and fabrics.

They'd had no time for a honeymoon; they'd had that on the ship, she supposed. Bruce had to get straight back to work in the mine as soon as they returned home. He was always up early and out of the house before she'd even come downstairs for breakfast. He worked long hours and only returned after dark. Alice had grown lonely all by herself in a strange place with just the servants for company. Again.

It was only three weeks or so after they'd arrived when she'd decided to go down to the mine office at lunchtime to take Bruce some food so they could eat together. She had asked Cook to pack him some snacks, she knew he took his lunch with him when he left in the mornings, then she'd asked Suleman if she could take one of the bicycles, stashed the tin of snacks in the basket and pedalled the mile or so through the jungle to the mine office.

When she'd entered, Bruce's assistant, a young Chinese man called Ah-Po, stood up stiffly.

'Mrs Lacey. What a surprise. What can I do for you?'

'I've come to see my husband. Is he around?'

'Tuan is out in the sheds,' Ah-Po said.

'I'll go to him,' she said, eager to see how the mine worked.

The man's face had clouded over. 'I don't think that's a good idea. Only workers are allowed on the mine. Tuan is very strict about that.'

'Oh, I don't think he'll be strict with me. I am his wife after all,' she replied. 'Is it through here?'

She opened a door at the other side of the office that said No Unauthorised Personnel and stepped out. She stopped on the step, stunned at what she saw. When she'd approached on the bicycle she'd had some idea of what the mine looked like: machinery towering behind the single-storey corrugated-iron office buildings, and beyond that the exposed soaring cliff of a great pit. Now her view was unimpeded by buildings and the scale and magnitude of the place took her breath away. The pit in which the mine was built was enormous and was a scene of constant movement. Groups of workers, clad in long, black robes and conical hats, were wielding pickaxes halfway up an incline on the far side, chipping away at the red earth, filling giant tipper trucks with their spoils. Those trucks formed a train which stood on a small railway that led down to a hulking great corrugated-iron building which was set in the middle of an enormous, yellow-coloured pond. The rhythmic rattling of machinery came from inside the building.

Alice stood there, taking it all in – the noise, the heat, the clamour – when she saw Bruce leaving the factory building by a side door and walking towards her. When he neared her, she was shocked by the look on his face. She'd only ever had smiles, laughter and loving looks from him before. But now, his face was red, clouded with anger. He stormed towards her.

'What in hell are you doing here, Alice?'

She took a step back. 'I... I'm sorry. I thought I'd bring you some food. I get lonely in the house all day.'

'I don't want to be disturbed at work, do you hear me? This is no place for a woman.'

'Alright. I'll go. But I don't know why you're so angry.'

'Just go now,' he thundered. 'And never come back here again.'

She left, trembling all over. She walked back through the office, leaving her basket of snacks on the desk, not saying a word to the manager. Then she got back on the bicycle and pedalled home. She was shaken by the encounter and by the discovery that her seemingly perfect husband had a temper he'd success-fully hidden from her for the first few weeks of their marriage.

After that, things between them deteriorated quickly. He was still angry when he got home that night and spent the evening locked away in his study, drinking. On subsequent days and weeks, Bruce no longer bothered to control himself at home. Any little thing Alice did that annoyed him would be greeted with an outburst. The most frightening thing about it was that when he lost his temper, Bruce reminded her so much of her father.

That night after dinner with Diana, Alice had been ashamed to admit how her marriage had been unhappy virtually from the start.

'The first time he hit me was when we came back from the club one day,' she went on. 'He kept saying I'd been flirting with someone. I can't even remember who it was now. Just someone I was talking to. He called me a whore and slapped me round the face when we got home. I just couldn't understand what had happened.'

Diana took a sip of brandy and put down her glass. Then she

took Alice's hand and looked her in the eye. 'The suffering in those Japanese prison camps did terrible things to men. I should know, I spent three years in one myself. Many couldn't stand it. They just gave up. Some even took their own lives. But the conditions for civilians weren't half as bad as they were for soldiers. The Japs treated those men like slaves. They were beaten, starved...'

'I know,' Alice said. 'He's never talked about it, but I knew as soon as I met him that there was something... something lurking behind his eyes that wasn't quite right.'

Diana squeezed her hand.

'I thought I could help him,' Alice said, feeling the tears overwhelm her again. 'But it's only now that I'm realising that I can't. I never will be able to.'

9

CHLOE

Kathmandu, 2018

CHLOE LAID down the latest letter from Alice to Anil on the desk and looked at Rajesh. 'Poor Alice,' she said, shaking her head. 'Her husband was obviously very bad news.'

'Yes. Poor, poor Alice,' Rajesh repeated. 'Perhaps the rest of the letters will tell us more.'

'I hope so,' Chloe said. 'Only, I think I'd better be getting back to the shop now. I'm sorry I can't stay longer, but Shova is very young and inexperienced, and I don't like to be away for too long.'

'Of course. I understand,' Rajesh said.

'I have an idea though. Why don't you come along to the shop next time? I could read the letters to you in between serving customers. I could keep an eye on things that way, and we might be able to get through more letters too.'

'I'd love that,' Rajesh said with a warm smile. 'Paradise Books is a wonderful place. You've made it so welcoming. I really enjoyed coming with you to help unload the books the other day.'

Chloe smiled, thinking back to when she'd driven Rajesh and the books across town in her little van. They'd navigated the busy streets of Thamel at walking pace, avoiding the throngs of locals and tourists, until she'd finally turned into the alley behind Paradise Books and reversed into her narrow parking space.

Kiran had been waiting there to meet them and he and Rajesh had shaken hands.

'Rajesh!' Kiran said. 'I didn't know you were coming. I was so sorry to hear about your father. He was a real character.'

'Thank you. It is a sad time. But my father lived a long, happy life. And, yes, I came to help stow the books downstairs. It was the least I could do. Chloe has been so brilliant about taking them all off my hands.'

They set to work straight away, heaving the boxes down the steep cellar steps and into the storeroom beneath the shop. Chloe was glad to see Rajesh and Kiran hit it off instantly; obviously they'd known each other since Kiran was a child, but it had been a long time since they'd had any real contact. They were chatting easily as they worked, catching up on news about family members, about their lives.

Moving the books was heavy work, and Chloe was soon out of breath and sweating in the warmth of the afternoon.

'You look exhausted, Chloe,' Kiran said after a while. 'Rajesh and I can do the rest of the boxes. You must have done your fair share of lifting already, and you probably need to check in with Shova.'

'Thanks! I definitely do. I'll bring you both a drink when I come back,' she said. She went into the shop through the back door and the two cats ran to her, miaowing and purring, rubbing against her legs. 'I'll feed you in a little while,' she told them, but undeterred, they followed her as she walked through to the front of the shop where Shova was showing a customer the section on Nepalese history.

Shova was about twenty years old. That day she was dressed in jeans and a baggy T-shirt, reminding Chloe of how she'd been at that age. The young woman was full of energy and had more confidence than experience, but she was a hard worker and willing to learn.

'How's it gone today?' Chloe asked when the customer had left.

'Absolutely fine,' Shova replied. 'No problems at all. It wasn't very busy, luckily. I thought you would be back earlier though.'

'There were a lot of books to pack,' Chloe said.

Shova smiled. 'Let me know if you'd like help sorting them.'

Chloe thanked her, but secretly wanted to save the job of sorting through the books to herself. She was still harbouring the notion there might be yet more letters that she and Rajesh had missed on their search and, besides, she was a little possessive about the bookshop. It was her baby, so she liked to make sure she was in charge and made all the decisions.

Now, she got up from where she was sitting at Anil's desk upstairs in the palace, and put the letters away in one of the drawers, which Rajesh locked up. Then he walked her through the corridors of the enormous house, down the sweeping staircase, across the grand entrance hall and out of the front door.

'Goodbye, Chloe,' he said, shaking her hand. 'And thanks for coming.'

'When do you want to bring the letters to the shop?' she asked.

'Later in the week? Only if you're sure you don't mind though.'

'Of course I don't mind. I'm intrigued by Alice's story and I want to find out more. Thursday would be good if you're free. Come in the afternoon. Auntie Gita always makes apple turnover on a Thursday afternoon, and it's a real treat.'

'Auntie Gita!' Rajesh said, his face lighting up. 'It's years since I last saw her. I'd love to catch up with her. I have some free time on Thursday afternoon, so I'll come at about three o'clock if that's alright.'

'Perfect, I'll see you then.' She went down the steps to the waiting van.

'And thanks again, Chloe,' Rajesh shouted from the top of the steps. 'Your reading the letters means so much to me.'

'It's no trouble at all, and I'm as fascinated as you are by the letters,' she replied, getting into the driver's seat.

She drove back to Thamel, parked in the alleyway behind the shop and let herself in through the back door. This time the shop was quite busy, buzzing with customers. A couple of backpackers were playing on the fortune-telling machine in the corner, there was a crowd of schoolboys in the geography section poring over atlases, and several tourists milling about upstairs. Shova stood by the till with a customer, looking a little frazzled.

'Thank goodness you're back,' she said. 'There was a power cut so I haven't been able to use the card machine for a while. I've had to take cash and add things up myself. I'm no good at arithmetic.'

'Don't worry. Do you want me to take over here and you can go and see if anyone needs help finding anything.'

Shova looked relieved and left the customer to Chloe, who counted out the change and wrapped the purchases in a paper bag. It was five o'clock by that time and the early evening crowds were thickening. Soon the streetlights would come on, the shops light up with candles and fairy lights, incense from the temple and aromas from the street vendors wafting on the air. It was when she was most thankful that she'd fallen in love with and married a Nepalese man, and could call this vibrant, fascinating city her home.

She stood in the doorway, watching the sun go down over the

rooftops, when a familiar figure emerged from the alleyway opposite.

'Kiran?' she said, pleasure and surprise running through her at the sight of him.

'Hi!' He came up the steps towards her and planted a quick kiss on her lips.

'What are you doing here?' she asked.

'The tour finished early, so I thought I'd come and see you. How's it going? It looks busy in there,' he said, looking past her and into the shop.

'It is quite. Which is good.' She smiled. 'I went to Rajesh's place again today to help him read his father's letters.' She'd told him the previous evening about the mysterious cache of letters they'd found beneath the floorboards in Anil's study.

'That's good. I'm glad you haven't been working flat out... I thought you were going to start taking things a bit easier.'

She looked at him, grasping his meaning, and her heart sank. She'd thought he'd forgotten about all this since he'd come back from the Annapurna trek. But clearly not. He'd just been waiting for the right moment to bring it up. To Chloe's mind this was hardly the right moment.

'Why don't we go into the kitchen, and I'll make you a drink. We can chat there,' she said. She didn't really want to leave the shop floor when it was so busy, but equally she wasn't keen on having this important conversation with Kiran in full view of so many people.

They walked through into the kitchen at the back of the shop and Chloe closed the door behind them. She put on the kettle.

'Tea? I think there's still some carrot cake left if you fancy it?'

'That would be good,' he said, settling on one of the stools at the breakfast bar. 'I did a lot of walking today and haven't eaten much.'

Chloe made them each a mug of tea and cut two slices of

cake, which she put on plates. Then she sat down on a stool opposite Kiran.

'Like I said' – he took a sip of tea 'I thought we'd agreed you would start slowing down. You seem to be working harder than ever.'

Chloe bit into the delicious, moist carrot cake and chewed it, giving herself time to respond to him calmly. She was determined not to let this conversation descend into bitterness, as so many others had.

'I don't think we did agree that, Kiran,' she replied, keeping her voice steady and looking him straight in the eye. 'You suggested it, but I told you I want to make sure the bookshop is up and running before I even think about slowing down.'

He frowned and bit into his own slice of cake. 'But time is ticking away, Chloe. It's not going to get any easier as time goes on.'

'I know that,' she said. 'And one day I *will* be able to slow down and take things easy. But now's not the time.'

'How long do you think it will be?' he asked.

'A few months. A year maybe. Things here are going really well, but if I step back they might *stop* going well. You've seen how busy it is this afternoon. We need to be able to capitalise on that. It's not the time to be handing it over to someone less invested than I am.'

'You could trust Rumi,' he said. Rumi was Kiran's twin sister.

'I'm sure I could. But Paradise Books isn't her business, that's all. She doesn't feel about it the way I do. It's hard to explain, Kiran.'

They stared at each other for a while, both full of emotion. They'd been at this impasse for months. Kiran desperately wanted to start a family. They'd started trying as soon as they'd got married, but nothing had happened for them. Then Chloe decided to buy Paradise Books and was so caught up in making a success of the business that they didn't discuss having a family for a while. She'd got busier and busier with the bookshop and getting pregnant was the last thing on her mind. But in recent months Kiran had started asking her to slow down at work, to even take a break to improve her chances of getting pregnant. She'd resisted, not wanting to relinquish control of the shop to anyone. Then he'd hit upon the idea of asking his twin sister, Rumi, to come to Kathmandu and manage the shop to enable Chloe to take a break. Rumi was capable and intelligent, and, as her and Kiran's mother was often sick, she practically ran the guest house in Pokhara that Kiran's parents owned.

'I do understand. My parents feel that way about the guest house. And I do about my work too. It's just... you mustn't let it take over your life.'

'It hasn't taken over my life,' she said. 'Look, I'm just not ready to step back yet. One day I will be, just not yet. Can't you accept that?'

'You could still work, but having Rumi here would let you relax more. You could reduce your hours and take things easier. I actually had a word with Rumi when I was in Pokhara after the trek, and she was all for it.'

'You did what?' Shock and outrage washed through Chloe. She could hardly believe he would have gone behind her back like that. They'd discussed Rumi helping, but Chloe had never agreed to the plan. She felt hurt and betrayed.

'I spoke to Rumi about it,' Kiran repeated. 'I thought we'd discussed that. Hey, you don't mind, do you?'

She stared at him; put down her plate. She'd suddenly lost her appetite.

'Yes, I do mind as a matter of fact. We never agreed you would talk to Rumi about it. I can't believe you did that without us discussing it first.'

'I'm sorry. I had no idea you'd mind so much. Rumi won't tell anyone.'

She looked into his eyes, incredulous. She'd felt like this

before on a few occasions – left out because of the special bond between Kiran and his twin sister. She'd told herself she shouldn't worry about it, that Kiran and Rumi were lucky, and the precious closeness of twins was a wonderful thing. She'd also told herself she'd never understand it, being an only child. But now she felt fully justified in feeling as she did.

'It's not just about Rumi not telling anyone,' she said. 'Don't you realise there are some things a husband or wife shouldn't tell anyone?'

'Look, Chloe.' He got down from the stool and, coming towards her, slipped his arms around her waist.

She pushed him away. 'You just don't get it, do you?'

He held up his hands and backed away. 'Look, I'm sorry. I really am. I was only doing what I thought was best.'

'Best for you, you mean. Not for me.' She got off the stool and emptied her teacup in the sink. 'I've got to get back to work now. The shop's really busy and Shova can't manage on her own.'

'Hey, Chloe, don't be like that. We can work this out.'

Again, he tried to put his arms around her, but again she moved away.

'I've got to get on, Kiran. We can talk about this later.'

Without a further word she walked back into the shop and over to the till where a customer was waiting. She took the book from him and checked the price on the back. She was aware of Kiran crossing the floor of the shop and going to the door. Then out of the corner of her eye she saw him walking across the court yard and disappearing down the alleyway opposite. Her heart ached to see him go like that. She hated that they had parted on bad terms.

After she'd served the customer, she stood at the window and watched the alleyway in case Kiran came back. Her mind wandered to Alice. Although she and Rajesh had only scratched the surface of the letters so far, it was already clear that Alice's marriage to Bruce wasn't a happy one. A sliver of fear went through her. Was that what might happen to her and Kiran? Surely not. Kiran was loving and caring. He would never treat her badly. And yet they seemed to be at loggerheads about an important decision in their lives only two years into their marriage.

They'd never really quarrelled before, and it felt alien and unwelcome. She felt alone for the first time in their marriage, and for the first time since she'd come to live in Nepal. She took a deep breath. She wasn't going to let this come between them. There must be a way to get through it.

10

ALICE

Rimba Valley Estate, June 1948

DEAR MAJOR DESAI,

Thank you so much for the shooting lesson this morning. It took me a while to get the hang of things and I'm sorry I was so nervous, but I think I made some progress. I won't feel so anxious at home anymore, now that I know how to shoot a gun.

You asked me to write to let you know when would be a good time for my next lesson. The answer is any morning this week. Whenever you're free and have time.

I look forward to hearing from you and am eagerly awaiting my next lesson.

Your sincerely,

Alice Lacey

ALICE SEALED and addressed the letter, smiling at the memory of her shooting lesson. Major Desai had arrived alone and, as he had when he came to dinner, exactly on time. He had driven her down the drive and through the gates, past the sentries and the checkpoints on the road. Neither of them had mentioned Bruce's behaviour at the dinner party. Alice was relieved the major didn't bring it up and that the trauma of that evening was firmly behind them.

He took her to a square of wasteland somewhere deep in the forest, where targets were already set up around the edge of the clearing. Tin figures of men were nailed to tall trees, their trunks already riddled with bullet holes, and there were bottles set up on tree stumps.

'This is where we bring our men sometimes to do target practice,' Major Desai explained. 'They also have ranges within the base, but sometimes it is good to practice in the field too.'

Alice looked around her in awe, wondering if she would actually be able to shoot a gun. She already felt nervous, her hands sweaty and shaking. She didn't want the major to think she was hopeless, and the thought that he might was making her even more anxious.

'We'll learn on a carbine,' Major Desai said. 'It's a type of rifle, although shorter and easier to handle. It's what you'll be using at your property.'

She swallowed. The way he was speaking made it sound as though an attack by the communist guerillas was virtually inevitable. So far, the Emergency, the attacks on the rubber estates and British planters, had all seemed remote from her life, as if they were happening in another place entirely and would never affect her. But when Major Desai handed her a loaded carbine, it all began to feel very real.

They walked to the firing spot, marked by some stones on the ground. Major Desai stood behind her.

'Hold the gun snug into your shoulder like this, stand slightly sideways to the target, rest your cheek against the handle and fix your eyes on the target.' He manoeuvred the gun, so the butt was against Alice's shoulder, then placed her hands on the smooth, wooden handle, one holding it steady, the other poised on the trigger.

Aware of him standing very close to her, coaching her through the process, she no longer felt nervous. Having him there had a calming effect on her.

'Now, fire!' he said.

She pulled the trigger and heard a ping as the bullet hit the metal target. The gun thrust against her shoulder, pushing her backwards, making her stumble. To her relief, Major Desai was there to catch her, otherwise she might have fallen over.

The lesson had continued for over an hour, and by the end she was exhausted. But by that time she was also confident enough to fire without the major standing behind her. She couldn't believe how quickly she had learned.

Later, when he dropped her off at the house, he said, 'You made very good progress today, Mrs Lacey. One more lesson and you should be ready to handle a gun on your own. Would you write or telephone the base and let me know when you're free?'

Now she took the letter and sought out Abdul, who was only too happy to pocket the ringgits she handed him and slip away on his bicycle to the Gurkha base unnoticed by Suleman.

As he pedalled away down the drive, she was surprised to see Bruce approaching in the opposite direction in his Land Rover. He didn't usually come home during the working day. She waited for him to get out of the vehicle and come up the steps.

'Where's Abdul going?' he asked.

'He's posting a letter for me,' she replied, her heart pounding, colour rising to her cheeks.

'Oh? Who are you writing to?' Bruce asked.

'Jamila. My friend at home,' she lied, crossing her fingers behind her back. He was aware she and Jamila regularly exchanged letters, and if he'd known she was writing to Major Desai it would probably trigger another jealous rage.

'Your friend at *home*?' he said coldly. 'This is your home now, remember?'

'I mean... I mean my friend in Barrackpur,' she replied, dropping her gaze to the floor.

He huffed and strode past her into the house.

'Why have you come back from work?' she asked.

'This is my house, Alice, and I can come and go as I please. But if you must know, I need to get changed. I spilled some acid on these trousers,' he said. Then he stopped and turned around. 'How did your shooting lesson go, by the way?' he asked in a sly voice.

It was the question she'd been dreading, but she'd known she would have to answer it at some point.

'It went fine,' she said, keeping her voice steady and her eyes on his face. 'I can actually hold a gun and shoot straight now. I learned how to load it as well.'

'Well, bravo for the major,' Bruce said. 'I expect you had fun making eyes at him all morning, didn't you?'

'Oh, Bruce, I wish you wouldn't say things like that,' she said.

To her dismay he strode towards her, took her hand and twisted her arm backwards at the elbow.

'And I wish you wouldn't look at other men the way you do. It's humiliating,' he said, pressing himself against her.

'Please let me go,' she said, wincing from the pain.

He dropped her hand and moved away. 'I'm trying to teach you a lesson,' he said. 'But you never seem to learn.'

She stared at him, shaking her hand to ease the pain. 'I don't know what you mean, and if you think those things about me I don't know why you married me,' she said before she could stop herself. 'You have no respect for me.'

He stood watching her, his hands on his hips, a sardonic smile on his lips. 'Don't you know why I married you?' he asked. And then a broader smirk spread across his face. 'Well, I'll tell you the truth, but you might not like it.'

What did he mean? She felt her scalp prickling.

He leaned in closely, a malicious glint in his eyes. 'I married you because your father offered you in settlement of a gambling debt,' he said. 'And because I thought you were pretty and harmless and that you might be good company for me out here in the back of beyond.'

Her hand flew to her mouth as she gasped, and tears sprung to her eyes. Could this possibly be right?

Then, remembering the conversation she'd eavesdropped on between the two men, she realised his story had a terrible ring of truth about it.

'But... but you said you loved me,' she said.

'I thought I loved you at first. But I didn't know you then. I wasn't prepared for what you were really like.'

She couldn't reply, the terrible admission he'd made was only just sinking in. She needed to get away from him, to calm down, to try to make sense of what he'd just told her.

She left him standing there at the bottom of the stairs, turning away and rushing out through the front door, onto the veranda. There, hanging on a chair, was her wide-brimmed hat. She pulled it on and ran down the steps to the drive. Without looking back she headed through the garden and up the hill through the jungle to her secret place on the edge of the mine. Desperate to put distance between herself and the house, she was almost running, tears blinding her vision. The boughs of jungle foliage brushed against her, insects and moths flew into her face, but she brushed them aside and pushed on. Soon, sweat was streaming down her face, and her clothes were sticking to her.

By the time she emerged from the trees at the top of the rise she was out of breath. She found her gap in the fence, ducked through it and flung herself on the grass on the other side. It was only then she allowed the tears to flow. She lay there on her belly, sobbing into the grass. Now she'd had a little time to digest it, the full extent of the pain and humiliation of what Bruce had told her was coming home to roost.

She thought about her father, and wasn't at all surprised by him striking such a bargain with Bruce. He'd hardly ever tried to be a proper father to her and had spent every hour he could away from the house, feeding his addictions of alcohol, gambling and women. And since Indian Independence the year before, Father didn't have the position or the influence in the community he'd once had. He was one of the few British officers to have 'stayed on', electing to spend his retirement in India. In one of her recent letters, Jamila had told her there were rumours that since Alice had left, her father had installed a young Indian woman in the house as his mistress, although he'd tried to pass her off as a maid. Alice could easily believe those rumours and it was partly because of that that she'd never even tried to visit Barrackpur. She knew she could never go back there, no matter how unbearable life in Malaya might become.

She didn't know how long she'd lain there feeling sorry for herself, when she heard a rustling sound on the jungle path. She lifted her head and listened carefully. Could that be footsteps? It crossed her mind that it might be a jungle beast, but she doubted a wild animal would venture so close to the mine. No, it would definitely be a human being. She sat up quickly and dried her eyes, dreading who might emerge from the forest, hoping against hope it wouldn't be Bruce.

To her surprise, it was a woman who walked out of the trees on the jungle path, ducked through the fence and approached her. The woman was petite with dark hair, and as she got closer Alice could see she was Chinese, not native Malay. She was dressed in shabby clothes – a wide-brimmed hat, a tight-fitting white blouse, baggy blue trousers, and on her feet she wore scuffed leather sandals. She knelt down beside Alice, her face full of concern.

'Are you alright, madam?' she asked.

'Yes, perfectly. Thank you,' Alice said, dabbing her eyes with a handkerchief.

'I saw you walking to the trees, and you looked as though you were in trouble,' the girl said.

'I'm alright, thank you. It's kind of you to check.'

She moved to get up and the woman held out a hand and helped her to her feet.

'Come, I will take you to my home,' the woman said. 'It's close to here. I will give you tea. Alright?'

Alice was about to refuse, then thought again. She didn't want to go back to the house while Bruce might still be there bathing and changing his clothes. From experience she knew it was best to give him a wide berth for several hours after an argument. And, in any case, she was curious as to where this woman's home was. None of the mine workers' homes were near here, they were on the other side of the mine buildings on a patch of flat land cleared from the jungle.

'Where do you live?' Alice asked.

'Just around here, on the edge of the jungle,' the woman replied. 'It is only a small kampong.'

'Alright,' Alice replied. 'I'll come with you. But I can't stay long, I'm afraid.'

'Of course, I understand. Follow me.'

Alice followed the woman's nimble frame around the rim of the mine, skirting the fringes of the jungle, until another path, obscured by giant ferns, opened up in the foliage. The woman walked quickly and deftly, she clearly knew the path well, and Alice had trouble keeping up with her. She'd heard of Chinese squatters' villages built on the edge of the jungle. Many Chinese itinerant workers had fled there during the Japanese Occupation in the war, to hide from persecution, and now they had nowhere else to go. She'd had no idea there was such a village within the mine complex though. She was convinced Bruce didn't know about it either, otherwise she would definitely have heard him complaining about it.

She followed the young woman down this new path between the trees, which was even narrower and more encroached on by jungle foliage than the one she was familiar with. It was so well hidden she guessed only the villagers knew about it. It twisted and turned, crossed jungle streams and wound around huge rocks as it descended the hill. Finally, she spotted daylight between the branches, and they stepped out of the dense jungle and into a clearing through which a fast-flowing stream ran.

'This is our kampong,' the woman said.

The kampong consisted of a circle of rickety bamboo huts on stilts, thatched with palm leaves. There were animals there, too: pigs, chickens, dogs and cats. Women and old men sat on the porches of their houses gossiping, and a group of skinny children played on the grass beside the stream. Alice was astonished. She'd had no idea this place even existed. It was completely surrounded by thick jungle, which hid it from the outside world.

'Come,' the young woman said, beckoning Alice to follow her into a nearby hut.

Alice did so. When she mounted the flimsy steps, the whole structure trembled.

'This is my home,' the woman said, smiling. 'I am Ying May. My mother is inside the house. She is very old.' She pushed aside some creepers that had been trained over the doorway to keep out insects.

Alice peered inside. After a few seconds, when her eyes had adjusted to the gloom, she saw a frail old woman, her face deeply lined, lay on a bundle of rags on the other side of the small space.

'Good morning,' Alice said.

The old woman croaked something.

'She doesn't speak English,' Ying May said. 'Only Cantonese, our language. Would you like a drink? I will make you tea.'

'That would be nice,' Alice replied, relieved. A pot of water stood in the corner of the porch, with a couple of tin mugs beside it, and she had worried it hadn't been boiled. Having spent her life in the east, she had a horror of drinking un-boiled water.

Ying May smiled and took a blackened kettle, filled it with water, then went out to the front of the hut where a charcoal fire was smouldering in the middle of the clearing. She poked it into life with a stick, and hung the kettle from an iron frame above the fire. When it had boiled, she brought it back up to the porch and made tea in a battered metal teapot.

'Best green tea,' she said, handing Alice a cup.

'Thank you,' Alice said, grateful for the hospitality of someone who clearly had so little, and took a sip of the aromatic liquid that tasted of smoke and herbs. 'Are you married?' she asked, wondering how these people earned a living. She'd noticed there were only women, children and very old men in the village at that moment. Surely some of the villagers must work?

Ying May smiled, exposing blackened teeth. 'My husband works in the mine sometimes. Sometimes on rubber plantations too. It is difficult to get work. We do not have papers, but some foremen will employ us if they need extra help. I work in the mine sometimes too, collecting earth for the dredger.'

'Really?' Alice was surprised. 'That is tough work.'

She'd sometimes seen women working amongst the men when she'd watched the activities of the mine from her crow's nest. They were well hidden by broad-brimmed hats and swathed in scarves and long tunics to protect them from the fierce sun. She knew Bruce was strict about who worked in the mine, insisting on proper documentation for all his workers, but perhaps his managers were less so when they were short-staffed.

'We are often hungry,' Ying May said.

Alice felt a surge of pity for her. The woman was tiny and looked pitifully thin, squatting there on her porch in the middle of the jungle. In fact, all the villagers looked the same; pale and wan from lack of nutrition and very thin. Guilt washed through

Alice. She and Bruce lived in luxury surrounded by servants, and always had more than enough to eat, while less than a mile from their home people were starving.

'I could bring you food,' she said, taking another sip of tea.

Ying May looked at her, surprised, but brightened instantly. 'Could you? Could you really?'

'Yes. We always have food left over from our meals and a store cupboard full of supplies. I could bring it to the top of the hill in my knapsack if we arranged when to meet.'

'Oh, that would be very kind. As you see, my mother is sick.'

'I have medicines,' Alice said. 'What does she need?'

'Quinine if you have it. She has malaria.'

'Of course. I'll bring some of that too.'

Ying May's face lit up in a grateful smile and Alice brightened a little. If she could do something good, if she could help even just a few people, it might make her life less desperate than it felt.

'You will keep it a secret, though, madam?' Ying May asked, frowning. 'We have to be secret here. If the police find us, we could be expelled.'

'Of course. I won't breathe a word to anyone,' she assured Ying May. 'It will be our secret.'

11

LATER THAT NIGHT, Alice found an old knapsack, crept into the pantry when all the servants were in their quarters, and filled it with rice, vegetables, eggs and cured meat. She covered her tracks by taking care to ensure she didn't open any new bags, and that none of the individual sacks or boxes of goods appeared too depleted by what she took. She went upstairs and slipped a bottle of quinine tablets into the knapsack. Then, she hid it in her wardrobe while Bruce was taking his nightcap in the study, covering it with a picnic blanket and some large summer hats.

She was excited about returning to the village the next morning with the supplies. It made her feel as though she was doing something useful, trying to alleviate the suffering of that group of desperate, forgotten people. When she went to bed that night, well before Bruce stumbled upstairs and slid between the sheets and started snoring, she lay awake thinking about the day. She'd spent time with two new acquaintances – Major Desai and Ying May – both of whom had shown her kindness, but both of whom intrigued her as well. It made her feel a little less isolated.

Despite the fact she had new bruises blooming on her lower arms, instead of dwelling on the bitter exchange she'd had with

Bruce after her shooting lesson, she thought about the lesson itself. She recalled Major Desai's kind eyes, his reassuring presence behind her when she first handled the gun, his steady hands on hers as he showed her how to fire the carbine. She also thought about the village; about the stick-thin old men and women pottering about on their porches, about the naked children playing in the mud. If she could help them in any way at all it might make her own existence feel a little less pointless.

The next morning she awoke at the same time as Bruce, but lay still until he'd washed and shaved, and gone downstairs for his breakfast of porridge and fruit. Then she got out of bed, and dressed quickly in the old skirt and blouse she sometimes wore for gardening or household chores. Once she heard the front door slam, Bruce stomp across the veranda and down the steps to his Land Rover, start up the throaty engine and roar away, she went downstairs herself.

In the dining room, Suleman was clearing the table.

'Memsahib?' he said, clearly surprised when she entered. 'You are early this morning. Would you like your breakfast now?'

'Just some coffee and toast please,' she replied, taking a seat at the table and ignoring his curious looks.

He brought it to her silently. She knew he was taking it all in, ready to report to his master later. But what could there possibly be for him to tell? She was going to spend some time in the flower garden, dead-heading roses; that was all there was to know.

When she'd finished breakfast, she went upstairs to collect the knapsack. Then, she crept back down to the hallway, making sure none of the servants were about. Instead of going out through the front door, she left the house by the patio doors in the drawing room and headed across the garden to the side gate. She didn't look back, she just prayed nobody was watching her.

Once through the side gate, she walked quickly across the scrubby land behind the garden and into the trees. There, she took her familiar, secret path. She hardly noticed the climb through the jungle, she seemed to have an excess of energy; her heart beating fast with excitement rather than exertion. She was surprising herself. She'd never done anything like this before. She'd always toed the line, terrified of first her father, then her husband. It felt as though she was striking a blow for freedom that morning, and it felt good. It gave her a surge of elation.

She'd arranged to meet Ying May in her crow's nest hiding place behind the fence at nine o'clock, but she was a little early. She put the knapsack down on the grass, leaned back against it and watched the mine spread out below her. As usual, the sound of machinery from the pit was deafening, and the whole area was a scene of frenetic activity. A group of workers were busy digging at the edge of the pit, gradually filling the railway trucks with the reddish-brown soil. A little train on the narrow-gauge railway chugged its way towards the factory, pulling ten trucks behind it, all loaded with the dirt.

The massive, corrugated-iron dredger was already at work in the great yellowish lake, sucking in water at one end, splurging it out at the other. Although she couldn't see them, Alice knew the great sluices were at work inside the hulking building, sifting through the soil again and again, extracting the minerals, finally spewing waste and water back into the lake at the end of the process. She was endlessly fascinated by the mine, partly because Bruce had made it quite clear that it was forbidden territory to her.

There was a tap on her shoulder, and she looked up to see Ying May standing beside her smiling broadly.

'I wasn't sure if you'd come,' Ying May said.

'I promised, didn't I?' Alice said, standing up and shouldering the knapsack. 'I knew you were relying on me.'

'Thank you. I know it is a risk for you.'

'Not really. It's my food. I haven't stolen it, only I don't think my husband would approve somehow.'

'No, perhaps not,' Ying May answered, her face darkening. 'Could I see what you've brought?' she asked.

Alice handed her the knapsack. Ying May opened it up and peered inside, taking out some of the contents, weighing them with her hand, scrutinising them, then nodding in satisfaction.

'Thank you. This is just what we need.' She looked up at Alice with a grateful smile. 'Would you like to come down to the kampong with me again? Have some tea?'

'I'd like that very much.'

Once again, Alice followed Ying May along the path that led round the rim of the mine, and then plunged down through the steep jungle. When they emerged from the trees and entered the kampong, they were instantly surrounded by the village women, clamouring around them, holding out their hands and asking for food.

Ying May turned to Alice and said, 'Don't give any food to them now. I will take it home and distribute it myself. Only that way can I do it fairly.'

When they walked up the rickety steps to Ying May's home, the women stopped and backed away, melting between the huts, returning to their homes.

Once again, Ying May gave Alice green tea on her porch.

When they had finished their drinks Ying May handed Alice the empty knapsack. 'I will show you back to our meeting place,' she said.

They set off again, climbing back through the jungle and up to the perimeter of the mine.

'I can't thank you enough,' Ying May said when they arrived at their meeting point.

'It's alright. I can come again in a couple of days if you like,' Alice replied.

'That would be very good,' Ying May said. 'Shall we say Friday? Nine o'clock again?'

They said goodbye and Alice watched Ying May leave – a

slight but determined figure, winding her way along the rim of the mine beside the fence. Then, Alice went back through the jungle, crossed the patch of land behind the house and let herself into the garden. There, she hurried to the little shed in the corner where she kept her gardening tools and spent half an hour dead-heading roses. At least if she was asked about what she'd done that morning, she could speak truthfully. It would be easier that way.

ALICE'S second shooting lesson had been arranged for the Thursday of the same week. She had looked forward to it, but on Thursday morning, when she glanced out the window, she was surprised to see not just Major Desai arrive in his jeep, but also two army trucks, each with four Gurkhas sitting in the cab. Major Desai strode up to the front door and Alice hurried to answer it.

'I'm sorry, Mrs Lacey. We will have our lesson a little later on, but first we must secure your property with sandbags.'

'Why?' she asked.

'Haven't you heard the news?'

She shook her head. She hadn't turned on the radio that morning and the paper hadn't yet arrived.

'Yesterday afternoon, two rubber estates in the vicinity were attacked by CTs.'

'CTs?'

'Communist terrorists,' he explained. 'Several rubber tappers were killed, as were the British managers of each estate.'

Alice gasped at the news. 'Which estates were those?'

He rattled off the names and she felt a brief surge of relief that neither of the victims was someone she knew, although these were still fellow ex-pats and it surely meant that she, Bruce and the mine were at greater risk of attack than ever before.

'Have you spoken to my husband?' she asked.

'Yes. I dropped in at the mine office just now. Some of my men are still there, putting sandbags in place around the buildings, although the place is so enormous it is almost impossible to secure. If you don't mind, we will start unloading more sandbags here. I suggest we put them along the front of your porch and on your veranda behind the house too.'

'Of course,' she said, wondering what Bruce might say about this.

At that moment his Land Rover roared into view and stopped in front of the house. Bruce leapt out.

'Mr Lacey,' Major Desai went forward to speak to him.

Alice couldn't hear what was being said, but saw with relief that, whatever it was, Bruce was nodding in agreement with Major Desai.

The soldiers began unloading sandbags from the lorries and stacking them along the front porch. Alice watched them from the doorway and before long her view of the drive and the surrounding jungle was obscured by a five-foot wall, several sandbags thick. They left a narrow gap for people to go in and out of the house, which could be filled with spare sandbags in seconds. Just looking at the fortifications brought home to Alice how serious their situation was. This place, that had once been a beautiful, peaceful home, was now a virtual fortress, vulnerable to attack.

Before the wall was finished, Major Desai went out to his jeep and brought a large black gun up the front steps. He asked his men to position it within the sandbag wall directly opposite the front door. He noticed Alice watching him.

'Don't be alarmed, Mrs Lacey,' he said, clearly seeing her expression.

'Is that a machine gun?' she asked, looking at the gun's stand and its large magazine.

'It's a Bren gun,' he said. 'A light machine gun. Your husband asked specifically if I could supply him with one. They are very effective and have a huge range.'

Alice swallowed. The presence of the huge gun with its long barrel and swivel mountings made the whole thing even more terrifying.

'It's actually easier to use than a rifle,' Major Desai assured her. 'But I haven't forgotten your lesson this morning. Although in view of recent events, I would prefer to teach you on your property today. Here we can be sure we are safe.'

'Of course,' she said. 'And thank you, Major Desai.'

He stood looking at her for a moment and she realised his eyes had, once again, settled on the fresh bruises on her arms. She'd forgotten to cover them. This time she was wearing a short-sleeved shirt and there was no hiding them. She put her right hand over her left wrist, but it wasn't enough. He held her gaze for a brief moment. There was so much meaning in his look. She thought he was on the point of saying something, but instead he cleared his throat and looked away.

'Will you be ready in half an hour?' he asked. 'I saw a place in the trees down near the mine where we could practice.'

The soldiers were still finalising the sandbag wall when Alice and Major Desai left in the jeep. He drove her away from the house towards the mine. She glanced back over her shoulder at the house and happened to see Bruce, standing there in an upstairs window, staring down at them as they left. Shock coursed through her, seeing him standing there like that. He knew she was having another shooting lesson that morning, but she hadn't told him she was leaving, and she knew now he would have something to say about it when she returned.

'Are you alright, Mrs Lacey?' Major Desai asked when she turned round again. 'You have gone rather pale.'

'I forgot to tell my husband we were leaving, that's all.'

'Do you think he'll worry? You will be safe with me.'

'I don't know...' she began, twisting her hands in her lap.

He said no more at that moment. When they reached the mine, he swung the jeep off the road and onto a rough track that led towards a stand of trees on the edge of the estate. When they reached it, he parked the jeep in the clearing, got out and came round to Alice's side. She gave him her hand and got out, but before he let go he peered closely at her wrist.

'These bruises look painful. How did you get them?' he asked.

She stared at him, shame and humiliation rushing through her. She wished he hadn't asked because she knew she couldn't face telling him the truth. She would be forced to lie, and she regretted and resented that.

'I fell over in the garden,' she said at last, lifting her head to meet his gaze. 'When I was pruning the roses.'

He frowned. 'Are you quite sure? It looks to me as though somebody has hurt you.'

'Quite sure, Major Desai,' she said coolly. 'Please don't worry about me. Now, shall we get on with our lesson?'

He continued to look at her for a few moments, his forehead pulled up into an anxious frown. Then he said, 'Of course. As you wish.'

He went to the back of the jeep and took out various cardboard targets, a hammer and some tacks. She watched him moving round the clearing, nailing the targets to the trees as he went. Guilt and regret surged through her. If only she'd been able to tell him the truth. What would he think of her if he knew? Would he think any less of her? And, more importantly, would he be able to help her?

12

ANIL

AFTER THE SHOOTING LESSON, Anil dropped Alice at the house, turned the jeep around and drove back down the long jungle road towards the mine. He thought about Alice, about how her shoulders had drooped as she went up the steps to the house and disappeared between the sandbags onto the veranda, about the bruises on her arms. All of that made him anxious for her safety. He wished she would let him into her world. Only then could he possibly help her. But he could see she was ashamed of what her life had become, and he didn't want to humiliate her further by forcing her to answer difficult questions.

He thought too about the spark of light in her eyes when she'd looked up at him during the shooting lesson. She was a fast learner; she quickly learned how to hold the carbine with a natural grip and had a steady eye for the target. There was no doubt in Anil's mind she would be able to handle a gun and shoot at the enemy with confidence. He would have liked to teach her how to use the Bren gun too, but knowing how difficult her husband was it would probably be diplomatic to speak to him about that first. He shook his head as he drove, resenting having to have any contact with that odious man. As it was, he was already on his way to speak to him again about security at the mine.

With a sigh, and filled with loathing, he pulled up on the drive outside the mine buildings. He got out of the jeep and went through the gap in the newly built sandbag wall and into the office, all the time dreading the upcoming encounter with Bruce Lacey.

He spoke to the manager in the office, who went to the mine to fetch his boss. Bruce arrived within a few minutes, wiping his oily hands on a cloth.

'Ah, Major Desai. You wanted to see me? I'm very dirty so I won't shake hands. Do sit down.'

Anil took a seat on a hard wooden bench and Bruce sat down opposite him and lit a cigarette.

'Yes, Mr Lacey. Thank you for your co-operation in erecting the sandbag walls here and around the house this morning. I came back to talk about what is needed for the security of your mine and workers in the coming days and weeks.'

'You're going to tell me the sandbags aren't enough, aren't you?'

'I'm afraid so. It's particularly worrying that the CTs have started targeting native workers on rubber plantations and mines in the past few days.'

'It is,' Bruce agreed, blowing smoke rings absently in Anil's direction.

'Previously, we thought it was only the British they were after. But now we're beginning to think differently. I'm not sure if you know this – it isn't common knowledge – but during the attacks yesterday, the CTs slit the throats of several workers on rubber plantations and left them bleeding to death. There seems no reason for it, other than to cause terror amongst the rest of the workforce.'

'Good God! I agree with you. It seems the bastards are hell-bent on terrorising those workers who are loyal to the British,'

Bruce said. 'What a hellish situation. So, what do you want me to do, Major?'

Anil took a deep breath. 'I would like you to select twenty or so men, the strongest and fittest in your workforce, to form a security detail for the mine, and then another four or five for the house. I will send some of my men over to train them, and we will provide them with arms.'

While he spoke, Anil watched Bruce's face warily, half afraid of another outburst like the one on Saturday evening. As he'd gathered from that ill-fated dinner party, this man was unpredictable. The bruises on Alice's arms came into his mind, as clear as day. His fists clenched involuntarily, but he tried not to think about it. He was here to do an important job, and he needed to put his personal feelings aside. If he let himself dwell on it, he would leap up and plant Bruce Lacey square in the jaw, and that would spell an end to his posting and possibly his career.

But to his relief, Bruce drew deeply on his cigarette, blew another smoke ring then stubbed it out in an ashtray.

'I appreciate the need to arm the workforce, but I don't want to lose that many men, Major. It will put the mine at a severe disadvantage.'

'The men could continue to work in the mine,' Anil assured him, 'but in the event of an attack they would need to be ready to take up arms.'

'Oh, I see...'

'And if you don't provide these men and the mine is attacked and overrun with CTs, you could lose many more men. Then the mine could be out of action for some time. The CTs have already damaged machinery on several mines in the region. They will stop at nothing.'

Bruce stood up abruptly. 'I need to get back to work, I'm afraid,' he said. 'The dredger has been playing up this morning. I understand what you're saying, Major, and I don't like it much, but I agree there is little option. When I've seen to the dredger, I will pick out a defence force from amongst the workers. They will be ready after lunch.'

Anil stood up too. 'Thank you, Mr Lacey. Your co-operation is much appreciated. I will send some of my men round at 3 o'clock this afternoon to start instructing them.'

Anil left the building and drove away in his jeep towards the checkpoint at the gate, feeling relieved. The encounter had gone far better than he'd expected. When it came to protecting his business, Bruce Lacey was a lot more sensible than Anil had thought he would be.

It was a tragedy he wasn't equally reasonable in his personal life. Once again, Anil's mind wandered to Alice. He thought about her winsome beauty, but also about the ugly bruises on her arms.

Now he'd taught Alice to shoot, there was no real reason for him to go back to see her, but he would have to invent something. He had an instinctive feeling that, although she wouldn't ask him directly, something deep within her was silently appealing for his help. He wasn't going to ignore that plea.

He rattled through the gates to the Lacey estate and slowed down as he neared the checkpoint. It was set up in a cutting in the jungle, just before a bend in the road. One of the Gurkhas manning the roadblock saluted him, the other slung his gun over his shoulder and walked over to lift the barrier. Anil was just about to accelerate towards it, when there was a sudden burst of gunfire from the jungle. The Gurkha's hand hovered over the barrier for a second, then he lurched forward and fell, his body half slumped over the bar.

Instinctively, Anil grabbed his rifle, jumped down from the driving seat and took cover behind the jeep. From where he was, he could see the remaining Gurkha crouching beside the wooden sentry hut, his rifle at the ready. Continuous fire was coming from the jungle on both sides of the road, bullets pinging off the metal of the jeep. The fire was heavy and continuous, and it was hard to judge how many CTs there might be, hidden away amongst the trees.

Moments later, Anil was alarmed to hear shots coming from the direction he'd just driven. They must be advancing towards the mine too. Frustration and anger washed through him. He was too late! The CTs must have been planning this attack before he'd even visited that morning. If only he'd got Lacey to ready his workforce a few hours before, they would have been ready to return fire with fire.

The CTs were clearly attacking the checkpoint to clear the way for an attack on the mine and the house. Anil focused on the jungle, trying to pinpoint exactly where the shooting was coming from. The CTs were clearly very skilful, they were hiding behind trees and in bushes, giving no indication of their positions. However, after a few minutes observing them, Anil saw one of them shift slightly, revealing that he was hiding in a clump of bamboo. Anil took aim and fired at the clump, shooting his rifle again and again into the same spot, and after an initial burst, soon no fire was returned.

He then focused on another point in the trees from which gunfire was coming. That way he managed to eliminate four out of the six or seven guerrillas surrounding them. He breathed more steadily knowing he was no longer completely outnumbered, but he realised he needed to get back to the mine and the house to help the Laceys defend themselves against the forthcoming attack.

He knew he couldn't stand up without drawing fire, but he realised, if he was careful, there might be a way for him to get away. Slowly, while his men continued to fire into the jungle, Anil inched towards the driving seat of the jeep. It was an open vehicle with no doors, so he eased himself into the well on the driver's side, squeezing his body into the space beneath the steering wheel.

It was now or never. Praying the engine would start first time, he turned the key and as the jeep choked into life, he jumped onto the driver's seat and pushed the accelerator to the floor. The jeep surged forwards, in a hail of bullets, and roared on through the gates of the estate. In seconds he was away and powering down the jungle road towards the mine buildings.

He stopped in front of the office and, leaving the engine running, leapt out and ran into the building.

'The CTs are on their way,' he said to the astonished manager. 'You need to fetch Mr Lacey immediately.'

The man rushed off and came back within seconds with Bruce. Anil repeated the message and watched the colour drain from the Englishman's face.

'You need to get your workforce into this building,' Anil told him. 'The CTs are on their way. Have you any guns here?'

Bruce nodded. 'I have a few rifles in the storeroom. I'll get them right now.'

'I'm going up to the house to warn your wife,' Anil said. 'When I've gone, put sandbags in the gap in the wall and make sure everyone is protected behind them. We've already shot several CTs, but there are probably more on their way. I will radio for reinforcements from the base, but it's going to take them thirty minutes or so to get here. Do you think you can hold them off until then?'

'Of course. You need to go right away. Get Alice to open my gun cupboard. Suleman and Abdul know how to shoot. I'll stay here and defend the mine,' Bruce replied.

Anil returned to the jeep and radioed an SOS message to the base in Ipoh. The line was crackly and for the first few tense moments he thought the lines had been cut by the guerillas, but he finally got through and relayed his message. He was assured backup troops would be dispatched straight away. Then he started the engine and roared back up the drive towards the house.

As he approached, he was relieved to see the house looked

still and peaceful apart from the sandbags on the porch. He parked up and pushed his way onto the veranda. After closing the gap between the sandbags with others behind him, he opened the front door.

'Mrs Lacey?' he called.

The old bearer, Suleman, appeared from the kitchen frowning deeply. 'Sir? I didn't hear you knock,' he said.

'Could you fetch Mrs Lacey straight away? The CTs are at the gate. They are bound to attack the house in a matter of minutes.'

The old man flushed, but stood staring at him obstinately, a belligerent look on his face.

'Did you hear me?' Anil asked, striding towards the bottom of the stairs. 'Mrs Lacey?' he called, wondering if he should go up. Despite the circumstances, his ingrained politeness stopped him.

Alice Lacey appeared at the top of the stairs. 'Major Desai?'

'There are CTs at the gate. I've come to help you defend the house. You need to open your husband's gun cupboard.'

There was only a moment's hesitation before she came running down the stairs, her eyes wide with shock. She ran past him to her husband's study and emerged seconds later holding a key.

'This way,' she said, taking him through the hallway to a lobby at the rear of the house where she unlocked a tall cupboard. Inside were four rifles, a couple of revolvers and several rounds of ammunition.

Anil took out each gun and checked they were loaded. 'Call the servants,' he told Alice. 'They can each have a gun.'

She left immediately and he followed her, carrying the guns into the hallway where, in the next few minutes, he handed them out to the four servants.

'I will defend the front porch with Mrs Lacey and one of you,' he said, pointing to Abdul. 'The rest of you must cover the back of the house. We don't know which way the CTs will approach, but my guess would be they will attack from the front.'

Anil went with Alice and Abdul to the front veranda, where they set up the rifles and carbine so their barrels poked through gaps in the sandbags.

'Remember what I taught you,' he told Alice as she positioned herself behind the carbine. 'Although you won't need to hold the gun on your shoulder, the principles are the same.'

He made sure Abdul knew what to do as well, then he took his position behind the Bren, which had been erected in the centre of the porch, in front of the door. He'd only just settled himself behind it, when the first shots rang out from the trees on the other side of the drive.

He fired the Bren at the spot where the shots had come from and, as he fired, he could hear Alice and Abdul shooting too. But enemy fire was coming from several positions and he saw there were probably six or seven CTs firing at the house from the jungle opposite. He was not afraid for himself, but he was for Alice and the others. He wondered if he'd been right to position Alice beside him. Perhaps he should have sent her to the back of the house? Or perhaps he shouldn't have given her a gun at all? But he knew they didn't have that luxury. They needed to use every gun they had to stave off this attack.

The firing from the trees opposite went on for several minutes, and Anil fired round after round back into the jungle. Soon he realised there were probably now only four CTs returning their fire from amongst the trees. His heart lifted a little. They'd managed to shoot at least three of them, which was a slight relief, but the four remaining were still firing just as aggressively.

He stole a sideways glance at Alice, who was kneeling in front of her gun, her eyes focused on the gap between the sandbags, her finger poised on the trigger of the rifle. He felt a swell of admiration for this diminutive woman. There hadn't been a trace of reluctance when he'd asked her to take one of the positions on the porch. Beneath her mild exterior, she clearly had a steely edge.

His attention immediately returned to the task in hand when there were a few seconds of ceasefire from the trees opposite. Anil's heart raced. He knew what that signalled and, as if on cue, four CTs burst out from between the trees and ran towards the house in a line, yelling at the tops of their voices, their guns blasting fire as they ran.

'Fire!' Anil yelled, and hammered bullets continuously from the Bren, the force of the vibrations making the whole veranda shake and shudder.

Alice and Abdul were firing too. Three of the CTs were hit and fell sprawling on the gravel, blood spreading from their bodies, but the other had managed to avoid the fire and ran on towards the house, leaping onto the sandbags at one end. His eyes were wild and his face filthy, a white bandana around his head. He was already on the wall, too high for the machine gun to reach him. As the man caught his balance and swung his gun in Anil's direction, Anil swiftly drew his own revolver and shot the man in the head. He tumbled off the sandbags and fell into the well of the veranda. And it was only then that Anil saw that Abdul had been shot, blood oozing from a wound in his chest.

Alice cried out in anguish and hurried to Abdul's side. Anil remained at the Bren, watching out for more insurgents. He knew the young man was past help.

Alice was feeling his neck for a pulse. She looked at Anil and shook her head, slumping back with tears in her eyes.

With one last glance around and satisfied that, for now at least, they were safe, Anil went to her. 'There's nothing you can do,' he said, looking into her tear-filled eyes. 'Come, get up. We've fought them off for the time being.'

He helped her to her feet, and as they went back into the house, his arm around her shoulder, he heard the sound of engines on the drive. It must be the reinforcements, coming just too late.

'Sit down here,' he said, helping Alice into one of the chairs. 'I'll find you some brandy.'

'Thank you,' she said, her eyes full of gratitude.

He stood for a moment, looking into her eyes. It was all he could do to resist taking her into his arms to comfort her.

Just then there was a sound from the porch. Sandbags being pushed aside. Then footsteps in the hall.

'I see you managed to kill the bastards.'

It was Bruce's voice and Anil sprang away from Alice abruptly.

'Damned shame about poor old Abdul though.'

13

ALICE

'I saw the way Desai was looking at you,' Bruce yelled. 'Don't deny it! I interrupted something. A moment between the two of you. You know it's true.'

Alice shook her head vehemently and protested again, just as she had been doing for the last ten minutes. But he wouldn't believe her. She was sitting on the edge of the bed, her arms folded tightly, and Bruce was standing in front of her, leaning over her, his every word making her flinch. She wanted to stay strong. She knew if she showed weakness in moments like this, it only made him worse.

It was about an hour after the CT attack, which had left everyone in the household deeply shaken. The place was quiet now. The Gurkha reinforcements, around twenty-five men, had arrived in two army trucks shortly after Bruce had returned from the mine. They had loaded the bodies of the dead CTs into one of the trucks to take back to their base, explaining that they needed to identify them. Under the supervision of Major Desai, they had carried out a thorough search of the house and gardens and concluded the place was secure.

After they'd all left, Alice had shrouded Abdul's body with a sheet, then, realising her blouse was smeared with his blood, had gone upstairs to wash and change her clothes. Bruce had followed her. As soon as the bedroom door was shut behind them he'd started haranguing her about Major Desai. Alice couldn't believe he was doing this. He'd lost three of his men in the battle at the mine and Abdul, who'd served him faithfully since he'd arrived in Malaya, had been cruelly murdered. Surely he had more important things to think about than the way Major Desai had looked at her?

The worst of it was, Alice had to admit to herself that his accusation had a grain of truth in it. There *had* been a moment between her and Major Desai, and that moment had been building since the day they'd first set eyes on each other. She'd been drawn to him from the start. Diana had been right; Major Desai was the exact opposite of Bruce in every way. He was kind and sensitive, and Alice knew he cared about her and that she could trust him implicitly. She also knew he'd guessed the reason for the bruises on her arm. She was desperate to tell him the truth, to let him help her. But something was stopping her. And that something was fear of Bruce and his temper.

'I couldn't believe my own eyes,' Bruce said. 'The battle with the CTs was only just over, and you were already fluttering your eyelashes at the major.'

'Oh, please don't say that, Bruce,' she said, wishing he would stop. 'You're imagining things. Just like you always do. I need to wash and change my clothes. Let me go to the bathroom, please.'

She tried to get up off the bed, but he pushed her back with some force and she fell onto her back. He leaned over her, his eyes narrowed, his mouth twisted, and to her horror he put both his hands on her chest and ripped her blouse open, the buttons flying everywhere.

'Bruce!'

'Shut up,' he said. 'You're still my wife, whatever you might think of me.'

'No!' she cried, his intentions suddenly dawning on her.

'Don't scream, or the servants will hear,' he said, pushing her legs apart with his knees. Suddenly he was pinning her down with one hand on her chest and ripping off her trousers and underwear with the other. His weight pressing down on her ribs was stopping her breathing.

'Please, Bruce. Don't do this. You're going to regret it.'

'I told you to shut the hell up,' he said, easing off her enough to unbutton his trousers.

How had it come to this in two short years? What had happened to the man she'd adored, the man she'd followed thousands of miles to marry? He'd become a monster in that brief time, or perhaps he'd just allowed the monster inside to surface.

Alice made a last attempt to close her legs and push away from him, but it was impossible. He was standing right between them, forcing them apart, and the next second she felt his flesh against hers and he was thrusting at her, inside her, the pain and the shock of it making her cry out. He clamped one hand over her mouth and continued his assault.

She was suffocating in the smell of oil and sweat on his skin, but she forced herself to look into his eyes while it was happening. He pushed into her violently, again and again, his face a livid red and bathed in sweat. She searched his eyes for some reminder of the man she'd loved, but it was as if that man had disappeared, and a wild, cruel stranger had taken his place.

When it was finally over, he went into the bathroom and slammed the door.

Alice could hear him running the shower, the splash of the water as he washed. She lay there limp, unable to move, unable to think properly. She felt numb with shock, humiliation and despair.

When Bruce came out of the bathroom, he didn't look at her. He dressed in silence, then, without saying a word, or even glancing her way, left the room. She heard his boots slamming down the stairs and his voice in the hallway barking out orders to the servants.

Shaking from head to foot, she dragged herself up into a sitting position and stared down at her thighs, which were grazed and bruised. Feeling sick and weak, and trembling all over, she slid down from the bed, peeled off her remaining clothes and went into the bathroom.

The shower was cold, but she forced herself under it and stayed there for a long time, scrubbing herself with carbolic soap and a rough sponge. But no matter how much she tried to wash away Bruce's sweat and odour, she knew she would never feel the same again. Something inside her had broken and she wasn't sure if it would ever mend.

IT WAS ONLY when Alice heard Bruce's Land Rover start up and roar away down the drive, that she was sure he had left the house to return to the mine. Tentatively, she opened the bedroom door, crept out onto the landing and went to the banister to look down into the hallway. The servants were all gathered there, and when she realised what they were doing she drew back and stayed out of sight.

Solemnly and slowly, they carried Abdul's body, covered in the sheet Alice had draped over him, through the house and towards the servants' quarters. From where she stood, Alice could see tears in Suleman's eyes as he shuffled along at the rear of the procession. He'd cared for Abdul like a son. Even though he was difficult and prickly, her heart went out to the old man.

She waited until they'd disappeared from view before going downstairs. She crept through to the drawing room and picked up the telephone receiver. To her relief, she heard the familiar buzz on the line; the telephone was still working. She dialled

Diana's number. A servant answered and there was a short wait while he fetched his mistress.

'Hello, Diana,' Alice said, her voice weak.

'Alice? Are you alright? We've been so worried. We heard there was an attack on your estate.'

'Yes, there was. We lost Abdul and three workers from the mine,' Alice said.

'Oh, how dreadful! You sound very shaky. It must have been a terrible shock,' Diana said, her voice full of concern.

Alice swallowed, fighting back the tears of self-pity that threatened to surface. 'I need to see you,' she said. 'Can I come over?'

'Of course. If you're able to. But it might be easier just to talk on the phone.'

'I'd prefer to see you,' Alice replied, knowing that speaking about her ordeal on a crackly line, with the possibility the servants might overhear, was something she simply couldn't do. 'I'll come straight away.'

She left the house, pushing her way between the sandbags on the porch, and headed round to the stable block behind it where the ancient Austin was parked in the old coach house. She hadn't used the car for months, but in her early days at the estate she used to love driving herself to the bazaar in Batu Gajah, and even into Ipoh sometimes, to buy fabrics and nick-nacks for the house. Occasionally, one of the servants might drive her, but today she would drive herself. They'd been through a terrible ordeal, and she didn't want to intrude on their grief.

The car door was stiff, but she pulled it open, got into the stifling vehicle and wound down the window. Then, she started up the engine. To her relief, the old car rattled into life. With some difficulty, she manoeuvred it out of the coach house, through the old stable yard, then headed off down the drive.

She held her breath as she drove, her heart thumping, hoping Bruce wouldn't decide to come back to the house just as she was driving away. But the road ahead remained empty, the thick jungle on either side still and quiet. The trees eventually ended, and the forest opened out into the mine clearing, but Alice didn't take her foot off the accelerator. She roared past the mine buildings and carried on towards the gate. The sentries nodded her past, but when she rounded the next bend and came upon the roadblock, she saw there were several soldiers standing around the sentry post conferring, and a couple of army jeeps parked up nearby.

She brought the car to a stop in front of the barrier. The Gurkha in charge held up a hand and came over to speak to her.

'I'm sorry, madam, but you must turn round and go home. It is too dangerous to take this road today. There may still be CTs in the forest, and there could be more attacks.'

Alice bit her lip, trying hard not to cry. 'Please,' she said. 'It's urgent. I need to see someone...' She couldn't think of an adequate explanation for being willing to run the gauntlet of enemy fire to visit a friend and cursed her ingrained honesty. She should have just lied and said Diana was desperately ill, but even in these circumstances she couldn't bring herself to do that.

'I'm sorry, madam,' the man said, shaking his head. 'We cannot let civilian vehicles through today. Perhaps try again tomorrow when things have calmed down.'

'Please...' she said again, feeling the tears well in her eyes. This time she was powerless to stop them.

At that moment a familiar figure detached himself from the group of soldiers standing beside the jeeps and approached the car. Alice's heart did a somersault.

'Mrs Lacey. Is everything alright?' He bent down to look in the car window.

'Major Desai!' she said, blinking away the tears. 'I need to see my friend, Diana Blanchard. Her place isn't very far from here, but your soldier won't let me through.'

He looked at her for a long moment and she could see the

puzzled look in his eyes. She was aware how pale and shocked she must appear. She hadn't looked like that when he'd left the house after the raid, despite having been fired on for over an hour and witnessing the death of Abdul.

'I will take you,' he said after a moment's thought. 'In my jeep. You can leave your car here at the checkpoint. My men are armed, and two of them can accompany us.'

'Are you sure?'

'Of course. Now... if you pull up over there, your car will be quite safe while we're gone.'

He waved her into a space beside the army jeeps and opened the driver's door for her to get out. She followed him to his vehicle, got up into the passenger seat and waited while he fetched two soldiers with rifles to accompany them. The two men sat on the back of the jeep, one facing forwards, the other backwards, and they set off down the jungle road towards the Blanchard estate.

The roar of the jeep was so loud that no conversation was possible on that thirty-minute journey to the Blanchards' gates. Alice was deeply grateful for that. She didn't know how she would have made small talk in such circumstances, neither did she want to be questioned about the reason for her trip. She knew from the way Anil Desai had looked at her that he must guess something was wrong, and she didn't want to talk for fear of breaking down.

No shots rang out from the depths of the jungle on that short trip and soon they were turning in through the gates of the Blanchard estate. The long drive swept through line upon line of rubber trees, planted on gently sloping hills that flanked the drive. Their grey-green leaves were soothing on the eye and between them the tappers moved slowly, collecting latex from the cups on the trunks. How much more restful this scene is than the tin mine, Alice thought – the great, ugly scar of the pit on the landscape, the constant clatter of the dredger and the rumble of the train. When they rounded a bend in the drive and drew up in front of Diana's beautiful, white-painted house, Alice saw that, like all others for miles around, it was fortified with sandbags.

Diana was already walking across the porch and coming down the steps before Alice had even got down from the jeep.

'We will wait for you here,' Major Desai said.

She thanked him, hardly daring to look into his eyes for fear he would guess the reason for her distress.

'Alice.' Diana came forward, arms outstretched. Even under siege she was elegantly dressed in a floaty, pink summer dress and large straw hat.

Alice allowed herself to be enfolded in her friend's embrace and, with her back turned to the soldiers, let the tears fall.

'Come into the house,' Diana said, leading her towards the front steps.

Once inside, Diana asked the bearer to bring tea, and they sat in the shade of her chintzy drawing room with the bamboo chik blinds pulled down over the windows.

'Now, Alice, tell me what's wrong. It's not just the CT attack that's bothering you, is it? Something else has happened. I know it.'

Diana passed Alice a handkerchief and she sobbed quietly for a while.

'Is it Bruce again, my dear?' Diana asked gently.

It was a few minutes before Alice was calm enough to speak. In the end, she took a deep breath and said, 'Yes. It's Bruce. He... he forced himself on me, Diana. After the attack.'

Diana took her hand. 'Oh, my poor dear girl...'

She didn't ask any questions, she just sat quietly and listened as Alice told her what had happened. When Alice had finished, there were tears in Diana's eyes too.

'I'm so, so sorry, Alice. You're being very brave... but why on earth would he do that?'

'He's convinced himself that I'm keen on Major Desai. He's so jealous... it's ridiculous.'

'It's a shame the CTs didn't get him instead of poor Abdul...' Diana murmured. 'But, seriously, you must come and stay here, my dear. No one can possibly live like that.'

Alice fell silent and thought about it. She wondered if she would have the courage to leave Bruce, even after what he'd done to her. It would be difficult to go in the midst of all this chaos, she reasoned. And then she remembered something else: the promise she'd made to Ying May to bring food to the kampong. She recalled the desperate state of the people there, the skinny children and withered old people, and the grateful clamour with which her knapsack of food had been greeted.

'I... I'm not sure, Diana.'

Diana frowned. 'But what's stopping you? Look, you don't even have to go back now if you don't want to. I could send one of our houseboys up to Rimba for your clothes.'

'Can I think about it?' Alice asked.

'Of course, but don't be afraid of Bruce's reaction. Once you're away from there you won't have to put up with his temper any longer.'

One of the servants brought a tray of tea in dainty china cups, and homemade biscuits on a plate. Alice sipped gratefully, and ate three biscuits in quick succession, realising she hadn't had anything to eat or drink since well before the raid. While they drank their tea, she told Diana about the attack, how terrifying it had been, and how Major Desai had been there to defend the house beside her.

'That man is an absolute godsend,' Diana said. 'He helped us set up the defences around the house and the latex sheds, and a few of his men are here even now training some of the tappers to shoot.'

When they'd finished their tea, Alice got up from her seat.

'I must go now, Diana. Major Desai is waiting for me. They

wouldn't let me drive here in my car and I don't want to waste his time. But thank you for listening to me. It's been a huge help.'

'I'm worried about you, Alice. It's your decision, I know, but I wish you would stay. Think carefully about what I said. You can come over anytime, roadblocks permitting, and I'm always here if you need to call.'

'Thank you,' Alice said. 'You're a true friend.'

SITTING beside Major Desai in the jeep as he drove her back through the jungle, Alice thought about her decision to stay. She would move into the spare room and lock herself in at night and, in the daytime, if Bruce was at home, she would make sure the servants were around and that she never went upstairs alone.

As they flashed past jungle trees and thick undergrowth, splashes of sunlight lit up the vehicle for a few seconds at a time. Looking down at her arms, Alice realised there were more fresh bruises beside the old ones, and she faltered. Was she doing the right thing? Was providing food for a starving village worth putting herself at risk?

14

CHLOE

Kathmandu, 2018

IT WAS late by the time Chloe had secured the bookshop and walked through the empty streets of Thamel to the apartment. Most of the shops were closed, but the place still had that magical atmosphere she'd always loved; dim streetlamps lit up the ancient houses and temples, giving the streets an ethereal quality. She climbed the stairs to her apartment and let herself in as quietly as she could. The place was still and silent, and when she crept through and opened the bedroom door, she knew from Kiran's steady breathing that he was already asleep.

She hadn't found time to eat that evening, so she grabbed a quick snack of cold pakoras from the fridge. Then, partly because she didn't want to disturb Kiran, and partly because she was still feeling bruised from the disagreement they'd had earlier, she found a sleeping bag in the hall cupboard and laid it out on the settee in the living room.

She slipped off everything except her underwear and wriggled into the bag. She closed her eyes and tried to sleep, but her mind kept wandering to Alice and her husband. So far, the letters hadn't said much, other than that Alice's husband had behaved badly at a dinner party, and Alice felt guilty and ashamed. But Chloe could tell, reading between even those brief lines, that there was a lot of pent-up emotion behind the words. She couldn't wait to read more; to see if later letters would let her into more of Alice's secrets.

Thinking about Alice and her unhappy marriage inevitably led her to think about her own situation. Anger still burned inside her at the knowledge that Kiran had let his sister into his confidence about having difficulty starting a family *and* had sought her help managing the shop. Chloe tried to imagine the siblings' conversation, but found it hard to envisage what words Kiran might have used to tell Rumi they'd been trying for a baby for almost two years now without success. It was all so hurtful.

Finally, she made an effort to put those thoughts aside, closed her eyes and let sleep steal over her.

When she awoke in the morning, bright sunlight was already flooding the apartment and she realised, dismayed, that she'd overslept. She'd intended to be at the shop early so she could spend some time in the basement going through Anil's books before opening time. She pushed back the sleeping bag, hauled herself out and pulled on a T-shirt, still feeling sleepy.

Kiran was in the galley kitchen chopping fruit for his breakfast.

'Good morning,' he said when he saw her. 'What happened to you last night?' He smiled at her, his beautiful, genuine smile that had first drawn her to him.

She almost melted, but the flint of pain from their argument yesterday was still lodged in her heart and she couldn't forget it. 'The shop was busy until late. Then I had to lock up,' she said stiffly, avoiding his gaze.

He paused, still smiling, but more warily now. 'Hey, you're not still angry with me, are you?'

She sat down on a stool at the breakfast bar, but didn't reply.

'Would you like some?' he asked.

She shook her head. 'No thanks. I'll have some toast in a while.'

She watched him eat his papaya and banana. Both remained quiet for a few moments, the question he'd asked her still hovering in the air. In the end, Chloe broke the silence.

'I just wish you hadn't spoken to Rumi about such a personal matter without talking to me first,' she said.

'So, you *are* still angry,' he said. 'I'm really sorry, Chloe. I had no idea you would be upset about it. It just didn't occur to me.'

She didn't reply at first, it was hard to articulate the extent of her discomfort.

Then Kiran went on. 'Maybe... well, maybe it's because you are an only child, Chlo. You don't have family, so you've never even had to think about what things it's OK to share with a sibling.'

'Perhaps,' she said. But his words didn't make it better, in fact they made it worse. It made her feel even more excluded from the bond Kiran had with Rumi and the fact he'd shared their secrets.

He came over and put his arms around her and nuzzled her hair. 'I'm sorry. Whatever I say doesn't seem right. Can we talk about this later? I need to get over to the Kathmandu Guest House and meet my new group now.'

'I suppose so.'

'Look, we're going to get through this,' he said, looking into her eyes. 'We just need to work it out together.'

'I know,' she replied, her spirits lifting a little. It's what she'd told herself only the day before.

Kiran picked up his backpack, lodged a metal water bottle in the side pocket and hoisted it onto his back. Then he came over to kiss her goodbye.

'Why don't you come out with us this evening? I'm taking the group to a restaurant at Boudhanath. You and I have been there before. Nani's Kitchen. Remember? Some of the group are Brits. It might be fun.'

She vaguely remembered he'd told her he was starting a new tour soon, but she'd been so busy it had hardly registered. He seemed enthusiastic about it. He'd always loved his job. Chloe reminded herself how good it was to see him like that after so many months of illness following the earthquake.

'Where are you taking this lot trekking?' she asked.

'Everest Base Camp,' he replied. 'Starting tomorrow afternoon.'

She stared at him, suddenly anxious. 'You didn't tell me that, Kiran. Are you sure you're ready for such a big trek?'

'I thought I *had* mentioned it. And, yes, I'm fine now, Chloe. It's not much more difficult than the Annapurna Circuit and I managed that without a problem.'

She frowned. Once again a vision came into her mind of him lying in hospital after the earthquake, covered in tubes and monitors. She'd feared for his life then for several days. And his recovery hadn't been quick. It had taken many months for him to get back to normal after his head injury. He'd had to relearn a lot of life skills.

'You're sure you're not doing too much too quickly?' she asked, prickles of alarm running through her.

'I'm sure, Chloe. Please don't worry about me,' he said. 'Look, I really have to go now. See you at seven at the restaurant? It would be great if you'd come along.'

'Perhaps,' she said, letting him kiss her cheek. 'If I can get away. See you later.'

She watched him go with a jumble of mixed emotions; fear for his safety mingled with the remnants of the hurt at what she felt to be his betrayal.

After breakfast and a refreshing shower, she walked back

through the already busy streets to Paradise Books. On her way she stopped at a teeming market to bargain for fruit. She loved the colour and clamour of the stalls, the press of locals jostling for space, the babble of conversation, and for a moment she was drawn into the scene and forgot about her sadness.

To her surprise, when she arrived at the shop, Shova had already opened up and was standing at the till serving customers. With a quick wave to make sure Shova had seen her, Chloe slipped down to the basement, where she switched on the light and stood in the middle of the room surrounded by the boxes of Anil's books. She sighed, wondering how long it would take her to get through them all. She thought again if she should ask Shova to sort through some of them, but she didn't want to miss the possibility of finding another letter or perhaps some other reminder of Anil and Alice's relationship.

She heaved the first box to the floor, knelt down and started sorting through it. In this box she came across novels and short stories by William Somerset Maugham. They were original hardback volumes, beautifully bound in tooled brown leather, and she imagined Anil reading them at home, being transported by the stories back to the steamy jungle of Malaya and its mysteries and intrigues. She flicked through the volumes carefully, looking for anything that might have been hidden between the pages, but there was nothing.

Then, putting them carefully in a pile, she turned to the next book. It was *Bhowani Junction* by John Masters. Turning to the front of the book, she saw it had been published in 1954. Then, on the title page, she caught sight of some handwriting. She looked closely.

To my dear Anil, This reminded me of India and I thought you would enjoy it. With love, Alice

· · ·

CHLOE STARED AT THE WORDS, written in neat, flowing ink. They must have been written in 1954 at the earliest, several years or so after Anil's marriage to the princess.

Inspired to discover more, she carried on sifting through the books, looking carefully at each title page, then leafing through all the pages to see if there were any letters she'd missed the first time round. She worked for a long time, sorting and classifying books into three different piles: ones she definitely wanted for the shop, ones she would look at again later to make a decision, and ones she would throw away.

She'd been through five boxes when something fell out of a volume of Shakespeare's *Julius Caesar*. Picking it up, she realised it was a newspaper cutting. Peering at the smudged print she could just about make out that it was from the *Straits Times*, dated 30 June 1948. She smoothed it out. The paper was soft and yellowed with age and the print was rubbed away in places. It was headed: DEATH OF SIR EDWARD GENT.

SIR EDWARD WAS RETURNING to London after having been relieved of his post as High Commissioner of Malaya, when his aircraft was in a collision at Northwood Aerodrome in North London...

THE ARTICLE WENT on to describe how Sir Edward had been High Commissioner for only two years, since the Federation of Malaya was formed in April 1946.

ALTHOUGH HE DECLARED a State of Emergency on June 16th, he was recalled to London because his early response to the insurgency was not seen as sufficient by the British government...

.   .   .

SHIVERS WENT through Chloe looking at the fading print. She thought of Anil, reading the newspaper in his quarters at the Gurkha base in Perak when the events described would have meant so much to him and everyone around him. Somehow, this little scrap of yellowing paper made the whole thing very immediate and real to her.

She put it aside and carried on. Later she found another newspaper clipping from the *Straits Times*, inside an ancient volume of the *Encyclopaedia Britannica*, dated 18 October 1948, which announced the arrival in Malaya of Gent's successor, Sir Henry Gurney. She didn't find any more newspaper cuttings in the boxes she was emptying, but she was sure there would be more when she looked in subsequent boxes. Perhaps Anil had wanted to chart the progress of key events in the Emergency by taking article cuttings. She wondered why he hadn't stuck them in a scrapbook.

Dusting herself off, she went upstairs to the shop, where Auntie Gita was just arriving, carrying her wicker baskets of cake ingredients. It was Tuesday, and on Tuesdays she baked custard tarts. Chloe loved Kiran's elderly great auntie, who was warm, generous and caring. The two cats rubbed themselves against Gita's green-and-gold saree as she walked through to the kitchen.

'Haven't you been fed yet, my precious ones?' Auntie Gita asked them in a singsong voice.

Chloe felt a stab of guilt. She'd been so anxious to get down to the basement and look through the books that she had forgotten all about the poor cats. She'd never done that before. The stress of the difficult exchanges with Kiran must be distracting her.

Chloe followed Gita through to the kitchen, and while the elderly lady bustled around, opening and shutting cupboards, getting her ingredients out and finding the utensils to start baking, Chloe hastily opened two tins of cat food and emptied them into the bowls on the floor. Then she topped up the milk saucer.

'It's not like you to forget, Chloe,' Gita said, frowning. 'Is something troubling you?'

Chloe bit her lip, wondering whether to confide in the old lady, but quickly deciding against it. She couldn't criticise Kiran for betraying confidences if she was going to do the same thing. Instead, she said, 'No, nothing at all, Auntie. I've just been busy in the basement. I collected a whole load of books on Sunday and I've been sorting them out. They belonged to a relative of yours, actually. Anil Desai.'

'Oh, poor Anil! I went to his funeral last month. He was very sick at the end, poor fellow. All alone in that great big old house.'

'Did you know him well?' Chloe asked. 'I realised you were related, but wasn't sure how.'

'Second cousins. Your father-in-law's father was another cousin. It's a big rambling family, as you know, my dear.' Gita covered her ample body with an apron, then turned to the counter and started weighing out flour.

'Rajesh is coming round on Thursday, actually. I'm helping him...' She stopped, realising Rajesh might not want Auntie Gita to know about his father's mysterious relationship with a British woman. 'With the books,' she finished.

'Oh, Rajesh! Such a lovely boy. So clever too. Takes after his father in that regard, but looks so much like his mother. Now, she was a real beauty in her day.'

Chloe smiled. 'Yes, I've seen pictures of their wedding.'

'Oh, I'd love to see the photos again. I was there, you know, although it was a very long time ago. They made such a handsome couple.'

'I'm sure Rajesh would bring the photographs along to show you. I'll call and ask him.'

'That would be wonderful dear,' Gita said, weighing out generous portions of brown sugar and tipping them into a large bowl with the flour. 'You know, the princess was a wonderful woman. She did a lot for charity, always throwing parties and receptions in her house. But...' Gita put down her wooden spoon, frowning as if trying to fix a memory in her mind. 'I never really got to know her properly. There was something distant about her. But even though she had so much to be joyful about, I always thought she looked rather sad.'

'Really, Auntie? And why was that do you think?'

Gita shook her head. 'None of us ever knew. And I guess no one ever will now they're both dead and gone.'

'I'd better go and check in on Shova,' Chloe said. 'I haven't spoken to her yet today.'

'Of course. But the custard tarts will be ready in about an hour. Be sure to come through and taste one.'

'I will. Thank you, Auntie.'

Shova seemed to be coping well, so Chloe asked her if she could carry on until lunchtime while Chloe went to the basement to sort through more of the books.

'Oh, and one more thing. Would you mind staying on a bit later this evening? Only Kiran has asked if I'll go for a meal with his group.'

Shova hesitated for a moment.

'I'll pay you overtime, of course,' Chloe said.

Shova's face brightened immediately. 'Alright then. It's a deal,' she replied.

After eating lunch with Auntie Gita in the kitchen, Chloe returned to the basement and continued sorting through Anil's book collection. She was disappointed that, despite searching thoroughly, she didn't find any letters or even any more newspaper clippings. But the good news was that by the end of the afternoon, she had several piles of saleable second-hand books that would look good on the shelves of the shop. The next stage was for her to price them.

At around six o'clock, she went upstairs and talked to Shova about feeding the cats and locking up the shop. By that time Gita had gone home and closed up the café.

'Are you sure you're going to be alright on your own?' Chloe asked.

'Of course,' Shova said. 'I'll manage.'

'What about getting home?' Shova lived with her parents in a far-flung suburb.

'I'll be OK. I'll catch the bus.'

'No,' Chloe said, suddenly fearful for the young girl's safety, remembering with a shudder some of her own bad experiences when she was travelling alone. 'Order a taxi, please. I will pay for it.'

'If you're sure,' Shova said, looking relieved.

'Of course. Now, I'm just popping to the cloakroom to get ready then I'd better be off. It can take forty-five or fifty minutes to get to Boudhanath from here.'

She went to the small bathroom upstairs on the first floor and peered critically in the mirror. She looked tired, and her face was smudged with dust from having handled the old books. She didn't want to meet Kiran's tour group looking like that.

She wiped away the worst of it, applied some eyeliner, a slick of lipstick and a touch of perfume to her wrists and neck, brushed her hair, then went back downstairs. To her surprise, there was a visitor standing beside the counter, chatting to Shova. It was Rajesh. He was dressed in his usual shabby suit and looked as though he'd just come from work, as he had a briefcase with him. He smiled when he saw Chloe. His eyes were shining with excitement.

'It's lovely to see you, Rajesh,' Chloe said, 'but I thought you were coming on Thursday.'

'I was, and I still am. I hope you don't mind me popping in today, though. I needed to come and see you,' he said, barely able to contain himself. 'I've made another discovery and I simply had to show you in person.'

'How exciting!' Chloe said, catching his mood. 'You'd better come through to the back where we can talk.'

Rajesh followed her through the shop to the little kitchen, where the two cats were asleep on their beds. Seeing Chloe and Rajesh enter, they got up, stretched and came forward to be stroked.

'Would you like a custard tart?' she asked Rajesh. 'Auntie Gita has gone home now, but she left some of her famous pastries.'

'I'd love one, thank you,' Rajesh said.

Chloe fetched a tart from the fridge, put it onto a plate and poured cream over it.

'Aren't you having any?' Rajesh asked.

She shook her head. 'I'm meant to be eating out this evening with Kiran and his tour group.'

Rajesh's face fell. 'Oh, I'm sorry. Am I holding you up?'

'Not at all.' She smiled, glancing at her watch. 'I've probably got ten minutes or so.'

'Where are you headed?' he asked. 'I could take you in my car. That way you wouldn't have to wait around for a taxi.'

'That's kind of you. OK, that would be great if you don't mind. I'm going up to Boudhanath. It might give me a bit more time,' she replied. 'Would you like a drink with that? Tea, jasmine tea, coffee?'

'Jasmine tea would be wonderful,' he said.

'So, what did you find?' she asked as she put on the kettle, not able to wait any longer.

'I was clearing out my father's room. An antiques dealer came round yesterday and made an offer for the bedroom furniture. There is a lovely old four-poster bed that belonged to my mother, and some matching chests. When he lifted the mattress to check on its condition, this is what was tucked under it.'

He dipped into his briefcase and pulled out a large, brown envelope, and from that he extracted a blue, hardback exercise book.

'What's that?' Chloe asked.

'It's a sort of journal. Part diary, part scrapbook. There are lots of press cuttings about the Malayan Emergency, and in amongst those, Pa's observations. I only read the first couple, but you'll be pleased to know they mention going to Rimba Valley Estate for the first time, and one of them contains his thoughts about that dinner party.'

'Oh really, what does he say?' Chloe asked, intrigued.

Rajesh took the book and riffled through the first few pages. 'Here it is. It's written in Nepali, but I'll do my best to translate it for you.'

Chloe made the jasmine tea and put the cup in front of him. Rajesh found the page and started to read, slowly and stumblingly, pausing every now and then to find the right word.

DINNER PARTY AT THE LACEYS' *house this evening. What a terrible oaf that man Bruce Lacey is! He was rude, overbearing, and very critical of the Gurkha operations. I was rather offended. To top it all, he started to insult his wife, saying how she made eyes at other men. I must say it was all I could do to stop myself from punching the man. Two of the guests actually left in protest! I do feel for his poor wife though. She's such a lovely woman and clearly doesn't deserve such treatment.*

I do worry about her. I'm sure I saw some bruises on her arms the first time I went there. Last night she'd obviously taken great care to cover them up with a long-sleeved evening gown. I will check in on her again. I want to make sure she's safe, but of course it is a pleasure to visit her. She is also beautiful and charming!

'POOR, POOR ALICE,' Chloe said, thinking about the bruises. 'It ties in with what Alice said about the dinner party in her letter to him. Gosh. How fascinating to hear it from your father's side too. I can't wait to read more.'

Rajesh sipped his tea. 'There's a great deal of historical material in here too. All the newspaper cuttings from the time, meticulously preserved, in date order.'

'That's amazing. By chance I found a couple of cuttings in the books I was going through today,' Chloe said. 'I wondered if he was making a scrapbook. He must have forgotten to include those two.'

Rajesh finished his custard tart and drained his jasmine tea. 'I think we'd better get going if you're not going to be late. Where did you say you're meeting Kiran?'

'Boudhanath,' she replied.

'The traffic's often very heavy out that way. Especially at this time. Come on. We should make a start now.'

They walked through the thronging early evening Thamel crowds to Rajesh's car, which was parked half a mile or so from the shop, and set off into the traffic. He was right: the queues were very heavy, and they crawled through the centre of Kathmandu and the few kilometres towards the suburb of Boudhanath. When her watch ticked round to half past seven, Chloe started to get agitated. At that point they had been stationary at some traffic lights for at least five minutes.

'Maybe I'd be better off walking,' she said to Rajesh. 'How far is it now?'

'Maybe another fifteen minutes? I think it's a bit far to walk, but it's up to you.'

She stayed in the car and texted Kiran to apologise for being late, but he didn't reply. When, at last, the car arrived at the gates of the pedestrianised square where the restaurant overlooked the great white Boudha Stupa, it was 7.45. Chloe thanked Rajesh, then ran across the cobbled square, dodging tourists and worshippers. The restaurant was on the top floor and when she reached it she was sweating and panting. As she entered the room, she saw Kiran's group sitting around a large table at the front overlooking the floodlit temple. They were all talking and laughing happily. She waved to Kiran and made her way over.

'Chloe!' Kiran stood up. 'You've missed most of the meal, I'm afraid, everyone's just ordering dessert.'

'Oh, I'm so sorry. The traffic from Thamel was terrible.'

'I know,' Kiran said.

Chloe noticed a slight tightness in his voice. Was he annoyed? She wouldn't have blamed him if he was.

He introduced her round the table to the group of ten tourists, six men and four women, Americans, Australians, British and one German. All looked to be in their thirties. Chloe smiled and shook hands, but she was so flustered she barely registered their names. She sat down beside Kiran and ordered some ice cream. She was hungry, but decided to eat more at home later.

The tour group were full of their upcoming trip.

'You know we have to fly into one of the most notorious airports in the world, don't you?' one of the Australian women said. 'How is everyone feeling about that?'

'The safety record at Lukla isn't really that bad. There hasn't been an accident for a long time now,' Kiran said, anxious to reassure the group. 'I think you'll find the flight exhilarating. Please. You mustn't worry.'

A frisson of fear for Kiran's safety and for that of his group went through Chloe, but she hid it with a smile, noticing how Kiran's words had reassured the travellers, remembering what a skilled guide he was. Listening to the conversation around the table, the palpable excitement in the air, she could tell how much he was already trusted and liked by them. She felt a swell of pride and turned to smile at him. Perhaps things were going to be alright between them after all.

But once they got home, he seemed distracted. Chloe made herself some pasta and sat at the breakfast bar to eat it. He came and sat beside her.

'You know, when you didn't show up this evening, I thought you must be punishing me.'

She looked up at him, her fork halfway to her mouth. 'Punishing you? Whatever do you mean?'

'For talking to Rumi. I know you're angry, and I thought you were protesting about it.'

'Not at all, Kiran. I told you. The traffic was bad.'

'It's always bad at that time. Why didn't you set off earlier?'

'Something came up at the shop.'

He sighed. 'I thought... just for once, that you might be able to put me first.'

She put down her fork. 'What does that mean?'

'That shop. You're there almost every waking hour. You're working so hard you're not looking after yourself like you promised you would. Honestly, Chloe. On this one occasion, I thought you might actually be able to shut the place up and spend the evening with me for a change.'

She hung her head. 'Look, Kiran, I'm truly sorry about that. I really didn't intend to be late. Rajesh came to the shop with a diary of his father's he'd discovered. I could hardly turn him away, could I?'

'No, I suppose not. I... I missed you, that's all. And I worry about you, working so hard.'

She laughed. 'Well, my job certainly isn't as dangerous as yours. Don't you think I worry about you too?'

'That's different. You know what I mean.'

Chloe finished her mouthful, then said, 'Yes, I know what you mean. And I've said when the business is on a more solid footing I'll take a step back, but that's not possible right now. And I'd be grateful if you didn't have any more conversations with your sister about it behind my back.'

Kiran's face clouded over with anger and hurt at her words, and Chloe immediately regretted having said them. But she was too proud to apologise. He left the kitchen without a word and went into the bedroom, where she could hear him opening and closing drawers and cupboards, packing his rucksack for the trip.

She finished her pasta, washed up the dish, then went into the bedroom and undressed. Kiran carried on packing in silence. When he'd finished, he got undressed too, slid between the sheets and put out the light without speaking. Chloe lay awake listening to his breathing, trying to think of the right thing to say. Finally, she put out a hand to touch him, but realised from his breathing that he was already asleep. Feeling wretched, she turned over, away from him. Then she tried to get to sleep herself, all the time wondering how they would get through this impasse. But sleep wouldn't come.

15

ALICE

Rimba Valley Estate, January 1949

ALICE SAT on the veranda at the front of the house in one of the planter's chairs, reading a novel. It was *I Capture the Castle* by Dodie Smith, which had been sent to her by Jamila. It transported her to a cold, grey Suffolk landscape that seemed a million miles from where she was now.

She'd always loved sitting in that position on the veranda, ever since she first came to the estate as a young bride almost three years before. It used to be a beautiful, peaceful spot, where she could relax and watch the jungle birds flitting in and out of the trees across the drive. But now all she could see was sandbags in front of her, blocking the view. She'd been thankful for their protection during the raid, several months ago now, but she resented them being there. Their very presence reminded her of Abdul's death, the precariousness of her existence, and of the guerilla war that was still raging on the peninsula.

One compensation was that a family of geckos, called

chichaks by the locals, had discovered the strange new wall and every so often one would dart out from a crack between the sandbags and wait for flies, chattering away. Alice was fascinated by them and loved to watch these tiny creatures scurrying about, finding food and making their homes. It warmed her heart to see evidence of thriving life in amongst all this killing.

The CT raids on rubber estates and tin mines had continued unabated and were as ruthless as ever: the senseless killings of British and Malays, the slitting of throats, the intimidation of workers, the burning and sacking of property. At least once a week Anil Desai would drive up to the house in his jeep to check on Alice's safety, and they would sit and chat and drink tea comfortably together before he drove back to his base. She was grateful for his concern and looked forward to his visits more than she wanted to admit to herself. He'd long stopped asking her about her bruises because there hadn't been any for some time. Since Bruce had forced himself on her that terrible day of the raid, he'd left her alone and hadn't touched her once.

Life on Rimba Valley Estate had gone on much as before, only Alice had moved out of the master suite and into the spare bedroom, without even a word from Bruce. They rarely spoke nowadays, took their meals at different times, and if they passed one another in the hall or drawing room, barely made eye contact. Christmas had come and gone. On that day, they'd motored to the club together as usual, travelling in silence in Bruce's new armoured vehicle. He'd had his Land Rover fitted with reinforced metal shutters that covered all the windows, and he drove peering through a narrow slit in the windscreen.

At the club Diana had taken Alice aside and asked her in hushed tones how things were.

'How are you, my darling?' Diana had asked. 'You're looking a little better than last time we met, I must say.'

'I'm alright actually,' she'd replied.

'And Bruce?' Diana had whispered. 'Has he... has he tried anything again?'

'No. No, as a matter of fact he avoids me nowadays and I far prefer things that way.'

'That's good to know, Alice,' Diana had said, looking relieved. 'But you must be on your guard.'

It was now late January and Alice hadn't ventured off the estate since Christmas Day. While she sat there reading, she was waiting for the servants to retire to their quarters for their afternoon naps. Then she would be able to slip out through a gap in the sandbags with her knapsack and walk up to her meeting place on the edge of the mine. She'd promised to meet Ying May there at three o'clock that day and she was cutting it fine. As if to scupper her plans, one of the servants was cleaning her bedroom where she'd hidden the knapsack. She could hear him banging the broom around up there. There was no way she'd be able to fetch the knapsack until he'd finished. She cursed her thoughtlessness for forgetting that it was his routine to clean her bedroom on Wednesday afternoons.

She'd been taking food up to the Chinese kampong twice a week for several months now, much to Ying May's joy and immense gratitude. The village women would surround Alice when she arrived, taking her hand and greeting her with smiles and laughter. She'd got into quite a routine with her visits. Just seeing their happy faces when she arrived had given her a purpose in life. It had also given her a reason for staying in the house and not taking up Diana's offer of a refuge. She loved sitting on Ying May's veranda and passing the time of day with her while sipping the earthy tea. Ying May was always friendly and hospitable, and Alice had begun to think of her as a friend. Sometimes it troubled her that the village children didn't look a great deal healthier than when she'd first met them, despite the risks she was taking, and sometimes she would pause and wonder if the food was actually getting to the right people.

Now, at last, she heard the houseboy bring his brooms downstairs and disappear to the kitchen. The house fell silent. She went inside, up the stairs and to her bedroom at the back of the house. She collected the knapsack, which she'd already filled with food from the pantry, from the bottom of the wardrobe. Checking that nobody was about, she went downstairs, out between the sandbags and then on her usual route through the garden and up into the jungle.

Ying May was at their meeting place before her that day, pacing up and down. When she looked up at Alice's approach, Alice caught a look of anxiety in her eyes.

'I'm sorry I'm late,' she said. 'I couldn't get to the knapsack because someone was in the room. I came as quickly as I could.'

'It's fine,' Ying May said. 'You don't need to come down to the village today. I can take it myself.'

'Oh.' Alice was crestfallen. Her walks to the village had become part of her familiar routine and seeing the joy on the faces of the women made the risks she was taking all worthwhile.

'Unless you really want to, of course,' Ying May said, relenting.

'I enjoy visiting,' Alice said. 'And there is the knapsack to bring back... But if you don't want me to come, I understand. I'll just go home. I can find something else to bring the next lot up in.'

Ying May looked at her for a moment, clearly weighing up something in her mind.

'Alright. Come along with me then,' Ying May said and set off around the rim of the mine without a further word.

When they arrived in the village, Alice noticed immediately that the atmosphere was different from usual. The village women didn't come and greet her as they normally did, and fewer people were sitting on their porches that day. Alice followed Ying May to her house and sat outside while Ying May prepared her tea as usual. When Ying May went to boil the kettle, Alice saw she stopped to speak to a couple of people who were sitting cross-legged before the fire. With surprise, Alice noticed they were men – three of them. All of whom looked able-bodied and of working age. That was an unusual sight in the village.

When Ying May returned with the hot water, her face was serious.

'Who are those men?' Alice asked.

'Oh, one is my husband, and the other two are just neighbours from the village. Today they have no work.'s

'I'm sorry to hear that,' Alice said, and wondered if the strained atmosphere in the village was because the men didn't have work that day.

'I wish I could help them get work in the mine,' she said. 'But as I mentioned, my husband is very particular about papers.'

Ying May looked at her with fear in her eyes. She shook her head. 'Please don't mention them to your husband. Your trips here are our secret, aren't they?'

'Of course. Yes, sorry. I wasn't thinking,' Alice said. 'I haven't told anyone at all that I come here, and I don't intend to, so please don't worry.'

She left soon after that, hoping things would soon pick up for the villagers and that when she returned in a few days' time, people would be prepared to come out of their houses to speak to her again.

When she got back to the house, she was surprised to see Major Desai's jeep parked on the drive. It wasn't his usual day to visit, and although she always looked forward to seeing him and enjoyed his company, she wondered why he had come. She put down her knapsack behind a bush in the rose garden. When she approached the porch, Major Desai was standing there, behind the sandbags.

'Mrs Lacey, good afternoon,' he said. 'I was a little worried about you. The servants weren't sure where you were.'

Her heart skipped a beat. 'I was in the back garden,' she said, keeping her face as straight as she could while she lied. 'I often spend time there in the afternoons. I'm surprised they didn't tell you that.'

He frowned. 'One of the houseboys went into the garden to look for you, but he couldn't find you.'

She was stumped momentarily. 'Oh... well, perhaps I was in the potting shed. I did go in there for a little while. He must have missed me.'

Major Desai remained silent, regarding her face with his steady, unnerving gaze. She looked straight back at him. What had she to be ashamed of? Walking into the jungle wasn't a crime. Giving away food from her own larder wasn't a crime either. But still... she wouldn't want him to find out about her secret village.

'You know it has become increasingly dangerous around these parts lately. You are advised not to stray off your property, Mrs Lacey.'

'I am well aware of that, and I can assure you that I was in the back garden,' she said, with an air of finality, lifting her chin in defiance. 'Now, what can I do for you, Major? Would you like to sit down? Have a drink?'

'I can't stop for a drink, but I will sit down for a moment,' he replied.

She led him along the veranda to the basket chairs. They sat down opposite one another and the major shifted in his seat. Alice realised he was feeling uncomfortable.

'Is everything alright, Major Desai?' she asked.

'I'm afraid things might get worse around here for a while, Mrs Lacey.'

'Oh, why is that? We haven't had an attack for several months.'

'Well.' He cleared his throat and looked down at his hands. It was almost as if he was ashamed of what he was about to say. 'A few weeks ago, there was what I can only describe as a massacre in a village in Selangor. Batang Kali it is called. The government managed to hush it up for weeks, but it's coming out now.'

'A massacre?' she repeated in alarm, chills of horror running through her. 'Whatever do you mean?'

'I mean just that. Some British troops went into a village, herded all the men into a hut, and sent the women and children away in trucks. The next morning, they forced the men out of the hut, lined them up on the banks of a river and shot them all in cold blood. There was only one man who survived, and that was purely by chance.'

'But why? Why in God's name did they do that?' she asked, trembling with shock. This was more terrible than anything else she'd heard of in all the long, hard months of the Emergency.

Major Desai shook his head slowly, and when he looked into her eyes, she saw the pain and shame in his.

'They must have suspected the villagers were collaborating with the guerillas. Many of them were of Chinese descent. But others say it was a village of rubber tappers who had no connection with the guerillas at all. The government has started an inquiry.'

Alice shook her head. 'I don't suppose they will be keen to accuse their own soldiers of murder,' she said. 'I haven't seen this in the newspapers.'

'No. There is a ban on reporting it currently, people are afraid of a backlash.'

'So is that what you're worried about now?' she asked. 'That they might take revenge on us here?'

'It's possible. I spoke to your husband on the way in and his men are standing ready for another attack on the mine. He said he would come on up to the house to set up things here too.'

Alice stared at him. She was finding it hard to take it all in. A vision of British soldiers lining up a group of ragged rubber tappers along the banks of a river and gunning them down kept going through her mind.

'I can't believe the British Army could do something like that,' she said, still reeling from the news.

'I know,' the major said. 'I'm finding it difficult to comprehend myself. I intend to speak to my colonel about it. I will protest to him in the strongest possible terms. I and my company are professional soldiers. We don't want to be associated with this sort of abuse... of innocent civilians.'

Alice looked at him with renewed respect. 'You're going to speak to your colonel about it?'

'I will. I have protested to him before about the conduct of some of the British soldiers,' he replied. 'We should be honourable in our dealings with the people here, even with the enemy. That hasn't always been happening.'

'It's very brave of you to speak up,' she said, looking into his eyes again. She knew what a committed soldier Anil Desai was, how loyal he was to the Gurkhas. He must feel very strongly to consider raising it with superior officers.

He must have seen the admiration in her gaze because he frowned and looked away.

There went another moment between them. It had happened several times over the past few months when they'd exchanged a look, loaded with meaning, full of yearning and hope that had no outlet.

Anil cleared his throat and got up. 'I'd better be going now,' he said. 'I need to get round all the mines and estates on my patch and let them know what is happening. I came to you first. Ten of my men are on their way. They will split themselves between the mine and the house and will stay with you until the immediate threat is over.'

'Thank you,' Alice said.

She walked him along the veranda to the gap in the sandbags. As she said goodbye to him, and watched him climb into his jeep, she heard the rattle and roar of Bruce's Land Rover approaching. It burst into view and he pulled up, waved briefly to the major and walked towards the house. Alice's heart started beating more quickly. It would be impossible for them not to speak. They would need to prepare the house and the servants for a possible raid. The thought of having to communicate with Bruce after so many months of silence filled her with dread. She stood aside and waited for him there on the veranda and when he appeared through the gap in the sandbags she stepped forward and took a deep breath.

'We need to prepare for the raid, Bruce,' she said. 'So we'll have to work together.'

He glared at her, his face already florid with anger. 'I saw you, standing on the porch, watching Desai leave like a long-lost lover,' he said. 'He's always up here, isn't he? You might not think I know, but I see him driving past the mine in his jeep and I know where he's going. You must think I'm a bloody idiot.'

She stared at him, amazed that he could still be fixating on this when armed guerillas could well be on their way to attack the estate.

'You're wrong,' she said, looking him in the eye. 'There's nothing between us, Bruce. I wish you'd believe that. But right now, we need to get things ready for an attack.'

He took a step towards her, and she took one back, realising she couldn't take another one because her back was against the wall of the house.

'I thought I'd taught you a lesson, but no, you can't resist a good-looking soldier, can you?'

'Taught me a lesson? Taught me a lesson? Is that what you call forcing yourself on me? Well, that's got another name in my book,' she yelled.

As soon as she said it, she regretted it.

He lunged towards her and slapped her hard on the cheek.

It stung and she gasped, reeling with the shock and pain of it. Then he grabbed her bodily with both arms and was pushing her inside the house, making her stumble and trip, propelling her across the hall, pinching and bruising her arms with his grasp. They reached the bottom of the stairs and, despite her attempts to stop him, he half lifted her, half pushed her up the steps, along the landing and into the master bedroom.

She hadn't been in that room for months. It was untidy now and smelled sour, with Bruce's dirty work clothes strewn over the chairs, the bed rumpled and unmade, the curtains half drawn. But there was no time to think about it, he was pushing her down on the bed backwards and she had a terrible dread in the pit of her stomach, a dreadful sense of déjà vu. He tore at her clothes and pawed at her body and she squirmed, trying to get out of his grip.

'Bruce! Please... no. Please don't! Not again!'

But her cries were in vain.

16

BRUCE GRUNTED and rolled off her; leaving Alice sobbing and trembling on the bed. Her whole body ached and throbbed with pain, but it was the shame and humiliation of his brutal attack that hurt her more. She felt wrecked, annihilated. How could this have happened again? She closed her eyes to stop the tears, but still they oozed out from between her lids. She should have seen this coming; if only she'd taken Diana's advice and gone to live with her and Tony, it would never have happened. She was such a fool, thinking she could avoid Bruce's jealousy and violence.

'For God's sake stop blubbing and get dressed,' Bruce said, buttoning his trousers.

She prised her eyes open, sat up and forced herself to look at him. 'I want to know why,' she said, her voice catching in her throat. 'Why do you need to do this?'

He didn't reply, so she went on. 'We could have been happy, you and me, but you turned against me. I don't understand why.'

He was buttoning his shirt and sat down heavily in an armchair. He looked at her, his face still red and sweaty, his eyes full of pain and anger. 'You've betrayed me, Alice, that's why. And I have every right to take what's mine.'

She stared at him, realising she would never convince him he was imagining all this, that his mind was playing tricks on him, that she'd never betrayed him. But what did it matter now anyway? He'd destroyed her love and her trust. She would never love him again.

All she could mutter was, 'It's not true. It's not true.'

He got up from the chair and came up close then. He put his flushed face right up to hers so she could smell his foul breath.

'I can take what I want from you any time I want, and I fully intend to,' he said through gritted teeth. 'And another thing while we're on the subject. You're to move back to this room this evening. I'll not have my wife sleeping in the spare room any longer.'

She shook her head. 'No. No, Bruce. I won't do that. I'm not going to let you do this to me. Not again.'

'I'd like to see you try to stop me,' he said.

He grabbed her by both wrists and twisted them together until searing pain shot up her arms. She cried out in agony.

Just then a shot sounded outside.

They both jumped and Bruce dropped her wrists and moved to the front window. More shots followed and a couple of upstairs windows shattered, the glass tinkling onto the roof of the veranda.

'Damn those bastards!' Bruce yelled. 'They're back. I'll give them what for.'

'We should have warned the servants!' Alice said, fastening her blouse with trembling fingers and pulling her torn clothes around her as best she could.

Bruce turned and glowered at her. 'Don't you dare blame me for this! I'm going down to give the boys guns right now. You can defend the front with Suleman and Omar. I'll go to the back with one of the others. If things get really bad, I'm going to take cover in the cellar.' He left the room.

The hammering of gunfire from the jungle in front of the

house carried on. Alice sat on the edge of the bed, trying to calm her shattered nerves, trying to brace herself for the battle to come. She knew she would have to find the courage to go downstairs and out onto the veranda, to crouch behind the sandbags and man one of the guns. But how could she do that in the state she was in, shaking and trembling all over, her mind filled with the horror and the humiliation of this latest assault?

But she had no choice.

She forced herself to stand up. There was a pitcher of water on the bedstand, and she staggered to it, steadied herself on the table and took a few gulps, then splashed some onto her tear-stained face. She glanced in the mirror. A white-faced ghost stared back at her. She looked away. What did it matter that her clothes were torn and she looked a wreck.

She left the bedroom and when she reached the top of the stairs, she looked down into the hallway. Suleman and another of the houseboys, Omar, were down there making their way to the front of the house, carrying rifles. She knew Suleman had been teaching Omar to handle a gun after Abdul's death, she'd seen them practising in the yard at the back of the house. But she still worried. The boy was very young, barely out of his teens, and she wondered how he would cope under fire.

But there was no time to think about that now. She ran down the stairs and followed the servants through the front door and onto the veranda, where bullets were whistling over the top of the sandbags and thumping into the wooden panels of the house.

She dived straight for the Bren gun, which stood ready, mounted on its tripod, while the others hastily set up their rifles either side of her. Anil had shown her how to use the Bren after the last raid, although she'd only ever fired a couple of rounds; they hadn't wanted to waste ammunition. Now, she knelt in front of it. The horror of what had just happened dissolved and she became totally focused on that moment. She put her eye to the sights, lined up the gun and cocked it. She fired several rounds straight into the jungle, then paused and listened. The firing from the trees carried on relentlessly, the bullets slamming into the sandbags and the wall above her head.

This attack seemed more ferocious than the previous one and Anil wasn't here this time. He'd said he would come back with extra men, but even when straining her ears she couldn't hear engines on the drive or tyres on the gravel above the rattle of the bullets. She hoped fervently the Gurkhas wouldn't be long.

After her first burst of fire, she waited for a few seconds, trying to pinpoint the gunmen through the sights of the Bren gun, as Anil had instructed her. It was tempting to just keep on firing, but she knew it was no use wasting ammunition shooting randomly into the jungle. Within moments, she glimpsed a slight movement in the trees, then a burst of fire came from a particular position. She fired straight back at it and immediately the gunfire stopped coming from that direction. She realised then she was out of ammunition, and in the few short seconds it took to change the magazine, it hit her that she may have killed a man. But there was no time for reflection. She felt numb. Right here and now it was kill or be killed.

The firing continued relentlessly from the jungle. Even though she'd knocked out one of the gunmen, there must have been at least two others aiming at them from the trees. She glanced over at Suleman. He was kneeling on the ground, his eye to the rifle-sights, completely focused on his task. On the other side of her, Omar was doing the same.

Between her bursts of fire, she could hear shots coming from the back of the house where Bruce and the other house-boy, Mohammed, were firing. The building must be surrounded. Her heart pounded and she imagined being captured by the guerillas. The stories of garrottings, of bayonet-ings, of throats being slit rushed through her mind, almost paralysing her with fear. With an effort of will, she turned back to face the jungle and carried on firing the Bren. Her hands were hot and slippery with sweat, her whole body vibrating from the rapid motion of the gun. This didn't feel real, it was like a bad dream, but she knew she wasn't going to wake up from this one.

It wasn't long before the two remaining gunmen burst out of the jungle and, as before, ran towards the house, yelling battle cries and firing bullets above the sandbags. Alice froze, and everything seemed to blur – the guerillas running wild-eyed towards her, the jungle behind them, her hands on the gun. Then she shook her head, swung the Bren round and fired at their attackers as hard as she could. One man dropped to the ground, but the other carried on running towards the side of the house, reaching the sandbags piled up at the end of the veranda. He was out of sight now, but she could hear him climbing the bags.

She turned to Suleman. 'What shall we do?'

Suleman just stared at her, paralysed with fear.

The next second, the guerilla's face had appeared at the top of the sandbag wall and he was over it and scrambling down, firing random shots around him. Suleman collapsed on the floorboards, blood pooling from a wound in his chest. The man lunged forward and grabbed Alice.

She cried out. 'Bruce! Bruce!'

That instant, three other guerillas appeared through the front door of the house. They looked wild and filthy, their clothes ragged. Two of them grabbed Omar and held him at gunpoint. Chills of shock and fear pulsed through Alice at the sight of them. It must mean Mohammed and Bruce had been shot too. She and Omar were alone. Alone with four guerillas who would stop at nothing. She prayed the end would be quick, that she wouldn't die in agony with her guts spilling out of her, or have her throat slit and bleed slowly to death.

The man that had grabbed her pinned her against the wall of the house. Up close he looked and smelled rough, of sweat and damp and the mould of the jungle, as if he hadn't bathed or washed his clothes for weeks. His face was sunken and pallid, covered in sores from mosquito bites and his breath was rank.

Still holding her against the wall, he barked some orders in Cantonese and two of his men scrambled to get the fallen guns. The others pushed down the sandbag wall and pulled the Bren out of its position. Dozens of spent cartridges rattled to the floor. Alice realised she must have fired hundreds of rounds in the few short minutes since she'd first knelt in front of the gun.

Then, another of them drew a knife, walked up to Omar where he was being held, and lunged at him. Omar dropped to the floor, holding his throat, blood spurting from between his fingers. Alice let out a scream of terror, her mind and body consumed with fear. She knew this was the end.

The leader turned back to Alice and shoved her against the wall again. Then, he drew a knife and held it against her throat. She could feel the edge of the sharp blade on her skin, almost cutting it, but not quite. One push and her throat would be slit. The fear she felt in that moment was intense. She couldn't think, she couldn't focus. Her body and mind were taut with terror. She hardly dared take a breath.

'Where is he?' the man asked in broken English. 'He not here.'

She stared at him, her eyes bulging with fear. Her thoughts were scrambled, scattered everywhere. She couldn't understand what he meant. Who he meant.

He pushed her again. 'Talk to me. Tell me where the tuan is and I won't hurt you.'

Tuan! He meant Bruce. She shook her head. Bruce must be lying dead on the porch at the back of the house.

'He not there. You tell us where he is,' he was yelling at her now.

The others stood behind him, pointing their rifles at her.

Suddenly it came to her, through the mist of fear and confusion that had paralysed her, she remembered what Bruce had said just before they separated.

I'll go to the cellar if things get bad.

That was where he must be now, showing his true colours like the coward she already knew him to be. He'd fled to save his own skin, leaving her and the servants to defend the place on their own.

She stared back at the guerilla's bloodshot eyes, her own wide with terror. Her mouth had drained of saliva. She tried to swallow, and as she did, she felt the blade move against her throat.

17

ANIL

Batu Gajah, Malaya, January 1949

FROM MAJOR ANIL DESAI's diary:

When I reached Rimba Valley Estate with twenty of my Gurkha troops that afternoon, the guerillas were already there, attacking the mine buildings. A fierce gunfight was going on when we drew up. The manager and several of the defence force that Bruce Lacey had put together were barricaded in the offices, fighting for their lives. I ordered the men out of the truck and told them to use it as a shield to fire on the enemy. We crouched there behind the truck, shooting into the jungle. I don't know how many guerillas there were, but from our vantage point on the road we were able to quickly pick off several CTs who were firing at us from the trees.

We fought on for about half an hour. Two of my men were shot and were carried off by others to the back of the truck where the medic treated them. I was worried for them, but I had to carry on shooting. Eventually the firing from the trees stopped. We waited for a few minutes. Then, asking my sergeant to cover me, I crept towards the mine building, my rifle cocked. There was another burst of gunfire from the jungle then, but fortunately the bullets missed me and pinged off the truck instead and I was able to make it to the building. Five of my men then ran into the jungle, firing ahead of themselves into the trees, to flush the last guerilla out.

I reached the door to the office. The handle was stiff, so I kicked it open. Inside was a scene of devastation and carnage. The windows were smashed, furniture was upturned and the front wall riddled with bullets. Three or four mineworkers lay on the floor in pools of blood, and were clearly already dead. The other four men in the room looked very shaken. The manager was crouched under a window, bleeding from his shoulder. I shouted for one of my medics to come and help him, then I called for a couple of men to join me, and we went through the back door and into the mine.

What I saw there shocked me to the core. Five Chinese mineworkers lay dead on the ground outside the office, caked in blood and buzzing with flies. Their throats had been slit and they'd been left to bleed to death. I knelt beside each of them to check for breathing, but there was no sign of life. The whole place was empty and still; the dredger stood silent, the train wasn't moving, and I couldn't see a soul in the entire expanse of the great pit. I realised the rest of the workers must have fled when the guerillas arrived. When I looked across the mine in the direction of the miners' village, the sky above it was filled with billowing black smoke.

Anil radioed for backup, then, giving orders for his lieutenants to take ten men to the miners' village and find survivors, he posted five at the office, and ordered five more to get into the back of the truck. He got into the passenger seat and asked the driver to take them up to the house. They covered the mile or so along the drive as quickly as the truck would take them, dust and gravel flying from the heavy wheels. Anil stared ahead of him for the whole of those few, tense minutes, his teeth gritted, his jaw tense. All the time willing the house to have been spared, trying not to think about what might have happened to Alice.

When the square, white house came into view, still standing, he let out a low whistle of relief. But when they drew closer, he was shocked to see that his worst fears had materialised. Some of the upstairs windows were broken. The sandbag wall had been breached; there were huge gaps in it, some of the bags had burst and sand had spilled over the drive. He knew then that it was too much to have hoped for the house to have escaped the attention of the CTs. With the attack on the mine, the guerillas were certain to have targeted the residence too.

When the truck stopped, he swung out of the cab while the other men jumped down out of the back. He picked out three men.

'Go round to the back of the house and secure it. We will take the front,' he ordered, nodding to the other two.

Followed by his two Gurkhas, Anil skirted the drive and crawled along the front of the house to the gap in the sandbag wall. There, brandishing his rifle, he peered over the barricade. He caught his breath. Two servants lay dead on the veranda, their blood soaking their white uniforms and running into the boards. He climbed carefully and noiselessly through the gap in the sandbags, then paused and listened. The house was still and silent.

But then he heard a sound. Someone was crying quietly, sobbing inconsolably. He knew it was Alice. He clambered over the rest of the sandbags and ran to her.

Alice was sitting hunched up against the wall of the house, beside the bearer's stricken body, her knees drawn up to her chest, her face in her hands. Anil knelt down next to her and put his hand on her shoulder. He could feel her body trembling.

'Alice? Alice, it's me, Anil.'

She lifted her head and looked at him blankly. It was as if she didn't know him. Her face was dirty and stained with tears; her clothes ripped and ragged. Several buttons had been torn off her blouse. A rush of anger and horror went through him.

'Whatever did they do to you?' he asked, aghast.

She shook her head, frowning. Still she didn't speak.

'What did they do to you? Did they assault you? Did they—'

'No... no,' she said, her voice cracked and shaky. 'They didn't touch me.'

'It's alright,' he said, putting his arm around her shoulders, holding her close. 'You can tell me. You're safe now.'

She shook her head. 'They didn't touch me,' she said again, in a stronger voice this time.

He took his arm away. 'Alright,' he said, but he didn't believe her. This wasn't unusual, in his experience. Many women who'd been assaulted by the enemy were reluctant to talk about it. His heart filled with pity. He knew she was suffering from shock; perhaps he would try to get her to talk later. 'I can take you up to the base,' he told her. 'There is a doctor there.'

'I don't need a doctor,' she said, wiping her tears away with the back of her hand, smearing the dirt across her cheeks.

Anil stood up and turned to his men who were now standing behind him on the veranda. 'Search the house,' he ordered. 'See if there are any CTs still here.'

He didn't want to leave Alice, and he was fairly sure there weren't going to be any guerillas left in the house. Otherwise, they would already be firing on them.

'How many CTs were there?' he asked, turning back to her.

She swallowed and took a shuddering breath. 'Three or four, I think. They started off shooting from the jungle and from behind the house. We managed to knock out a few of them. One of them came for us over the sandbags, and then others came through from the back.'

'Where did they go?'

'I don't know. They... they just disappeared into the jungle.'

'What about your husband?' he asked.

She shrugged. 'I don't know,' she said in a whisper.

In all probability, Anil thought, Bruce was lying dead or wounded on the back porch. His men would find him.

There was a shout from inside the house and one of the soldiers came running.

'What is it, Private?' Anil asked when the man appeared in the doorway.

'You need to come, sir,' the man replied.

Anil glanced back at Alice who was still sitting on the floor, her face in her hands.

'I'll be back in a moment,' he told her, then he turned to another soldier and told him to stay with her.

He followed the man through the house to the back porch where there were two more bodies, sprawled on the floor, riddled with bullet wounds. Neither of these men had their weapons; the guerillas would have taken them. He stared at the bodies, puzzled. Both these men were clearly servants, in their white tunics and trousers, covered in sand and blood. Where on earth was Bruce Lacey?

'This way, sir.'

His private beckoned him on, through a gap in the broken wall of sandbags which were riddled with bullets, the sand falling from the hessian sacks and onto the boards. They went down the steps of the porch and out into the garden where the full glare of the afternoon sun hit him with a physical force.

'Look, sir. Over there.' The man pointed across the lawn to a tall, spreading mahogany tree that dominated one corner of the property, its shade darkening the pink hibiscus and rose bushes in the borders below it.

Anil shaded his eyes and looked towards the tree. What he saw there churned his stomach.

The body of a man was hanging from a rope slung over a high

branch. It was swaying gently with a faint creaking sound, although the air was heavy and still, without the whisper of a breeze. The head was slumped forward, the dirty blond hair flopping over the eyes. All that was visible of the face was a swollen, protruding tongue, but it was unmistakeably Bruce Lacey. He was dressed in his work overalls, smeared in mud and diesel from the mine.

Anil felt the blood draining from his own face. He turned to his soldier and saw three of the others had joined them and were staring up at the swaying body as well.

'Climb up there, Private, and cut the man down. You other men, stay on the ground and help him.'

His men were adept at climbing trees as well as rocks and mountains. It was part of their training. He glanced back at the house. They'd better be quick. He didn't want Alice to see her husband like that.

The private drew his kukri, laid down his rifle and pushed his way through the flower border to the tree. The others moved forward and stood beneath the body. Anil watched as the man scaled the trunk deftly and swiftly, until he reached the branch. The dark green leaves of the old mahogany tree shivered and shuddered under the soldier's weight. The next minute, the man was shimmying along the branch, and, balancing there, he worked his knife on the rope until it snapped, and the body dropped towards the waiting Gurkhas.

They caught Bruce Lacey, staggering slightly as his body landed in their arms, then they laid him down gently on the grass. Anil forced himself to go over and look at the body. Bruce's hair had fallen away from his face, revealing red, purplish skin, bulging, bloodshot eyes and a swollen tongue. Underneath the frayed rope that was still tight around his neck, were purple bruises and trickles of blood from broken veins. Anil had seen hanged men before, but there was something particularly shocking about this. Only that morning he'd been talking to

Bruce about defending the mine, and here he was, dead, in the most grotesque way imaginable.

'Find a tablecloth or a sheet from the house and cover him up,' he told his men. 'I need to speak to Mrs Lacey.' He headed back to the house, wondering how to break the news to Alice. She was hardly in a fit state to receive it, but he knew she must be told.

When he went onto the veranda, she was still sitting on the floor, staring blankly ahead of her. The soldier Anil had left with her was standing nearby with his rifle at the ready. Anil nodded to him to withdraw, and the man saluted and went inside the house. Anil crouched down on the boards beside Alice.

'Bruce is dead, isn't he?' she said, looking at the floor.

'I'm afraid he is,' Anil replied, knowing he would have to say more.

She was silent for a few moments, then said, 'Was he shot?'

'No... No. They didn't shoot him.'

She turned towards him, terror in her eyes. 'What did they do to him? How did he die?'

Anil cleared his throat. 'I'm afraid... and I'm sorry, this will come as a shock to you, Alice. They hanged him.'

Alice gasped and froze; she went stock-still, like a trapped animal. He looked into her eyes and they were ravaged with pain. He waited for her to dissolve into tears, but instead she fell into a tense silence. She drew her knees up to her chest and hugged them to her, rocking back and forth. Anil put his arm around her shoulder, wondering desperately what to do, how to comfort her. What he did know, was that the shock and grief she must now be experiencing must take their course.

They stayed like that for several minutes, but he knew he didn't have the luxury of time. He needed to clear the bodies from the property, get back to the mine to check on his men there, then return to base to make his report to HQ. But he couldn't leave Alice alone in this state.

She stopped rocking back and forth, looked up at him and

said, her voice racked with pain, 'It's all my fault. It's my fault he died.'

'How could it possibly be your fault?' Anil asked, puzzled.

She didn't answer, just looked away from him again and let out a long, deep moan, as if she was in severe physical pain. She fell silent, a few more seconds ticked past, then she started to get to her feet.

'I need to see him,' she said. 'Where is he?'

Anil helped her to get up. 'I don't think that's a good idea. He looks...'

'I don't care. I need to see him.'

'Please, Alice. There's no need to. Why do this to yourself?'

She didn't answer, just headed straight along the veranda and through the front door into the house. Anil followed her. She had every right to see her husband's body, but what effect would that terrible sight have on her? He put his hand on her arm and tried to stop her again, but she brushed him off.

'Is he out here?' she asked, walking straight through the house and onto the back porch. She stopped and gasped when she saw the bloodied bodies of the two servants lying there.

'But he's not here,' she said. 'Where is he?'

'He's in the garden,' Anil replied, 'on the grass. Prepare yourself, Alice, please.'

She pushed through the gap in the sandbags and ran across the lawn towards the little mound under the tree, covered by a gingham tablecloth. Two of the Gurkhas were still standing beside the body.

Alice walked up to it, knelt and pulled the tablecloth aside. Anil was right behind her. He was again sickened by the sight of the once handsome face, bloated and livid, with its grotesquely distorted features. Again, he was prepared for tears, for sobbing. He knew the man had hurt her and treated her badly, but he'd been her husband, her companion, and she must have loved him once.

But instead of bursting into tears, Alice lifted her head and let out a scream; an animal cry of anger, despair and horror. It bounced off the walls of the house and echoed around the surrounding jungle-covered hills, and all Anil could do was drop to his knees and take her in his arms.

18

CHLOE

Kathmandu, 2018

CHLOE STOOD ALONE in the corner of the bookshop that Friday evening. She'd just closed up for the day after saying goodbye to Shova, who'd gone off with a group of friends to a café. The cats were in the kitchen, gobbling their food contentedly, and Chloe had completed her usual evening round of the building; watering all the plants, putting stray books back into the shelves, straightening the furniture, tidying up in readiness for the lady who came to clean early in the morning.

Now she stood in front of the fortune-telling machine contemplating the all-too lifelike model inside, shrouded in veils and hung with gaudy jewellery, who seemed to stare back at her, as if mocking her. It was that time of the week when Chloe normally treated herself to a dabble on the machine. But somehow, today, she didn't have her usual enthusiasm for it. All the joy seemed to have gone out of her world these past few days and she was wondering what the point of her ritual was.

She was feeling a little reluctant to go home to an empty flat. Kiran had left for his trek to Everest Base Camp two days before, and things had still been frosty between them.

'I'll see you in about ten days' time,' he'd said before he left, 'weather permitting.' He'd grazed her cheek with a cursory kiss.

After the sound of his footsteps had faded away down the stairs, Chloe's heart ached with regret. She wished they'd resolved their differences before he'd left. It didn't feel right to be spending time apart when their disagreement was still simmering. It had made her feel miserable, and she'd found it hard to pick herself up and go to work that morning. But once she'd walked through the bustling, clamouring streets and arrived at the door of Paradise Books, she'd felt a little better. And as the morning went on, she began to feel almost normal. Although the sorrow was still there in the back of her mind, she got so busy putting on a brave face for customers she'd managed to stay cheerful.

Later that morning, she asked Shova to help her bring the books of Anil's that she'd selected to keep up to the shop. They spent time between customers putting the books back into boxes, carrying them up the narrow staircase into the shop and finding space on the shelves to display them.

That first evening she'd worked as late as she could to avoid returning to the flat alone. She'd been checking her phone all day, waiting for Kiran to text her. Eventually he did – while she was walking home through the darkened streets – telling her he and his group had arrived safely at the airport at Lukla and were staying the night in the town before trekking on to the village of Phakding the next day. Chloe glanced at his words on her screen as she walked. They were curt and factual, she realised, and lacked the warmth and humour of their usual exchanges.

She stopped walking and responded to the text – *Glad to know you're safe* – then put her phone in her bag, discouraged. She *was* happy to know he'd arrived safely, but the tone of his text had lowered her spirits again. This time even further than before.

Kiran didn't reply to her text. She knew it was difficult for him to keep in touch, that there was often little or no phone signal up in the mountains, but she wondered if that was his real reason for not responding.

The next day was Thursday, the day Rajesh was coming to the shop in the afternoon. Since he'd come to show her Anil's diary earlier in the week, Chloe had been looking forward to the moment when they would have a chance to read it. The shop was busy that morning, but at lunchtime she slipped out for a quick meal of rice and dahl at her favourite food stall in a tiny side street, where smells of herbs and spices floated on the air and a crowd of regulars jostled to be served. Afterwards she found herself standing beside the till in Paradise Books, staring out the window, waiting for Rajesh to appear from the alleyway opposite. Eventually, he did, hurrying towards the shop, looking flustered, wearing his crumpled suit and carrying his battered briefcase.

She'd greeted him at the door, her heart going out to him as usual. He looked lonely and a little defeated.

'Sorry if I'm late, Chloe. The traffic was terrible.'

She'd taken him through to the kitchen at the back, where he and Gita greeted each other warmly and Gita had served him some fresh apple turnover. Rajesh had brought his parents' wedding photographs and they left Auntie Gita poring over them, while Chloe and Rajesh found a secluded corner table in the courtyard.

Alice had written several letters to Anil between June 1948 when they'd first met, and the end of January 1949. These letters were very short, just notes really, mostly telling Anil times when it would be convenient for him to drop in to the house. As she read them out to Rajesh, Chloe wondered at first why Anil had kept them. But looking more closely, she realised there were small clues to Alice's life scattered throughout these hastily scribbled notes and that was possibly why Anil hadn't thrown them away.

Those glimpses into Alice's world made the notes even more intriguing to Chloe. In one of them, Alice had written:

PLEASE DON'T WORRY *about me, Major Desai. As I told you, I slipped over in the garden yesterday and bruised myself. But it is nice that you are concerned, and that you are happy to drive out here and check I'm alright from time to time. I do value your visits.*

ON ANOTHER OCCASION, she wrote:

I'M sorry I wasn't there when you came to the house today, Major Desai. We hadn't made an arrangement, had we? I had been working in the garden, but decided on an impulse to take a walk into the jungle. That land is also the property of the mining company, and I didn't go outside the estate boundary, so wasn't doing anything you've advised me not to. I'm always very vigilant when I go out of the garden, but I'm sure you will have something to say about it when we next meet.

TO CHLOE, both these comments seemed significant. Why would Alice go to the trouble of mentioning her bruises if they were genuinely accidental? Perhaps her husband had hurt her? Anil's diary had also mentioned the bruises and from earlier correspondence Chloe knew Bruce Lacey to be a belligerent, aggressive man. And why did Alice leave the relative safety of her house to walk in the jungle where guerillas were known to be hiding?

'There's quite a gap in the letters,' Rajesh said. 'My father didn't seem to keep any letters from Alice between mid January and sometime in late February 1949. So I thought we could start on the next batch another time. But why don't we look at the diary and see if it sheds any more light on what happened then?' Rajesh opened the battered exercise book, turned to the first page and began translating from Nepalese to English.

It soon became clear that Anil had started the diary soon after he'd arrived in Perak in May 1948. The first few weeks contained factual entries about his trips to the various estates and mines in the district, and his impressions of the British people who ran them, few of which were favourable. Then, in mid June, came an entry which read:

TODAY WENT *to Rimba Valley Estate for the first time. Enormous tin mine, owned by United Tin, employing hundreds of workers, mainly Chinese. It will certainly be a target for the CTs, so will clearly need additional security measures. The manager, Bruce Lacey, is arrogant and rude. But his wife, Alice, seems a delightful person, who is also very beautiful. She seemed a little on edge, though. What a shame she is married to such an odious individual. I pity her.*

THEN CAME Anil's entry about the dinner party a few days later, then it moved on to Alice's first shooting lesson. Of that he wrote:

A VERY PLEASANT *interlude teaching Mrs Lacey to shoot a carbine this morning. She is a quick learner and picked up the techniques in no time. But I couldn't help noticing she had a couple of bruises on her arms, which she was quick to cover up. I wonder if her husband hurts her. It wouldn't surprise me. She seems so vulnerable and alone. I wish I could protect her.*

. . .

WHEN CHLOE READ that she looked up at Rajesh. 'I thought that must be it, didn't you?'

He nodded. 'I did. Poor, poor Alice.'

Later, came an entry about an attack on the house, when Anil had helped Alice defend the front porch, and a servant had been killed:

I ADMIRED HER COURAGE. She knelt there firing away like a seasoned soldier. And she kept her cool even when one of the houseboys was shot dead and a CT stormed the house. But later, when she turned up at the checkpoint driving an old car, quite alone, I was sure something else must have happened. She was shaking all over, she'd been crying, and she was desperate to see her friend, Mrs Blanchard, so I drove her over there. She didn't say, but I could tell her husband had hurt her again. There were new bruises on her arms which confirmed what I thought I'd seen before. I worry for her, and whatever Lacey might say, I'm determined to check on her regularly. It will be fairly easy to do that on the pretext of checking on security on the estate.

OVER THE NEXT FEW MONTHS, came several entries detailing attacks on mines, rubber plantations and other British buildings in the area. All followed roughly the same pattern: the CTs would surround the building, storm it with guns, then shoot or slit the throat of whoever they found there, including servants and workers whether Malay, Tamil or Chinese. They also sabotaged mine buildings, rubber factories and the homes of workers, setting them on fire and leaving them to burn to the ground.

'People must have been terrified,' Chloe said as Rajesh translated his father's words into English. 'Did he ever tell you about it?' She tried to imagine what it must have been like during the Emergency, living on a remote plantation or estate in the middle of the thick jungle, in the knowledge that ruthless guerillas could attack at any time.

Rajesh shook his head. 'Pa didn't talk about his time in action. He hardly even mentioned the battles he was in during the war. I do remember him saying once that he didn't serve in Malaya to the end of the Emergency. That he left sometime in the early fifties. I'm not sure why though. Perhaps these entries will explain it.' He turned back to the diary and carried on translating.

There were descriptions of British people being ambushed on jungle roads in their cars, dragged out and shot at point-blank range, of workers and servants having their throats slit by the CTs. Finally, on 20 January 1949, came a chilling entry, describing a second raid on the Rimba Valley mine and house, the slaying of all the servants and the hanging of Bruce Lacey. Rajesh went pale as he translated the story set out in his father's words, and Chloe was filled with horror.

MY MEN REMOVED the bodies from the house and grounds, all except Bruce Lacey's, and put them in the back of the truck to take to the police station. I watched the truck leave, then my driver arrived at the house with the jeep. Mrs Lacey came out onto the front porch with her suitcase and I helped her into the vehicle. She had calmed down by that time, but her face was completely white, and she didn't say a word. She sat in the front seat between me and the driver, and we pulled away. She stared ahead of her and didn't look back at the house once. She remained silent for the whole journey to the Blanchard estate. I wanted to comfort her, to help her somehow, but she seemed to have retreated a long way into herself and there was nothing I could do to reach her.

RAJESH CLOSED THE LITTLE BOOK, shaking his head.

'That's just terrible,' Chloe said. 'I had little idea about what happened in Malaya after the war. Poor, poor Alice, witnessing those terrifying scenes and all the people around her being murdered. She must have thought she would die herself. And then Bruce being hanged. How terrifying. Whatever she might have felt about him, that must have been a dreadful shock.'

'Simply terrible,' Rajesh agreed.

They were both silent for a few minutes as they reflected on what they'd just read.

'It's so frustrating that there's such a gap in the letters. I'll have another look.' Rajesh rummaged through the envelopes in his briefcase and pulled one out. 'Ah! There is one letter after the date of that last entry, but after that one there is still a gap of a few weeks. Alice must have gone to stay with her friend. Perhaps there was no need for her to send notes from there.'

'When's that one dated?' Chloe asked, glancing outside at the darkening sky. She knew she should really go back and relieve Shova, but perhaps there was time to read just one more letter.

'Here. It's dated 25 January 1949,' Rajesh said. 'Will you read it to me?' He handed Chloe the letter.

DEAR ANIL,

I HOPE you don't mind my calling you Anil now and not Major Desai? It seems so formal, and you have been such a pillar of strength to me these past months, I feel I can now call you a friend.

I wanted to thank you for your support at today's service. It was even more painful than I imagined it would be, and so hard to stand there in what was once a happy place, shaking hands and listening to all the condolences. I'm glad it was possible for Bruce to be buried in his own garden. He loved the house and the mine, and would have wanted that.

You know my husband was sometimes a difficult man. I'm not sure if it explains it, but he went through some terrible times during the war.

I believe he was once tortured by the Japanese. Despite everything, his death has still come as a shock to me.

I hope you will continue to visit the Blanchard House. I'm not sure I could cope without your visits.

YOURS SINCERELY,
Alice Lacey

'THEY WERE CLEARLY GETTING close at that point,' Chloe said, folding the letter and slipping it back into its envelope. She handed it to Rajesh. 'This is so intriguing. I'm dying to carry on, but I need to get back to the shop and start cashing up for the evening.'

'Of course. Of course,' Rajesh said, jumping up from his seat. 'Let's continue next time. My apologies for having kept you so long.' He began putting the letters and diary back into his suitcase. 'Give my regards to Kiran, won't you?' he asked.

There was an awkward pause. 'Actually, Kiran is off on another trek at the moment,' Chloe told him, trying to keep the emotion out of her voice. 'It's up to Everest Base Camp, and it's quite difficult for him to keep in touch.'

'Everest Base Camp! What an adventurer young Kiran is. I've never been up that way myself. I hear it can get quite crowded with trekkers nowadays.'

'I'm sure it does. I haven't done that trek myself either...' Chloe said, biting her fingernail.

Rajesh leaned forward, peering into her eyes. 'Are you worried about him, my dear?'

'A little. Yes, I suppose I am.' She looked into Rajesh's kind eyes and wondered whether to confide in him about the argument, but held back, just as she had from talking to Auntie Gita, reminding herself that to speak about it to anyone would feel like a betrayal.

'You mustn't worry,' Rajesh went on. 'Kiran's an experienced climber. In fact, he's more than that. He's a native, born in the mountains, who has a unique feel for the terrain. He knows his own limits and he understands the conditions.'

Slowly she nodded. Rajesh was right, of course. 'But... you know about his accident during the earthquake three years ago, don't you?'

'Oh yes. His mother, Ehani, kept us informed. I understand he was very ill for a time.'

'He had bleeding on the brain. He had a couple of operations, and it was touch and go for months. He's only just got back to full fitness.'

'You're bound to worry about him, but he's a sensible man.'

She bit her nail again, not able to tell Rajesh that she wasn't just worried about the trip, she was worried about the way things had been left between them.

Now, as she thought back over the exchanges, standing there in front of the fortune-telling machine, she still hadn't had any further messages from Kiran. Perhaps there was no reception where he was, or perhaps he was remaining silent for a reason. She had no way of knowing and it was eating away at her.

With a sigh, she put her coin into the slot and waited while the machine whirred and clicked, the fortune teller inside stood up from her seat and turned full circle, and the little piece of paper was churned out from the slot. She pulled it out and looked down at the flowing writing. This time without her usual sense of anticipation.

THE SEED of yesterday is the fruit of tomorrow.

. . .

WHAT DID THAT MEAN? she wondered, looking at the words until they blurred before her eyes. She was tempted to screw up the paper and throw it in the bin, but instead she folded it neatly and slipped it into her pocket.

Of course it was all nonsense, she reminded herself. But, still, she would look at it again later to see if it rang any bells. She couldn't help wondering if it actually had any significance.

19

ALICE

Blanchard Rubber Estate, Perak, February 1949

DEAR ANIL,

Thank you for taking me back to Rimba Valley to collect my things today. It was very kind of you and, as you know, I didn't want to trouble Diana. She has been so good to me since Bruce died, offering me a roof over my head and endless support.

I hope you will visit me at the Blanchards' house again very soon. As you know, I really value the time we spend together.

Yours,

Alice

Alice felt a little disingenuous writing a letter of thanks in those terms to Anil. She hadn't been honest with him about her reasons for wanting to go back to the house. It was true she'd arrived at Diana's that first terrible day with hardly any belongings, and she badly needed some more clothes, as well as a few of her treasured personal items, particularly books. Diana and Tony weren't great readers and she'd already raced through the meagre stock of novels in their house. But, truth be told, she could have done without any of those things. The real reason she needed to go back to Rimba Valley was because she was desperately worried about Ying May and the other villagers living in the secret kampong deep in the jungle. She knew they'd become reliant on her for a regular supply of rice, flour, potatoes and green vegetables, and it was over a month since she'd taken them any. She felt a huge responsibility towards them, and she was plagued with guilt at the thought she was letting them down.

She'd toyed with the idea of asking Diana if the Blanchards' driver could take her home, but had decided against doing that. She knew Diana would, out of kindness, insist upon coming with her, and then it would be impossible for her to slip out of the garden and up through the jungle to the village.

So when Anil had dropped in after lunch one day, for one of his increasingly regular visits, and Diana was down at the estate office helping Tony with his monthly accounts, Alice hit upon the idea of asking Anil to run her back to the house on the pretext of collecting some belongings. She'd felt terrible lying to him – although it was only a little white lie, she told herself. He'd been such a rock for her since Bruce's death, and she'd even begun to trust him enough to start to tentatively confide in him about the way Bruce had treated her. Of course, she would never be able tell him everything and he must never know her terrible secret. They had grown close, though, so she felt doubly guilty for hoodwinking him, but she simply couldn't think of another way of getting to the kampong.

'Are you sure you'll be alright in that house on your own?' he said, frowning, when she'd asked if he would drop her there for a couple of hours and return to pick her up at the end of the afternoon.

'I'm quite sure,' she replied. 'I just feel... I feel I need to be alone there for a while, to... well, to come to terms with what happened. And, actually, thinking about it, I won't be totally alone. The new servants will be there too, won't they?'

Alice had last been at the house for Bruce's funeral a few days after his death. Even in that short space of time the mining company, United Tin, had repaired the bullet-riddled façade of the house, replaced the broken windows and rebuilt the sandbag walls. Alice hadn't gone inside the house that day; the funeral had been held in the British church in Batu Gajah, and two vehicles, the first a hearse and the second a limousine, had driven sedately along the jungle roads to Rimba Valley for the burial, with a heavy army escort of armoured cars and jeeps carrying armed soldiers.

Alice had felt numb going back there that day. She'd stood between Tony and Diana, and watched the coffin being carried by four of Bruce's mine workers around the front of the house and into the garden, where a large grave had been dug beside one of the rose beds.

Since then, United Tin had installed a new bearer and a houseboy to look after the place until Alice's return. A relief manager was living in the miners' village, to supervise the rebuilding of the burned houses, the repair of the mining equipment, and to get the mine up and running again after the attack. She knew that one day they would appoint a permanent manager, and she would have to leave the house for good. But that was bound to take time; it was difficult to get men to commit to such a task in these dangerous times.

'Alright. I'll take you,' Anil had finally said.

She'd hastily scribbled a note to Diana, letting her know where she was going, and that she would be back by the end of the afternoon.

As Anil drove her out of the rubber estate, past the armed guards on the gate, and out onto the rough jungle road in his jeep, he was broodingly silent. He was often pensive, but today his silence unnerved her. Was he reflecting on her reasons for going back to the house? She didn't want him to question her too closely about it. She glanced at his face while he stared ahead at the rutted road. But, as so often before, she couldn't discern what he might be thinking. Perhaps something had happened at the base, or perhaps there were some new orders afoot he was mulling over...

She recalled the time he'd told her, on one of his visits to the Blanchard estate shortly after Bruce's funeral, that he'd spoken to his superior officer about the massacre at the village of Batang Kali. It was that incident that had sparked the violent retaliation that had led to the raid on the mine and house and Bruce's death. She recalled Anil had worn a similar expression on that day, brooding and pensive, and Alice had eventually managed to extract from him the reason why.

'I was told not to question what had happened,' he'd told her. 'A British government investigation had concluded the killings were justified. When I protested again, the colonel dismissed me and ordered me not to raise the matter with him again.'

Alice had been impressed that Anil had spoken out. She knew he was a loyal officer, and that it must have taken a lot for him to question authority. Although she wasn't completely surprised; she'd never met anyone as fearless and honourable as him. Which was why she was now filled with shame for not being able to tell him the truth. Both about Bruce's death and her reasons for returning to the house.

When they approached the checkpoint near the entrance to Rimba Valley, the Gurkhas in charge saluted Anil and raised the barrier – Anil hardly had to slow down. The soldiers at the gate to the estate itself saluted too as they sped past. They drove on towards the mine offices, which had been repaired and repainted. They raced by, and Alice noticed the mine was back in operation. Even above the roar of the jeep's engine, she could hear the familiar rumble of the great dredger at work.

On they went, through the thick, dark jungle towards the

house. Alice stared straight ahead, and when the house came into view looking exactly as it always had, a chill went through her.

When they drew up in front of the house, Anil jumped down and ran round to open Alice's door. He held out a hand to help her, peering at her with a concerned look on his face. She could see he was still puzzled by her behaviour.

He said, 'Are you quite sure you don't want me to come inside with you?'

'Quite sure,' she said, dropping her gaze. 'But thank you. As I said, I need to do this on my own.'

'Alright,' he said. 'I do need to get back to base, but I will send one of the men from the checkpoint to guard the house while you're here.'

Alice felt her cheeks heat up. 'There's no need, really,' she said, wondering furiously what she could say to dissuade him. 'I'll only be here a little while,' she went on, 'and things have quietened down a bit now, haven't they?'

Anil rubbed his chin. 'We did make a number of arrests after your husband's death, it's true...'

She laid her hand on his arm. 'So, it's alright then. If I hear or see anything suspicious, I will call you at the base.'

'Alright... I have a briefing, but someone will raise the alarm.'

'Thank you,' Alice said, breathing again.

'I'll be back to collect you in two hours' time,' he said, glancing at his watch.

Alice stood on the drive and watched the jeep turn around and speed away in a cloud of dust. Then, gritting her teeth, she walked slowly towards the house, and up the wooden steps. She pushed her way through the gap in the sandbag wall and stepped onto the veranda. Pausing there, she closed her eyes for a second. She'd rehearsed this moment over and over in her mind, but now she was there, the horrors of that fateful day came flooding back. An image of the guerilla's face shoved up against hers flashed into her mind. She staggered slightly and put her hand on the front wall to steady herself. She'd known it would be hard coming back to the house, especially alone, but she hadn't expected this. She took a deep breath and, with an effort of will, banished the image from her mind.

She opened her eyes, walked towards the front door and stopped. Under her feet were bloodstains where Omar had bled to death. Someone had tried to scrub them away, but the deep-red stains had seeped into the wood. Nausea and faintness washed over her. She took another deep breath, opened the front door and stepped inside.

'Hello?' she called, standing in the empty hallway. Uncannily, it looked just as it had the day Bruce had brought her to the house for the first time almost three years ago.

Footsteps approached from the servants' quarters and a man appeared. He was slimmer and younger than Suleman, and lighter on his feet, but wearing a white tunic and red fez just as his predecessor had. Alice felt a wave of sadness for the old man and for the other servants who had died on that fateful day. They hadn't deserved to lose their lives defending their employer's property.

'Good afternoon, madam,' the man said with a puzzled smile. 'I'm afraid Mrs Lacey is not here at present.'

She couldn't help smiling. 'I *am* Mrs Lacey,' she said.

'Oh! I'm sorry, memsahib. Please forgive me. I am Ibrahim, the new bearer.'

'Salaam Alaikum, Ibrahim,' she said. 'Nice to meet you. I've just come home to collect a few things. And I was wondering...' She was thinking quicky now, needing to make an excuse for raiding the pantry. 'Supplies of food are a bit low where I'm staying. I thought I might take some basics back with me.'

Ibrahim looked at her with a polite but fixed smile. 'Of course, mem,' he said. 'The food is yours. The houseboy will help you with it.'

'No. No thank you. There is no need for that. I can manage,' she said, trying to slow down her voice. 'I'll just pop upstairs and pack a few clothes first.'

She could feel his eyes on her back as she walked up the stairs.

She hesitated outside the master bedroom, then gripped the handle firmly and went inside. The room had been tidied and the bed made, but even so, the memory of being dragged through the door and thrown onto the bed resurfaced, sending shivers of horror through her. She hurried over to the wardrobe and took out a few of her dresses, found a suitcase and packed them into it quickly with a few other items. Then she left the room, banging the door shut in her haste.

She crossed the landing to the spare room, where she'd slept for the months leading up to that last terrible day. That room too had been tidied and the bed made neatly. She opened the cupboard. Her knapsack was still there, under her sunhat. She pulled it out and held it to her face and breathed in. The dank smell of the jungle and the woodsmoke from the kampong she remembered so well lingered in the fabric. She felt a stab of guilt. She needed to get up to the kampong as soon as she could. She hadn't long before Anil returned.

Hurrying downstairs, she left the suitcase in the hall and went through the passage towards the kitchen and servants' quarters. She could hear Ibrahim and the new houseboy chatting away in Malay in the kitchen. Even though she'd mentioned it to Ibrahim, she still felt awkward about raiding the pantry. She hesitated in front of the pantry door, feeling a different sort of guilt creep through her.

Once inside she inspected the shelves. Stocks had dwindled since she'd last been in there, but there were still bags of flour, rice and a sack of potatoes, although there was no meat in the safe. She filled the knapsack as quickly as she could and stole back to the hall. She left the house by the front door, squeezed her way out through the sandbag wall, and crossed the drive towards the side gate that led into the garden.

Crossing the garden was the hardest part. The sun beat down fiercely, but still Alice trembled at the memories that danced before her eyes. Bruce's bloated, blotchy face, the distended tongue, the rope marks on his neck. She put her head down and plunged across the lawn towards the rear gate, trying not to look at the mahogany tree in the corner and the mound of earth marked with a wooden cross beside the rose beds, now covered in spindly new grass.

Once she'd left the garden behind her and started to climb, she breathed a little more easily. Shrugging the knapsack more firmly onto her shoulders, she headed into the jungle on the old familiar path. The humid air quickly enveloped her; the rank smell of damp and mould filled her nostrils. The hum of insects and the chattering of jungle creatures was oppressive, but she pressed on, panting with the effort, and was soon out of the trees at the top of the hill and skirting the edge of the mine, heading towards the path to the village. She'd rarely done this part of the walk alone before. She was almost sure she knew the way, but it had been a while since she'd been there and she had to concentrate hard not to get lost. Losing your way in the jungle could be a death sentence.

At last, she came to the edge of the trees again and the kampong clearing spread out in front of her. Wiping the sweat from her brow, she looked down at the circle of rickety houses, the smoke curling up from the campfires. Relieved, she headed towards it.

Two skinny women waved and hurried towards her from their porches when she entered the clearing, broad smiles on their faces, exclaiming with delight in Cantonese. Others joined them as she made her way between the huts towards Ying May's house. When it came into view, she saw Ying May wave and get up from her veranda. She ran down to meet Alice. As she got closer, Alice noticed that Ying May was thinner than ever. She also looked troubled, her cheeks were hollow and there were dark smudges beneath her eyes.

'Mrs Lacey,' she said. 'You haven't been to see us for a long time.'

'I know. I'm so sorry,' Alice replied. 'You know we were attacked, don't you?'

Ying May frowned. 'Yes. We heard about that.'

'My husband and all the servants... were killed. I... I had to go away for a time. But I've brought some food for you now.'

'I'm very sorry to hear that. Thank you for bringing the food. Come...'

Ying May shooed the other women away, yelling at them rapidly in Cantonese, then took Alice's arm and guided her up onto the porch of her house. There, Alice sat, as she had so many times before, while Ying May took the kettle and went down to the fire with it. The other women had dispersed by now, returned to their porches, where they sat watching anxiously, waiting for the food to be distributed.

Alice's eyes strayed to the edge of the clearing where she was shocked to see something new. Four fresh mounds of earth. Four villagers must have died since she'd last been here. Perhaps of malnutrition? Again she felt a stab of guilt. If only she'd come sooner, she might have been able to save those lives.

Ying May returned with the boiling kettle and made a pot of the pungent, earthy tea. She handed a chipped mug to Alice.

'Those graves are new, aren't they?' Alice asked, taking a sip of the hot liquid.

Ying May nodded. 'The headman and his wife... they died,' she said. 'And two others as well.'

'How terrible,' Alice said. 'What happened?'

'Natural causes,' Ying May said sharply, dusting a mosquito off her shirt. 'They caught fever.'

'Oh! I'm so sorry,' Alice said. Ying May clearly didn't want to be drawn about the deaths. Perhaps it was painful for her to speak about it. Alice changed the subject and they chatted for a while, just as they used to, and Alice realised how much she'd missed coming to the village.

'I promise to bring food again very soon,' Alice said. 'I'll try to come again next week. And I expect I'll move back to the house in a couple of weeks. It's time I went home.'

'Thank you,' Ying May said. 'We have missed it badly.'

At that moment, a man emerged through the hanging creepers over the doorway of the house. He was dressed simply, in peasant's clothes like Ying May, but Alice had the impression he was more educated than most of the people around here. He and Ying May exchanged a few words in Cantonese, then he nodded to Alice and went back inside.

'My husband,' Ying May said. 'Today he has no work.'

'I'm sorry to hear that,' Alice said. Ying May seemed subdued, Alice thought, not her usual self at all. But it was understandable, in the circumstances.

'Let me see what you've brought,' Ying May said, interrupting her thoughts.

'Oh, of course.'

Alice handed her the knapsack and Ying May took out each paper bag carefully, inspected and weighed the contents in her hand, as she always did, then placed it down beside her on the bamboo slats.

'Ying May?' the old woman croaked from inside the hut.

Ying May got up.

'I'll go now,' Alice said, taking this as her cue to leave. Ying May clearly didn't want her to linger and, in any case, Alice had to get back to the house. She'd been away at least an hour already and she didn't want Anil to come back and find her missing. 'There's no need to come with me,' Alice said. 'You need to go to your mother.'

'Thank you for coming,' Ying May said. Then she brightened a little and said, 'You look better now.'

'Better?'

'Than before. You not so worried now.'

Walking back through the jungle, Alice reflected on Ying May's words. Did she really look better? These days, when she looked in the mirror, she sometimes saw a change in her face since Bruce's death. She was no longer on edge, terrified of offending him or of sparking a violent outburst. It was true, she was more relaxed now – despite living under constant threat from the guerillas – because she was no longer under siege in her own home.

She was just going into the house through the back porch, when she heard Anil's jeep approaching. She rushed into the drawing room and threw a few books into the empty knapsack, then went back out into the hall. She was standing beside her suitcase, trying to look composed, when Anil knocked at the front door.

She heard Ibrahim's footsteps behind her. 'It's alright, Ibrahim, I'll get it.' She opened the door to Anil who stood there, his hands behind his back, regarding her with a puzzled smile. She smiled back.

'Are you quite alright, Alice?' he asked.

'I'm fine, thank you. Why do you ask?'

'Well, you look very hot, and you've got cobwebs in your hair.'

Her hand flew to her head, and she felt herself blushing. 'I... I went into the garden. It's hot out there. And I must have brushed against a bush. I haven't looked in the mirror.'

He laughed and picked up her case. 'I was just teasing you. You usually look so cool. So... well, so perfect. I mean, you look different, and I couldn't help noticing.'

She relaxed a little and followed him out to the jeep where he swung the suitcase onto the back and took her knapsack from her and did the same with that. They got into the jeep and as Anil turned it round in front of the house she noticed another vehicle parked in the corner of the drive.

'Did you see my soldier?' he asked.

She turned to him, the hairs on the back of her neck slowly rising. 'Your soldier?' she asked, her mouth dry.

'Oh, didn't he knock at the door?'

'No. I didn't hear anything. I was in the back of the house for a long time, talking to the servants. I thought you weren't going to send anyone.'

He glanced at her. 'I changed my mind when I was driving back to the base.'

She fell silent. The soldier must have turned up while she was walking up to the village. What if he'd spotted her leaving the garden or coming back down from the jungle? Her heart started pounding, but she tried to tell herself not to worry. She was entitled to walk where she wanted to within the estate. On the other hand, what if the soldier told Anil? What if he discovered she'd secretly been taking food to an illegal Chinese kampong, deep in the jungle? She'd recently read in the *Straits Times*, delivered daily to Diana's house, that Chinese communities were all under suspicion. She'd thought when she read it that it was unfair and wrong, that just because the CTs were Chinese, it didn't mean the whole community were terrorists. It was clear to her that Ying May's family and her neighbours were simply desperately poor, living on the margins of society with no one to help them. But would Anil understand that?

'Did your briefing go well?' she asked, searching for a change of subject.

They were driving past the mine buildings now, heading out towards the gates of the estate. Anil changed gear and slowed the vehicle.

'There's a new order from the British government,' he said. 'It's been hush-hush until now, but it will be in the evening newspapers, so I am able to tell you.'

'Oh?'

'They are going to clear all Chinese squatters' kampongs and move the villagers away from the jungle and into detention camps. Some of them will be deported.'

'What?' Alice asked, aghast. 'Why?'

'It's High Commissioner Gurney who came up with the plan. Most Chinese villages are helping the guerillas. The idea is, if they are moved and kept under guard, they won't be able to do that. Anyone proved to be helping the CTs will be deported. Quite soon, the CTs will be starved of supplies and have to surrender.'

Anil slowed for the checkpoint while the barrier was raised and saluted as they drove through.

'But surely... not all villages harbour CTs,' Alice said.

'Perhaps not. But they are all being cleared anyway. All those we know about, that is.'

Alice didn't reply. She simply stared out at the endless green of the jungle flashing past and thought about her own secret village. Of poor Ying May and her sick mother, of all the starving women and children, of the men with no work. How could she prevent them being uprooted and torn from their homes?

20

March, 1949

Dear Anil,

It's very kind of you to offer to drive me back to the estate in your jeep tomorrow, but there is really no need. Diana is insisting her syce should take me there, and she is actually coming along with me herself! It is kind of her, and as you know she's been a tower of strength over the past few months.

I'm very much hoping you will come and see me now and then once I'm installed. I know you have many demands on your time, but I so value your company.

Yours,

Alice

A week after Alice had been back to the house and visited the secret village, she decided to return there for good. She'd told Anil about it when he'd dropped in on one of his security checks two days beforehand. He'd immediately suggested he should take her in his jeep, but after he'd left, Diana had been insistent that there was no need to take up Anil's valuable time.

'I'm quite sure Major Desai has more important things to do than act as a taxi. He's far too kind to you for his own good, Alice. Our syce can take you.'

'If you're sure,' Alice had said.

'Of course I'm sure. And I will come with you myself and get you settled in. It will feel very strange going back there to stay all by yourself for the first time. I can even stay the night with you if you like. Abdullah can sleep in the servants' quarters. I'm sure there's space.'

Alice hesitated. Anil had already said he would send soldiers to guard the house day and night when she returned. But even so...

'Would you mind terribly?' she asked.

Diana patted her hand. 'Of course not. It would be utterly ghastly for you to spend the first night back in that place all alone. And I can stay as long as you like.'

'That's so kind, Diana,' Alice replied, then went on hastily, 'but I *will* need to get used to being by myself. And the sooner I do that, the better.'

Diana looked into Alice's eyes with a searching, puzzled look. 'You're very brave, Alice darling,' she said. 'But please don't worry. I won't hang around and get under your feet. Abdullah and I will leave for home straight after breakfast.'

Since she'd heard about the government plan to resettle all Chinese squatters in newly built villages, Alice had decided she needed to be near the secret kampong again. That way she would be able to go up there and warn the villagers about what might happen. Perhaps some of the men who worked on the local rubber estates might have already heard about the resettlement policy, but Alice wanted to talk to them about it in person. That way she could reassure Ying May and the others that they could trust her not to betray them.

She wouldn't breathe a word to anyone about them, she decided. Not even Anil; perhaps especially not Anil. That way, the village might remain undiscovered, and the villagers may get to stay where they were. But then, another thought struck her. It might be difficult for the men to continue to get itinerant work in the mines and estates in the area without raising suspicion, if all the other Chinese villages had been cleared. How would they manage for food and supplies then? One knapsack of rice and flour per week wouldn't keep them going. She would have to try to do more, but that could be difficult.

She was mulling all this over in her bedroom in the Blanchard house while packing her belongings into her two suitcases. She was trying to cram too much in. While she'd been staying at the Blanchard estate, she'd collected a few bits and pieces from the local bazaar and some clothes Diana had insisted on paying the local tailor to run up for her. Now the lid of the first suitcase wouldn't shut.

She pushed it down as hard as she could and forced the fasteners to close. She sighed, sat beside it on the bed and wiped perspiration from her brow. Despite the electric fan whirring overhead, the room was hot and sticky. Through the open window, the rain beat down relentlessly and monotonously. It was building up to the southern monsoon, the heat rising like a pressure cooker, and as it got hotter, it got more and more humid. Just packing the suitcase had sapped her energy, and her skin was covered in a fine film of sweat.

In a few minutes she would be leaving with Diana to go back home. She'd been grateful to Diana and Tony for their hospitality, but as well as wanting to get back to help the villagers, she felt she couldn't impose on the Blanchards any longer. She was also tiring of the strain of living a lie each and every day. She'd not been able to tell Diana what had really happened when the guerillas burst into the house on the day Bruce died. She hadn't told anyone, and the truth was eating away at her.

Whenever she thought back to that terrible day, she would break out in goosebumps, despite the stifling heat, so she tried her best not to think about it. But the memories refused to be banished. Images would break through unbidden, just as they were now; flashes of the guerilla leader's scarred and sweaty face as he pinned her to the wall, the feel of the blade against her neck, the smell of his rotten breath. By rights she should be dead now; he should have killed her, if she'd not been as weak as she was. Every time she started thinking about it, she ended up exactly where she was now, feeling wretched and guilty, a weak-minded fool, unworthy of the life she'd been gifted that day.

There was a gentle knock on the door and Diana put her head round. 'Are you ready?'

'Of course,' Alice said getting down from the bed and reaching for one of the suitcases.

'Leave that where it is, darling, one of the houseboys will bring them down to the car. Now, are you quite sure you want to do this? You can always change your mind. You can stay here as long as you like, you know.'

'I'm quite sure, thank you, Diana. I'm so grateful to you and Tony for putting up with me for this long. But I really need to get home.'

They went out onto the landing and down the sweeping stair-case together. Just then, the front door opened, and Tony entered, mopping his brow with a handkerchief, dark patches on his khaki work clothes from the downpour.

'Good God. I wish the monsoon would break,' he said. 'These infernal showers. As soon as they're over the heat becomes unbearable. Still...' He looked up and smiled. 'Are you really leaving us, Alice?'

'Yes. I'm sorry to go. I've loved it here. You've both been so kind.'

'Our pleasure. You know you can always come back again if you don't fancy it once you get home.'

'Thank you,' Alice said.

'Why don't I come along with you both?' Tony said. 'I know things seem to have settled down a bit, but I don't like sending you two off into the jungle on your own.'

'Nonsense, Tony,' Diana said. 'We've been out on our own before. It's not far. And Alice and I both know how to shoot if the worst comes to the worst.'

'You're too intrepid for your own good, my dear,' he said, kissing his wife fondly.

Alice kissed Tony goodbye too, then followed Diana out onto the porch, squeezing through the narrow gap in the sandbags and down the steps to the waiting car. The rain had just stopped, and the sun was already blazing down. Steam was rising in clouds from the front lawn and the rubber plantation beyond.

The syce, Abdullah, opened the back door of the car, Alice slid inside, along the back seat, and Diana got in next to her. The houseboys loaded the suitcases into the boot, then Abdullah went round the car, fastening the metal bullet-proof screens to the windows and windscreen. Once he'd finished, it was eerily dark inside, the only light coming through slits at the top of each window. She and Diana had been driven like that before, to the local bazaar and to the tailor's, but Alice knew she would never get used to it. It felt like being inside a coffin. It was already heating up and would soon be stifling and as hot as an oven in there.

'Here, take this,' Diana said, handing Alice a carbine she'd picked up from a long box which had been installed behind the driver's seat, before bending to get her rifle from the box.

Alice glanced down at the loaded carbine. She'd carried it on her lap on each outing they'd made in the car, but now she was going back to Rimba Valley Estate, it somehow held greater significance. Holding the smooth handle brought to mind the rattling vibrations of the Bren gun as she'd fired into the jungle that day. She closed her eyes to banish the memory.

Abdullah got into the front, started up the car and pulled slowly away from the house, leaning forward and peering through the narrow slit in the windscreen.

'Gosh, I hope we're not attacked on the way,' Alice said.

Diana patted her hand. 'It's not likely, but we always have to be prepared, don't we?'

Alice didn't reply. She didn't want her friend to think she was afraid. That would risk Diana insisting on either Alice staying at the rubber estate or Diana staying on with her at Rimba Valley for an extended period. Much as she loved her friend, she really wanted to be alone.

The car moved slowly down the gravel drive between the lines of rubber trees. Through her peephole in the side window, Alice gazed out at the uniform grey trunks sliding by at regular intervals. Tappers were at work in the grey-green light, emptying the latex from the cups fixed on the trunks beneath the wide, diagonal black scar on each tree.

'They're very brave,' Diana said, seeing Alice peering out at the tappers. 'They go out every day, and they know there could be CTs lurking in the forest and that some tappers have had their throats slit on other estates.'

'It must be terrifying for them,' Alice said, then added, 'but I suppose they don't really have much choice. After all, they do have to work, don't they?'

'They *want* to work,' Diana replied. 'They are as angry about the insurgency as we all are. It's *their* country those guerillas are destroying, after all. Their livelihoods. They don't want the place to be ruled by Chinese communists any more than we do.'

Alice was silent for a few moments reflecting on this, then she asked, 'Have you ever thought about going home? Just giving it all up and going back to England?'

Diana gave a short laugh. 'I was born in Malaya. England isn't my home. This place is.'

Alice knew that unlike many of the local planters who worked for corporate owners, Tony and Diana owned the plantation themselves; Tony had inherited it from his father. They had a stake in the country, Alice thought, so no wonder they were determined to weather out the Emergency.

'Have *you* ever thought about going back to India?' Diana asked. 'I mean, now that Bruce is... well, Bruce is no longer with us?'

Alice shook her head. 'I miss the country... desperately sometimes, and my lovely friend, Jamila, but... she's married now and has moved away from Barrackpur. And, well, I've told you about my father, haven't I?'

'You've told me some of it,' Diana said.

The car slowed for the estate gates, which were being drawn back by the soldiers on duty as they approached.

'He never really wanted me around, to tell you the truth,' Alice said, glancing through the peephole, 'I got in his way. He liked to drink and gamble, to shoot tigers, and to bring women back to the house. I think he's even got a young woman living there with him since I left. And now India has its independence... It sounds strange, but despite the Emergency, and everything that's happened, I actually feel more at home here.'

'But Malaya will be independent too soon,' Diana said with a wry smile. 'Perhaps we'll all have to make our homes in England. Live respectable lives in the home counties.'

'I sincerely hope not,' Alice said with a shudder, remembering her schooldays in a chilly boarding school in Hertfordshire – shivering in the freezing depths of winter, always an outsider, constantly pining for the country she called home.

The car slowed again for the checkpoint. One of the soldiers spoke briefly through the slit in the driver's window to Abdullah, then waved him through.

'Everything alright, Abdullah?' Diana asked, leaning forward to make herself heard above the rattle and roar of the engine.

'He says there is a local bus up ahead, carrying workers for the Windy Ridge plantation.'

Alice and Diana exchanged glances. Anil had told them there had been a guerilla raid on that plantation a few days beforehand. A group of Chinese tappers had been shot, and the rest of the workforce had refused to return to work afterwards, fearing for their lives.

'The company must be bussing in some replacement workers from somewhere else,' Diana said. 'Jolly good for them!'

The jungle was dense here, thick branches met and entwined overhead, enclosing the road under a green canopy, making the inside of the car even darker than before. Abdullah slowed and changed down a gear for a bend. Then he slammed on the brakes. Alice was thrown forwards against the front seat, the gun slamming into her chest.

'What is it?' Diana shrieked.

Abdullah didn't reply. Alice saw his hand fumbling on the gearstick, shaking and slippery with sweat. He was clearly trying to put the vehicle into reverse. Her heart thumping, Alice pulled herself forward to look through the slit in the windscreen.

'Oh my God!' Diana saw it at the same time. Framed in the peephole, a single-decker bus blocked the road ahead. Flames leapt from its broken windows, clouds of smoke billowed all around. A line of workers stood under the trees at the side of the road, their heads bowed, hands behind their backs. Two guerillas stood in front of them, their rifles trained on the prisoners. Then Abdullah crashed the gearstick home, and the car screamed backwards, the engine whining, the vehicle skidding and swaying from side to side.

Shots rang out from the jungle on either side of the road and instantly there was a sickening, hissing sound from underneath the vehicle.

'Tyres are burst!' Abdullah shouted.

'Keep going if you can,' Diana said.

Abdullah revved the engine, but on the loose, gravelly surface of the road, the rims of the wheels began to stick, and within seconds the car was marooned in the ruts, the engine roaring; it was unable to move forwards or backwards. Then the engine stalled.

All three of them stared at each other in horror. Diana's face, deathly white in the gloom, a mask of terror. Abdullah's bathed in sweat, his eyes wide with fear.

'We've got to do something!' Alice broke the silence. Then, shaking so much she could barely move, she grabbed her carbine and swung round towards the back door, about to thrust the gun through the slit.

Before she could do that, the door flew open and she had a fleeting glimpse of a guerilla's face staring in at her – scarred and pasty, covered in jungle sores, his mouth covered by a filthy bandana. Rough hands grabbed the gun and wrenched it from her. Another man stepped forward and grabbed her arms. She was pulled from the vehicle. She screamed and struggled and could hear Diana's and Abdullah's screams as they too were dragged out of the car.

Alice felt a gun in her back. She, Diana and Abdullah were being prodded forward by the guerillas to the side of the road.

'Stand there!' one of the men commanded. Then he said something in Cantonese to one of the others, who ran back towards the burning bus.

The air was filled with smoke from the fire. Alice was soon coughing and choking, her eyes stinging. She hardly dared lift her gaze from the rutted surface of the road. Were these the same men who'd raided her house, who'd killed Bruce? She wasn't sure she would recognise them even if they were. She was trembling all over and she could feel Diana's arm against hers, shaking too. This time was really the end. Why had she given in to Diana instead of insisting on Anil taking her home? In his army jeep with his armed soldier riding on the back, they would never have been attacked. Anil would have known what to do.

It was too late for regrets now, though. She lifted her head and found herself staring into the barrel of a rifle. The two guerillas were standing in front of them, their rifles trained on them. Alice shivered. They could open fire at any moment. Both looked ragged and wild, skinny and hollow-cheeked beneath their face coverings.

The third man, the one who had run towards the bus, was coming back, accompanied by another man. This one was a little taller than the others. He strode towards Alice and her companions with an air of confidence. As he got closer, Alice could see that his uniform was cleaner and smarter than the rags the others wore, but he too wore a bandana around his face, hiding his features. He conferred briefly with the other man. What were they saying? Alice braced herself for the order to fire.

But then the leader nodded, dismissing the other man, and strode forward to inspect the three prisoners. He walked along in front of them slowly, peering into their faces. When he reached Alice, he stopped. She bowed her head, her eyes cast to the ground. The man's muddy boots were almost touching her open-toed sandals. She hoped he wouldn't see that she was shaking. Alice tried to control her breathing, remembering what had happened before; the blade on her throat, the terror of being manhandled by those rough, pitiless fighters.

The leader reached out, took her chin in his calloused hand and lifted her face so she was looking straight into his hard, black eyes. She fought the urge to close hers and forced herself to stare back at him.

They stood like that for a few seconds, then he grabbed her by the arm and pulled her towards him. Alice shrieked as he dragged her away from Diana and Abdullah and towards the burning bus.

Alice found her voice. 'Let them go!' she said. 'They're only here because of me. It's my fault they're here.'

The man pulled her on, away from the others, but she dug in her heels and kept on pleading with him. She couldn't bear the thought of Diana and Abdullah suffering because of her.

Finally, the man stopped and he turned back to the others. 'You can go,' he yelled, pointing to Diana and Abdullah with his gun. 'You two. Walk back along the road. The way you just came. Don't look back.'

Alice breathed again for a second, but then the man pushed her forward towards the fire. She tried to resist, but she felt the barrel of his pistol in her back and had no choice but to stumble forwards into the clouds of billowing smoke, her heart hammering. Getting closer to the burning bus, the heat on her face was intense and she could feel her skin burning, her eyes stinging. What was he doing? Was he going to push her into the flames?

When they were a few yards from the bus, the smoke was so thick she could hardly see ahead of her. She strained to see the line of terrified workers who'd been standing along the side of the road. Had they been shot? Their throats slit? Or were they just engulfed in smoke?

The guerilla leader pushed her onto a path that led through the trees. 'Keep going!' he ordered.

She had no choice but to do as she was told. She stumbled on along a muddy, winding path coughing and spluttering from the smoke that curled between the bushes, the hard pistol digging into the small of her back, leaves and tendrils wet from the rain dragging against her clothes, soaking through them. There was one thought in her mind: He was taking her into the jungle to kill her.

But she walked on, pushing through the giant ferns and clumps of bamboo and gradually she realised that instead of taking her deeper into the forest, the path was winding round and back towards the road. They stopped in front of a rocky embankment where the road began to rise.

'Get up onto the road,' the man ordered.

She scrambled up the bank, breaking her nails and grazing her knees on the rocks. Finally, she was standing on the rough surface of the road looking back at the burning bus.

'You can go,' the guerilla said, making a jerking motion with his head, indicating for her to walk along the road. 'That way,' he said waving his gun. 'Don't look back.'

Alice stared at him, momentarily paralysed, wondering if she'd heard correctly. But she didn't stay there for long. She turned in the direction of Rimba Valley Estate and, feeling numb, began to walk.

When she'd gone a few paces, she had a terrible thought: He's going to shoot me in the back. That's why he said not to turn around.

She wanted to run, but her legs wouldn't move any faster. Instead, she stumbled along the rutted surface towards a curve in the road, barely noticing the pain from the stones through her flimsy sandals. It seemed an age before she reached the bend. Every step she took, she was sure was her last. But she kept her eyes on the road ahead.

When she'd rounded the bend, she still didn't look back. She just kept putting one foot in front of the other, and every step took her a little further away from the horrifying encounter and closer to Rimba Valley Estate and home.

21

ANIL

Malaya, March 1949

From Major Anil Desai's diary:

A workers' bus was ambushed by CTs today on the main road leading to the Windy Ridge rubber plantation. It was a savage and brutal attack on the relief workers who were travelling from Ipoh town to the rubber estate to replace the tappers who were too afraid to work because of recent guerilla attacks. In retrospect they were an obvious target for the CTs.

The local police and fire service were first at the scene. They radioed through to the Gurkha base for backup. Our radio operator reported that the policeman who called in the incident sounded shaken. He said that within a few minutes of arriving at the scene, his men had discovered the bodies of all nine of the workers from the bus a few yards into the jungle. They had been dragged into the trees and their throats had been slit.

I set off from the base shortly after the call came in with a group of twenty soldiers. Our job was to track down the CTs responsible for the

attack. Of course, they had vanished into the jungle by the time the
police had arrived on the scene, so we knew that by the time we came
along, they would have had plenty of time to disappear completely.

BUMPING along beside his driver on the jungle road towards the
scene of the bus fire, Anil's mind turned to Alice. This was the
very stretch of road she and Diana would normally travel along
between the Blanchard estate and Rimba Valley. What if they'd
got caught up in the attack? His fists clenched involuntarily. If
only Alice had taken up his offer to drive her home. Why had he
let her be persuaded to go with Diana? He should have been
more insistent.

Staring through the juddering windscreen at the bumpy road
ahead, he tried to reassure himself that Alice would be safe. After
all, the policeman who'd called for backup hadn't mentioned
anything about any Europeans being involved... that was a good
sign, surely? Anil comforted himself with the thought that Alice
and Diana had probably enjoyed a leisurely breakfast at the
Blanchard house and waited until the early morning rainstorm
was over before they'd started out on their journey, therefore
being too late to encounter the workers' bus. He relaxed a little.
He couldn't imagine Diana Blanchard being an early riser.

He was still mulling over the possibilities when the truck
rounded a bend in the road and the driver braked sharply. Anil
had his first glimpse of the chaos left by the attack. It was
instantly clear the bus fire had been fierce. The road surface and
verges on either side were scorched and still smoking, while the
surrounding branches had been burned to blackened stumps.
The bus itself was now a smoking black skeleton, skewed across
the road, clouds of smoke still rising from it. And beyond it, Anil
spotted another vehicle still burning fiercely. The flames
engulfed it so he couldn't make out whether it was a van or a car,
but the sight of it made him even more anxious for Alice's safety.

The driver parked the truck a few yards short of the wrecked bus. Anil swung out of the cab and went round to the back of the vehicle where his men were already jumping down, carrying their weapons and equipment. They knew the drill – they had carried out identical exercises many times before in recent months. Their task was to spread out in a broad line and make their way painstakingly through the dense jungle, scouring the undergrowth for any sign of tracks or debris left behind by the guerillas: spent cartridges, a broken twig, a footprint – anything that might help lead them to the CTs hideout.

Anil was just moving to the head of the column to lead his men into the forest when one of the senior policemen strode towards him. It was William Manners, the police inspector from the station in the nearby town. A tall, lean, Englishman, deeply tanned. Anil knew Manners from the many dealings they'd had during the Emergency. He was normally affable and good humoured, but today he looked troubled.

'Ah, Major Desai. Good of you to come so promptly. Could I have a word?'

'Good morning, Inspector Manners.' Anil saluted the policeman. 'Of course. One moment.' Anil walked down the line of soldiers and asked one of his lieutenants to lead the men into the jungle. 'I will follow on shortly,' he said.

'Bloody awful business this,' Manners said when Anil rejoined him.

They watched Anil's Gurkhas melt away, disappearing between the trees. The jungle closed around them instantly, almost as if they had never been there.

'Poor blighters, those tappers,' Manners went on. 'Just trying to do a decent day's work to feed their families. They didn't deserve to be bundled into the forest and have their throats slit.'

'Indeed. It was a vicious attack,' Anil said.

'You know, two of our men were riding with the workers in the front of that bus.'

'Your own men?' Anil asked. 'What happened to them, Inspector?' No wonder Manners looked upset.

'Shot, we think, and burned with the bus,' Manners replied through gritted teeth. 'My men are removing their bodies from the wreck as we speak. It's cold-blooded murder, that's what it is. Two young men, boys really. Just joined up, straight out from Blighty. Their whole lives ahead of them. Bloody awful.'

'I'm so sorry, Inspector,' Anil said.

'I hope to God your men can track down those murdering bastards,' Manners said, his forehead puckered into an anxious frown.

'They will do their best,' Anil replied. 'But you know the difficulties we face each time we go into the jungle, Inspector. The CTs are skilled at hiding their tracks.'

'I know they are. It's bloody infuriating.'

'I'm wondering though, if this is a *new* group of CTs,' Anil went on. 'This attack seems far more professional than some of the amateurish raids we've seen in the area before.'

'Very perceptive, Major,' Manners said, pulling out a pack of Craven A and a lighter from his pocket and lighting up with shaking hands. 'You don't smoke, do you, Major?'

Anil shook his head and Manners went on.

'As a matter of fact, CT activities *have* started to escalate round here in the last week or two, although we've been trying to keep things hush-hush so as not to alarm the local residents. The attack on the Windy Ridge Estate wasn't the first, and now this.'

Anil sensed the man had more to tell him, so he kept silent and waited. Sure enough, after he'd taken a few drags on his cigarette, Manners cleared his throat. He moved closer to Anil and lowered his voice.

'I'd be grateful if you'd keep this under your hat for the time being, Major, but word is there's a new man at the helm of the local rabble. It's clearly someone skilled and well organised. We think he must have come to this area recently because, as you mentioned, there has been a marked change in tactics in recent days. He appears to be reorganising and revitalising the local groups.'

'Do you have any idea who he is?' Anil asked.

'Intelligence sources think it might be one of the higher ups in the Communist Party with links back in China. They think it could well be a chap called Ah Ping. He was responsible for a number of brutal attacks in Padang last year, but his camp was discovered and annihilated by the British Army. Somehow, he managed to escape and he's been on the run for several months now. The attacks we've seen here in the past ten days seem to be following the same pattern as the ones in Padang. It's a worrying turn of events and we need to catch this man before things escalate beyond our control.'

'Of course, Inspector. Do you have any information about where he might be hiding?'

'Not at the moment, but we might have something shortly. As you know, normally the CTs try not to leave any witnesses behind. But by some quirk of fate we might be lucky on this occasion.' He paused to draw on his cigarette again, then blew the smoke out in a thin stream sideways.

'There are three people still living who must have seen at least *something*. Two British women and their driver had a narrow escape. Mrs Alice Lacey from the Rimba Valley tin mine and Diana, Tony Blanchard's wife. I believe you know both ladies. That's their car burning up ahead there. Tony Blanchard's old Austin...'

'My God!' So they *had* set off early. They *had* been caught up in the attack after all. Anil was aware of the blood draining from his face. He stared at the flames leaping from the vehicle. 'Are they alright? Where are they now?' he asked, doing his level best to keep the panic from his voice.

'As luck would have it, I came across poor Mrs Lacey walking along the road towards Rimba Valley when I was on my way here.

She was in a very dazed state. I asked my sergeant to take her home. She didn't say much to me, but from what she did say, it seems the guerillas let all three of them go.'

Anil blinked at the Inspector, trying to process this information, relief mixed with confusion running through him. He needed to go to Alice, to talk to her, to comfort her. He could imagine what she must have been through, and she was only just recovering from the attack when Bruce was killed. But even with knowing all this, he didn't want to display any emotion. He didn't want the policeman to suspect he might have feelings for Alice.

'What about Mrs Blanchard and her driver?' Anil asked, deflecting the subject from Alice, though he was genuinely worried for Diana and Abdullah too.

'I radioed through to HQ and one of the men from the station went out to collect them. They will be back at the rubber estate by now. I'm sure they would have been as shaken up as Mrs Lacey was. When I've finished here, I'm going to interview all three of them. I'll drive out to Rimba Valley first and then over to the Blanchards' place. They must have got a good look at whoever was leading this attack, and I'm hoping they will be able to give us enough information to confirm the man's identity. If it is Ah Ping, then at least we'll know who we're up against.'

'Of course, Inspector. I'll radio my senior officer at the base to send more men out to reinforce security at both estates straight away. As you know, we haven't been providing a full guard at either place lately because things had appeared to have settled down.'

'Thank you, Major. That's reassuring to know. Now, I need to get on to Rimba Valley. Keep in touch. We'll be waiting to see if you are able to find their hideout. I'll let you know what the witnesses have to say.'

William Manners saluted and turned away to leave, but when he'd walked a few steps, he stopped and turned back towards Anil, rubbing his chin.

'Frankly, it's a bit of a puzzle as to why the three of them were allowed to leave at all. They were lucky to escape with their lives, if the truth be told. If it is Ah Ping, maybe he has a civilised streak. Who knows? He certainly didn't before, but I suppose he might have changed since he left Padang. Perhaps all will be explained when I speak to our witnesses. Now, I need to get off to talk to Mrs Lacey. The sooner I get there the sooner we can track down our man.'

Anil watched the policeman go, shaking his head. He was as baffled as William Manners was as to why the CTs had allowed Alice and the others to walk away from the scene. He closed his eyes and briefly thanked God that they had. Then he shouldered his gun and walked forward into the trees. He needed to catch up with his men and help them track down the guerrillas.

As ANIL HAD FEARED, the hunt through the jungle was fruitless. He and his men scoured the undergrowth systematically for three hours and eventually emerged from the forest and onto the Kuala Lumpur road a couple of miles from where they'd started. In all that time the only settlement they came across was one small Malay kampong on a winding track in a clearing a little way back from the main road. The villagers, mostly women, children and old men, stood on their porches looking terrified at the approach of the soldiers. Anil spoke to the head man, and it was clear to him this wasn't a village of Chinese communist sympathisers and that no one here would be helping the CTs or harbouring a Maoist terrorist.

As they left the village, Anil radioed to his driver to collect him and his men, and they began their long, hot weary march in the direction of the junction with the Windy Ridge road. They'd marched about a mile when it started to rain; great splashing drops that ran down the back of their necks and seeped through their uniforms. Anil bowed his head and trudged on. His men were hardy and tough. No one even paused or remarked on the deluge.

The truck eventually appeared on the road ahead of them. Anil's spirits lifted at the sight of it through the slanting rain-drops. When it pulled up, he stood in the rain and watched his men climb onto the back. Their heads were bowed, and they looked soaked and dejected. Another seemingly wasted day being thwarted and outmanoeuvred by the CTs. Anil couldn't blame them for looking frustrated.

By the time they arrived back at base, it was mid afternoon. After standing down his men, Anil would have liked to get into his jeep straight away and drive over to see Alice, but first he needed to go into the office and make his report of the incident to his senior officer.

Colonel Bristow registered no surprise when Anil told him what Inspector Manners had revealed about Ah Ping.

'I heard about it this morning while you were on your way to the scene,' he said. 'As a matter of fact, I've just put the phone down from speaking to Manners myself. He called to debrief us on his interviews with the witnesses.'

'Good news?' Anil asked.

Colonel Bristow shrugged. 'They couldn't tell him much. The leader was wearing a mask, apparently. The whole group were. The witnesses were a bit vague, according to the inspector. It must have been a terrifying ordeal for them. But from what Manners was able to extract from them, the leader spoke good English.'

There was a pause while Anil digested this information.

'Are the witnesses alright?' he asked, his voice studiedly casual.

The colonel looked up and frowned. 'Of course, Desai. Manners briefed you earlier about that, didn't he? They were allowed to leave unharmed. A bit shaken up though. Particularly

Mrs Lacey, for obvious reasons. But I've dispatched the extra men you requested to boost security on both estates, so they should all feel safer tonight.'

Anil cleared his throat. 'I think I'll look in on both estates myself before nightfall, sir,' he said.

'Good idea, Major,' Colonel Bristow said. 'A reassuring presence and all that. But I wouldn't spend too long over it. Orders came in this afternoon that we're needed to supervise the beginning of the Chinese squatters clearance programme tomorrow morning. That will mean an early start for you and your men.'

The clearance programme. The transfer of Chinese villagers from the fringes of the jungles to purpose-built new villages where they could be protected from the CTs' influence and guarded by the British.

'Of course, sir,' he said. He saluted and left the office.

Crossing the parade ground to fetch his jeep, a sliver of doubt entered his heart. He was a soldier, trained to fight an armed enemy on equal terms, not to drive unarmed civilians – women and children even – from their homes. Alice's words came back to him as well as the fear and outrage in her voice when she'd heard about it. *It sounds terrible. Moving families away from their homes. That can't be right.*

It had taken a lot for Anil to admit to Alice that he too had misgivings. He'd felt disloyal to his regiment, even telling her that. He'd tried to reassure her the resettlement programme was for the best, but deep in his heart he knew she was right.

22

It was early evening by the time Anil drove through the roadblocks outside Rimba Valley Estate. He saluted the soldiers manning the gates, and splashed through the puddles towards the mine buildings. The two Gurkhas, who were now guarding the place with their rifles drawn, saluted him. Behind the wooden office buildings loomed the shadow of the great, hulking dredger. It stood silent now. The setting sun stained the corrugated-iron roofs a deep, rusty red and cast a glow over the darkening jungle. Anil switched on his headlights, put his foot to the floor and accelerated along the forest road towards the house.

By the time he emerged into the clearing in front of the building, the sun had gone down and the place was enveloped in darkness. Swinging the jeep round on the gravel to park, he was surprised to see William Manners' old Ford police car standing in front of the sandbag wall. That was strange. Hadn't Colonel Bristow told him Manners had already interviewed Alice? If that was right, what had brought him back? With a prickle of concern, he jumped out of the jeep and strode towards the front steps. Two more of his men who were patrolling the front of the house, saluted him as he passed.

He squeezed through the gap in the sandbags, crossed the veranda and knocked on the front door. It was opened quickly by a houseboy Anil hadn't met before.

'Mrs Lacey is busy. She is speaking to a policeman,' the man said, eyeing Anil with suspicion.

Anil could hear the rise and fall of voices from the drawing room.

'Could you ask the inspector if I could join them, please?' Anil asked. 'I'm Major Desai from the 6th Gurkhas. Inspector Manners knows me.'

The man pulled the door back reluctantly and left Anil standing in the hallway holding his cap while he knocked on the drawing-room door and relayed the message. Anil recalled the first time he'd waited there in that very spot to see Bruce Lacey. He'd felt so apprehensive. That was less than a year ago, but so much had happened since that day, it seemed far longer.

'You can go in,' the houseboy said, turning back to Anil and holding the door open for him.

The drawing room was hot, even though the ceiling fan was turning so fast it looked as though it might spin off its axis. The room was lit by lamps and the bamboo chiks were pulled down over the windows.

Alice was sitting in a rattan armchair in the far corner and the police officer sat opposite her with his back to the door. She wore a cream safari dress, belted round the waist, emphasising her tiny frame. Her face was ashen, her shoulders drooped. She was clearly exhausted. When she looked up and saw Anil, the relief on her face was plain to see.

'Anil... Major Desai. Do come in,' she said straightening in her seat.

Inspector Manners stood up and turned to greet Anil. He too looked drained, his face grey and drawn.

'Ah, Major,' Manners said. 'Good to see you. I briefed Colonel Bristow earlier about my interviews with the witnesses to the bus fire, as you're probably aware. I came back to talk to Mrs Lacey to clarify a couple of things that weren't crystal clear when we first spoke. Would you like to join us, Major?'

'Yes. Thank you, Inspector.' Anil sat down on the chintzy sofa. 'Good evening, Mrs Lacey.'

'Good evening. Would you like a drink, Major?' Alice asked. 'The Inspector is having a whisky.'

From the tone of her voice and from the way her eyes lingered on his, Anil could see that Alice was willing him to agree. He wasn't quite sure why.

'I'm on duty, Mrs Lacey. But I will join the inspector in a small glass. Thank you.'

'Ibrahim...' Alice nodded to the bearer who was still hovering in the doorway. 'Please bring the major a single shot of whisky.'

Manners sat down beside Anil and cleared his throat, but he waited until the servant had placed Anil's glass on the table beside him and left the room before speaking.

'Now, Alice, my dear,' he said, leaning forward. 'As I was saying before Major Desai arrived, we're all trying to get to the bottom of what happened today. Two young policemen and several workers lost their lives.'

'It's terrible,' Alice said, biting her nail.

'It is... When I came to talk to you before, you were understandably very shaken and couldn't recall some of the details. That's why I came back. I hope you've managed to get some rest now so that we can talk properly.'

'I've had time to have a bath and a change of clothes,' Alice replied. 'I feel a lot better now. Thank you for being patient, William.'

Anil took a sip of the whisky and felt the unfamiliar heat of it course through his veins. He watched Alice's face. He knew her so well now, it was easy to forget she was part of the British establishment, a member of the Royal Ipoh Club. She was on first-name terms with the police inspector, the chief of police, the local judges and resident commissioner, in fact the whole British community.

'So, could you please tell me,' Manners went on, 'in as much detail as you possibly can, exactly what you saw of the CTs who attacked you.'

'I told you before, William. I didn't see much,' Alice replied. 'They were all wearing face coverings. Bandanas or bits of filthy cloth...'

'Yes. So I understand. But I'm wondering, could you possibly describe their leader to me again? Anything you remember about him. Anything at all. We've got an idea who he might be, but it would help enormously if you could tell me as much as you can.'

Alice hesitated and took a drink from the glass beside her on a coffee table. Her eyes flicked towards Anil and back to the inspector before she spoke again. Anil smiled gently, trying to give her reassurance.

'I don't remember much, but he was quite tall,' Alice said, her voice stronger this time. 'Yes. Taller than the other CTs. And he wasn't like them.'

'What do you mean?' said Manners, leaning forward eagerly. 'Not like them?'

'I mean he wasn't dressed in rags like they were. He had a clean uniform on. And... well, the others seemed to respect him. At least... they took orders from him.'

'Did you hear him speak?'

'Not much, but yes, I did. A few words.'

'Could you tell me what he said?'

Alice took a breath. A shudder pass through her. 'He... he touched my face. He had rough hands, and he lifted my chin so I was forced to look at him. Then... he told Diana and Abdullah to leave. To walk away...'

'Do you recall what his voice was like? Mrs Blanchard seemed to think he spoke quite good English.'

Alice paused once again, frowned for a moment, deep in thought, then her face cleared.

'Now I come to think of it, yes, he spoke good English. Almost without any trace of a Chinese accent. I hardly noticed at the time, I was so afraid, but... well, now you ask, I realise he spoke exactly like an English gentleman.'

'Are you sure?'

'Yes, of course.'

A broad smile spread over William Manners' face. He turned and beamed at Anil, triumphant. 'That's our man!' he said. 'Thank you, Alice. You've been very brave. Very brave indeed. It must have been a heck of an ordeal for you.'

'It was,' Alice said. Then she heaved a sigh and seemed to slump, as if all the tension she'd been bottling inside had suddenly left.

'I'll go back to the station and get things moving right away,' Manners said getting to his feet. 'Are you going to be alright here on your own, Alice? I really think you should go back to stay with the Blanchards. I could run you over there right now. Or I'm sure Major Desai would be happy to if you need time to pack.'

'I'll be fine, thank you, William. I've been wanting to come home for a while now. And now I'm here, I want to stay.'

'You're a very plucky girl, Alice,' Manners said, 'but I really don't think it would be wise for you to stay alone here. Not tonight. Not after what has happened to you today.'

'The servants are here, and Major Desai's soldiers have the house under constant guard. I'm afraid I just can't face going anywhere else tonight.'

Manners hesitated. 'You'd be very welcome to come and stay with me and Hattie in town.'

'That's very kind of you, but I'll be fine here.'

'If you absolutely insist, I can't make you leave. I'm afraid I have to make a move now. Major Desai, perhaps you could stay a little while longer, keep Mrs Lacey company?'

'I'd be glad to, Inspector,' Anil replied.

'Well, goodnight then, Alice,' William Manners said. 'No, please don't get up. I can see myself out. Perhaps though, before I leave, the Major and I could have a quick word in private about security matters?'

'Of course.'

Anil followed Manners out of the room. Manners shut the drawing-room door firmly behind them. The bearer hovered in the hall, his eyes full of curiosity.

'If you don't mind, the major and I will just pop into Mr Lacey's study for a quick word,' Manners said to him.

Bruce Lacey's study was considerably tidier than the last time Anil had been in there. The desk had been cleared and polished, there were no papers strewn around, no overflowing ashtrays or empty glasses. Was Anil imagining it, though, or did the smell of Bruce's cigarettes and whisky still linger on the air?

Manners closed the door and walked over to the desk. 'I was sure it was Ah Ping as soon as Mrs Lacey mentioned his accent,' he said. 'We know he was educated in England. He went to Eton and Oxford.'

Anil digested this new information, then he said, 'But how can you be sure it is *him*, Inspector? He might not be the only Chinese communist in Malaya who was educated in England.'

'It's him alright, Major,' Manners said, gritting his teeth, 'which is good news because he's a big enough fish for me to be able to request more men to track him down and root him out. And their blood will be up, I can tell you. After the death of those two young policemen... There's still one thing that I don't understand about this business, though.'

'What's that, Inspector?'

'Why the devil did he let the two women and their driver go? It doesn't really fit the pattern of Ah Ping's previous form.'

Anil pondered the point. He agreed with Manners – it did

seem strange. The odd encounter Alice had described seemed out of character for a hardened CT leader.

'Perhaps it isn't Ah Ping after all,' Anil ventured.

'No, it's him alright. Look, Major,' Manners went on. 'I got the impression Mrs Lacey was holding things back. Why don't you try to have a quiet chat with her after I've gone? You probably know her quite well, don't you? After all, you were here at the house the day her husband died, weren't you?'

'Indeed. Yes, I was here then,' Anil replied, keeping his voice and his expression neutral. 'I'm happy to have a word with Mrs Lacey.'

Relief spread across Manners' sandy features. He patted Anil on the shoulder. 'Good man. Now, I have to crack on. I'll leave you to it. Let us know if you do get anything out of her.'

Anil went into the hall with Manners. After they'd said good-bye, he went back and tapped on the drawing-room door before entering. Alice was standing in the middle of the room, and as soon as he walked in and closed the door behind him, she walked quickly towards him. Without thinking, he automatically opened his arms and folded her to him. They stood there silently, their hearts beating together, listening to the sound of the inspector's car turning round on the gravel drive.

'Oh, Anil. It was awful,' Alice said, letting the tears fall.

He held her to him, feeling the shudder of her sobs pass through his body. 'It's alright. You're safe now,' he said.

Neither of them spoke again for a few moments until her sobs finally subsided. Then she looked up at him, her eyes red and swollen. They widened a little in surprise, as if she was only just realising his arms were around her. He let her go and she took a step back, all the time looking into his eyes.

'I'm sorry,' she said. 'I don't know what I was thinking.'

'Please,' Anil said. 'There is nothing to be sorry for.'

She dabbed her eyes with her handkerchief. 'I'm not thinking straight at all,' she said. 'Shall we sit down? Do you want another drink?'

'No. I really shouldn't,' Anil said, sitting down on the sofa. 'But you go ahead. You've had a terrible shock.'

She walked over to the sideboard and he noticed how her hands shook as she poured herself another brandy from the decanter. He yearned to hold her again, but he knew he shouldn't think like that, that he had to try to get her to talk about the bus fire.

She came and sat beside him and took a sip of her drink. He cleared his throat. He hated having to quiz her.

'It must have been a terrible shock for you when the car was held up,' he began.

Alice blew her nose. 'It was terrifying. I really thought they were going to kill us.'

Anil closed his eyes for a second and took a breath. What if they had killed her? How could he have borne that? He swallowed.

'But they didn't,' he said. 'They let you go. Can you think of any reason... any reason at all why they might have done that?'

Alice shook her head, then blinked and looked at him with a frown. '*He* asked you to ask me these questions, didn't he? Will Manners. That's what he wanted to talk to you about. He doesn't trust me.'

'He does trust you. Of course he does. He's just desperate to track this man down. Two of his men died today.'

'I know,' she said, taking a shaky breath. 'It's simply awful.'

'Perhaps Inspector Manners thinks there might be details you haven't yet remembered that could help the investigation.'

Alice shook her head, frowning deeply. Anil studied her face, worried he was upsetting her further, that she might start crying again.

'So, if you do remember anything else. Anything at all, you will tell me, won't you?'

'Of course. Of course I will, Anil.'

She looked up at him then, her eyes full of pleading and that deep sadness that tugged at his soul, and he couldn't help himself. He leaned in and kissed her on the lips, and she kissed him back quite naturally. A lingering kiss full of longing and emotion, and the love neither of them had spoken of, but that had been building since the first day they'd met.

23

It was after nine o'clock when Anil finally tore himself away from Alice. Before he left, they'd shared one last, passionate kiss. When they moved apart, she straightened her hair and got to her feet. He followed her to the door of the drawing room and Alice showed him across the hall and to the front door herself.

The new bearer still hovered at the bottom of the stairs.

'It's alright, Ibrahim,' Alice said. 'I will show Major Desai out.'

The man turned on his heel and retreated to the servants' quarters, but not before darting a suspicious look Anil's way.

'Goodnight, Major,' Alice said, opening the door.

'Goodnight, Mrs Lacey. My men will be on watch outside the house all night, but don't hesitate to call the police station or the Gurkha base if you are at all worried.'

He crossed the veranda and squeezed through the sandbag wall, glancing back at her. She was watching him go, that yearning, soulful look still in her eyes.

Anil spoke briefly to the soldiers guarding the house, then set off in the jeep down the long jungle road towards the mine buildings, his rifle beside him on the seat. He hadn't wanted to leave Alice alone, but he knew he must – more to shield her from malicious gossip than to protect himself. But self-preservation had played a part in it too. He was well aware he would be severely reprimanded for his conduct if it ever got back to his superior officers.

His dimmed headlights lit up the bumpy road ahead and he drove on quickly and expertly, but his mind was full of Alice and the kisses they'd shared. It was madness, he knew, jeopardising his career and her reputation. What had he been thinking of, letting his guard down like that? He changed gear and splashed through the puddles past the mine offices.

His mind wandered to his mother and father back in Kathmandu and he felt a stab of guilt. He was an obedient son, and when his tour of duty was over he was expected to go home and marry the daughter of a family friend; a girl he'd known since childhood. She was descended from the Rana princes – intelligent and spirited, beautiful too. She would bring property and prestige to the family. Before he met Alice, he'd had no qualms about agreeing to do what was expected of him – he'd even welcomed it. But now... he clenched his jaw and pushed the thoughts of home away. He could hardly bear to imagine the pain on his parents' faces if they knew what was happening here.

Perhaps he should ask Colonel Bristow for a transfer? But what possible excuse could he use? And, in any case, how could he bear to abandon Alice when she seemed to need his friendship more than ever before? Friendship? How had it become more than that? He told himself it was quite natural to have taken her in his arms, to have comforted her when she was clearly so distressed. Their kisses had simply been a natural progression of their closeness. But that loving expression of their friendship must never go any further than hugs and kisses, he told himself. And it wasn't likely to either, with the ever-vigilant servant constantly on the prowl.

He hadn't got very far with questioning Alice about the attack on the bus, he realised, annoyed with himself for his lapse of professionalism. He wondered what Inspector Manners had wanted Alice to say. How could she possibly explain why the CT leader Ah Ping (if indeed it was Ah Ping) had let her escape? Perhaps the man had simply taken pity on her, Anil thought. That look in her eyes was enough to melt any man's heart, even a hardened guerilla. Perhaps the man simply couldn't bring himself to pull a knife across her lovely throat.

He slowed the jeep as it reached the Rimba Valley gates and waited, the engine idling while the sentries dragged them open for him. Once through the gates and clear of the nearby road-block he put his foot to the floor; it was late and he needed to get back to base. The colonel's words echoed in his mind: *we're needed to supervise the beginning of the Chinese squatters clearance programme tomorrow morning. That will mean an early start for you and your men..*

As they'd sat together on the drawing-room sofa, holding each other close, he'd confided in Alice about what he'd be doing the next day, partly to explain why he needed to leave when he did. The clearance programme wasn't a secret anyway, the villagers had been informed about the move and told to have their belongings packed by dawn.

Alice had drawn in a sharp breath when he told her. She'd put her hand on his and squeezed it. 'I can't believe the government is actually going ahead with that appalling, inhumane scheme. How terrible for you, Anil, and for those poor villagers. I can only imagine how distressing it will be.'

He'd watched her face while she spoke. She was suddenly animated, full of conviction. How extraordinary she was, he'd thought, finding compassion in her heart for Chinese squatters when she herself had already been the victim of two CT raids and she could easily have died at their hands that very day.

'The squatters are helping the CTs,' he'd told her, mechanically repeating what he'd been told at his briefings, not being able to meet her gaze. 'Even if they don't want to help them, they do it anyway. They're being coerced, threatened with death and torture. Moving them away from that threat will be better for the villagers in the long run.'

She'd stiffened and shifted away from him a little. 'But surely not all the kampongs are involved in helping the CTs?' she said. 'That can't be the case. Why not let those who are in Malaya peacefully to make a living, simply stay where they are?'

'It's part of a wider scheme to starve the guerillas out of the jungle,' Anil had said. 'To cut off their support network. Those villages who aren't helping CTs at the moment soon would be if all the others around them were moved.'

She'd put her hand on his cheek then and looked deep into his eyes. He'd felt the softness of her fingers against his skin. He'd wanted to look away, but was compelled to keep looking back at her.

'You're a good man, Anil. The kindest, most decent man I've ever met,' she'd said. 'I'm quite sure that, deep down, in that generous, loving heart of yours, you don't believe this is the right thing to do.'

He'd flinched at the intensity of her look, torn his eyes away. She was right. Of course he had doubts about it. He'd already told her as much. But he felt uncomfortable about expressing them, even to her. It wasn't his role to question orders or to raise objections about the methods employed. He'd already stuck his neck out about the Batang Kali massacre, which hadn't gone down well with Colonel Bristow. He was here to serve the British government, whatever their policy might be. And, at the moment, their aim was to stamp out Chinese communism in Malaya; to stop it in its tracks.

But Alice's words had struck a chord deep within him, and driving the final few miles through the dark jungle back to the Gurkha base, he found himself dreading what the morning would bring.

IN THE MORNING, Anil got up before dawn to make offerings and say prayers at the Gurkha temple in the camp. He presented flowers to the god Varuna. He felt the need to atone for his actions in some way.

After a swift breakfast in the canteen, he set off with his men. It was after eight o'clock and the sun was already high in the sky when they finally arrived at the squatters' village. It had taken them over two hours to reach it from their base. When his final orders had come through before dawn, Anil had been surprised to see that the village his company had been allocated couldn't be reached by road. It was deep in the jungle, on the banks of the wide, fast-flowing Kinta River.

They travelled the first few miles by army truck, turning off the main road and continuing through the jungle on rutted unmetalled tracks. Finally, they reached a wide bend in the river where the water was shallow and the current fast. A group of Orang Asli tribesmen were waiting for them with bamboo rafts, moored beside a pebbly beach. Anil led his soldiers through the shallows with their guns and equipment. They climbed deftly onto the slats of the flimsy craft and squatted down two abreast so as not to overbalance them. The tribesmen then jumped on board, leaned on their poles and pushed the rafts off into the current.

They were poled expertly by the tribesmen who skilfully navigated round rocks and driftwood, and through rapids, moving silently with the fast-running river between towering teak trees draped with creepers and vines, and interspersed with stands of giant bamboo that leaned out over the river.

Anil travelled on the first raft. His men were tense and silent on the journey, their rifles cocked. All were keenly aware that they could be fired on at any moment by guerillas concealed in the thick undergrowth, but the journey passed without incident.

Finally, the village came into view; a collection of twenty or more dilapidated huts on a wide bend in the river. The dwellings were hidden between the teak trees, thrown together from uneven planks of wood or bamboo, and thatched with palm leaves. Several empty rafts and flat-bottomed boats were pulled up on the muddy bank, waiting to take the villagers downstream to their new homes. Malay boatmen sat beside them, smoking cheroots and chatting amongst themselves.

The tribesmen jumped off the rafts and steadied them. Anil leapt off first and helped hold the front of his raft as the soldiers stood up one by one and clambered off the precarious bamboo slats onto dry land. The villagers were already coming out of their huts and assembling beside the boats, carrying whatever they were able to take with them. Old men walking with sticks, their belongings on their backs or heads; young women with bundles bouncing from poles across their shoulders; older women in huge circular hats shrouded in black gauze carrying cooking equipment or baskets of chickens; children struggling under enormous loads, hauling babies or toddlers on their backs, bound to them with lengths of cloth.

While the villagers assembled on the riverbank, Anil spoke to his men.

'We're here to help these people move to their new home as best we can,' he told them. 'We want to make sure the operation goes as smoothly as possible.'

His Gurkhas peeled off and moved towards the lines of struggling villagers to relieve them of their loads, to help the children and old people walk to the boats. They picked up packages and bundles, furniture and equipment, puppies and kittens, heavy boxes of household goods, carried them down to the riverbank and stowed them in the boats.

Most of the villagers went quietly. They had no choice. But Anil couldn't help noticing the bewilderment and reluctance in their eyes. Their ramshackle houses, the rough vegetable plots on the riverbank beside the landing, the scrubby area in the clearing in the centre of the huts where they must have cooked their meals, where their breakfast fires still smoked, was their home.

One of the two policemen who had arrived at dawn came to speak to Anil. He was a burly, ginger-haired Scotsman.

'Most of them are going quietly, as you can see, Major. There's just one house where we've encountered a bit of trouble. We might need your help with that one. It's on the edge of the village.'

Anil followed the two policemen between the ramshackle huts. They disturbed some stray chickens a boy was trying to round up. The chickens cackled and fluffed their feathers, and a couple of dogs still tied up and straining on chains barked at them. The hut stood a little apart from the others, some of its thatch was missing and one of the woven bamboo walls had half collapsed.

'It's an old couple. They won't move,' the policeman said, standing aside for Anil to enter. 'We're going to have to find a way of getting them out.'

Anil stooped under the low doorway and allowed his eyes to adjust to the gloomy interior. The stench caught the back of his throat; the place smelled of the familiar decay and mould of the jungle, but of sickness too, and of death.

On the far side of the hut lay an old man on top of a pile of rags. He wore a stained blue tunic. His leathery, skull-like face was beaded with sweat and a wheezing sound came from his chest. Beside him, on the floor, crouched an emaciated old woman. She stared up at Anil with blazing, terrified eyes. The skin that stretched over her nose and cheekbones was as thin as parchment, her cheeks hollow.

'They won't budge,' the police sergeant said. 'They'll have to be carried. There's only me and my colleague, and we didn't want any trouble before you came. Could you get two of your men to help?'

Anil paused. His orders were unequivocal. They were to clear the village of its population and move them to their new home on the edge of the town, which was in effect a detention camp. There, the British government would provide the villagers with makeshift homes and vegetable plots so they could grow their own food. And they would be away from any possible influence from the CTs. But looking at these two old people, it didn't make sense to him. This hut had probably been their home since the Japanese invasion in 1941. Surely, sick and weak as they were, they posed no threat to the British here?

'Major?' the policeman asked.

'One moment.' Anil put his hand out and steadied himself against the doorpost. Alice's passionate words were ringing in his ears; he remembered the sincerity in her eyes. He looked at the old couple for a moment longer, then straightened up. He was a soldier with orders to carry out. What was he thinking? Why was he hesitating?

'Of course. I will ask two of my men to help,' he said.

He went outside and picked the first Gurkhas he saw. They were helping a family carry a bed towards the rafts. He waited while the bed and the family were stowed safely on board then gave the men their orders. He watched them jog away through the clearing towards the hut on the edge of the village, then he turned away towards the bank. He didn't want to witness the sick old couple being torn from their home.

The first boat cast off downriver with its cargo of villagers and furniture. It moved into the fast-flowing current in the middle before being swept away from his view. Soon, he heard the pitiful, rasping cries of the old lady coming closer and he turned to see one of his men carrying her towards the river. She kicked and screamed in the soldier's arms, but he contained her easily. Behind him, the policeman and the other Gurkha carried her husband on a plank of wood, one at each end. The old man lay immobile and silent.

The villagers who were waiting on the bank to get into the boats, all turned to stare at the struggling woman's approach, murmurs of discontent rumbling through the crowd. As the soldier carried her down the bank to the raft, she was still crying and writhing in his arms.

A little boy huddling amongst the people on the bank let out a cry and, detaching himself from the crowd, scampered back towards the huts. His mother dropped a heavy box she was carrying and ran after him, a baby bouncing around on her back. The villagers were restless now, muttering amongst themselves, several of them glancing back longingly towards their homes.

Anil knew he had to contain the situation. He gave orders to his men who were on the bank to stay on guard there and prevent any of the villagers from going back to the huts.

'Make sure they get onto the boats as quickly as possible,' he said. Then he strode after the boy and his mother, who he'd seen disappearing into one of the huts in the middle of the clearing.

He climbed the rickety wooden steps and stopped in the doorway. The boy was sitting in the corner of the empty room on the bare slats, his mother standing over him, speaking rapidly in Cantonese. The boy was cradling a tiny white kitten in his lap, which was mewing pitifully.

When the mother saw Anil, her eyes narrowed in anger. 'We want to stay,' she snapped in English. 'This our home. We've done nothing wrong.'

'I'm sorry, but our orders are that everyone has to go,' he told her. 'You will be moving to a new home. There will be food there. You will be looked after. Come... please don't make it difficult.'

She straightened up and eyed him suspiciously, hands on hips. 'Why do you work for the British?' she asked.

At that moment, the baby on her back began to cry.

'Come,' Anil said, reaching out to take the woman's arm.

But she pulled away from him. 'Don't touch me!'

The baby started to scream then, distracting the woman, who twisted round, trying to comfort it.

Anil turned to the boy who was still crouched in the corner of the hut, staring up at him, fear and confusion in his eyes. Anil smiled at the child, trying to defuse the tension.

'That's a pretty kitten,' he said. 'Is that why you came back?'

The boy nodded.

'Can I stroke her?' Anil asked.

The boy nodded again, this time tentatively with a quick glance at his mother, who was still tending to the screaming baby. Anil knelt and stroked the soft fur of the little animal. The kitten began to purr, and the little boy's face creased into a smile.

'Will you come with me? You can bring the kitten,' Anil said. He stood and held out his hand to the boy who, after a second's hesitation, grasped it and got to his feet. Quickly, Anil led him past the distracted mother to the door.

Going out into the daylight, Anil turned back towards the woman, assuming she would follow her son. Realising what was happening, she lunged towards them and spat in Anil's face. Startled, Anil put his free hand up to his cheek and wiped the globule of spit away.

'Running dog!' she yelled, then pushed past him, snatched the little boy's hand out of his, clambered down the rickety steps and marched back towards the riverbank, the baby on her back still wailing at the top of its voice.

IT WAS WELL after sunset when Anil and his men arrived back at the Gurkha camp. The colonel was waiting to be debriefed and, having seen his men out of the truck and back to their quarters, Anil went straight to Bristow's office.

For the entire journey home, bumping along in the cab of the truck beside the driver, he'd been plagued with images of what had happened that day: the screaming children, the dying man forced from his home, his angry and terrified wife being carried onto the boat, struggling in the soldier's arms.

When all the villagers had either left or were safely on board the boats, Anil had climbed onto the final flat-bottomed craft. The policemen were staying behind in the village. The Scotsman had told Anil his orders were: 'To burn the place to the ground. Every last stick of it.'

Anil had no idea if the families who were being taken on rafts to a new life behind barbed wire knew this.

The boat cast off, and when they had travelled a little way downriver, Anil turned to look back at the forest. Clouds of black smoke billowed in the sky, darkening the narrow river valley behind them.

The colonel was smoking his pipe when Anil entered the office. Anil saluted.

'Ah, Major Desai. I've been waiting for you. I've just spoken to the inspector of police again. We sent two platoons out into the jungle today with the police to try to track Ah Ping down, without success I'm afraid. The inspector mentioned you might have got further information out of Mrs Lacey last night. I think he was grasping at straws. I told him you would have passed it on if you did.'

'Of course, sir. I'm afraid there wasn't anything else. Mrs Lacey was sure she'd told Inspector Manners everything she knew.'

'I thought as much,' the colonel replied. 'We'll have to keep sending search parties out until we track Ah Ping down. It's a drain on resources, especially now we're being asked to supervise the evacuation of the squatters, but we don't have much choice. Orders are coming directly from the high commissioner.'

'I see, sir. And are the men still guarding Rimba Valley... and the Blanchard estate?'

'Yes. In fact, I stepped up the number of men at Rimba Valley today to four instead of two. I don't like the thought of a British woman living in that house on her own. She needs extra protection.'

'Of course, sir,' Anil said, relieved.

'Did all proceed smoothly with the evacuation today, Major Desai?' the colonel asked.

'We evacuated around a hundred inhabitants, mainly women, children and old people from the village, and took them by boat and lorry to Detention Camp No. 3 outside Ipoh, sir,' he replied, keeping his face impassive as he always tried to when speaking to his superior officer.

'Good. Any fatalities?'

Anil blinked at him. 'Of course not, sir.'

'Well done, Major. There were pockets of resistance in other villages, resulting in the need to use a certain amount of force...'

Anil stared at him. An image of Alice's face came into his mind; he recalled her outrage at what was happening to the squatters, her bravery, her conviction. Without thinking he cleared his throat.

'Force, sir?' he asked. 'Do you mean people were injured while they were being dragged from their homes?'

The colonel took his pipe out of his mouth and stared at Anil. 'Not like you to be squeamish, Desai. These are *not* innocent people, you know. They have been harbouring terrorists, feeding them, supporting them. In doing so, they are as good as terrorists themselves. They must either be detained or deported. This is a war we are fighting here. Drastic times call for drastic measures.'

'A State of Emergency, sir,' Anil corrected him in a quiet voice. 'Not a war.'

The colonel banged a fist on his desk. 'As good as a war! Now, I take it from this that today's operation has put considerable strain on you and your men. I will overlook your comments in view of that. Go and get some rest, Major, and report back to me in the morning.'

Anil saluted and left the office, surprised at himself. He would never have spoken like that before he met Alice. Knowing her had changed him.

Walking across the parade ground to his room in one of the wooden huts, reaching his jeep, he lingered beside it for a second. Should he drive out to Rimba Valley now? He ached to see Alice. But then he thought of the four soldiers guarding her house. What excuse could he give them for going there now? They would be bound to be suspicious and tongues would soon start wagging. He quickly decided he couldn't take the risk and walked on past his jeep towards his quarters.

24

CHLOE

Kathmandu, 2018

Several more days had passed without Chloe hearing from Kiran. She'd carried on with her daily routine, doing her best not to think about him, but finding it difficult not to. His lack of communication was impossible to ignore, and her heart ached to hear from him, to know he was safe. As she struggled through those days, sorting through yet more boxes of Anil's books in the basement of the shop or chatting to customers, she couldn't ignore the thoughts that were plaguing her. Kiran was either deliberately ignoring her or something terrible must have happened to him and his group of trekkers.

When she woke on the fifth morning after another restless night, she couldn't wait any longer. She dragged herself up early and, without eating breakfast, walked straight to the shop and opened up. When Shova arrived at nine o'clock, Chloe asked her to take charge for a while.

Chloe made her way through the bustling streets of Thamel, passing street vendors already busily peddling their delicious-smelling wares, to an ancient square nestled in the heart of the district. This was where the trekking agency Kiran worked for, Durbar Treks and Tours, had its offices in a tall, narrow building, sandwiched between a nightclub and a restaurant. A shop on the ground floor sold trekking equipment and the offices were above. Chloe climbed the tiled staircase to the second floor, ignoring the enticing aromas of cooking wafting from the restaurant.

The young man on the reception desk, who was evidently new to the company, didn't recognise her. When she asked him if he had any news of Kiran's group, he looked at her with a blank face.

'Kiran who?' he asked, squinting.

Her anxiety levels soared. 'Kiran Rai? He's taking a group to Everest Base Camp.'

'Wait one moment, madam,' the boy said and disappeared to fetch his boss.

Chloe knew Bikram, the owner of Durbar Treks and Tours, quite well. He and Kiran had been friends since boyhood, and Kiran had worked freelance as a guide for Bikram's company for many years. Bikram had even been one of the guests at Chloe and Kiran's wedding.

'Chloe!' Bikram greeted her with a smile and shook her hand warmly. 'Come through to my office. I've just made a pot of coffee. How are you?'

'I'm fine, thank you.'

She followed Bikram down a maze of passages to his cluttered office, which looked out over the street. The window was open, and the sound of motorbike horns and the hubbub of morning shoppers floated up from the street, mingled with chanting from a Hindu temple in the middle of the square.

He moved a pile of papers and offered Chloe a seat, poured

her a coffee from a jug on his desk and sat down. Chloe took a sip and when he pushed a plate of sel roti, Nepalese rice doughnuts, her way, she took one gratefully, suddenly realising how hungry she was.

'I haven't seen you for a while, Chloe,' Bikram said. 'Kiran told me you are very busy with your shop.'

Chloe paused and put down the sel roti, wondering briefly what else Kiran had said about her and Paradise Books, before telling herself not to be overly sensitive.

'I *have* been busy,' she replied with a forced smile. 'But at least it seems to be beginning to pay off now.' She took another sip of coffee, which was earthy and strong.

Bikram was looking at her with a slightly puzzled expression. No doubt waiting for her to tell him why she was there.

'I was wondering if you've heard from Kiran in the past few days?' she asked.

Bikram relaxed and smiled. 'Ah, I heard from Kiran the day before yesterday,' he replied. 'He was just setting off from Namche Bazaar towards Tengboche with his group.'

Chloe digested this information before replying, 'I've only heard from him once since he left, when they first reached Lukla,' she said. 'I've been a bit concerned... this is only Kiran's second trek since his accident.'

'I know it is, but I'm confident he's fit enough for it, Chloe, or I wouldn't have let him go. Our doctor has given him the all-clear, as you know. I have a responsibility to my clients, after all.'

'I know. I know that. It's just...'

'Please' – Bikram held up a hand – 'there's really no need to worry. It's difficult to keep in touch up in the mountains some-times. Kiran will be busy with his group. As you know, guides have many demands on them. They often don't have much time to themselves.'

She couldn't work out whether to be reassured by Bikram's words or more anxious than before. She was a little more satisfied that Kiran was likely to be safe, but if that was the case why hadn't he got in touch with her when he texted Bikram? Was he not texting her on purpose? Surely Kiran wouldn't do that to her?

'He normally checks in with us most evenings,' Bikram went on. 'He didn't last night, but I don't see that as a cause for concern. But if you really are worried, I could check with the lodge owner at Tengboche to make sure the group set off safely from there this morning.'

'Oh, could you? Just knowing he's alright would really set my mind at rest.'

'Of course. Now, please stop worrying and eat your sel roti, Chloe. You look as though you could do with some comfort food this morning.'

Chloe bit into the sel roti and chewed the delicious sweet pastry hungrily. 'Is it that obvious?' she asked between mouthfuls.

Bikram laughed. 'You did look a bit drawn when I first saw you. Please, like I said, there's no need to worry about Kiran. I'm going to text the lodge owner right now and I'll get in touch with you as soon as she comes back to me. Alright?'

At that moment the phone on his desk started to ring.

'Do you mind if I answer this?' he asked.

Chloe shook her head, realising how busy he must be at the height of the trekking season.

Bikram's hand hovered above the receiver. 'Like I said. I'll be in touch as soon as I hear back from the lodge owner. Take another sel roti with you, please, Chloe!'

That was Chloe's cue to leave. She thanked him, dropped a sel roti into her handbag and walked out of the office, down the tiled steps and out onto the street. She felt a little better than when she'd entered the building ten minutes beforehand, but not completely free from anxiety.

She headed back towards Paradise Books and again the thought came to her: If Kiran had been in touch with Birkam, why hadn't he been in touch with her? She needed to face her fears, she told herself, walking quickly back through the thronging streets. She knew it was guilt driving her emotions. Guilt at the way they'd parted. She was terrified something had happened to Kiran and that she would never have the opportunity to make things right between them. How she regretted the bitter words they'd exchanged before he'd left and the way they'd parted without saying a proper goodbye.

When she got back to Paradise Books, she couldn't resist checking her phone for texts from Bikram every five minutes. She tried to busy herself by going down to the basement and sorting through another box of Anil's books, but even this task didn't fully distract her.

She'd developed a routine for checking the books she'd brought from the Rana palace. First, she leafed through each one for stray letters or envelopes. Then she checked the inside cover and title pages and even the back cover to see if any messages from Alice to Anil had been scrawled inside.

What had become of Alice? she wondered. She still wasn't sure what had actually happened between the two of them, though whatever it was had been serious enough for Anil to keep Alice's letters and his diary, even concealing them from his family for the rest of his life. From the early letters, Chloe had expected to discover a hidden passionate love affair, but although the letters and diary entries she and Rajesh had read so far had contained expressions of love, she was beginning to wonder if it had ever developed into anything more than friendship.

And why had their story captured her imagination so much? she wondered, pausing between books. She'd become desperate to know it, and looked forward to reading the letters and diaries with Rajesh obsessively. In a sense, she supposed she was researching family history again, just as she had in her pursuit of her grandmother's wartime story. It was what had brought her to Nepal in the first place.

But it wasn't just about family history, although Anil was a relative of Kiran's and therefore hers too. It was, she thought in a moment of clarity, because if Alice and Anil had actually become lovers, there were parallels with her own life. Alice was a British woman forming a close bond with a Nepalese man, albeit sixty years ago in a very different world. These thoughts had been in the back of her mind since the start, but it was only now that they had crystallised enough for her to understand.

If the bond had been that close though, what had driven them apart? Was it the fear of something similar driving her and Kiran apart that was compelling her to uncover what had happened to Anil and Alice? Was she pursuing it so she could try to prevent the past repeating itself? It was clear Anil and Alice hadn't stayed together – that Anil had come home to Kathmandu and married Rajesh's mother. So what *had* happened to that close bond the two of them had forged in those turbulent days at the end of British rule in Malaya?

Chloe closed the book she was looking through. Her phone pinged and she quickly pulled it out of her bag. It was a text message from Bikram.

LODGE OWNER SAYS *Kiran and his party set off from Tengboche yesterday morning no problem. I will keep you updated, Chloe. Please don't worry! Namaste, Bikram.*

CHLOE LET OUT a deep sigh of relief. If Kiran hadn't been able to text Bikram to tell him this news from Tengboche himself, then in all likelihood he was having problems with his phone. That must be it. A chink of light opened in her mind. Maybe he wasn't avoiding communicating with her after all, perhaps it was just that technology had failed him. She breathed a little more easily.

That evening, after she'd closed the shop and Shova had left,

she wandered around the rooms, up and down the creaky stair-
cases, touching the quirky pieces of art, the stuffed parrot, the
sculptures, the fortune-telling machine. She was followed by the
two cats, who rubbed themselves against her legs as she walked.
She loved this place. She'd created it because she was settled here
in Nepal, because she wanted to be part of the community and to
make her life here, she reminded herself, so why was she feeling
so unsettled and alone right now?

She sat down beside the boxes of Anil's books she'd brought
up from the basement, fished in her handbag and took out a
photograph of her grandmother. It was the one of the young,
slender, beautiful Lena taken in 1944, her dark hair tucked under
the cap of her uniform. She was in her early twenties and had
just joined the Women's Auxiliary Service, Burma (the Wasbies as
it was known). It was the discovery of Lena's diaries and that
particular photograph that had first brought Chloe to India and
Nepal to uncover the wartime past her grandmother had never
spoken about.

'Oh, Gran. I wish you were here,' Chloe said, kissing the
photograph, knowing Lena would have understood just how she
felt.

'Tell your old gran about it,' Lena would have said with a
warm smile. She would have lent Chloe a sympathetic ear and
have said something wise that would have guided her and reassured her at the same time.

Chloe felt a wave of homesickness for England, for her grandmother's old vicarage in Hampshire where she'd spent her
teenage years after her mother had died of cancer, and for the life
she'd left behind. She thought again about Alice and Anil, how
the odds were stacked against them being together. Perhaps
things were equally stacked against herself and Kiran being
happy. Had she rushed into marriage with him without thinking
it through? Without considering the differences in their back-

ground and upbringing; the ancient culture and traditions that underpinned Kiran's whole being?

She glanced at her watch. It must be five o'clock in the evening in England. She pictured her friend, Sophie, coming towards the end of her day's work at the estate agents' office and had a sudden urge to speak to someone from home. She called her father in Australia now and again, and although relations were cordial between them now, he'd walked out of her life shortly after her mother had died, and she still didn't feel she could confide in him fully. She took her phone out of her bag and scrolled through her contacts to find Sophie's number when suddenly it buzzed in her hand. Her heart gave a lurch. Was that Kiran? Or Bikram with more news?

But it was neither of them. It was Rumi, Kiran's sister, whose name was flashing on the screen. Chloe answered.

'Chloe? How are you?' Rumi's voice sounded warm and loving.

'Oh... so-so.' It was hard to fake cheerfulness. She pictured Rumi, with the same beautiful features as Kiran's, sitting in the office in the family guest house in Pokhara.

'Missing Kiran I expect?'

'Yes. I'm missing him a lot, Rumi. Actually...' Chloe paused. She was desperate to talk to someone about how she was feeling. But Rumi of all people... she was still smarting from the bruising revelation that Kiran had spoken to his sister behind her back.

'Is everything alright?' Rumi said. 'You sound a little upset.'

Chloe swallowed, fighting back the tears. 'It's just that Kiran hasn't been in touch with me for a few days. I think he's having trouble communicating, but...'

'We haven't heard from him either. Do you think he's OK?' Rumi suddenly sounded alarmed too.

'Yes. I went to see Bikram and he checked with the lodge owner. They were safe and well this morning. So please don't worry.'

'Oh, that's a relief... I called to check if you were OK though. Kiran told me you'd been working very hard,' Rumi said. 'He was worried about you.'

'Worried about me?'

'Yes... he loves you so much, Chloe. He would never have mentioned anything to me otherwise. I could tell he felt bad about talking about your relationship with me. But he was so worried about you and he didn't know who to turn to. You know if you're feeling low you can always talk to me, Chloe. You're a long way from your home. Kiran knows you gave up a lot to be with him.'

Chloe couldn't hold the tears back any longer. She took a deep shaky breath and let out a huge sob. 'I'm so sorry, Rumi,' she said between sniffs.

'Don't be sorry. Please. We are family. I'm your sister now. Please tell me what is wrong.'

So Chloe sat down on an old armchair beside the boxes of Anil's books and told her sister-in-law everything: how Kiran had been trying to persuade her to take things easy at the shop just when she wanted to build up the business, how they both wanted a baby, but nothing had happened, and in any case it didn't seem quite the right time, and how this whole issue had put them at loggerheads and driven them apart.

'To tell you the truth, Rumi,' Chloe said – now the floodgates had opened she wanted to be completely honest with her sister-in-law. 'I was upset he'd talked to you about it and asked you to come and help out in the shop. I took it rather badly.'

'Oh, Chloe, I only offered because I thought it might help both of you. I didn't mean to intrude or to cause you any pain. That was the last thing on my mind. I know how hard you've worked building up the business and I admire you for it. We all do. I would only ever come and help out if you, yourself wanted me to.'

Chloe felt a rush of love for Kiran's sister, mingled with guilt for the way she'd misinterpreted this gesture of kindness. What had she been thinking of? She knew Rumi to be a kind, generous person with an open, loving heart.

'I'm sorry, Rumi. I overreacted, and I'm afraid Kiran and I parted on bad terms. We didn't even say goodbye properly.' She took another shuddering sob.

'And that's why you're so worried about him not being in touch?'

'Yes,' Chloe said miserably.

'I understand. Kiran can be a bit stubborn sometimes. But like I said, he loves you so much, Chloe. I'm sure things will be right again as soon as he's back and you can have a proper talk.'

Chloe felt a lot better after they ended the call. She remembered that Kiran's family had always been good to her and welcomed her into the fold without hesitation. They'd always helped and supported her. Why had she thought anything different? She wiped her eyes with her handkerchief, then picked up another of Anil's books. She would finish this box and then lock up and go home.

She opened the book and a note that had been tucked inside the dust jacket dropped out. It was dated March 1950.

MY DEAREST ANIL,

I am so, so sorry for what has happened. I don't know how I could have been such a fool. You must feel betrayed and humiliated, and I don't blame you if you never want to see me or speak to me again. Please know, everything I've done has been with the best of intentions. I was trying to do something good and kind amongst all this horror. I know it's too late to ask for your forgiveness, but I will live in hope.

Your ever loving,
Alice

· · ·

CHLOE STARED at the note and read it over and over again. What did this mean? She needed to speak to Rajesh. It had been a few days since they'd met. She'd been so absorbed with her concerns about Kiran she hadn't registered the passing of time. But this letter was important. It could be a clue as to what might have happened to drive Anil and Alice apart.

25

ALICE

Rimba Valley Estate, March 1949

A FEW DAYS after the attack on the bus, Alice got up early, determined to make it to the jungle village that morning. She waited until the servants were having breakfast together in the kitchen before sneaking into the pantry and loading her knapsack with supplies. Now the government's resettlement policy was underway, it seemed more important than ever that her visit to the village should remain secret.

She wondered if news of the CT attack on the bus had filtered through to the village. If the villagers were aware she'd been involved they might think she would abandon them, that she would think it too risky to go there. That made her even more determined to keep their faith with her. And she had another reason for going, too. She needed to warn them about the resettlement programme so they could be prepared. If their village was discovered, they would certainly be moved from their homes.

Anil's men were still guarding the front of the house, so

Alice crept out through the back door, hurried across the garden, slipped out through the gate and onto the jungle path. As she walked, her mind turned to Anil, to the kisses they'd shared on the night of the attack, the way he'd held her and looked into her eyes. He hadn't returned since then. What did it mean? Was he regretting what had happened? Or was he worried about his soldiers finding out? Either way, Alice ached to see him.

Gradually, her mind turned to William Manners and the British ex-pats at the club. She was well aware what she was doing was against Emergency regulations. She tried to picture their faces if they discovered that she, Alice Lacey, shy, retiring widow, an exemplary citizen, was breaking the law to provide sustenance to a starving Chinese village. The thought made her smile, despite the tension she was feeling as she pushed her way through the ferns and bamboo encroaching on the jungle path towards the top of the hill.

Ying May didn't know she was coming that day, so Alice walked along the boundary and carried on down the path that wound through the second patch of jungle towards the village. Finally emerging into the clearing, she looked around her, surprised. The village seemed unusually quiet that morning. There were no children playing in the mud, no one sitting gossiping beside the fires between the huts.

Nobody came out to greet her, but she noticed a few people sitting on their porches who waved tentatively as she passed. When she approached Ying May's house, she saw someone get up from the porch and go into the hut. Ying May soon hurried down the steps to greet her.

'Hello, Mrs Lacey, I didn't expect you today,' she said, looking a little flustered. 'Come and sit. I will make you tea.'

Alice handed her the knapsack. Ying May took a peek inside before stowing it on the porch. Alice sat down cross-legged as she always did, while the other woman brewed tea.

'Who was that who went inside?' Alice asked as Ying May handed her a mug of the steaming liquid.

Ying May hesitated before saying, 'Oh, just my husband. He has no work again today. I'm afraid he's too tired and grumpy for visitors.'

'I understand,' Alice said. 'I'm sorry I haven't been here for a while,' she went on. 'I intended to come before, but unfortunately I was caught up in a CT ambush on the road a few days ago.'

'Yes, we heard about that,' Ying May replied, dropping her gaze. 'I'm so sorry, Mrs Lacey. That must have been very frightening for you. We even thought you might not come again.'

Alice smiled. It was just as she'd anticipated. 'Of course I would come. I will always come here. As long as you need my help.'

'Thank you. You are very brave,' Ying May said with a grateful smile.

Alice took a deep breath. 'Do you know anything about the government's resettlement policy?' she asked.

Ying May's forehead creased into a frown. 'Yes,' she replied in a low voice. 'We heard about it from our men who work on the mines and rubber estates. We are very worried about it.'

Alice reached out and patted her hand. 'Your secret is safe with me,' she said. 'I would never breathe a word to anyone about this village.'

Ying May's smile reached her eyes. 'Thank you. You are so kind to us.'

'It's the least I can do,' Alice said. 'I can't stand by and see you suffering when I'm in a position to help.'

Ying May emptied the knapsack and handed it back to Alice. 'Thank you again, Mrs Lacey. We are so grateful.'

'I only wish I could bring more,' Alice said, finishing her tea.

They walked together back up the path to the edge of the mine, where they said goodbye. Alice hurried back through the last stretch of jungle. She'd been away from the house for almost an hour. The servants would have finished breakfast by now and might well be wondering where she was.

As she emerged from the edge of the forest and headed towards the garden gate, she noticed an unfamiliar blue Ford parked on the drive. She stopped and frowned, then walked on more slowly. As she drew closer, she realised it was Diana's spare car; one she rarely used and was kept in a barn on the Blanchard estate. Diana must have come to visit her. Alice's mind started racing. Whatever would she tell her friend about where she'd been?

Diana was sitting on the veranda, reading a magazine and sipping coffee when Alice walked up the front steps.

'Good God, Alice,' Diana said putting down her magazine. 'Where have you been? I was worried about you.'

Alice felt a guilty blush creeping into her cheeks, but she decided to brazen it out. 'I've been for a walk,' she said. 'Just up into the jungle to the edge of the mine. I often go up there in the mornings.' She was surprised at how easily the lie tripped off her tongue.

Diana got up from her chair and kissed Alice on both cheeks. 'You know how dangerous it is to stray far from the house,' Diana said with an anxious frown. 'I would have thought you'd be more cautious after the other day.'

'I don't go off the property,' Alice said. 'I just feel the need to get out of the house sometimes.'

'I know,' Diana said. 'I feel the same, but I'm trying to be more careful.' She sat down again.

'But didn't you just drive over here?' Alice asked, sitting down in the rattan chair beside her friend and tucking the empty knapsack discreetly beside the chair.

'Arif brought me over. He's in the kitchen having tea with your servants. Abdullah is still in shock, the poor thing. Tony won't let me drive alone. Not at the moment, anyway, but I wanted to see how you were getting on.

Talking on the phone isn't enough after what we went through together.'

'No, you're right,' Alice said. She'd tried not to dwell too much on the horror of the bus hold-up, but the fear still lurked in the back of her mind; the memory of the gun pointed at her, the feel of the leader's rough hands on her face, the fire, the terrified workers. She shuddered at the memory and tried to focus on what Diana was saying.

'William Manners has been to see me several times,' Diana said. 'He can't understand why the CT leader let us go. He keeps questioning me about it. He clearly thinks I'm holding something back, but I'm afraid I simply have no idea.'

'Me neither,' Alice said. 'But thank God he did let us go... or we'd all be dead.'

Diana gave a shudder. 'When I was walking down the road, away from the bus with Abdullah, I really believed he was going to shoot me in the back. I was bracing myself for it.'

Alice closed her eyes, not wanting to remember. She'd felt the same way.

'William Manners has been back here too,' she told Diana. 'He thinks I'm hiding something. He even tried to get Anil to question me.'

Diana looked at her sharply. 'Has Anil been to see you?'

'Only that evening,' she said. 'He came to see how I was after the attack. William Manners asked him to stay on for a few hours to keep me company.'

Diana gave her a sideways look and Alice dropped her gaze.

'You need to watch your step, Alice,' she said. 'I've told you before. I can see you and Anil are falling for each other, but no good will come of it.'

'Falling for each other?' Alice repeated, her heart thumping, her cheeks warm with embarrassment. Was it so obvious? 'I don't know what you mean.'

Diana gave her an incredulous look. 'The ex-pat community

here is terribly stuffy, Alice. You must know that. A British woman who has an affair with a foreigner like Major Desai would be an outcast. And it would ruin his career. You don't seriously think it would ever work, do you?'

Alice stared at her hands. She knew what Diana said was true and that her friend was only trying to protect her, but what did she care about a few bigoted ex-pats at the club. Why did it have to be like that anyway? Life was so unfair.

'I'm not having an affair with him, Diana. He's been very kind to me and we're friends. That's all there is to it.'

Once again, Diana gave her a sceptical look. 'You know he would never marry you, don't you? Even if society would tolerate you being together. He'll already be betrothed to someone back home. Someone his parents chose for him when he was a boy. And knowing what a decent, honourable man Anil is, I'm sure he wouldn't want to disappoint his parents. You mark my words.'

Alice's heart thumped sickeningly. She'd not thought of that angle, but she realised it was probably true. She felt a fierce pang of jealousy for the mysterious girl back in Kathmandu who would one day be his wife. She would be a beauty, Alice was sure of that.

'You'll never be able to marry him, Alice. I don't want to upset you, I'm telling you this for your own good because I love you and I don't want you to get hurt.'

At that moment, Ibrahim appeared in the front doorway with a tray.

'Coffee, memsahib?' he asked Alice. He brought the tray to the table and poured fresh coffee from the pot for her.

When he'd gone back inside the house, the conversation moved on to other things – gossip about neighbours, the recent attacks on British property, speculation about the new guerilla leader. They chatted comfortably for an hour or so, then Diana got up.

'We should make a start back. I've got lots to do at home. I just wanted to make sure you were alright.'

They embraced and Diana held Alice at arm's length and smiled into her eyes.

'I didn't mean any harm by what I said about Anil,' she said. 'But it's good advice and I hope you'll take it.' Then she went into the house to call for Arif.

Alice stood waving on the veranda, watching the car disappear down the drive and into the jungle, her heart heavy with sadness. If only her friend hadn't been so perceptive. Everything she'd said was true, Alice was aware of that, but how could she swim against the great tidal wave of love for Anil that had already knocked her off her feet? Even if she wanted to stop it, she didn't think she could. Ever since their first kiss she hadn't been able to get him out of her mind. She'd been desperate to see him again. She'd gone over and over that evening, the way he'd held her, the feel of his lips against hers, his arms around her, pulling her close. She knew Diana was right and there was no future in their love, but that didn't stop her aching to be with him.

She was restless for the remainder of the day, trying to occupy herself by working in the rose garden, and later by reading, but her mind kept wandering. Diana's words rang in her ears, but – worse than that – she couldn't help reliving the CT ambush over and over again. Vivid memories of it would come to her unbidden, stopping her in her tracks.

A few minutes after Alice had finished her evening meal, she heard the sound of a vehicle on the gravel outside. She assumed it was the new soldiers arriving to replace those on duty for the night watch. She went to the window, pulled the chiks aside and looked out. Her heart leapt. It was Anil, getting out of his jeep and crossing the gravel to the front door, his head bowed.

She went into the hall calling, 'I'll get the door, Ibrahim.'

She opened the front door before Anil could even knock and

looked up into his eyes. They were full of love for her and looking at him she knew there was no holding back the tide.

'Mrs Lacey.' He gave a nod before glancing at the two guards, seated behind the sandbags. 'May I come in?'

'Of course, Major.' She stepped aside to let him past, her heart racing madly.

He closed the door on the guards, and drew Alice into his arms.

He kissed her then, his lips hot against hers, and she returned the kiss with fervour. She wanted to take him upstairs, but that would be impossible with Ibrahim and the other servants still in the kitchen, so they went into the drawing room and sat side by side on the settee and kissed again.

'Will you stay with me tonight?' she asked.

He stroked her hair. 'Oh, Alice, I've been wrestling with my conscience,' he said. 'We both know this can't last, that it will ruin your reputation and my career. I came to tell you that, as gently as I could, but when I saw the look in your eyes something inside me broke. My heart overruled my head, and I couldn't resist you.'

She looked away. What he said was true, but it was still painful to hear their love was doomed, especially from Anil himself. She didn't know how to respond. She turned towards him and looked up into his eyes longingly and they kissed again.

They sat there together, their bodies entwined, for the rest of the evening, kissing and embracing, murmuring words of love. At one point Alice poured them some drinks from the cabinet and put a Chopin record on the gramophone.

Later they heard Ibrahim and the others lock up and go to bed in their quarters behind the house. Then, without a word, hand in hand, they crept upstairs together.

Alice hesitated at the door of the bedroom she'd shared with Bruce, shuddering at the memories. 'Not there,' she said, and guided Anil to the guest room.

There they fell on the bed together, and kissed slowly,

running their hands over each other's bodies, not wanting to rush the moment they'd both been anticipating for so long.

He pulled her close, unbuttoning her blouse, his lips exploring her body, and in turn she unbuttoned his shirt, slipped her hands inside, relishing the feel of his hot skin against hers. Then he was on top of her, kissing her, stroking her hair, loving her with his eyes, and without the need for words their bodies were moving together in a seamless expression of their love.

It was after midnight when, with one last, lingering kiss, Anil announced it was time for him to leave.

'I have to go, or the soldiers will start asking questions,' he said. 'But I'll come back soon.'

After he'd left, she lay there on the bed, listening to the sound of his jeep fading into the distance and looking up at the stars through the open window, her mind and body flooded with love and happiness.

AFTER THAT FIRST NIGHT, Anil drove to Rimba Valley as often as he could, sometimes every other day, sometimes two or three times a week, and they would make love in the spare room. Both were wary of discovery, aware of the consequences for them both. Alice wished they didn't have to be so covert; it pained her deeply that they couldn't celebrate their love in public.

The months flew by and soon 1949 was over and 1950 had begun. Alice could hardly believe that a year had passed since Bruce's death. When Anil wasn't with her, she went about her days in a near euphoric state, her mind suffused with the memory of him, of the loving words he'd whispered, of the touch of his lips, of the wonderful way he made love to her. Her only regret was that even now they were lovers – and she was closer to Anil than she'd been to anyone before in her life – there were still things she had to hide from him. She simply couldn't risk telling him about the squatters' village, and she continued to go there every couple of days to take food. She knew the villagers relied on her; that they waited anxiously for her visits. She looked forward to chatting with Ying May, who she now counted as a friend.

She wished she could be honest about it with Anil, but that was impossible due to his heavy involvement in the resettlement programme. Not that he was happy about that. Whenever he came to see her, he told her of the latest atrocities he'd witnessed as squatters were evacuated from their homes to either be detained in camps or deported to China. He seemed torn. He was a dutiful soldier; half of him supported the British effort, but the other half hated the injustices he'd witnessed, hated having to tear families from their homes and force them into concrete compounds under guard.

But her visits to the village weren't her only secret; Alice kept others too. She would never reveal the dark events around Bruce's death that she'd buried deep inside. She hated the fact she couldn't bring herself to tell Anil about either of those things.

One day, Anil looked more troubled than usual, and when Alice asked him what was wrong, he sighed and said, 'The British are losing patience with the squatters. They want this resettlement programme to be over and done with. So they're stepping up efforts to clear the entire country of squatters.'

'What are they going to do?' Alice asked, alarmed.

'They want to root out the remaining villages that are hidden deep inside the jungle. For the past few days, RAF planes have been sent up on reconnaissance missions to fly low over the jungle to look for them.'

Alice bit her lip and looked away, nerves sweeping through her body. What if the planes discovered her village? She couldn't bear the thought of Ying May and the others – whom she now knew quite well – being torn from their homes by soldiers, marched through the jungle to waiting lorries and ferried to distant compounds at gunpoint. Surely they had a right to live their lives in peace. They weren't doing any harm where they were.

Now, at every waking moment, Alice's eyes and ears were on alert for the sight and sound of RAF reconnaissance planes flying over the jungle – though she realised if a plane were to approach from the other direction she wouldn't even hear them, and it was possible for a plane to spot the village without flying over her house. That made her even more nervous.

The day after Anil had told her about the flights, she set off early in the morning towards the kampong with her knapsack. Anil had said he would visit her at noon, so she wanted to be back in time to see him. But first she was going to warn the villagers. Although what they might do to prevent themselves from being spotted, she had no idea.

She pushed through the errant ferns, bamboo and creepers impatiently and walked up the path as quickly as she could. The sun was high in the sky and the heat under the dense canopy of trees was clammy and intense. When at last she reached the fence that bordered the mine, she was sweating and panting, but she was anxious to get to the village and pressed on, into the second patch of jungle and downhill towards it.

This time she hurried between the flimsy huts, waving briefly to a couple of people on their porches, but she had no time to waste.

As she neared Ying May's house, she noticed movement on the porch. Instinctively she slowed down and paused beside another hut. There was a man standing on Ying May's porch speaking to her. It was the man Alice had seen there before, the one Ying May had said was her husband, but something in the way he moved made Alice's heart thump in her chest. She was rooted to the spot, unable to take her eyes off him.

She knew this man. He was taller than most of the villagers, dressed in neat khaki fatigues, his black hair cut short, and he held himself erect. As she watched, he turned around and started

down the steps towards the open fire in the clearing and a bolt of
recognition went through Alice; it was the guerilla leader who'd
set her free after the bus ambush. She stared at him open-
mouthed; there was no doubt in her mind. This was Ah Ping.

Everything around her seemed to go into free fall – the
houses and trees became a blur, her legs felt suddenly weak –
and she steadied herself against the wall of the hut. Her hand
flew to her mouth and, in that moment, everything became clear.
How could she have not seen? How could she have been so naïve?
The truth had been staring her in the face. These villagers, the
ones she counted as friends, had been hiding Ah Ping all along
and had been using her to supply the CTs with food. She'd been
unwittingly supporting the murderous guerilla cause for
months now.

She turned on her heel and ran back towards the trees,
plunging into the jungle and hurtling up the path towards the
mine as fast as she could, stumbling over roots, pricked and
scratched by brambles and thorns, her clothes tearing on sharp
bamboo. Her breath came in gulps and tears blurred her vision,
but she ran on, constantly checking behind her to see if anyone
was following.

At last, panting and sobbing, she reached the top of the hill.
She stopped and bent double to catch her breath, then straightened up and ran on beside the fence that bounded the mine.
When she reached the other patch of jungle she dived into it
without stopping, hurtling down the path towards the house.

Emerging from the jungle, scratched and bleeding, she ran
towards the house, her eyes scanning the drive for any sign of
Anil's jeep. She needed to talk to him, to tell him what she'd
done, to explain to him and apologise before the secret was out.
He would know how to help her. He would tell her what to do.
But as she ran towards the drive, she saw it was empty. No jeep
stood in front of the house.

She would wait for him, she decided. She would wait on the

porch and as soon as he arrived she would come clean and tell him all about the village. She would tell him she could see how naïve she'd been, how she'd only been trying to help; she would plead for his forgiveness.

She sat there in the basket chair watching the drive for a long time. The sun moved overhead, making the gravel shimmer in the heat. The minutes ticked by. Noon came and went. Soon it was half past and still he hadn't come. Anil was never late. What had happened to him?

One o'clock came and went. Ibrahim asked her if she wanted lunch. She could barely respond because a terrible thought had occurred to her. Anil wasn't coming to see her. He might never come again. He had heard all about the village and about her duplicity, and he would never forgive her.

26

ANIL

March, 1950

From Major Anil Desai's diary:

It is very difficult for me to write about the events of the past few days, but I'm hoping putting it down on paper might help me make sense of what has happened.

Two days ago, one of the RAF reconnaissance flights spotted a squatters' village deep in the jungle, a few hundred yards from the edge of the mine on Rimba Valley Estate. When soldiers on the ground went in to check on the village and did a thorough search of all the dwellings there, they discovered the notorious CT leader, Ah Ping, hiding in one of the huts. The squatters in this hidden village on the Rimba estate had obviously been harbouring him for months.

William Manners, the local police chief, took Ah Ping into custody, along with a number of villagers suspected of assisting him. It didn't take long for those villagers to reveal something else. Something that was a huge shock to me. They told the police that Alice Lacey was regularly supplying the village with food, and that she'd been doing that since well before her husband died. She'd actually been taking those supplies up to them herself, on foot. The soldiers found a well-trodden path which led all the way through the jungle directly to her house.

I was shaken to the core when I was told of this. I could hardly believe my dear, good, beautiful Alice, could have done such a foolish thing, but the truth was staring me in the face. There is no hiding from it, and my heart bleeds as I write these words.

Something else gradually became clear when the villagers were questioned. The reason why Alice was released by the guerillas after the CT attack on the bus was because Ah Ping recognised her as someone who'd supplied them with food. I can hardly believe that my sweet Alice, whom I love with body and soul, has been carrying this secret with her all along. Each time we saw each other, each time we kissed, each time we made love.

As well as the terrible shock of discovering she was doing such a thing, what hurts more than anything is that she kept it a secret from me. I thought we were soulmates, that we had no secrets from each other. That is the most painful thing about all this.

WHEN NEWS BEGAN to emerge of the shocking discovery in the village, and about the details of Alice's involvement, Anil drove straight up to Rimba Valley. He had to talk to her, to get her side of the story, to understand why she'd done what she'd done and why she hadn't been able to confide in him.

But when he knocked at the front door, it was opened by Ibrahim, who gave him a stony look.

'Memsahib is not here,' he said.

'Do you know where she is?' Anil asked.

The man shook his head. 'Captain Manners took her away to the police station yesterday. She hasn't been home since.'

Anil got into his jeep and drove straight to the police station in Ipoh. The officer on the desk told him Mrs Lacey was being questioned and that he'd been given strict instructions she should have no visitors.

'What about tomorrow? Can I see her then?' Anil asked.

The man shook his head. 'No visitors, anytime,' he said.

Anil turned away in dismay.

As he drove out of the yard he passed Diana Blanchard driving a blue Ford into it. He wondered if Diana would get the same treatment he had. He hoped not and that she would be allowed to talk to Alice. She must be feeling very anxious and lonely.

He returned to his camp, his heart and mind in turmoil. As well as the shock of discovering what Alice had been doing behind his back, he was deeply worried about her state of mind and how she would cope in police custody. He was well aware of the brutal tactics the British police sometimes employed to get the answers they wanted. Surely they wouldn't do that to one of their own. Especially a young woman like Alice, all alone in the world. He spent a sleepless night worrying about her.

First thing the next morning he was called into Colonel Bristow's office. Normally the colonel would have asked him to sit down, but this time he left Anil standing to attention in front of his desk and kept him waiting while he signed some papers. When the colonel finally looked up, Anil saw his face was clouded with anger.

'To say I'm disappointed in you, Desai, is an understatement,' the colonel began.

Anil felt shame wash through him. He respected the colonel, loved his regiment and he'd always been a conscientious, dutiful soldier.

'When we questioned the Gurkha soldiers who'd been guarding the Lacey estate to ascertain Mrs Lacey's whereabouts, to double-check that what the villagers had said was true, it emerged that you have been a frequent visitor to her home for months, and that often you don't leave until the small hours.'

Anil hung his head. He couldn't meet the colonel's eye.

The colonel banged on his desk. 'Damn it, Desai, I didn't say "at ease". Stand to attention while I speak to you. It has become clear that you have disgraced your uniform and your regiment by conducting a clandestine affair with a woman you were assigned to help and protect. This woman lost her husband in terrifying circumstances, she's been the victim of several brutal CT attacks, she was clearly vulnerable, and yet you saw fit to get into her bed. Shame on you, Desai. I expected more from a decorated officer.'

Anil remained silent. Was he expected to respond?

'Well? What do you have to say for your pitiful self, Major?'

Anil cleared his throat. 'It wasn't as you describe, sir. We became friends. Her husband used to beat her and assault her regularly. He was a brute. She felt safe with me…'

'And you took advantage of her,' the colonel finished.

Anil shook his head. 'No, sir. It wasn't like that.'

'Either way, you were assigned to protect Rimba Valley Estate, and this is how you conducted yourself. I am sorely disappointed in you. Now, if you were a lesser soldier, Desai, you would be out of the regiment, out of the Gurkhas altogether, but your service record is impeccable and you served with distinction throughout the war. In view of that, your punishment is this: you will be sent back to Kathmandu forthwith and reassigned elsewhere. Your tour in Malaya is over and done with.'

'But sir,' Anil protested. This couldn't happen. It would mean his relationship with Alice was over. He would never hold her in his arms again, never comfort her, make love to her. They'd both known it would have to end one day, but this was so sudden. How would he bear it?

'I've already arranged your passage. You will sail from Butterworth to Calcutta in two days' time. You'll catch the train tomorrow.'

'Sail?' Anil repeated.

'Yes. All aircraft are currently engaged in essential reconnaissance missions.' Colonel Bristow paused and looked at him. 'You've been given this chance, Desai. You've been lucky. Make sure you don't waste it.'

When Anil left the office, he went straight to the base and gathered his men around him. He gave them the news that he'd been posted back to Kathmandu. As he spoke, he could see the puzzlement and dismay on their faces. They'd been through a lot together, and he knew they trusted him and looked up to him. He couldn't bring himself to spell out the reasons for his transfer – he didn't want to see the disappointment in their eyes – but he guessed the gossip would filter through to them eventually.

When he'd dismissed the men and watched them drift back to their quarters, shaking their heads, he returned to his own room. Opening the door, he noticed a letter slipped underneath it. It was how Alice usually communicated with him. He snatched it up, tore it open and read it quickly.

My dearest Anil,

I am so, so sorry for what has happened. I don't know how I could have been such a fool. You must feel betrayed and humiliated, and I don't blame you if you never want to see me or speak to me again. Please know, everything I've done has been with the best of intentions. I was trying to do something good and kind amongst all this horror. I know it's too late to ask for your forgiveness, but I will live in hope.

Your ever loving,
Alice

It was written on Rimba Valley notepaper. That meant she'd been allowed home. Anil got straight into his jeep and drove the familiar road to Rimba Valley Estate. As he accelerated away from HQ and into the jungle, he realised with a pang of regret that he would miss this country; the verdant greenery, the relentless heat, the looming hills, the whoops and cries from the jungle creatures, the gentle locals, and even the British planters and miners he'd got to know and respect. It was hard to think that soon all this would be just a memory.

He drew up outside the house and before he was out of his jeep the front door opened and Alice came running towards him. He took her into his arms and held her close as she sobbed against his chest.

'Come, let's go inside and talk,' he said.

They went together into the drawing room where the chiks were down and the fan turning, the room shady and cool.

'I'm so sorry, Anil,' Alice said as they sat down on the sofa. 'I wanted to tell you about the village, but I just couldn't think of a way of doing that. I had no idea any of them were guerillas. They seemed so genuine.'

'Almost every squatters' village will have come under the influence of the guerillas, whether they wanted to or not. They will have been threatened with torture. Some of them may have even been killed to bring the others into line.'

Alice went pale. 'The village headman and three others died very suddenly recently. I saw their graves, and when I asked about it I was brushed off. I was told they'd died from natural causes.'

'I expect they tried to resist helping the CTs, maybe even hiding Ah Ping,' he told her. He'd seen similar brutal killings in many other villages in the area.

'I can't get over how they tricked me. I saw Ying May in the police station. The woman I thought was a friend. She looked terrible, Anil, – thin and haggard, and so different from how I knew her. She spat at me, yelled that I'd betrayed them. I was so shocked to see her like that.'

'It was her who betrayed you, Alice. You know that don't you?'

'I suppose so, but I still can't believe what a fool I was,' Alice said. 'How I didn't see it. I just thought I was doing something good. You must be very angry with me.'

He took her hand and kissed it tenderly. 'I wish you'd told me, that's all. I might have been able to prevent all of this. But I understand why you didn't. And I forgive you, Alice. I'd forgive you anything.'

She looked up at him, her eyes brimming with tears.

'But I have to tell you,' he went on, 'I've been ordered back to Kathmandu. I'm leaving by train to Butterworth tomorrow.'

Alice gasped and her hand flew to her mouth. 'No! Oh, Anil, it's all my fault.'

He put his arm around her and pulled her to him. 'Please don't think like that. I'd have had to leave at some point anyway.'

'But so soon... you must be furious with me.'

'What happened at the police station?' he asked to change the subject.

'They questioned me for a long time, but in the end they released me without charge.'

'Really?' Anil was a little surprised at this. Alice's conduct had been a clear breach of Emergency regulations. Supplying the enemy with sustenance was a serious offence.

She hung her head. 'I feel very bad about it. I know it's because William Manners took pity on me. I'm part of the community here and probably, even here, my father's name and status have some influence.'

Anil was silent for a moment. He knew it was true and, while he was glad Alice hadn't been charged, it was a bitter pill to swallow. The British Army and the British establishment would always protect their own.

As if reading his thoughts, Alice said, 'It's so unfair, isn't it, that I've been allowed to walk free, but you are leaving under a cloud? I feel guilt-ridden about that. It's only because of me that you're having to leave.'

'It's the world we live in, Alice. It's not your fault,' he said, trying to reassure her.

'I wish I could take it all back, Anil,' she said. 'I wish I'd never been to that wretched village. But you know, I think I was trying to make amends somehow.'

He looked at her with love in his eyes. 'You don't need to apologise, Alice, you *are* good,' he said. 'You are good through and through. You didn't have to prove that. To me you are perfect.'

She began to cry properly then with great gulping sobs, shaking her head, tears streaming down her cheeks. 'You don't know me, Anil. You don't know half of what I've done. What I'm capable of. I'm not good. I'm weak... and selfish, and—'

Anil couldn't bear to see her like that. He wouldn't let her finish. He put his finger over her mouth to stop her words. He refused to believe she could be anything other than good and innocent.

'Could I come with you, Anil?' she said after a long pause.

'Come with me?'

'To Nepal? So we could be together.'

He held her close and kissed her hair. 'If only you could. But we both know that would be impossible.'

They went up to the guest room and made love. It was bittersweet, tinged with regret and longing, and when he kissed her for the last time before getting into his jeep and driving away, they were both distraught beyond words.

THE NEXT DAY, Anil said a formal goodbye to his men, then boarded the train in Ipoh for Butterworth with his pack, feeling very low. His sergeant, who'd driven him to the station, saluted as they said goodbye. As the train pulled out of the station, he stared out at the encroaching jungle, his heart full of remorse for what he was leaving behind.

The following day he left the barracks in Butterworth, feeling wretched, and made his way to the docks to board the liner, HMS *Rajula,* that was being readied to set sail for Calcutta.

As he walked along the dock towards the gangplank, through the little knots of well-wishers who'd come to see off passengers, he heard a shout from the crowd and turned to see Alice waving and running towards him, dressed in a white lace dress and wide-brimmed hat. His heart soared.

'Anil! I had to come and see you off. I got one of the house-boys to drive me here.'

'Alice!' He swept her into his arms and, not caring who saw them, gave her a long, passionate kiss.

He lingered beside the gangplank with her as long as he could, neither saying very much, the silence between them laden with sorrow, but the ship's horn was blasting for passengers to board. With a heavy heart, he stole one last kiss, then tore himself away and went up the plank, tears blinding his eyes.

He climbed straight up to the deck and stood by the rail as the ship cast off and pulled away from the dock. He waved, and Alice waved back and blew him kisses as the ship drew away from the land, until eventually she faded softly into the mist.

27

Kathmandu, 1950

ANIL HAD BEEN HOME in Kathmandu for a couple of months and was finding it hard to adjust to being back in his home city. Since he'd left Malaya everything seemed to have taken on an air of unreality.

For the first few days, he'd tried to reacquaint himself with the narrow, cobbled streets of Durbar Square and the centre of the city on foot. He'd breathed in the familiar aromas of spices and incense, feasted his eyes on the beauty of the ancient pagodas, listened to the cacophony of sounds from the temples, and tried to acclimatise himself to the smoky atmosphere of the place again. But he couldn't forget the steamy heat of Malaya and that country's many contrasts: the cobalt blue of the sky, the emerald green of the jungle, the stark, pearly white of the buildings. He'd never imagined he would miss it, but he found himself yearning for it on a daily basis.

Now he was home, his long-anticipated wedding had been

brought forward. He was in the throes of preparing for it, but although he tried his best, his heart wasn't in it.

He'd been heavily involved in preparations for the groom's procession to the temple, contacting all his old friends and the guests his parents had invited. All of them had greeted him with love and affection, and all had asked him the same question: 'Are you going back to Malaya after the wedding?' He'd had to shake his head each time, shamefaced, not knowing how to explain to them why not, when the Emergency raged on unabated.

His mother was in a frenzy of preparation. She was ordering new outfits for herself and Anil's father and she'd wanted Anil to go to the tailor as well. But he'd told her there was no need. 'I will wear my uniform,' he said. 'No need for a new outfit.'

He'd met his future bride, Manjula, a couple of times since his return. Once in the company of both sets of parents at an awkward tea party at her parents' home, Rani Durbar, the grand palace in Lazimpat. When he'd arrived, walking between his parents, they'd rounded the bend in the drive and stared up at the edifice of columns and windows in awe.

'This will be yours one day, my son,' his father said.

Anil could hardly believe it, but it was true. Manjula was an only child, and her ageing parents had already undertaken to move into a side wing of the building after the wedding so that the young couple could occupy the main rooms in privacy. It was so grand, the thought of living there made Anil a little nervous. He came from a modest, middle-class home on the outskirts of the city, and he wondered how it was possible to lead an ordinary life in that gracious, cavernous building.

The second time he'd met Manjula was at her Svayamvara, or 'choosing ceremony', when he and a group of his male friends met her at the temple. Prayers were said and offerings made, and she'd picked him out of the group, as was the tradition. When she'd laid her hands on him, she'd smiled at him from behind her veil, and Anil had felt deep shame coursing through him.

How could he be marrying this woman when his heart belonged to another? It wasn't fair on either of them.

If he looked deep inside his heart, he realised he was actually afraid of getting married. His future wife was beautiful in a bold, daring way; the exact opposite to Alice's winsome, quiet beauty. Manjula had flashing brown eyes, full lips and luxuriant black hair. She was educated, articulate and impressive. She intimidated him a little too, although he didn't like to admit it to himself. The thing that worried him most was that he wouldn't be able to love her, or make love to her, that the memory of Alice would be too overwhelming.

He'd done his level best to forget Alice. She was like a mirage, a dream; just like the oppressive heat and the encroaching jungle of Malaya. He assured himself he would get over her in time. He just needed to give himself a chance.

He'd been home a few months and was beginning to settle into things, when he received a letter from her.

MY DEAREST ANIL,

I HAVE ADDRESSED THIS C/O your Gurkha HQ in Kathmandu because you didn't leave me an address.

There is something I want you to know. You wouldn't let me tell you before you left Malaya, even though I tried to. Once you do know this, it might convince you that being sent away from me was the best thing that could have happened to you, that I wasn't worth jeopardising your career and your life for.

So, this is it. This is what I wanted to say to you before you left: It was me who killed Bruce. I as good as killed him anyway, and it has been eating at me ever since.

When the CTs stormed the house that day, it was I who told them where he was hiding. I did it because they held a knife to my throat and

I thought they might kill me if I didn't, but that wasn't the only reason. Something deep inside me wanted the guerillas to kill Bruce.

I could never tell you this directly, Anil, but Bruce used to hurt me. I was too ashamed to talk about it to you, but I think you guessed anyway. He would hurt me physically and mentally, and on the day of the raid he had forced himself on me for the second time.

I told the guerillas where he was hiding. I knew they would go straight to the cellar and drag him out. If I hadn't done that, Bruce might still be alive today. If I hadn't told them exactly where to find him, he might have had a chance of escaping, or at least have had more time to prepare to defend himself.

So, you see, I never deserved your love, Anil. I never told you the truth about what happened that day, I let you believe in the image you'd built up of me in your mind. I suppose it's because I wanted to believe in it too. But you deserved better than that.

I hope you are settling back into life in Nepal and that you can now put everything that happened in Malaya behind you.

Your ever loving,
Alice

ANIL STARED AT THE LETTER. What she'd told him didn't surprise him. He'd wanted to kill Bruce at times too and he didn't blame Alice for wanting that violent, odious man dead. Why should she have let the guerillas slit her throat in order to save Bruce?

He wanted to write back straight away, to reassure her that he didn't blame her. That he had half suspected what had happened and that he understood.

He found paper and pen in his mother's desk and started to write, but try as he might he couldn't articulate what was in his heart. He wanted to explain how he felt about her, how he thought about her every moment of every day, how he didn't know how he could live life without her, but the words wouldn't come.

Frustrated, he screwed up his first attempt and threw it away. His English wasn't up to what he wanted to say, so instead he decided to write a simple note. He told her he understood exactly why she'd done what she had and that she shouldn't blame herself. He addressed the envelope and, as he sealed it up, he felt overwhelmed with wretchedness and loss. Writing the letter had brought back so many memories. And mixed in with those was a feeling of guilt that Alice was alone, bearing all her anxieties and regrets without his presence and support.

Two days later, he was married. The ceremony passed in a blur. It felt to Anil as if it was happening to someone else, that he was hovering above himself, watching from afar.

He arrived at the temple in the centre of the bridegroom's procession, a group of friends and family walking through the streets together, bearing cakes and food, accompanied by a full brass band of trumpets and horns playing discordant but joyful traditional music. Before they'd set off, several garlands of sweet-smelling flowers had been placed around his neck and his fore-head smeared with tilaka. By the time he arrived, his future wife and her family had been at the temple for several hours praying and making offerings. As he entered the temple, well-wishers threw petals and rice at him for good luck.

He met Manjula under a canopy of flowers. She was waiting there patiently, shrouded in a red veil and bedecked with jewellery. They placed garlands around each other's necks, smeared their foreheads with more tilaka and exchanged rings. As he slipped the ring on Manjula's delicate finger, he closed his eyes and prayed their future would be a happy one.

After the ceremony, more festivities took place at the palace in Lazimpat in the beautiful front garden, which was decorated with fairly lights, bunting and colourful garlands. There seemed to be hundreds of people milling about, invited by his or Manjula's parents. All afternoon people he barely knew came and bowed before the newlyweds and presented them with gifts, congratu-

lating them heartily. By the end of the day Anil's jaw ached from
the smile he'd been forcing for hours.

He was vaguely aware of Manjula by his side throughout,
dressed in an elaborate red saree embroidered with gold, her face
covered by the filmy red veil. She was being embraced by female
relatives and congratulated by everyone. Guilt gnawed at Anil,
and he felt pity for his new wife. Unwittingly she'd married a
man whose heart belonged to someone else.

Manjula was a spirited, beautiful woman and she didn't
deserve that, but he hadn't had the heart to tell his parents he
couldn't marry her. He knew it was cowardly not to speak out, but
his father had been looking forward to this liaison with Manjula's
father and his business interests for decades. Anil couldn't let
them down. He'd already done enough damage to other people's
lives through his selfish actions. So he accepted the marriage as a
sort of penance for what he'd done in Malaya.

After the formalities were over and everyone had eaten their
fill from the banqueting table, traditional dancing to the band
took place in the garden. Anil sat beside Manjula under a silken
canopy, watching proceedings. When they got up to dance,
everyone cheered, and Anil felt the weight of his family's expectations on his shoulders. Towards the end of the day, when too
much alcohol had been drunk by all, he was hoisted onto the
shoulders of his friends and paraded around the garden to much
cheering and laughter.

When all the guests had departed and he was finally alone
with Manjula, he was suddenly overwhelmed by nerves. It was
almost night-time and in the next few hours he was expected to
take her to bed and make love to her. How could he do that with
the way he felt about Alice? The memory of her lithe, slim body,
still so fresh in his mind?

They were sitting alone in the garden beneath the fairy lights,
under the twinkling stars, the distant sounds of the city floating
in over the garden wall. Manjula pushed her veil back over her

head and he saw her face properly for the first time that day; those liquid brown eyes, her full lips, her high cheekbones. But in her eyes he sensed a nervousness too. She leaned forward and took his hand. Hers were covered in elaborate hennaed drawings from the temple.

'Do you mind very much if we don't do anything tonight?' she asked, her voice timid. 'I'm exhausted and I wouldn't want the first time to be a disaster.'

Relief washed through Anil, and he was instantly grateful for her bravery and frankness. 'Of course not. I understand,' he said. 'I'm exhausted too. Let's just go to bed and sleep, shall we?'

He took her arm, and they went up the front steps and through the entrance hall, where servants were clearing up the debris from the reception, climbed the sweeping marble staircase to their suite of rooms on the first floor, where the lighting was low and their bed was covered in petals. They undressed modestly down to their underwear and lay down side by side. Anil put his arm around Manjula and she snuggled against his body, and they went to sleep like that, like two best friends at the end of a long, exhausting day.

A few months later, Anil was on the move again. This time he was flying out to join the 51st Gurkha Infantry Brigade in Hong Kong. He said goodbye to Manjula with a pang of regret. By the third night of marriage, she had overcome her shyness, and they had made love for the first time, tentatively and tenderly. Anil was grateful Manjula was the opposite of Alice in every way, so he wasn't reminded of her.

Manjula was sad to see him go so soon into their marriage, but she was a practical soul and was already preparing to busy herself with redecorating parts of the palace and with the various charitable causes she already championed. He knew she wouldn't be lonely or bored while he was away.

He wasn't sorry to leave as his military transport plane sped down the runway at Kathmandu airport and took off over the mountains that surrounded the valley. At least he had a chance to be a soldier again, to resurrect his damaged career, to start to put the past behind him.

The flight to Hong Kong took over five hours, and when he landed he was driven in an army Land Rover straight to his barracks in Kowloon. Exhausted, he went into his spartan, soulless room and sat down on the bed.

His batman knocked on the door, came in and saluted. 'A letter came for you this morning, sir,' he said and handed him an envelope.

Anil didn't need to look at it to know it had come from Alice and, sure enough, there was a Malaya stamp on the envelope and the address written in her familiar hand.

'Thank you,' Anil said, his heart racing.

When the man had left, he opened the letter and stared at her words. As he read, and the truth became clear to him, he knew he would never be able to leave her behind.

28

CHLOE

Kathmandu, 2018

CHLOE WAS SITTING beside Rajesh in the coffee shop at Paradise Books. It was Thursday evening and the shop was winding down for the day. As usual, Rajesh had brought another batch of letters with him for them to read together. Chloe was feeling happier now, and since her chat with Rumi, far more relaxed about her relationship with Kiran. Although there was a niggle in the back of her mind; she was still waiting for more news of his trekking group from Bikram.

It was the day after she'd found the letter in the flyleaf of a book in which Alice had mysteriously apologised to Anil for everything that had happened that had resulted in him been sent home to Kathmandu. That evening, through the letters and diary entries they'd read together, Chloe and Rajesh had worked out that Alice's apology was about her taking food to a village of Chinese squatters, and that Anil had been posted back to Kathmandu as a result of her actions. It was all set out in Anil's diary.

When they'd finished reading the entry which detailed Anil's conversation with Colonel Bristow and his final meeting with Alice, Chloe looked at Rajesh. His eyes were clouded with sadness.

'What a tragic story,' she said. 'But I suppose they both knew it could never last.' She bit her lip, her mind drifting to her relationship with Kiran. Would that end in a similar way? But things were different now, she assured herself. This was the modern world, customs and expectations had moved on since the 1950s, and there was nothing to stop her and Kiran making a success of their marriage.

'Do you remember the first ever letter we found from Alice?' Rajesh asked. 'I'd like to read it again.'

He rummaged in his briefcase and produced it. 'It was the one that got us wondering – wanting to find out what happened between them.' He put it on the table between them and opened it.

Chloe remembered the thrill of discovery she'd felt when she'd first seen that envelope. Now, she picked up the letter and read it out loud again, and this time the words meant so much more to her. She could picture both Alice and Anil. She now knew what they looked like and what they had meant to each other, the depth of their love. The words had so much more poignancy, they almost brought tears to her eyes.

IT WAS SUCH a wrench to say goodbye that last day in Butterworth. I stood on the quayside watching your ship until it had completely disappeared over the horizon, not quite believing that you were gone! And I still can't believe the army sent you home before your posting was finished. It seems so unfair, especially in the light of your outstanding record.

· · ·

CHLOE COULD PICTURE them waving to each other as the ship pulled out of the harbour, both with tears in their eyes, both of their hearts breaking.

'There are several more letters here,' Rajesh said. 'They obviously kept in touch for years. I've brought them all. Here, I think this is the next in the sequence.' He handed Chloe a letter bearing Alice's handwriting and addressed to the Gurkha Barracks, Hong Kong.

Chloe opened it, and something dropped onto the floor. She picked it up and stared at it, shock flooding through her. It was a small black-and-white photograph of a tiny baby.

Wordlessly, she handed it to Rajesh. He took it and stared at it, frowning. Chloe began to read the letter.

MY DEAREST ANIL,

I HAVE MANAGED to last several months without writing to you. I wanted to give you a chance to get settled in your new life. I know by now you will be married, and I hope with all my heart it brings you joy, and that you are happy and content. I have some news that I've been debating with myself whether to tell you. I know it will come as a shock, and for that reason I've kept it to myself for months. However, I bitterly regret having kept secrets from you in the past. If I hadn't done that, who knows where we both might be now.

So, this is my news: two days ago, I gave birth to our baby, Anil my love. A beautiful baby girl. She is so gorgeous, with your eyes and features, and already I can see she has your gentle nature too. I have called her Zara because that name seems to suit her so well.

I'm not telling you this because I want anything from you, Anil. On the contrary, I didn't tell you before because I didn't want it to alter the course of the life you went home to, which you have every right to embrace to the full. It is simply because I now know the damage secrets can do and I don't want to keep the truth from you any longer.

I am staying on the Blanchard estate with Diana and Tony, and Zara was born here in their house. They have been the very model of kindness and discretion, and I owe them so much. However, I can't stay here for ever. A permanent manager has now been found for the tin mine, and the company want him to be able to live in the house. They were really very generous letting me stay on there so long.

I will be moving to Kuala Lumpur in a month or so. I need to make a life for myself and Zara there. I have experience as a secretary from my time in Barrackpur during the war, and United Tin have offered me a job in their headquarters in KL. Living on a tin mine for all these years must have given me some sort of insight into the industry! With the money Bruce left me and the compensation from the government, I will be able to buy a small apartment in KL and employ an amah for Zara.

CHLOE LOOKED up from the letter. Rajesh was sitting beside her looking dumbstruck, a smile slowly spreading from cheek to cheek.

'I have a sister,' he said slowly, shaking his head in amazement. 'If she was born in 1950, she will be a year or so older than me. I can hardly believe it. I wonder where she is now?'

'It's incredible, Rajesh. Who'd have thought we'd discover something like this when we started reading these letters?'

Rajesh was silent, deep in thought, then he said, 'That is what Pa's will must be all about. He wanted to make some sort of provision for her... for Zara. But why on earth didn't he tell me about her and how to contact her? I need to find her, Chloe, wherever she is. I wonder if she knows anything at all about me?'

'Shall we go through the rest of the letters?' Chloe asked. 'There are only a few more. Shall I open them?'

'Yes, go ahead. In date order, as we have been doing.'

The next letter was from a few months later. Chloe opened the envelope to find a tiny silk embroidered baby's bootie inside. She handed it to Rajesh who took it gently and stared at it as if mesmerised, tears in his eyes.

MY DEAREST ANIL,

IT IS SO wonderful to know that you are coming to KL for a short visit. I can't wait to see you and to introduce Zara to you. In the meantime, here is a little keepsake. Of course, she has grown out of the booties now. She is growing so quickly!

THEN ANOTHER. A year or so later.

MY DEAREST ANIL,

I HOPE YOU ARE WELL. As soon as you left the last time, my heart ached to see you again. I know you are posted to Indonesia now, and that things there are dangerous. Please take care of yourself. I always worry about you, as you know. It is wonderful news that your wife is expecting. I hope your baby brings you as much joy as Zara has brought me.

THEN CAME a few more scribbled notes, showing that they had written to each other every few months for several years, exchanging news, much of it about Zara and baby Rajesh. It was obvious from this correspondence that Alice was excelling at her job. In the three years spanned by the final letters, she worked her way up from secretary to shipping clerk, then to manager of a

section of the company. She was clearly enjoying life in Kuala
Lumpur. The Emergency was not over, but the CTs had been
severely weakened by that time and, through her letters, Alice
told that her life in KL was far more interesting than being buried
away on Rimba Valley Estate. It was also clear from the correspondence that Anil made several visits to Alice and Zara while
the little girl was tiny, his last visit taking place in 1954.

Then, Chloe opened a letter dated September 1955.

MY DEAREST ANIL,

*I WANT you to know that I'm going away from KL for a few months.
I've taken a leave of absence from the company. My father is very sick
and only has weeks to live, so I'm returning to Barrackpur to be with
him in his final days. I intend to stay on there to sell the house and
wind up his affairs.*

THERE WERE NO MORE letters for several months, then, in early
1956 came the final blow.

MY DEAREST ANIL,

*MY FATHER DIED a couple of months ago and I'm now back in Kuala
Lumpur for a short stay and to sell my apartment here. It is well over a
year since we last saw each other, although it seems far longer.*

*There is no easy way to say this, dear Anil, but I think now is a
good time to tell you that I'm going to remarry. It is an old friend I got
to know again in Barrackpur. He is Vikram, the brother of my childhood friend, Jamila. We have known each other since we were small,*

and he is now a lawyer with a well-established practice in Barrackpur. He helped me a great deal with the sale of Father's house and the arrangements for his funeral. He is a good man, Anil. He loves Zara and she loves him too.

It breaks my heart to say this, but I don't think we should write to each other again. I need to make a go of my new life, and you need to forget all about us and embrace your life in Kathmandu with your own family.

You will always have a special place in my heart, Anil. You saved my life in more ways than one.

Your ever loving,

Alice

CHLOE PUT down the letter and checked her phone, which had buzzed while she was reading. It was a text message from Bikram.

No CAUSE FOR IMMEDIATE ALARM, but Kiran's group didn't check in to Namche Bazaar yesterday. They may have stayed elsewhere en route. I'm doing my best to find out.

29

WITH SHAKING HANDS, Chloe tapped Bikram's number into her phone. He answered straight away, and she could tell from the sound of his voice he was rattled.

'Chloe. Thank you for calling.'

'Have you heard anything?' she asked.

'I'm sorry to say that Kiran and his group didn't report into the next lodge on their route.'

'My God, Bikram. What does that mean?' His words were like a stomach punch.

'The lodge owners say there's bad weather on the trail, but... well, most of the trekking groups made it to their destination that evening. Unfortunately, Kiran's group didn't. But I wouldn't worry unduly. Kiran is bound to be in touch as soon as he can get somewhere where there's a phone signal.'

'Isn't there anything we can do?' she asked, feeling helpless. She couldn't bear the thought of Kiran and his group shivering in the snow, injured, or lost and alone somewhere on that remote, pitiless mountain.

'Not at the moment, Chloe. In all likelihood they'll have

found somewhere safe to stay, and they'll be back in touch as soon as they can. We need to sit tight. I just thought you should know.'

'Thank you, Bikram. But please let me know as soon as you hear anything. Whatever time it is.'

'Of course I will. Take care, Chloe.'

She rang off, then realised Rajesh was watching her, his forehead puckered with concern.

'Has something happened?' he asked.

Chloe fought back tears. 'It's Kiran. Bikram thinks he might be lost somewhere on the Everest trail.'

'Is he sure?'

She shook her head miserably. 'No, but Kiran hasn't been in touch today and the group didn't go to the lodge they'd booked last night.'

'Oh, Chloe, I'm so sorry. But try not to worry. Kiran is an experienced guide. He's unlikely to let his group get into trouble.'

'I know,' she said, biting her nail. It was true, but it didn't make the terrible uncertainty any easier to bear. She wiped away a tear.

Rajesh gave her a warm hug. 'I know it's hard, my dear, but you have to be positive,' he said. 'You must believe in Kiran. He'll get out of this.'

She smiled at him, grateful for his kind words, but at the same time wishing she had his optimism. 'I'd better lock up now, Rajesh,' she said. 'It's way past my normal closing time.'

'And I'd better leave you in peace,' Rajesh replied, picking up his briefcase and moving towards the door. 'As I said, please don't worry, Chloe. And, remember, if you need anything, I'm just a phone call away.'

'Thank you,' she said, 'I appreciate that.'

'And thank you,' he replied with a warm smile, 'for helping me discover I have a sister somewhere!'

After putting up the 'closed' sign and bolting the door, Chloe went through to the kitchen and fed the cats, who seemed oddly jumpy and nervous. They hung back and didn't rub themselves against her legs as they normally did. She knew they were sensitive to the moods of those around them; perhaps they could tell something was wrong.

Passing the fortune-telling machine on the way out, she paused. What would it tell her, she wondered, if she put a coin in the slot right now? But the very thought made her skin prickle. Not wanting to tempt fate, she hurriedly left the shop and pulled the metal shutters down over the front.

SHE SPENT YET another restless night thinking about Kiran. Her mind went into overdrive, imagining the worst; that he had slipped and fallen off the trail, that he was trapped between two rocks, that he was injured, unable to move, unable to make anyone hear him. Or, even worse, that he'd suffered another blow to the head and was lying somewhere, concussed. She recalled when he was unconscious in hospital after the earthquake, covered in tubes, surrounded by machines. Try as she might, these images refused to abate and she twisted and turned all night, only drifting off in the small hours.

As soon as she awoke, she called Rumi.

'Is everything alright?' Rumi asked as soon as she heard Chloe's voice. 'Only, I've been having these strange feelings.'

Chloe gasped. If Rumi could feel it with her twin's intuition, something terrible must have happened to Kiran.

'Kiran and his group have gone missing,' she said, her voice breaking. 'They didn't check into their lodge yesterday. There's bad weather up there on the trail, apparently...'

'Oh no! I knew there was something,' Rumi said. 'I'll get on the next bus to Kathmandu. I'll be with you this evening.'

'Are you sure? What about the guest house?'

'Ammah and Baba can manage for a few days.'

'Don't tell them anything, will you, Rumi?' Chloe asked. 'I wouldn't want them to worry.'

'Of course not. I'll text you when I arrive. See you later, Chloe.'

Relieved to know Rumi was on her way, Chloe forced herself to get dressed, then, without eating, left the flat and walked through the half-empty streets to the shop. Shova arrived shortly after she'd opened up, and later Auntie Gita bustled in with her shopping bags and her bright, cheerful manner. Chloe didn't want to worry the old lady, so kept the news about Kiran to herself.

The hours dragged. Chloe found herself clock-watching and checking her phone continually for messages from Bikram. She was plagued with the same worries that had kept her awake all night and she found it difficult to concentrate on anything. At lunchtime, Gita made Tibetan momos, which smelled delicious, but Chloe could only pick at them and eventually returned the half-empty plate guiltily. Gita looked at her with concern in her kind eyes but said nothing.

At five o'clock, Rumi sent a text to say her bus had just arrived at Gongabu terminus in northern Kathmandu and she was getting a taxi to Chloe's flat. Leaving Shova in charge, Chloe hurried home, glad for once to be away from the shop. She'd found pretending to be cheerful too much to bear.

She hadn't been home long when Rumi knocked on the door. When Chloe opened it, her sister-in-law's eyes were full of sympathy. They flung their arms around one another and hugged for a long time, and Chloe let the tears that had been building all day, finally fall. Rumi had tears in her eyes too.

'Come on in,' she said to Rumi when she'd recovered enough to speak.

Chloe made tea and they sat down, side by side on the settee.

'Have you had any more news?' Rumi asked.

Chloe shook her head. 'Bikram would have texted if he'd heard anything. He promised he would. He sounded hopeful when I spoke to him, but...'

'Have they sent a helicopter to search for them?' Rumi asked.

'Not yet. They still think they'll turn up. Maybe they'll send one tomorrow if there's still no news...' she said, twisting her wedding ring absently.

Rumi put her hand on Chloe's. 'You know, Bikram has a good instinct for these things,' she said. 'He knows the conditions and the trail. And he knows Kiran better than anyone.'

'Yes, I know. It's just that waiting is agony,' Chloe said. 'Especially as...'

Rumi was watching her with questioning eyes now. 'As?' she asked.

'Well, as I said on the phone the other day, things weren't great between us when he left,' she said. 'I keep thinking... if something happens to him, I'll never have a chance to tell him I'm sorry, to make things right between us.'

'But you will have a chance, Chloe. Kiran will come back, and you'll be able to talk to him.'

'I hope so. I've been so obstinate, Rumi. I overreacted when I discovered he'd talked to you about coming to help out at the shop. I felt betrayed. I suppose it's because I don't understand families very well.'

'Nepalese families in particular can be a minefield to navigate.' Rumi smiled. 'And Kiran and I are twins. It must be so difficult for you sometimes. I'm very sorry we made you feel that way.'

'I was cross with Kiran, not you. And now we've spoken about it, I understand he was only trying to help. I've made such a mess of things.'

She felt Rumi's arm around her shoulder then, drawing her close.

'No, you haven't. You've been very brave, and strong. You've given up your whole life to move halfway across the world to make a life with Kiran. It must be very hard.'

Chloe drew a shaky breath. 'Sometimes I think we're doomed to fail. That our backgrounds and cultures are so different we'll never be able to make a success of things.'

'Why do you say that?' Rumi asked.

'Your distant cousin, Rajesh Desai, came to me after his father's death and asked me to take some second-hand books from his home. When I went through them, we discovered some letters written by a British woman in the late 1940s and 50s, to his father, Anil. He'd been stationed in Malaya and she lived on a mining estate there. It was clear from the letters they became lovers.'

'That's amazing! I'd never have thought it of Uncle Anil.'

'I know. Rajesh was stunned too. But, Rumi, right from the start, they both knew there was no future in their relationship. They were well aware the difference in their situations and nationalities meant they could never marry and be accepted by society. And in the end, when their relationship was discovered, he was sent back to Kathmandu in disgrace.'

'How very sad,' Rumi said. 'Poor Uncle Anil.'

'I can't help thinking that perhaps mine and Kiran's relationship is doomed in the same way. That no matter how hard we try, the odds are stacked against us succeeding. That our cultures and backgrounds are just too different for it ever to work.'

'Chloe, you mustn't think like that. You and Kiran are worlds apart from that situation. The world has changed a great deal since the 1950s. You're not living in a stuffy colonial outpost, and you and Kiran are both modern people, educated and free-thinking.'

'But Kiran is traditional in his own way, you have to admit. Or he wouldn't want me to give up my business to concentrate on having a baby.'

Rumi smiled. 'Nepalese society *is* quite traditional in some ways, I suppose, and all Nepalese men have a streak of that tradition in their veins. Some of that will have rubbed off on Kiran. But he's open-minded enough to understand about your hopes and dreams. When he gets home, talk to him again. I'm sure you will be able to work things out between you.'

'I want to talk to him, Rumi. I'm desperate to talk to him. I'm so worried he won't come back.'

'You must have faith in him, Chloe. He'll come back to you. You'll see.'

Chloe smiled at her sister-in-law. A warm feeling crept over her. She felt genuinely loved and accepted by Kiran's family as she never had before. She couldn't believe how much she'd overreacted when Rumi had offered her help before. She bit her nail, remembering some of the harsh things she'd said in the heat of the moment to Kiran, regretting them bitterly.

THEY WAITED all evening for Bikram to get in touch, but it wasn't until dawn the next morning that he finally texted Chloe. She heard the text come in and grabbed her phone, pulling herself out of a deep sleep to look at it.

GOOD NEWS FINALLY! *Give me a call when you get this.*

SHE DIALLED his number straight away.

'Bikram, it's Chloe.'

'I've heard from one of the lodge owners in Namche Bazaar. He texted me to say Kiran and his group have turned up there. They were delayed by a snow storm, and had to hole up in a tiny lodge for two days, riding it out. There was no phone signal there, but the weather was so bad they couldn't move.'

'Thank God,' Chloe said, relief washing through her.

'I need to get back to them to see if I can actually speak to Kiran now. I'll call later,' Bikram said.

Chloe leapt out of bed and ran through to the living room where Rumi was asleep on the settee. 'Rumi! Rumi! Wake up! Kiran is safe!'

Rumi pushed back the covers and rubbed her eyes. 'Thank goodness. What a relief!'

They celebrated by having a big breakfast. Scrambled eggs on toast and orange juice, papaya and mango. Chloe ate hungrily, realising she'd been so wound up about Kiran, she hadn't eaten properly for days.

After breakfast, Rumi said, 'I should be getting back to Pokhara. Ammah and Baba probably need my help by now. It's high season after all.'

'Don't you want to stay and see Kiran?' Chloe asked.

Rumi shook her head. 'I think you and Kiran need some time alone. I can see him another time. Just to know he's safe is enough for me.'

Before Rumi left, Chloe hugged her tight and thanked her for coming all that way, and for listening to her.

'Why wouldn't I do that? We are family after all,' Rumi said, before picking up her bags and leaving.

Immediately after Bikram called.

'Chloe! I thought I'd let you know I'm flying to Lukla this morning to meet Kiran and his group. I was wondering if you'd like to come.'

'Lukla?' She paused and her heart began to speed up. Lukla was high in the Himalayas, the jumping-off point for the Everest Base Camp trek. She'd heard the flight through the mountains to get there was a white-knuckle ride, but if she did brave it and go along with Bikram, it would mean she would get to see Kiran that afternoon.

'Yes,' she said. 'I'll come. Shall I meet you at the airport?'

'No, I'll book you a ticket and if you come round to the office, we can go there together. Can you be here by ten?'

'Of course.'

CHLOE COULDN'T STOP her stomach fluttering with nerves as she took her seat beside Bikram on the small propeller plane that was bound for Lukla.

'Why don't you sit by the window,' Bikram offered. 'The views are magnificent.'

It wasn't long before all the passengers were on board. There were only fourteen of them, all the others western trekkers and their Nepalese guides, chatting and laughing, clearly excited about this journey into the heart of the Himalayas.

The plane hurtled down the runway and with a soft bump was airborne and rising rapidly over the city. Chloe looked down over the crowded buildings; the houses, apartment blocks, temples and shanty towns that made up this huge metropolis. She wondered where Thamel was, but couldn't make it out in the confusing tangle of streets below.

Soon they had left the city behind and were flying over the wooded mountains that encircled the Kathmandu valley. Chloe gasped at her first sight of the high Himalayas up ahead; a long, wall of jagged, snow-capped peaks that seemed to float on the horizon, glowing white in the cobalt sky. They flew on into the blue towards the high peaks, over cloud-filled valleys and more darkly wooded foothills, zigzagged with pale roads and paths.

Bikram pointed out some of the distinctive peaks to her, those that rose above their neighbours. 'There's Mount Ganesh Himal, there's Shishapangma, there's Mount Gauri Shankar.'

She smiled at him. 'It's incredible, Bikram.' Her fear had dissolved, replaced with incredulity at the fabulous scenery.

Soon there came the most magnificent view of them all.

'There's Mount Everest,' he said. 'Or Sagarmatha as we Nepalese call it.'

In twenty minutes or so they were descending; down through the bumpy cloud cover towards the granite foothills, seeming to skim the treetops and rocks as they cleared the forested hills. Chloe held her breath and remembered an entry from her grandmother's diary. Lena had written about a flight from Kathmandu to Darjeeling where they'd flown so close to the rocky mountains she was able to make out the striations in the granite.

Now, between wispy clouds, Chloe could see stepped rice terraces, the roofs of village houses, a waterfall plunging through a forest, a rope suspension bridge dangling over it precariously. Then they were flying over a steep river valley and passing more huts and houses, then with another bump and a screech of tyres they were on the tarmac and she could hear the rush of the reverse thrust as she was thrown forward in her seat as the little plane braked sharply on the short runway.

There were no formalities at the tiny airport, so they were soon on their way, trekking through the narrow alleys of Lukla, between the guest houses and hotels, alongside trekkers with their walking poles and backpacks, passing mule and buffalo trains carrying supplies to villages higher up on the trail. They passed rows of colourful prayer wheels and walked under lines of prayer flags. Then they passed under the final arch that marked the edge of Lukla, welcoming those entering the town from the other direction.

Once out of the town, they followed the trail which descended the side of a valley down a flight of steep stone steps, and walked along the valley bottom, criss-crossing the river on flimsy suspension bridges. Sometimes they were accompanied by village dogs, sometimes they walked alone, past farms and cottages, lodges and teahouses.

Chloe was reminded powerfully of the trek she and Kiran had done together in search of her grandmother's past. They'd been following in the footsteps of her grandparents, who'd trekked into the hills behind Pokhara to recruit Gurkha soldiers for the Burma campaign during the Second World War. On that trail, she and Kiran had grown close, and she'd been struck by the beauty of the landscape and the friendliness and hospitality of the villagers, who had so little and were yet so generous. She must go trekking with him again, she realised, their shared love of the hills always brought them close.

After about three hours, the village of Phakding finally came into view; a group of teahouses and lodges straddling a steep river valley with a monastery on the hill behind. Chloe's heart beat faster. It was here that they would meet up with Kiran and his group.

'Where have you arranged to meet them?' she asked.

'They'll be waiting at the teahouse,' Bikram said.

They walked on between the buildings, along the narrow stone alleys of the little settlement, then there was only one more suspension bridge to cross.

As she put her foot on the bridge, she noticed someone else step onto it at the other end and as she walked across the swinging, creaking structure, her heart sped up. It was Kiran coming towards her, smiling broadly.

She couldn't run, it was impossible to do so on these bridges, and it was agony, having to walk slowly. But she kept going, and at last there were only a few steps to go.

'Kiran!' She rushed into his open arms, tears running down her cheeks as he hugged her.

'Chloe.' He kissed her hair, her face.

'I'm so sorry,' she said. 'I was so worried about you. I felt so guilty about some of the things I said before you went.'

'I'm sorry too,' he said. 'When we were stranded in that lodge, all I could think of was you and how unreasonable I'd been towards you. I couldn't wait to get back to you to say sorry.'

They kissed then, a long, tender kiss. She was aware Bikram must be somewhere behind her and that Kiran's group might arrive at any moment, but none of that seemed to matter. All that mattered was that Kiran was here with her and that things were going to be alright between them.

30

A FEW WEEKS LATER, Chloe was about to close Paradise Books one evening when she spotted someone hurrying through the alleyway towards the shop. Her heart sank. She'd been looking forward to getting home early and spending a quiet evening in with Kiran over a pizza and a bottle of wine. He was arriving home from another trek that day and she couldn't wait to see him.

Things were good between them again; as good as they'd ever been. On their return from Lukla, they'd talked openly about their disagreement. Kiran had apologised for trying to railroad Chloe into stepping back from her business. He'd agreed they should wait until she decided the time was right.

'It's your decision, Chloe. I know that now, and I respect that,' he'd told her. 'I was wrong to push you and I'm deeply sorry.'

They'd rekindled their early love, and Chloe felt about him just as she had when she'd first met him; she already had butterflies in her stomach at the thought of seeing him again that evening.

So it was with a sigh that she waited in the doorway for the latecomer, but as he got closer, she realised it was Rajesh. She opened the door for him, and he rushed up the steps and into the shop, looking as dishevelled as ever, but brimming with excitement.

'Chloe. I've got some fantastic news!' he said breathlessly. His face was red from running and he was brandishing a letter.

Chloe stared at him wordlessly, hoping the letter was from whom she guessed it might be.

As soon as she and Kiran had come back from Lukla and things had settled down, Rajesh had asked her to help him track down his half-sister, Zara.

'You're probably better at internet research than I am,' he'd said. 'After all, didn't you manage to find out all about your grandmother's mysterious past?'

'Yes, that's true,' she'd said slowly, 'but that was mainly from her diaries that an old friend of hers gave me after her death, and from visiting the places she'd lived. I'm not sure the internet figured that much in my research to be honest.'

'Oh, but still. You're young, Chloe. You're far more familiar with technology than I am.'

She'd smiled. 'You don't have to persuade me, Rajesh. I'd be happy to help you. Honoured, in fact,' she'd told him, and she'd set to work that very day to try to track down the man Alice had married when Zara was a little girl. She was sure that would eventually lead them to Zara herself.

But it wasn't the internet she turned to at first, it was Alice's letters. From reading them again, she discovered that Alice's childhood friend, Jamila's, surname was Bannerjee, and, knowing that Alice's second husband was called Vikram, and that he'd been a lawyer in the 1950s, she turned to the internet and looked up all the law firms in Barrackpur, and scanned the lists of partners and consultants. Of course, Vikram was likely to be long retired, if he was even still alive, but some of the firms had included a page about their histories on their websites.

Her heart pounded when she found the history page of website for a firm called Ghosh, Bannerjee and Partners.

THE FIRM WAS FOUNDED in 1950 by two friends, Raj Ghosh and Vikram Bannerjee, who specialised in property transactions. From those humble beginnings, the firm blossomed and grew into the multi-partner practice it is today, with a raft of prestigious clients from near and far, both commercial and private.

RAJESH HAD GIVEN his lawyers the information, and they'd contacted Bannerjee and Partners in Barrackpur, saying they were administering the will of Major Anil Desai from Kathmandu, and needed to get in touch with Miss Zara Bannerjee, the daughter of one of Ghosh and Bannerjees' founding partners, whom they thought might be one of his benefactors. Bannerjee and Partners had got back to Rajesh's lawyers the very next day, saying they'd been in touch with their client, Zara Bannerjee, and that she could be contacted at an address in Darjeeling.

In the meantime, Chloe had done some more digging in online public archives and discovered that Alice and Vikram had married in Barrackpur in 1956 and that Vikram had formally adopted Zara shortly after that.

Rajesh wrote to Zara at the address in Darjeeling, saying he thought they were related. He told her she had been remembered in his father's will, and asked if he could visit her. He'd held back from breaking the momentous news that he was her half-brother in the letter.

'It would be a huge shock, hearing that out of the blue from a stranger. She might not believe it,' he'd told Chloe. 'It would be far better to do it in person I think.'

So, now standing there in the shop, holding the letter from Zara, he showed it to Chloe.

. . .

MY DEAR RAJESH,

How wonderful to hear from you, and it's fascinating to know that we might be related. I was intrigued when my lawyers got in touch and told me you were looking for me. I've always wondered about my true family. My mother never told me who my father was; she simply said he was a good, brave man. I always thought of my father as Vikram Bannerjee, who was wonderful. But since my parents both passed away, within the last couple of years, I've started to think more about my real family, and then your letter came out of the blue.

You didn't say directly, but could Anil Desai possibly have been my father? I live in hope that he was, and would love to welcome you to Darjeeling, although I live very simply here, I have to tell you, and don't have space for visitors. But there are many excellent hotels in the town.

I'm looking forward to meeting you and to hearing from you very soon.

Yours,

Zara

CHLOE FINISHED READING and looked up at Rajesh. 'That's amazing! Darjeeling. That's where my grandmother grew up, met my grandfather and where they got married.'

'Do you know it? I've never been there myself. Why don't you come with me?' Rajesh asked.

'I'd love that,' Chloe answered. 'Perhaps Kiran could come too. We've never been there together, although I know he used to take tour groups there sometimes. That's how we met.'

'Oh really? I didn't know that.'

'Yes, on the bus from the Indian–Nepalese border to Kathmandu. He saved me from an unscrupulous rickshaw driver, actually.' Chloe smiled thinking back, but then pulled herself up.

'But, Rajesh, this is your journey. You might not want others along with you.'

'Nonsense, Chloe. You've been so much a part of this, it would be wonderful to have you along. And Kiran too. I'd love to spend some time with him. We've all been far too busy lately.'

A WEEK LATER, the three of them boarded a plane from Kathmandu to Bagdogra, a town nestled in the plains beneath the Darjeeling hills. Kiran had managed to get a few days off between treks, and Rumi had come from Pokhara to manage the shop for Chloe.

When they landed at Bagdogra they hired a taxi to take them up to Darjeeling. The car strained up the hills, struggling round the interminable bends, which switched back and forth up the steep mountainside through forests and tea plantations. At one point they stopped at a level crossing to let the Toy Train to Darjeeling puff past in clouds of white smoke and steam, amid a fanfare of whistling and tooting.

'I came up on that train the first time I visited,' Chloe said wistfully.

'But it takes seven hours,' Kiran said with an incredulous smile.

'It was worth it though, Kiran. It's how my grandmother would have travelled in the 1940s, and I really wanted to see what it was like.'

A couple of hours later they arrived in the little town of Darjeeling, that spilled up and down the steep hills against the stunning backdrop of the snowy peaks of Kanchenjunga. As they drove through the colourful streets, full of painted wooden buildings, with shops and stalls overflowing onto the pavements, her previous trip and everything she'd discovered on it came back to Chloe with a rush. The place felt so familiar now she knew all about her grandmother growing up here. Lena had been sent by her father to a harsh boarding school for the Eurasian daughters of British officers, but her mother, a determined Indian woman from Calcutta, had moved up to live close by, to be on hand to support her daughter through those difficult days. It was where Chloe's grandparents had met, on an army base in the hills, and where her grandmother had got to know a British soldier, whom she'd followed on a fateful trip to the front in Burma.

'You look miles away,' Kiran said, squeezing her hand. 'Are you thinking about your grandmother?'

She nodded. 'Coming here has brought it all back,' she said.

They arrived at the Elgin Hotel on the edge of town, where Chloe had stayed on her first visit. After they'd checked in and had a welcome pot of Darjeeling tea, Rajesh said, 'I think it's time to go and look up Zara.'

'Where does she live?' Kiran asked.

Rajesh pored over her letter and his map of the town. 'She actually lives in Lebong,' he said, 'which is a ten-minute drive back along the road we came in on. Her street seems to be inside some sort of complex... ' he peered more closely at the map, then looked up. '*The Tibetan Refugee Centre*... Gosh. I hadn't really noticed that before.'

'Shall we get reception to call us a taxi?' Chloe asked. 'And are you sure you want me to come along?'

'Of course,' Rajesh said. 'I told you before. It was you who first found Alice's letters and it was you who finally tracked Zara down. Without you, none of this would ever have happened.'

'If you're sure...'

They'd already discussed their visit to Zara and although Rajesh had also invited Kiran, he had tactfully bowed out. He had a friend in the town, another tour guide with whom he'd been in touch lately, and was going to spend the afternoon with.

The taxi retraced their previous journey along the road that skirted the side of the mountain and ran along the railway, with yet more fabulous views over the hills which stretched towards Kanchenjunga. In the village of Lebong, they finally turned off the road and into a courtyard, surrounded on all sides by two-storey wooden houses with carved doors and windows.

They got out of the taxi and went into a shop which sold Tibetan crafts and clothing. The shelves were crammed with colourful fabrics and quirky artefacts. Rajesh asked the woman behind the counter if she knew Zara Bannerjee.

Her face lit up. 'It's me!' she said. 'You must be Rajesh, and Chloe too. How wonderful to meet you. Come, let's go to my rooms.' She spoke quickly to the other woman serving in the shop, then came round from behind the counter to join them, kissing them each effusively on both cheeks.

As soon as Chloe saw Zara's face close up, she was reminded of the portrait of Alice – the shape of her eyes and face, and there were hints of Rajesh there too. Zara was tiny; slim and dark with twinkling brown eyes, and she moved impulsively with quick, emphatic movements. She was dressed in a colourful Tibetan skirt and blouse, with a woven red shawl pulled around her shoulders.

They followed her out of the shop and along an alleyway that led between wooden buildings, workshops and houses, until they reached a staircase. Zara beckoned them to follow, and they arrived on an upper floor where she showed them into a bright living room, furnished simply with wooden pieces covered with colourful throws. There was a magnificent view of the mountains from the front window. Zara asked them to take a seat and brewed them jasmine tea at a galley kitchen in the corner of the room.

'I can't thank you enough for coming,' she said, handing them cups of tea and sitting down between them. 'I couldn't believe it when your letter arrived, Rajesh. So, please, do tell me, do you think Anil Desai is my father?'

'Yes,' Rajesh said. 'I'm sure of it. I brought your mother's letter telling him about your birth to prove it.'

'Really?'

Rajesh leaned forward and, with trembling hands, gave her a yellowing envelope. She pulled out the letter, opened it up, then bowed her head and read. When she looked up, there were tears in her eyes.

'That's amazing, Rajesh. Thank you so much for bringing it to me.'

'We have Chloe to thank for that,' Rajesh said, nodding in her direction. 'Chloe is married to a distant cousin of mine. And she runs a second-hand bookshop in Kathmandu. She discovered your mother's letters to my... *our* father, when we were collecting books from his home after his death.'

Zara hung her head. 'It's so sad I never met him, but Ma was obviously determined to keep him a secret. I treated Vikram as my father for years, in fact she didn't tell me he wasn't my father until I was a teenager. He was a lovely man. It all worked out very well, but once I knew, there was always this question in my mind about my true parentage.'

'When Alice married Vikram, she asked my father not to write to her anymore. It was then that she moved back to Barrackpur, I think,' said Rajesh.

They both fell silent for a while then Zara spoke.

'I understand why she did that, but I'm glad we've finally found each other. What was he like, my father?' she asked.

'He was a wonderful man. Kind, honourable, strong and intelligent. I suppose first and foremost he was a soldier. A brave soldier at that, who served with distinction in the Second World War and in many conflicts around the world. I will show you his diary, which I brought with me. He saved your mother's life on more than one occasion.'

'I would love to read it,' Zara replied.

'And you know, he wasn't afraid to speak out. He would stand up to his superiors against injustice, even if it might not always have been good for his career.'

Zara smiled. 'That must be where I get my stubborn streak from,' she said.

'And your love of the Himalayas!' Rajesh replied.

'How did you come to be living in Darjeeling?' Chloe asked.

'We used to come here for holidays from Barrackpur,' Zara replied. 'Ma, Pa and me. I didn't know why, exactly, but something drew me to the mountains. Now I'm beginning to realise that the Himalayas are in my blood.

'I qualified as a teacher in Kolkata, and when I saw an advertisement for a primary school teacher in the Tibetan Refugee Centre here, I jumped at it. I retired from teaching a few years ago, and now I help out in the shop sometimes. This is my home. I love the people, and I love the place too.'

'Perhaps you'll come and visit us in Kathmandu sometime?' Rajesh asked. 'I'd love to welcome you there. And you'd be able to see your inheritance before it's sold.'

'Really?' Zara asked, wide-eyed.

Rajesh nodded. 'My father owned a former Rana palace. He left it jointly to his *children*, which is why it became really important to find you.'

'That's incredible,' Zara replied. 'I had no idea about a palace.'

'It's all in his diary. Would you like to see it now? I've brought that, and all Alice's letters to show you,' Rajesh said.

Zara nodded.

Chloe cleared her throat and stood up. 'Why don't I leave you two to talk? I'll get a taxi back to Darjeeling and wait for Kiran at the hotel. Perhaps we could all meet up later for dinner?'

'Oh yes,' Zara said instantly. 'That would be wonderful. I know a fabulous café in the town that makes the best Tibetan momos ever.'

THE LIGHT WAS FADING as Chloe and Kiran walked hand in hand up a winding path towards the Mahakal temple on top of Observatory Hill. They ducked under lines of prayer flags and turned each prayer wheel as they climbed.

'I came up here on my first visit,' Chloe said. 'It's a magical place, especially at this time of day.'

They were each carrying lotus flowers and candles they'd bought at a stall on Chowrasta Square for offerings at a temple. When they neared the top, they sat down on a bench, overlooking the mountains, while the setting sun streaked the sky with pink and orange light.

'This is where my grandfather proposed to my grandmother,' Chloe said. 'It could even have been on this very bench.'

Kiran put his arm around her shoulders, pulled her to him and kissed her hair. 'If I hadn't already, I would propose to you, Chloe,' he said.

They both laughed.

'We could renew our vows,' she suggested.

'That's a beautiful idea,' he said, kissing her gently.

They sat in silence for a while, watching the sky lose its colour and the scattered pinpricks of white light emerge from the darkness in the valley below them. When dusk finally enveloped the mountain, they got up from the bench and walked, their arms entwined, lit by fairy lights and drawn by the chanting of the monks and clanging of discordant bells, to the temple on top of the hill.

There, at Mahakal temple, where Buddhists and Hindus worshipped side by side, they turned the prayer wheels, then lit their candles and knelt before a golden statue of the Buddha, placing their lotus flowers on the altar in front of it.

As they knelt, Chloe smiled. Alice and Anil suddenly came into her mind, and she remembered how Alice had told him in a letter that he'd saved her life in more ways than one. It made her think of something the monk had said at her wedding.

She leaned towards Kiran and spoke the words softly to him, 'In true love, you attain freedom.'

And as they walked out of the temple, hand in hand, into the soft, dark night, she knew this journey represented a new beginning for both of them.

EPILOGUE
CHLOE

Kathmandu, 2018

A MONTH or so after that momentous visit to Darjeeling, Chloe was closing up the shop one evening. It was a Friday, and she was doing her usual round of putting books back on the shelves, checking everything was tidy and shipshape, and feeding the cats. She was thinking about Alice and Anil again. They were never far from her thoughts, even though it was over two months since she and Rajesh had first discovered their letters.

She wandered past the framed photographs of Anil and Alice, which hung side by side, next to another of Rajesh and Zara, smiling together, taken in Darjeeling on their recent visit. Zara was due in Kathmandu that very weekend to see the Rana palace before it was sold. Chloe was looking forward to seeing her and getting to know her better.

Rajesh had given Chloe a badge from Anil's Gurkha uniform, which she'd had framed. She'd been meaning to hang it that day, but the shop had been busy, and it was only now that she had the time. She took it upstairs and hung it in the section of the shop which sold books about the Gurkhas, alongside a photograph of her grandparents' wedding. Her grandfather, Charles Harper, had been a recruiting officer for the Gurkhas during the Second World War, and her grandmother, Lena, was his assistant and travelled by pony with him into the mountains. Chloe smiled at them. Charles looked proud and handsome in his uniform, and Lena looked beautiful standing beside him in a lacy white dress, bursting with happiness.

'Goodnight, Gran,' she said, touching the image of her grandmother.

Then she headed to the fortune-telling machine for her usual end of the week ritual. She dropped the coin in the slot and the fortune teller turned its mechanical head to stare at her. That always sent a shiver down Chloe's spine; it looked so lifelike. The puppet waved a hand, gave a nod, and the machine clicked and whirred into action before a piece of card dropped out of the slot underneath. She'd read all the cards before, of course. She had to replenish them every now and then, so she knew all the prophesies, or at least she thought she did.

She picked up the card and read it, the two cats looking on, both of them strangely curious. It was the same one she'd read a couple of months before and she stared at it, trying to work out its meaning.

THE SEED of yesterday is the fruit of tomorrow.

HER HAND automatically went to stroke her belly, and another shiver went through her as the realisation hit her.

'Oh my God,' she said, knowing unequivocally that it was true. She was expecting her first baby, and she realised with a chill that she must have already been pregnant when she'd first read the words two months ago. 'Thank you,' she said with a bow of the head to the puppet behind the glass.

As she pulled down the shutters, eager to get home and tell Kiran about the strange coincidence, the monk's words from their wedding came back to her once more: *In true love, you attain freedom.*

With one hand on her swelling belly, she hurried through the streets unable to stop smiling. She felt that freedom more than ever. Freedom to live life to the full, to love and be loved. And for the sake of Kiran and their child, she vowed there and then to grasp life with both hands.

ACKNOWLEDGEMENTS AND AUTHOR'S NOTE

As I mentioned in the acknowledgements to *The Fortune Teller of Kathmandu* I was inspired to write about Nepal when I first visited as a backpacker in 1987, but it has taken me a long time to do so. I so enjoyed writing that book, that I decided to write another one set partly in Kathmandu, and to follow Chloe's life for a little longer.

I've long been fascinated by the Gurkhas, living close to their HQ in the UK, and wanted to research more of their history. To discover more about their role in the Malayan Emergency, I visited the reading room at the Gurkha Museum in Winchester, a fascinating place, and read a couple of Regimental histories, including *The Steadfast Gurkha, The Historical Record of the 6th Queen Elizabeth's own Gurkha Rifles* by Charles Messenger, and *Jai Sixth! The Story of the 6th Queen Elizabeth's Own Gurkha Rifles 1817-1994* by James Lunt. I also found *The War of the Running Dogs* by Noel Barber very informative and readable.

I'd like to thank Arjun Rijal and his team at Outfitter Himalaya for guiding us around the Kathmandu Valley once again earlier this year. I'd also like to thank my editor Lauren Finger for her invaluable input, Mandy Lyon-Brown for her eagle-eyed proofreading, and everyone who read and commented on an Advance Reader's Copy of the book. And huge thanks also to everyone who's read my books and supported my writing down the years.

ABOUT THE AUTHOR

Ann Bennett is the author of several historical novels, many set in India or Southeast Asia. *The Bookseller of Kathmandu* is her twentieth book.

Her first novel, *Bamboo Heart: A Daughter's Quest*, was inspired by her father's experience as a prisoner of war on the Thai-Burma Railway. *Bamboo Island: The Planter's Wife, A Daughter's Promise, Bamboo Road: The Homecoming, The Tea Planter's Club* and *The Amulet* are also about WWII in Southeast Asia. With *The Fortune Teller of Kathmandu,* and T*he Lotus House,* they form *The Echoes of Empire Collection. A Rose in the Blitz*, the first book in the *Sisters of War* series is set in wartime London.

Ann is also author of *The Lake Pavilion* and *The Lake Palace,* set in British India during the Burma Campaign in WWII, and *The Lake Pagoda* and *The Lake Villa*, both set in French Indochina during WWII. Ann's other books, *The Runaway Sisters, The Forgotten Children, The Child Without a Home, The Orphan List, The Stolen Sisters,* and bestselling *The Orphan House*, are published by Bookouture.

A former lawyer, Ann is married with three grown up sons and a granddaughter and lives in Surrey, UK. For more details please visit—

www.annbennettauthor.com

A LETTER FROM ANN

Dear Reader,

I'd like to say a huge thank you for reading *The Bookseller of Kathmandu*. I hope you enjoyed reading it as much as I loved writing it.

If you did enjoy it, I'd be very grateful if you could write a review. I'd love to hear what you thought, and reviews help new readers discover my books for the first time.

Please sign up for the newsletter on my website for news and updates. If you sign up you will be offered a free download of one of my books.

You can also follow me on Facebook for information and previews of future books.

I always love hearing from readers, so do get in touch via social media or through the contacts page on my website.

BOOKS BY ANN BENNETT

Printed in Dunstable, United Kingdom